D1731445

HOW THE HEART BREAKS

USA TODAY BESTSELLING AUTHOR
S. MARIE

All rights reserved. Published by: Twisted Fairy Publishing Inc.
Layout by Judi Fennell (www.formatting4U.com)
Cover by: Jay Aheer (www.simplydefinedart.com)
Edited by Mo Siren's Call Author Services (thescarletsiren.com) and Emily Morgan of Guardian City Creative, LLC

For all those who've had a broken heart…
That's what alcohol was made for.
Drink until you forget that shit.

Table of Contents

Chapter 1
Emery

"Emery?"

My name rang out from the living room, followed by a frustrated huff. "Have you seen my running shoes?"

"You mean the ones you left at the back door?" I responded, not lifting my gaze to the dirty shoes I already knew were behind me. I continued to slice the juicy tomatoes from our garden, dumping them into the salad I was making.

"Right." My husband, Ben, strode into the kitchen, his lean body pressing into the back of mine. Ben was only a few inches taller than me, and he was thin but solid muscle. "What would I do without you?" His hands gripped my waist, his lips grazing my neck. "Maybe when I get back, I can get both our heart rates up." He softly kissed the curve of my shoulder.

"You're going to make me slice off my finger." I leaned back into him, a smile playing on my mouth.

"And that's something new? Probably better if you leave the food prep to my mom." He lifted the knife from my hands, placing it on the board.

"Shut up." I elbowed him softly, a laugh puffing out from him. Cooking was *not* my forte. It wasn't something I found fun or relaxing. I could make a mean salad, and I enjoyed growing my own vegetables, but not much past that. We had a lot of takeout in the last few years while he was studying for the bar exam.

"Your mother is handling everything else. The least I can do is make a salad."

"I'm sure she'll have one of those anyway."

Yes, his mother was a take-control kind of person. Even if I said I'd be making a salad, she still would bring one, giving me a passive-aggressive response of, "I just wanted to make sure there would be enough, and Ben loves my Caesar salad." *More than yours.* She left that part unsaid, but I heard it loud and clear.

Ben's arms circled my body. "Can't wait to take you upstairs tonight. Start on our family."

"Why not start now?" I countered over my shoulder with a wink. I would throw my to-do list out the window if he took me up on my offer. I wanted him to yank my shorts down and take me roughly against the sink because he couldn't help himself. I loved him more than life, but he wasn't the most adventurous or spontaneous when it came to sex.

A satisfied noise hummed in his throat. Ben twisted me around and leaned my 5'7" frame against the counter, brushing my long, dark hair from my face. "I don't want to be the perpetrator getting in the way of my own party." He wrapped his arms around me with a happy smile. "So, proceed, counsel."

"Wow, you sound like a lawyer." I stared at the kind face and light blue eyes I loved so deeply. "Have I told you how proud I am of you?"

He just passed his bar exam and already had offers from reputable practices in the area. Many of them he was familiar with from the golf course his family owned. Benjamin Roberts came from money, but he wanted to make sure he made it on his own merit, taking no handouts from his parents. Though his family connections at the club didn't hurt getting him a job right out the gate, we both worked long hours to get him through school. I was a dental assistant, which I can't say I loved, but it helped him get through law school and put us in this comfortable three-bedroom, one-and-a-half-bath house. Including a tiny garden of my own and enough lawn to give me fantasies of having rescue dogs running around in it.

It was a fantasy because Ben was allergic… to almost *every* animal.

"How about when I get back from my run? You can show me how much in the shower. Maybe start on a family." He nuzzled my neck. "Then I can help finish setting up."

All our friends and family were heading over for a dinner celebration in honor of his milestone. After years of hard work, the family we put on hold and the places we wanted to travel were tangible options now. I wasn't in a hurry to have kids yet, wanting to travel first and experience more than this town, but Ben was anxious to start one now. He'd have me pregnant already if it was up to him.

"Oh fuck. Can you guys stop making me want to slit my wrists?" A

2

voice came from the side door, my older sister stomping in with her arms loaded with grocery bags.

Ben sighed, kissing me quickly before he backed away. "Hey, Harper."

"Hey, Ben." My sister's tone matched his. They liked each other okay, but they weren't huge fans either. He felt she was too overbearing and opinionated, and he was too dull and vanilla for her.

Harper really had no room to judge. She had married a guy she met at a sleazy bar. He was supposed to be a one-night stand, but she got pregnant with my niece, Addison. They married right before Addison was born, and Harper suffered fourteen years in a turbulent relationship, only to find he had been having affairs with an endless string of women the whole time.

They were trying to work it out right now, but it was messy.

She followed in our mother's footsteps. Where I preferred safe, comfortable, and reliable, Harper leaned toward the dangerous and wild. Ben might be boring to some, but he made me feel secure and warm. Something I didn't have a lot of growing up.

"I brought extra tequila." Harper yanked two bottles out of the grocery bag.

"You know what Emery is like on tequila." Ben winked at me, his eyebrow cocking, sending a twinge of embarrassment through me. I tended to get a little horny on tequila. I attacked him last time, trying to play out one of my fantasies. It didn't go over as well as I had hoped.

"It's been a crappy day. It demands tequila." My sister cracked the top.

"Where's Addison?" I asked, pushing off the counter.

"At a friend's house. Joe and I had another fight." Harper's mouth lined.

I bit my lip, struggling for the hundredth time not to ask why she hadn't kicked his ass to the curb. She always seemed to forgive him. They'd be good for a while before the cycle started all over. Addison was everything to my sister, but unfortunately my niece had front row seats to her mother and father's battles her whole life. She was only fourteen, but she was already getting into trouble with boys and school. Another reason Ben got upset with Harper. He criticized how my sister was raising my niece, and Harper not only felt his opinion acutely, but the judgment of his entire snobby family.

"She'll be here later. You know she wouldn't miss it." Harper motioned to Ben. Addy idolized Ben, to the point she came here to hang out with him more than with me sometimes. I think she was desperate for a solid father figure, and Ben was as stable as you could get.

"Should I ask what you and Joe were fighting about this time?" I unpacked one of the grocery bags.

"That's my cue to leave." Ben shoved on his shoes, coming back over to me. "I love you."

"Love you too." I kissed him quickly before he headed out the door.

"Be back in an hour!" I yelled after him. "Everyone will be here at seven!"

"Okay, babe." The screen door slammed, the warm summer breeze drifting in. I watched him jog down our drive, my heart filling with so much love. Feeling so lucky to have found the love of my life.

"Where's Ben?" Alisa, Ben's mother, asked the moment she stepped into the house, her soft, honey blonde hair perfectly quaffed, her husband John in normal country club golf attire, smiling behind her, holding a stack of food dishes in his arms. Where Ben's mother was intense and did not exactly approve of me, John was much more laid back and gave me the warmest hugs every time he saw me. He never acted as if I was beneath them. He felt like the dad I never had, always checking in on Ben and me.

Thankfully, Ben took after him.

"Um." I peered down at my watch, noticing he was gone more than his usual hour. "He went for a run. He should be back soon."

Alisa frowned, hustling John to the kitchen. "We need to get the steak and ribs on right now. And my dessert needs to go in the fridge."

"The grill is set up in the back." I motioned to the back patio.

"Hey, kid." John leaned over, kissing my cheek. "Good to see you."

"Good to see you too."

"John!" Alisa called to him.

John rolled his eyes playfully, rushing off to the kitchen, not wanting to get any more grief from Alisa.

I peered over at my sister. She was trying not to show how she felt about my mother-in-law before she looked back at me, taking a shot of tequila. Harper was six years older than me, but we'd always been close. She had raised me when mom got sick. We shared the same body frame and hazel eye color, but my sister was blonde, like Mom, whereas I was dark-haired, like our father. Though he was only briefly in my life, my memories of those moments were strong. Both of our parents were gone now.

So, even though Alisa was a lot sometimes, I still clung to her and John as my family. Ben gave me the stability I had been searching for all my life.

Snorting, I strolled over to Harper. She poured another drink, handing it to me. "Can I say I'm thankful Joe's mother is cross country?"

We clinked glasses, shooting down the liquor.

"Someone else is at the door." She nodded to Ben's friends waving at me through the screen door, loaded with beer and chips.

Why wasn't Ben back yet? It was so unlike him.

Something in my gut fluttered, and the back of my neck prickled, but I quickly pushed it away. Pinning a smile on my face, I motioned them inside, telling them the same thing. "Ben went for a run. He should be back soon."

Where are you, Ben? Irritation furrowed my brows. This was all for him. He should be back.

Yanking my cell out of my pocket, I hit his number. A ring chimed from the sofa, my gaze landing on his mobile. Dammit. He had a habit of leaving it behind no matter how many times I asked him to carry it with him.

With every guest who arrived, my stomach twisted more. My irritation and fear plowed head-on into each other. Ben was never late, and he especially wouldn't be late tonight. He knew everyone was coming over. The party was for him.

"Did you try calling him?" Harper came up beside me.

"Yeah." I swallowed, the lump growing in my throat. "He forgot his phone."

"He'll be back soon." Harper patted my arm. "Knowing him, he probably stopped to get more beer and ice."

My head bobbed in agreement, but I couldn't let go of the tightening in my gut. *Please, Ben... walk in now.* I could picture him slamming through the side door, all smiles, his face sweaty, his arms carrying beer and ice, greeting everyone with boisterous cheers. Doing exactly what Harper had said. It was totally something he would do. He always thought to bring flowers to me when I had a bad day or add chocolate to the cart if I was on my period.

When my eyes spotted his wallet on the side table next to his phone, my lungs clenched. The taste of panic coated my tongue like battery acid.

A knee-jerk reaction from my past, the reason I sought stability. Permanency. Love.

Ben's fine, Em. He'll be back full of apologies, claiming he got wrapped up in his head and lost track of time. He sometimes tended to do that when he went running. It was how he escaped all the pressures of work and school life.

I heard someone turn music on in the backyard, voices curling around me in a happy timbre, the gleeful celebration already starting as my smile felt more and more forced.

He's fine. He's fine. I'm going to kill him when he comes in, though.

A knock hit the front door in three solid strikes, the thump echoing down my spine. My head snapped to the screen door, instinct locking up my lungs as my gaze made out the forms standing on my stoop.

Two policemen stared back at me, their faces stern.

I went numb, my feet shuffling me to the door, my mind rolling with the simple reasons why they were standing there. My heartbeat thumped in my ears, my body prickling with both hot and cold.

"Can I help you?" I swallowed.

"Did we already get a noise complaint?" Harper laughed from somewhere behind me, but I felt everything growing farther and farther away.

"Are you Mrs. Roberts?" one officer asked.

"Yes." I heard the tremble in my voice.

"There has been an accident," the tall blond one said.

"Accident?" My defenses stacked up.

"I'm sorry, but your husband has been taken to the hospital."

"No." The word flew from my mouth, my head shaking, denying. "You are mistaken."

"The store clerk identified him as Ben Roberts."

My muscles locked up, and the terror I tried to shove away earlier came roaring back in my ears like it had been warning me.

"What do you mean, accident?" Harper came up beside me.

The officer's mouth pinched. "He was found collapsed near the liquor store on Union Street. It's all I know."

That was on the route he ran every day. Bob, the owner, knew us. We went there often. He would know Ben.

Air heaved in and out of my lungs, my legs wanting to bow underneath me. "Is he okay?"

The blond officer shifted on his feet. "We can drive you to the hospital, Mrs. Roberts."

My brain didn't think past the need to get to Ben. I tore out of the house after the cops, my feet bare.

Harper yelled back at people as Alisa shrieked for John. In my peripheral, I could see them running for their car while Harper hopped into the back seat next to me.

"Emery?" She leaned over, slipping my flip-flops onto my feet, taking my hand. "He will be fine. Ben is young, healthy, and strong."

I only nodded, my mind a whirl of panic and desperation, tears flowing down my face. "Ben..." I uttered his name as though he could feel me calling to him. That I was coming. I stared blankly out the window, everything feeling as if it were going in slow motion. The streets stretched out, the red lights longer. I fought to keep it together, my nails cutting into my hands, when we finally rolled to a stop in front of the emergency room.

Bolting from the car, I darted inside and straight to the desk.

"My husband..." I croaked. "He was brought in."

"Ma'am, slow down," a nurse responded, her expression holding no ounce of worry, her boredom clashing against my distress.

"No!" I bellowed. "My husband! I need to see him! Is he okay?" My voice rose, panic claiming my body and taking over.

"Ma'am, who is your husband?"

"His name is Ben Roberts." My sister jumped in. "He was just brought in."

The nurse tapped away at her computer leisurely. A slight pinch tapped her brows. "A doctor will be out with you shortly."

"No!" I screamed again. "Tell me if he's okay?" Tears of fear and frustration poured down my face.

"Please, have a seat. A doctor will be out shortly," she repeated.

Harper yanked me back from the desk to the sitting area, my arms whirling, wanting to fight the receptionist and my sister. I needed to see Ben. It was a desperation so deep that I felt vomit coming up into my throat. The notion I couldn't be by his side shredded through me. He was my heart.

My everything.

Alisa, John, and several others from the party rushed into the emergency room, but I couldn't do anything to ebb their fears. Harper let them know everything we did.

It wasn't long before Alisa turned into her demanding self, barking at the nurses to let us see him, to give us some kind of update. For once, I was okay with it, hoping she'd break through and they'd allow us back.

The door to the surgery area opened, and a woman in scrubs and a white coat stepped out, her expression pinched.

My muscles locked up, knowing we were getting what we demanded. The doctor was here for us.

Her eyes met mine, her steps steady as she walked up. "Mrs. Roberts?"

"Yes?" Alisa and I said in unison, her curvy figure moving next to me.

The doctor's gaze went to her, then back to me with sorrow.

And I knew.

My ears started to buzz, my mind and soul separating, feeling like I was leaving my body.

"I am sorry." Compassion was written over her face as she delivered the news. "Ben suffered from a pulmonary embolism. We did everything we could…"

I know she kept talking, explaining what happened, but I no longer heard anything. I know I screamed, but it didn't feel as if the guttural wail came from me. And I know I collapsed because I could feel the cool tile against my face.

Vomit burned my throat as howls of grief erupted around me.

My brain wouldn't let me absorb the truth, sheltering me from the agony dropping on me. It felt so foreign when he was kissing me just a few hours ago, talking about starting our family—our whole lives ahead of us.

He was supposed to come back from his run, and we should be celebrating right now, surrounded by his friends and family.

He was supposed to be my forever…

Now, all I felt was everlasting darkness.

Chapter 2
Emery

"I'm so sorry for your loss."

"It was a lovely funeral."

"Ben was a wonderful person. He will be greatly missed."

"So sad. He was so young with so much ahead of him."

Walking through the stream of people trying to comfort me, I nodded and smiled at their condolences. I felt as empty as their words were. I know they didn't know what else to say to a grieving widow, but if I heard "I'm sorry" one more time, I was going to lose it.

"Looks as if you need this." Harper handed me a glass of wine.

"Thanks." I took it, finding even such a simple reply was hard for me. It had only been two weeks since Ben's death, and everyone expected me to stand here like a pillar of strength, pretending my entire world hadn't crumbled under my feet. That the love of my life—my rock—didn't just leave me. I felt lost, as if I were floating, nothing holding me down.

"Please eat something." Harper pushed a plate of cheese and crackers to me.

My hand went to my stomach, rolling with acid, my head shaking. Food tasted like ash.

Arms came around my waist, and Addison leaned into me, her eyes streaked red with tears. I squeezed her back wordlessly. She had taken Ben's death badly, as if she had lost her rock as well.

Addison met her grandmother before she passed from cancer, but she was too young to remember. She never knew her grandfather. I barely knew my dad before he was shot and killed when I was six. Her own father was a dickhead and never around.

And now she lost Ben too.

Damn you, Ben, for leaving her also. The flare of anger at him dissolved quickly into guilt and sadness.

"Where are your salad plates?" Alisa marched up, her hair and makeup perfect, as she took over my house as the hostess. She wanted to have the funeral gathering at their large home, but I stood my ground. This was Ben's house. This was where he'd want it.

"I'll show you." Harper gave me a look, downing more wine.

"Thank you," I mouthed to her. She had her issues, but I couldn't have asked for a better sister. She had been with me every step of the way.

Harper took a deep centering breath before trailing Alisa back into the kitchen.

"I miss him so much, Aunt Emery." Addison leaned her head on my shoulder, her long blonde hair brushing my arm.

I dropped my cheek on her head. "Me too," I whispered, my eyes blurring as my gaze landed on our wedding photo on the bookshelf. We looked so happy, oblivious to what was in our future, and what little time we had. I'd give anything to go back to that day. To go back to any day with him. Never taking a moment for granted.

Kissing Addy's head, I pulled away, needing a moment, panic wrapping around my lungs. Slipping into my bedroom, a sob heaved from me, my legs buckling as I slid down the back of my door to my ass.

"You left me. You promised you'd always be there for me." My eyes took in where his clothes hung. His shoes were lined up in the closet. A t-shirt of his was still draped over the dirty laundry basket. I hadn't touched a thing because deep down, I hoped this was all a bad dream. That he would walk in as if nothing happened, and life would continue on.

"Damn you for deserting me, Ben," I gritted out. More guilt hiccupped tears from me. He was the one dead, and I was furious at him for being so. I felt like I was breaking, and nothing would be left of me.

This past week had been a blur of signing forms at the hospital, with words like pulmonary embolism and organ donation, then going straight into funeral arrangements, which led to tension between Alisa and me. She wanted him buried in a plot near their house, but Ben had told me he'd rather be cremated.

I won the argument only because John finally stepped in, siding with what his son really wanted. Alisa was still pissed, but she settled on taking the ashes they had and putting them in a grave marked with his name.

Rising slowly, I ventured to the closet, grabbing his favorite hoodie and putting it to my nose. It still smelled like him. Cuddling it in my arms, I dropped onto the bed, tucking up in a ball. I rested my head on his pillow, eyes closed, pretending he was still in my arms.

A deep wail came from my soul, my body convulsing as my sorrow took over.

He was supposed to be the father of my children. The one who was my forever.

Now, we would never have kids. Never travel to Europe. I'd never feel him making love to me. He'd never win his first case as a lawyer. I'd never hear his laugh, see his smile, smell him fresh from a shower, taste his kiss, feel his arms around me.

Never.

Final. End. Over.

That's exactly how I felt now.

Ben was dead, but I was the one no longer living.

Chapter 3
Emery

1 year later

Today would have been our wedding anniversary.

Last month was the anniversary of his death.

I sat on the bed holding our wedding photo, wearing his sweatshirt, sobbing my heart out behind closed doors.

People thought I was getting better. They'd see my smile and hear my laughs as a sign I was moving on.

It was all a lie.

Can you drown slowly while everyone thinks you are swimming? Can you fake being a living person when you're dead inside?

Everyone was over it. Not that they didn't miss him, but they've moved on and continued their lives. And they wanted me to do the same. They were tired of walking on eggshells. They didn't want to be around someone stuck in constant sadness.

I was tired of it as well. But I couldn't get out of this hole. I couldn't breathe. I couldn't let him go.

I was seeing a therapist, and she said it would take time, but nothing felt different. Another day I hid my pain and agony. I pretended I was okay. An endless *Groundhog's Day* of faking I was alive.

One of our dental patients, an elderly woman, told me not long after his death, "You're young and beautiful. Don't worry, you'll meet someone new."

A woman I worked with hinted her brother was newly single. She wanted to fix me up.

I curled up, staring at his clothes still in the closet, his razor still on the sink, the pillow that no longer smelled like him.

Could I even be fixed? Or was this how it would always feel?
Just empty darkness in front of me.

Chapter 4
Emery

3 years later

"I said you should move out of this house, not out of the state!" Harper trailed after me, following me into the kitchen, where I had boxes, tape, and bubble wrap covering every inch of the counters and floor. "Em..." She folded her arms. "Don't you think this is a bit extreme?"

"Funny, you accused me of being stagnant, keeping myself sheltered in my own misery. Now I'm over the top?"

"I meant get your own apartment across town, not move out of state! This house is keeping you stagnant." She motioned around the house. "Look around you, Em... you haven't changed one thing. You live in a tomb."

The dagger went straight to its target, and I nearly hissed as I spun around.

"Don't tell me you don't. I know his clothes are still hanging in the closet."

"So?"

"It's been three years."

"Oh, I'm sorry, am I supposed to stop loving him now? Be over it?"

"No." Harper sighed. "Of course you won't stop loving him, but this is not healthy. You can't move forward if you're set on living in the past."

I fiddled with a packing box, my teeth gritting together. She sounded exactly like my therapist.

"Is this about Matt from your office? I'm sorry I canceled on him. I didn't feel good." I bristled, focusing on bubble wrapping a plate.

"This isn't about Matt, though he is cute, nice, and really likes you."

Harper tucked her blonde hair behind her ear. She was right. He *was* cute and nice, but I felt nothing for him. "This is about every date any of us try to set you up on. You find a reason not to go or not to like them."

"I keep telling you I'm not ready."

"Okay, but someday you need to be." Harper exhaled, trying to control the blunt comments I could see growing daily on her lips over the past year. "You can't live like a dried-up old widow forever." She held up her hand, stopping my rebuttal. "I know you loved him, Emery, but he is gone. And we both know Ben would not want you wasting your life, ticking down the days until you die."

My head bowed, the truth sinking in and burning up the back of my throat.

She wasn't the only one who thought I should be moving on by now. All my colleagues at work had tried to set me up with their single guy friends. This forty-something widowed man kept coming in to get his teeth cleaned. They would all elbow me, their eyebrows wiggling, as though I should leap at the chance to go out with him just because we both lost our spouses. As if it was kismet or something. We clearly were meant to be because we were both widowed and single now.

I felt nothing for him either. I was a wasteland.

The few times I felt sexual lately, I would close my eyes and try to pretend my vibrator was Ben. But I could no longer picture his face clearly, just the featureless man I had in many of my fantasies even before Ben passed. The fact I could no longer see my husband above me, feel him around me, inside me, made me feel sick and horrible. I'd end up in tears, curled into a fetal position, feeling worse than I had before.

I had been on two dates with good-looking, nice enough men, and I wished to be anywhere else the whole time. It scared me that no one stirred anything in me, and I had dried up at the age of thirty, as if my life was already over.

This realization was what made me decide to leave everything. I couldn't do it halfway. I needed a fresh start. A place no one knew my story, no one knew me as Ben's wife—or Ben's widow. As much as my friends wanted me to find someone new, I knew all the people associated with Ben would secretly judge me if I did. Ben's ghost would always be with me here.

"It's why I decided to move." I twisted around, leaning against the counter.

"But why so far?"

"Because it's where I found a job." That was true. No one in this area was hiring dental assistants. The job offer was only four hours away, close, but far enough away to feel as though no one would know me. "Plus, it's not just this house. It's this town. Everywhere I go is a reminder of Ben. Where we got married, where he proposed, where we loved to go to dinner. Where he died. I constantly run into his friends, his parents, all the people from the golf club, who stop me every time to talk about him. You tell me I need to move on, but I can't here."

I was terrified to let him go, to leave this house, but deep down, I knew I would waste away here if I didn't. I would never move on.

Harper rubbed at her face, her own problems weighing on her shoulders. "I don't want you to go. I need you right now, Em."

"I know." I blinked the tears away. "But I'll only be a few hours away."

"What about Addison?"

I exhaled.

In the last three years, Addison had become out of control.

In this last year, Harper and Joe filed for divorce. It was ugly. As much as Harper was trying to protect Addison from Joe's petty vengeance, she couldn't keep her from all of it. Her father was a real S.O.B.

Addison had completely lashed out. She stayed with me more than not, claiming she hated her parents, especially Harper right now, blaming the divorce on her. Addison was an angry teenager who had gone through a lot and was not handling it well. She hurt her mother because her father was never around to punish.

"She got kicked out of school. Permanently." Harper fought back tears, her cheek twitching. She didn't cry much, except when it came to her daughter. Harper was trying so hard, but the more she tried to help Addison, the more her daughter pushed back. "I don't know what to do with her. I'm at my wit's end. She snuck out again the other night. She's going down this destructive path, and I can't seem to reach her."

I wrapped my arms around my waist, an idea bubbling up. "What if Addison moved with me?"

"What?" Harper stiffened.

"She can't go to school here anyway. This might be exactly what she needs too. A fresh start for both of us. A new school, new friends." I emphasized, knowing how much Harper hated the group Addison had started to hang around with. "You said it yourself the other day. You wish you could keep her from all this divorce crap."

"Yes. But she can't go with you." Harper wagged her head.

"Why not?" I countered. "Don't you want your own fresh start? Not dealing with an uncontrollable teenager? You know I'm strict. She'd have to follow my rules."

"She's my daughter! My problem. Not yours. You have enough to deal with."

"And you know I want the best for her. Honestly, Harp, the more you try to rein her in, the more she's acting out. This might be the smartest thing for your relationship."

Harper slumped against the fridge, her face looking like she wanted to break down.

"So, I lose both you and Addison?"

"You're not losing us. We'll be four hours away."

"Maybe I move with you guys."

I tilted my head. My sister loved her job, and it gave her really good benefits. She couldn't afford to leave right now. Plus, not only did I suspect my sister was already seeing someone, but she loved this town too much. She never wanted to leave it.

Harper sniffed, wiping a tear from her face. "I don't want to, but I don't know what else to do."

Her sentiment echoed in my head long after she left, my heart breaking as I packed up some of my things, deciding to leave most of it behind. I carried Ben enough with me. I didn't want the new place to be another echo of all I had lost.

This would be a fresh start. A new beginning for Emery Campbell, which felt like a betrayal to Ben, as if I had turned away from the man I planned to spend the rest of my life with.

"I don't want to…" I grabbed Ben's old hoodie, which I wore every night, holding it to my chest. "But I don't know what else to do."

Chapter 5
Emery

"I love it!" Addison squealed, her face glowing as she bounced around her new bedroom. I watched pain streak over Harper's face at seeing her daughter so happy. Addison seemed thrilled to be moving away from Harper, but my sister forced a smile on her face, absorbing the rare moments Addison smiled anymore.

"You must follow every rule your aunt Emery lays down." Harper wiggled her finger at her daughter.

"Yes, of course." Addison rolled her eyes, turning back to the small but adorable bedroom she would live in for the school year.

My house sold quickly, and I was able to secure an adorable two-bedroom, two-bath cottage near my new job and the high school Addison would be attending next week. The cottage was small and old, but it had a large garden/backyard. The couple before had developed it into an English dream garden, with wildflowers, vegetables, and cobblestone pathways. The deck overlooked the stunning backyard, with a grill and hot tub. The backyard was the reason I bought this house. The inside needed work, but the garden more than made up for it.

"I'm not kidding, Addy. One call telling me you skipped school or broke one of her rules, you are coming back home."

Addison exhaled an exaggerated breath. "Yes. I. Get. It."

Harper's jaw clenched at her attitude, and she looked over at me like *you sure you want to take this on?*

I smiled a yes, though my nerves jumped up and down. I could be making this worse, but we were in too deep now. All I could do was take it day by day with her.

Addison's mood flipped again in a breath as she jumped with a squeal on her full bed, the white and purple comforter puffing up.

"You have all your schoolbooks and stuff you need?" Harper asked.

"Yep." Addy looked down at her watch. "Oh shit! I got to go. Cheerleading tryouts start in fifteen minutes." She bounded back up, heading for the door.

"Hey?" Harper frowned. "Aren't you going to say bye? I'm heading back soon."

"Bye, Mom." She hugged her mom briefly before darting out the door, not even sounding a bit remorseful.

When the front door slammed, I moved to my sister, rubbing her arm. "She's a teenager."

"And fuck, does she make sure she gives me the full experience." Harper scoured her forehead, fighting back her tears.

"She loves you. She needs to work out her anger and hurt. Remember what you were like at her age?"

"I think that's why I'm getting punished." She huffed. "What goes around comes around."

Being six years younger, I watched Harper go through her rebellious teenage years and what it did to our mom. They weren't even as close as she and Addy.

"I'm so happy she's trying out for cheerleading. Honestly, I'm shocked at how excited she got when she saw the flyer at the school. I'm happy for anything getting her back to things she used to love." Harper swallowed, forcing a smile on her lips. "No matter how much it hurts, I think being here is the best thing for her. She needed to get away from the crowd she was hanging around with and her father. Maybe here she can get back on track."

I nodded, hoping both Addison and I could get back on track.

—⎍⎍⎍⎍♡

A few hours after Harper left and the house was quiet as I went through the last of the boxes. My heart squeezed as I pulled out the framed picture of my wedding day, my fingers sliding over Ben's smiling face. A surge of anxiety and terror climbed up the back of my throat. Did I do the right thing? I walked away from my life, from my friends and family. From everything of his. Alisa had taken a lot of Ben's items. Her resentment over me leaving, walking away from her son, was never expressed, but it was felt. John was the only one who still called me, who tried to act as if I were still part of their family, but without Ben, both seemed to struggle to keep me part of it. There were no kids to tie us, nothing but memories of Ben. She saw me as a traitor now, hating me for leaving, but she resented me more for being there. A reminder of the son she no longer had.

What she didn't keep went to the Home Hospice Thrift Store. Some stranger would wear his suits, walk down the street in his shoes. Someone's life was put into a box and given away to someone else to live in.

My gaze went down to my hand, the diamond wedding band still on my finger. I kept his in my jewelry box. I also held onto our photos and his sweatshirt. The rest I forced myself to leave behind, and now a part of me was regretting it.

Grief cracked open my chest as I leaned over the photo of a time when we were so happy. I cried, feeling the panic of letting him go. Why didn't I beg him to make love to me right then instead of going on his run? Why was getting his party together more important than taking a moment with him? Would he still be alive if he didn't go?

The guilt and what-ifs circled me, hounding me like demons come to life.

"Aunt Emery!" An excited screech jolted me up, and I hastily wiped my eyes as Addison barrelled into my room. "Guess what?"

"What?" I sniffed, putting on a false smile I was used to wearing now, acting as if I wasn't about to lose it.

Addison's gaze went to me, then to the photo in my hand, her shoulders sinking, her excitement evaporating. I hated I could rip joy from her so quickly.

"What?" I placed the picture down, my voice bouncing with eagerness I didn't feel, needing to see that smile back on her face.

"I made the squad!" Her cheer was half of what she came in with.

"Oh my god!" I exclaimed, wrapping her up in a quick hug. "That's so exciting. I'm so happy for you."

Her light brown eyes glittered with more enthusiasm. "I can't believe it, but the head cheerleader came up to me after, telling me I was the best tryout they had seen." She jumped up and down. "I'm so excited. I'm getting my uniform tomorrow, and practices start later this week. We can be ready when school starts next week."

"Wow. You need to call and tell your mom. She will be so excited for you." Harper had been the cheerleader. I had been the girl reading books and volunteering at animal rescue centers. When everything was going to shit with Mom, I found comfort in animals, putting all my energy into finding them homes. If I could make their life happy and find them the perfect family, it would make up for mine.

"Yeah." She swished her hand. "I will." Sounding more like *I'll do it if I have to.* "But…" Another squeal came from her. I seriously hadn't seen Addison this happy in a long time.

"There's more?"

A blush covered her cheeks, a slight embarrassment fluttering down her lashes.

"The head cheerleader, Elena, well, she wanted to introduce me to the football team. You know, meet the guys we'll be cheering for."

"Of course." I grinned playfully, though a small knot tied in my stomach. Addison had gone full boy crazy, which had gotten her into trouble. She was caught cutting school and found drinking and smoking. A boy is why she fell into the wrong group at her last school. She acted tough but seemed easily swayed.

"And oh my god." Her cheeks went bright red, fanning herself.

"They're cute?"

"The football team? Yeah, tons of really cute boys, but they aren't who I'm talking about." She blew out like she was going to faint. "The assistant coach."

"Addison!" I balked at her.

"No! No! He's a student. A senior. He was held back a year or something," she quickly explained. "Elena heard before he moved here two years ago that he was a top football player, like really good. But he quit for some reason. He was so good, the coach here wanted him to assist in games."

That sounded odd. Why would a kid at the top of his game quit? And then help coach instead?

"Oh my god, Aunt Emery. I seriously think I'm in love." She twirled her long hair, letting her head fall back. "Mason James…" She cooed. "He's like six-foot-three, dark hair, dark eyes. He seriously is one of the hottest guys I have ever seen. In. My. Life. He has this sexy, mysterious vibe going."

"You really are your mother's daughter." I laughed, herding her out of my bedroom.

During school, I may have crushed on the bad boy from afar, but he was never the guy I went for. Somehow, I sensed they would only hurt me. Leave me. Move on to the next girl and shatter my heart. I liked the Bens. The ones I knew would be there the next day.

"He totally checked me out. I'm sure of it." She paraded into the kitchen. "Our eyes met. And I felt it all the way to my toes."

I hummed in response, opening the fridge, though I knew there would be nothing more than leftovers from last night's takeout.

"I could tell all the girls on the squad want him. Sophie told me he hooks up with a lot of girls but doesn't actually date any of them."

"Sounds like a charmer." I already didn't care for this kid. "Please, don't be another one on that list." I whirled around to her. "You are worth so much more."

She fluttered her eyes at me. "I know."

This was the exact response Harper would have before jumping headfirst after the boy, getting her heart crushed. I knew I could warn Addy over and over, but at this age, she wouldn't listen. You wanted to be the one who nabbed the hard-to-get guy. The one everyone wanted but no one could get. Every girl believed they might be the one.

As much as I wanted to protect Addison, I couldn't, because I learned even the good guy could break your heart.

Chapter 6
Emery

"Hey, Emery."

I brushed the crumbs away from my mouth and scrubs, straightening up when my boss entered the room. "Hey, Dr. Ramirez."

"Please. Call me Daniel." He shot me a soft smile, heading over to the staff fridge, grabbing a yogurt and apple while I picked at my stale chocolate croissant. "I was hoping to catch you." His smile was warm but held something that made an alarm go off in the back of my head. "I wanted to see how you were doing here?"

I had been here for about a month. The staff was welcoming, and I had already been invited to drinks with some of them next week. Once a month they got together for a happy hour night.

"Good." I nodded. Dr. Ramirez ran a small but very highly rated practice. He was everything a dentist should be. Calm, kind, and spoke to every client as if they were important. He remembered everyone's names and asked about their children and what they were up to.

Several of the assistants had crushes on him. He was single, in his mid-to-late thirties, with a handsome face, tan skin, and soft caramel eyes. Only a few inches taller than me, he wasn't fit by any means but was in good enough shape. He was the type I would normally have a crush on.

Once again, I felt nothing except this strange panic to leave the staff room, to get away from the way he looked at me.

"I'm glad." He nodded. "I've heard nothing but praise about you so far. The patients love you." He twirled his spoon. "You fit right in with us. I'm glad you came to work here. Everyone already adores you." His eyes landed on me. Not sleazy, not even flirting, but my stomach still knotted up, sensing more to his words.

"Oh. Well, they're all sweet. Everyone has been very welcoming."

He dipped his head, spooning yogurt into his mouth. "You're coming to cocktail night next week?"

"You're going?" I almost choked on my baked good.

"I don't all the time, but it's nice to hang out with everyone outside of here, where I'm not the boss."

Why did every word he uttered feel poignant and full of more meaning than he said?

"Um. Yeah. I think so." I peered at the clock on the wall. "Oh, I better get back to work." I stood up. "Don't want to get in trouble with my boss."

"I think he'd let this one slide." He grinned at me.

The smile I had perfected curved my mouth before I practically ran from the room. No one here knew my full story. I didn't want pity-filled eyes and the standard *I'm sorry for your loss*, response. Or even worse, the shift in them when they learned it's been over three years ago. That seemed to be the line for people, where their compassion stopped, and they looked at me like something was wrong with *me*.

"Hey, girl." Marcie tapped her long nails on a folder, handing it to me. "Your next cleaning is here. Billy Thomas." She lifted a brow. "Let me warn you, he bites and kicks."

"Great." I exhaled.

"Now, if it was Billy's father, I'd be into that. Grab me by the hair kind. You know what I mean?" She winked playfully, her laugh trailing after as she walked away.

No, I didn't. Ben had been nowhere near that type. He wasn't the first guy I slept with, though he might as well have been. The first guy in college I hardly remembered, the second was good, but we had no real connection. Then it was Ben. Sweet, slow, always making *love* to me.

Though Marcie's words scraped a fantasy through the back of my head, I had an image of someone doing just that. Yanking my hair, pounding into me from behind. I had secretly wished for Ben to do it to me the night he died. Taking me hard and ruthless against the kitchen counter.

The imagery emerged fast and severe. I could feel him towering over me, sinking deep inside me, taking charge, making me lose all control as he consumed me.

Desire singed over my cheeks, a tingle sliding between my legs, throbbing through my core. Sucking in, I flushed again at the fact I was extremely turned on for the first time in years.

By a fantasy man who was not my husband.

"Aunt Emery?" Addison's voice called through the house, the sound of her bags dropping onto the floor.

"Out back!" I yelled, enjoying the last days of summer. A crispness was already hinting in the air, the leaves changing colors. My favorite time of year.

"Hey!" She slid open the screen, popping out to where I lounged on the deck with a glass of wine and a book.

"Have a good day at school?" I lifted my head to see her dressed in her cheerleading uniform, her face full of smiles. In school, Addison had done a 180. She was finishing her homework, getting good enough grades, and seemed ten times lighter and happier than she had even a month ago. She had new friends, loved cheering, and would not shut up about this kid, Mason. Every day she got gigglier and more crazed over him, though I think they had barely spoken a handful of times.

"I did." She plopped down in the chair across from me. "We have a game tonight. So just getting something to eat before I meet up with my squad."

"Don't forget to call your mother."

Addy flicked her eyes. They talked on the phone every few days, but Addison's mood toward her parents was the one thing that hadn't changed much. Though she couldn't hide her happiness when telling her mom about her friends here. I knew it hurt Harper, knowing her daughter was happier here than with her, but I also knew she was relieved Addy was doing so much better.

"Are you coming to the game tonight?" She stole a cracker from the bowl I had next to me, munching on it. "You have to come. I'm going up in the pyramid. Elena sprained her ankle, so I'm taking her spot tonight."

"Well, then I guess I have to come." I took a sip of wine.

"You will finally see Mason." She wiggled in her seat. "He said hi in the hallway to me today."

"Wow, it must be love."

"Shut up." She laughed, hitting my arm. "Seriously, I'm crushing so hard on this guy." She tucked her legs up on the chair, her eyes lowering, giving me her puppy-eyes expression.

"What?" I knew that look. It was only when she really wanted something. The last time I got it was when she wanted her ears pierced.

"You know you are the best, most amazing, beautiful aunt in the whole world."

"Oh Jesus, someone is laying it on thick. What do you want?"

"Let me first say, it would only be a handful or so…"

"Addison."

"I was wondering if I could have a few people over after the game?" She put up her hands, not letting me respond. "It will be totally chill. A few of us hanging out in the hot tub."

"You want to have a party?"

"No. No alcohol or anything. Just a few friends over."

"You mean Mason." I tilted a brow.

"Hopefully." She nipped at the end of her nails. "Please, please, please, please."

I had a hard time saying no to my niece. "You follow every rule, no alcohol, no drugs, and everyone is gone by midnight."

Her head nodded, knowing she had already won.

"I must be insane."

"Ahhhh!" She leaped up, hugging me. "Thank you, thank you. You are the best!"

"I know. I already have the World's Best Aunt mug to prove it."

Chapter 7
Emery

Addison spotted me when I settled down on the bleachers, holding her hand up and pointing me out to her friend, Sophie, then darting over to me.

"You made it!"

"Told you I would." Though I did drink another glass of wine before walking over here. Football was never my thing. This was Harper's scene in high school while I was occupied with making business plans for my future animal adoption center. It was still one of those dreams I had tucked away when life dashed those aspirations... when the need for food, rent, and stability came first.

"So, some football players and the cheer squad are coming over after." She talked like a speeding train. "I haven't seen Mason yet to ask, but I will after the game." She peered over her shoulder. "He's not out yet. But I will let you know when he does."

"Okay." Did they serve alcohol at these things? Probably not.

She re-joined her squad as they pepped up the crowd. The announcer came on as the football players from both teams came out onto the field.

"Aunt Emery." Addy mouthed at me, her hand trying to slyly point across the field behind her pom-poms. "There he is."

My gaze lifted to where she pointed, sliding over the older coach to the man beside him.

I sucked in sharply, a strange feeling trickling down my chest as my gaze locked on him. She had told me he was tall and built, but my head still imagined a young teenager, the same as all the other ones around here. A cocky high school boy who young girls would swoon over.

There was nothing high school-like about him. His frame towered over almost all the boys, including the coach.

Wearing dark jeans, a black t-shirt—which his broad shoulders filled out way too well—a baseball hat, and black boots, he looked nothing like an assistant coach or a student here. Under his cap, I could make out his dark hair and eyes, his scruff lining his chiseled jaw. And fuck, even I wasn't dead enough inside. He was the kind of gorgeous who turned smart people stupid.

No way was this guy around Addison's age. He screamed danger. Trouble. Sexual confidence. Years older than any other kid here. And that's what he made them all look like—kids.

Forcing my gaze back to Addy, she patted her heart, sighing before turning around to face the field, starting their cheer routine.

Hell, no. He was not touching my niece. He was far too old, even if it wasn't in years. He was way too "advanced" for Addison.

Unable to fight the pull, my attention darted right back to him. Watching his mouth move talking to the coach, the way his body shifted. He spoke with complete confidence, the coach nodding in agreement to his instruction as if Mason was the one making the calls.

Dominant. Self-assured.

Heat coated my skin under my jacket, and I frowned as I pulled it off. The night was abnormally warm, and I did drink two glasses of wine before I left. That had to be it.

Purposely looking everywhere else, I still found my attention landing right back on him, like a magnet.

His eyes lifted, and I swear they found mine across the field, air halting in my lungs. I could feel them on me, peeling at my layers.

Right below me, I saw Addison wave at him, her smile growing wider.

Oh my god, you idiot. He was looking at Addison. I shook my head, anger and disgust rising in my throat. My skin still itched as if his eyes were on me, but I refused to look back and check. *What the fuck is wrong with you? You're a thirty-year-old woman,* I chastised, repulsed at myself.

Putting all my attention on Addison and the game, I still had no clue who was winning. I tried to ignore the fact I was fighting to keep my attention off him, going overboard to cheer Addy on and act as if I was so into the game, only wishing for it to be over.

"We won!" Addison leaped over to me.

"Finally," I muttered to myself, rising and leaning over the railing to address my niece. "You were amazing, Addy."

"Thanks!" She hopped on her toes. "Everything still good for tonight?"

"Of course."

"Great. I'm gonna go ask Mason right now." She darted away before I could respond, my gaze tracking her as she bounced across the field up to Mason.

He showed no reaction to her presence while she exploded with hyper energy around him, rustling her pom-poms and flicking her ponytail. Her head nodded back to me, and my lungs clenched as his eyes followed, landing on me.

My heart thumped in my chest, my skin flushing hot, and my core throbbed. *Oh. My. God.* The heat turned instantly to ice. Absolute disgust and shame ripped me away from them, moving me down the stairs and out of the stadium. What the hell was wrong with me?

Pulling out my cell, I texted Addy. ***See you at home***. I knew she was getting a ride with Elena and Sophie back to ours, though it was only a few blocks.

My body shivered, but I kept my jacket off, flogging myself mentally. I never had this kind of response to anyone before, not even Ben. It terrified me, making me feel even more disoriented, as if nothing made sense anymore.

"Ben," I whispered his name out loud. "I miss you." I missed how safe and happy I felt. How easy. How it all made sense.

My mind settled into the memories of Ben like a warm bath. Him holding me. Loving me. It was safe. Secure. I shut down any thoughts beyond him.

Whatever moment I had was a fluke. A wine-induced reaction to something my body needed, or maybe a chemical imbalance in my hormones.

Nothing more.

I strode for the cottage, ignoring the fact that for the first time in over three years, a man had my nipples pebbling painfully against my shirt.

Laughter came from the deck, along with music and splashing from the hot tub. The kids were all carefree and happy, thinking the dramas of high school were so dire, not realizing life hadn't even gotten close to fucking them yet.

Cutting into another slice of cheese, something for them to nibble on, I felt even more divided from the youth outside.

29

More than a dozen had shown up, mainly cheerleaders and football players, probably treating this as the warm-up house before they headed to the real party, which was unchaperoned. It wasn't that long ago I was going to house parties and drinking.

I knew they would be. It's what you did at their age. Except it wasn't happening under my roof. I would not be liable for anyone getting drunk or hurt.

"Dude, your throw tonight. It was fuckin' sick," a boy's voice boomed out.

"Right?" another responded.

"Oh my god! He's here." I heard Addison yelp, running into the house, her cell in her hand. Her eyes found mine in the kitchen, doing a little dance before rushing to the front door.

I turned back to the cheese, slicing the entire block. Did teenagers even eat Gruyère?

"I'm so glad you came. Come in."

"Thanks," a deep voice rumbled, barely audible from where I was, but I felt it sink into my skin.

"Come out back. Everyone's outside. Did you bring a suit?"

"No."

"That's okay. I don't really feel like going in either." Though she was wearing her bikini with a thin short dress over it. Her bare feet padded to the back door. "Oh, this is my Aunt Emery."

My head turned to them; my smile ready to be cued up. It got stuck as his eyes met mine. His face showed no feeling, but his gaze pierced intently into mine as if he could shred through me, pick out every dark secret, leaving nothing but bones.

Stop it right now. Act like a fucking adult.

"Nice to meet you. It's Mason, right?"

He dipped his head, his eyes not leaving me. "Nice to meet you too, *Aunt* Emery." The way his tone rolled over the last two words, they sounded utterly sinful. His low gravelly voice hit something inside, rolling a drop of sweat down my spine.

"Go! Have fun." I motioned to the door. "Pay no attention to the old lady in the kitchen."

Addy wrinkled her brow at me like I lost my mind, motioning him out the door, his dark eyes moving back to me before he stepped out, a slight smirk hinting on his mouth.

Exhaling out, I dropped my head in mortification. I wanted to slap myself. One, I sounded so lame, and two, why did I feel this need to make sure he knew I was way older than him?

"Mason!" The echo of the entire backyard cheered at his arrival, the girls' voices going up a notch trying to get his attention and the boys' voices going down, like they wanted to emulate and/or compete with him. I could already tell everyone followed Mason. Wanted to be where he was.

After dumping plates of cheese, crackers, chips, and some soft drinks off, I planted myself in the kitchen, letting Addy have her privacy, staying out of her way.

Or avoiding him? A voice crept into the back of my head, rolling my hands into balls.

"Where do you want me to put these?"

"Shit!" My entire body locked up, my head jerking up at his voice, almost jumping out of my skin.

"Did I scare you?" Mason stepped into the room, his hands loaded with empty plates, his huge frame filling the kitchen entry. His hat sat low over his eyes, but I still felt them on me.

"Oh. Um. A little," I mumbled, getting up from the chair. "Just put them in the sink. The dishwasher is broken, as are many things in this house."

His tongue slid over his bottom lip, his attention dropping to the dishwasher as he placed the dishes inside the basin.

"I appreciate that. You didn't have to bring them in."

"My grandma raised me to do so." He turned to me, his physique looming over me, making me feel tiny. A smile tugged one side of his mouth.

"Then your grandma raised you right." My voice came out breathier than I intended, my pulse beating against my ribs. "Well, thank you." I motioned for him to leave, needing him out of this room. And definitely not smiling at me like that.

"I can fix your dishwasher."

"Oh." My mouth stopped working. "Um. That's okay. I was going to get someone in to fix it soon anyway."

"Why pay someone? I can do it for free. Just pay for the parts."

"You don't even know what's wrong with it."

"With this model, probably the motor. Buildup of soap can burn it out."

I blinked up at him.

"I've had to become a handyman around my house." He leaned against the sink next to me, lifting one shoulder, the bad-boy half smile snapping my head away again.

S. Marie

"I appreciate it, but I'll just get—"

"Mason?" Addison yelled, coming in from outside. I noticed she had changed her clothes into a short black dress and sandals, her head swiveling to us in the kitchen. My immediate reaction was to step away from him. Her attention went over him, then to the items in the sink. "Oh my god, did you bring in the dirty plates?" She strolled toward him. "Such the gentlemen."

Mason pushed off the counter, his voice low, meant only for me to hear. "Not even remotely."

Oblivious, Addy grinned up at him, squeezing his arm. "Come on, everyone wants to head over to Alex's house. You're coming." She pulled on his arm as if he had no choice.

"Addison?" I tilted my head.

"Please?" She scuttled over to me, her hands pressing together in a plea. "I promise I'll be home by one. And I won't drink."

Right. How many times had I said that?

"I'll watch her." Mason's almost black eyes latched to mine, the air in my lungs sticking in my throat.

It was a promise. An assurance. Then why did it feel more than that?

"Pleasssse," Addy begged.

"Okay, but be home by one." I responded to her but found my attention going back to him, like we were silently communicating with each other.

Watching me, his head dipped in acknowledgment. Then he turned, following his friends out of the house.

Addy bit down on her lip, trying to hold in her excited squeal, looking at me like, *couldn't you just die?*

"Thank you!" She kissed my cheek. "I swear I'll be home by one." She moved for the door, then twirled back, pointing at him, mouthing, "Isn't he so hot?"

He didn't look back as they all headed out, the door slamming behind them, leaving the house empty and quiet.

My shoulders dropped, the sickness I felt earlier punching back into my chest as my heart continued to pound. My skin itched, and I wanted to crawl out of my body, feeling restless and wrong.

Like I woke up after years of being in a coma.

Chapter 8
Mason

Bass thumped through the speakers, vibrating the windows. The constant pulse grated on my nerves, making me feel older than I was. I never went to parties anymore, feeling more comfortable in the garage, fixing up my 1964 GTO, listening to my grandpa's '70s rock station.

Sighing, I leaned against the wall, sipping the warm beer I had been holding for the last hour. Pretending to drink it more than I actually was and pretending to have an okay time when I wasn't. I kept my face neutral, which I had gotten good at.

Blonde hair flipped over a shoulder, light brown eyes slipping to me as Addison wiggled her body to the music with her friends, giving me every sign she wanted me.

Addison Lewis wasn't subtle. She had been nipping at my heels from day one, not hiding she wanted to be next on my list. It wasn't much of a secret at school; girls talked too much for them not to know I had been through most of her group of friends.

For a while, it distracted me from all my past shit, letting me believe I was a normal teenage guy. Then it became more of a habit until I realized I was bored out of my mind, and hanging with my grandpa in the garage was where I'd rather be. Girls this age were so eager to please, so willing to be or do anything to gain the attention of the popular, unattainable guy they all became alike. They thought playing coy made them different from the last girl, trying to be so sexual and willing when they had no clue who they were or what they wanted. They really didn't know what they were doing. They blended together in a faceless, forgettable haze.

I never lied to them. They knew where they stood but still would get clingy after. That's why I never hooked up with the same girl twice. I already sensed Addison's desperation to be wanted. To be loved.

Taking another small sip, my gaze went over the room. Everyone was dancing, playing beer pong, sitting out by the pool, making out on the sofa, or sneaking upstairs. They all seemed happy to be here.

I felt I was the one who didn't belong.

I didn't just feel over a year older than everyone here; I felt fifty years older, my past aging me beyond any of them. Beyond even what a nineteen-year-old guy in college would be.

"Mason?" Addison walked up, taking my hand and pulling on it. She tried to sound sexy, but it came out whiney. "Come dance."

"Fuck no." I snorted.

She pouted her lip. "Please? For me?"

My lids narrowed, wondering when I gave her the impression I was into her. I mean, she was cute and would absolutely be no challenge, which was exactly why I wasn't. I was here because I promised I would watch over her.

The picture of Emery flashed through my mind before I could stop it, instantly hardening my dick. Her long, dark, silky hair, the pain and knowledge in her hazel eyes, the way her chest puffed and cheeks flushed when I was next to her. I had seen her at the game talking to Addison, and the moment I looked at her, I felt this strange draw to her, my eyes going to her over and over.

She was *stunning*.

I couldn't concentrate the entire game, and when Addison invited me over, I didn't say no. I found any excuse to go into the kitchen where Emery was hiding out... and the next moment, I was promising to watch over Addison. *For her*. I didn't even want to be at this fucking party.

"Mason?" Addison tried again, her lip curling lower in a sulk.

"I don't dance." I pushed off the wall. "Think Mateo would be happy to, though." I nodded at my friend, who couldn't stop gawking at her. The coach had yelled at him at practice for staring over at the cheerleaders. We all knew he was looking at one in particular.

I brushed by her, heading outside, needing to get away from all of them. The cool night eased my shoulders down. Everything in me wanted to leave, but I couldn't. Not until Addison got home. For some reason, I needed to keep my word. To have a woman I didn't know, nor should care about, trust me.

Why the hell did I care whether some girl's aunt thought I was a dick or not? I *was* a dick. Though all I felt was relief when Addy introduced her as her aunt and not her mother. There was no way she could have been, anyway. She was older, but not old enough to have had Addison.

Not the point, jackass. She's still way too old for you.

Exhaling, I sagged into a lounge chair, staring at the sky. Life was too damn short, and I resented I was wasting it here. Yet, it was all of my own making. What I wanted was to get my GED and be done with it, but I knew my grandparents wanted to see me graduate. A few times, my grandmother had told me she wanted me to experience all the things I might have missed out on. That it was such a crucial, exciting year for a person.

My dad never graduated from high school, dropping out after junior year, and I know deep down it always bothered them. School was very important to my grandfather. This was my way of repaying them. To give them something they missed with him.

I owed my grandparents everything. They stood by me at my worst, had been there for me, and even moved from the home they loved to this town two years ago for me.

A fresh start. A place where no one knew me. Knew my past.

Where I could be normal.

Except tonight, once again, showed me I wasn't.

Chapter 9
Emery

"Dammit!" I kicked at the washer, my shoes soaking from the water still leaking out of it, flooding the garage. This was the result of buying a cottage from an elderly couple who probably hadn't updated their appliances since they got married in the '70s.

A lot of my money had gone into moving here so I didn't have a whole lot to spend on updates. The thing about death no one tells you is how expensive it is. I was grateful to the Roberts for paying for a lot, but there were still many little things that ate away at my balance I wasn't expecting, and I would never have asked Alisa and John for money.

Another thing people don't understand was that until you win cases and become a big-time lawyer in a firm, which was rarer than TV wanted you to believe, you were broke. Ben had been clerking for free for a while, living off my wages, wanting to do it without his parents. Just because Ben came from money didn't mean we had any of it.

"Asshole." I kicked the machine again, my mind trying to figure out which credit card would allow me to put a new washer and dryer on it without exploding.

"I hope you were talking to the machine." A deep voice hitched the air in my lungs, spinning me around to the open garage door. I pushed it up to drain some of the water inside.

"Shit." I clasped my chest. My lungs pitched, my cheeks instantly flushing.

Mason James stood in my driveway, looking like everything he shouldn't. His 6'3" form was clad in jeans, t-shirt, hat, and boots, similar to what he wore the other night. "You scared me."

"Sorry," he replied. One word said with no inflection, yet I felt it everywhere. I ground my teeth, hating I couldn't seem to stop my reaction to him. It was wrong. "Addison's not here. She's at cheer practice."

"I know." Again, he didn't make it lewd or with any hidden double meaning, solely matter of fact, but I still felt heat cascade down my shoulders. It pissed me off. "I came to fix your dishwasher, but it looks as if I need to add the clothes washer to the list too." A tool box and parts were clutched in his fingers, his dark gaze finding mine under the brim of his hat, making me feel the yoga pants and sports bra I had on were no more than underwear.

"Oh, you don't have to do that. I can call someone. Or get new ones." Although I couldn't afford to replace them all right now. "Think these came original with the house."

He watched me for another beat, and I swear I saw his gaze drop to the wedding ring on my hand, making me itch to explain or hide it. He strolled toward the washer, his body brushing mine. I hopped out of the way, hearing my own intake of air.

"Let me take a look first." He lifted the lid, flexing the muscle in his arms. His hands were rough, like he worked with them a lot. They could easily palm a football... *or my ass.* The thought shot into my head so quickly I jerked back.

I blinked my eyes in anger and shame and backed away more, trying to erase the thought from my head. *Seriously, what was wrong with me?* Resentment flooded me for being some sleazy cougar stereotype. He made me feel jittery and unstable because he didn't look like a normal high school boy.

But he is, Emery. *He is in high school.*

"I'm fine. I got it handled." I practically barked. "Aren't you supposed to be at practice or something too?"

Please leave.

Mason slanted his head to me, his eyes always so fucking intense.

"I should." He grabbed a drill from his tool bag. "There are a lot of things I should be doing."

I folded my arms. "What does that mean?"

"We spend most of our lives doing what we should and not what we truly want."

His sentiment raced through my gut, stirring up all those dreams and ideas I put to the side, flooding me with shame, like I had been called out.

"You'll learn when you grow up and join the real world that life doesn't work out so simply." I shot back. Leaning down, I grabbed a basket, hauling out all the wet clothes still in the washer. "You can't live life doing just what you want to do."

"Why not?" He spoke low, not moving as I grabbed the clothes, his frame so close to mine it crossed the invisible line of intimacy that society wordlessly drew.

"Because if everyone did what they wanted, we'd have a very selfish, ugly world."

"Even if you only had so much time left?" He peered down at me.

My body froze, every muscle stiffening. He peeled back every layer I had, yanking out that question from the pit of my soul.

What would I have changed if I had known Ben and I only had so much time together? How would we have lived? Would I have yanked him into bed instead of letting him go on his run? I know I would have been more forward with sex—more daring and spontaneous. I probably wouldn't have worked so many hours at a job I didn't really care for.

But this was fantasy. Not the real world.

"I try to live life to the fullest, but not selfishly."

"I didn't say anything about being *selfish*," he replied, his dark eyes burrowing into mine. I could feel the implication burn under my skin, squeezing my thighs together with the idea of what someone like him could do to me.

Emery, Stop it!

"Is that why you aren't at practice? Is fixing my washer living life to the fullest?"

His lips curved up, a laugh rumbling from him. "Maybe."

Swallowing, I glanced away. "I heard you used to play football. Why did you quit and become a coach instead?"

I noticed the tendons in his arms flexing and tightening, his expression staying completely neutral.

"I couldn't play anymore… and my grandpa thought assisting would keep me involved in a game I loved."

"But you don't want to coach." It came out as an observation, not a question.

It was so subtle, but his mouth pinched together, his throat bobbing. It took him several moments before he replied. "No."

"You do it for your grandfather." Again, not a question.

"I owe both of them everything."

"So, living for what *they* want?" A smirk danced on my mouth, my eyebrow lifting.

"As I said, I never said I was selfish." His gaze slid to mine, the irrelevant word lighting up every nerve of my body, oxygen thinning out of my lungs as I held his gaze, my head spinning.

"Mason?" Addison's voice pitched from the end of the drive, her eyes squinting against the sun as she peered into the garage. I jolted back, putting a huge buffer between us, which should have been there the whole time, my lungs filling with shame. I was the adult here. I needed to draw the lines.

"Oh my god!" Addison grinned ear to ear, darting inside the garage, her backpack thumping against her. "What are you doing here?"

For a moment his eyes slipped to me, but went right back to her. Completely impassive. He showed no sign he was happy she was here, but no resentment she was either.

"I promised your aunt I'd fix the dishwasher."

"Now, the washer as well." I secured the fake smile on my lips, indicating the film of water on the ground.

Addison's eyes widened, glowing with complete adoration. "Oh my god, that is so sweet. Seriously, Mason, it means so much."

His mouth flattened, not responding to her.

"I can help you," she declared, tossing her pack down on the dryer, fluffing her ponytail like she was preparing for some cheer-off.

"Okay, I'm going to go hang these on the line." I picked up the laundry basket. "And don't worry if you can't fix it. Probably beyond repair," I threw out with an aloof tone, strolling past.

"I enjoy fixing *older*, broken things." His deep rumble hit my spine as I stepped inside the house. Closing the door, a jagged breath scraped through my airways, feeling a pulse drop between my legs.

I slammed my lids together, my knuckles squeezing around the plastic basket until I heard them pop. Addison's giggle could be heard; the thrill of finding him here couldn't be hidden. I had no doubt she thought he came here for her.

She was my priority. He was hers to crush on. No matter if I foresaw him breaking her heart, she had the right to flirt with him. Who knows, maybe they would become an item?

Denying the burning sensation in my heart, I marched to the backyard, dropping the basket in the grass by the clothes line, the late afternoon rays glinting off my diamond ring.

I stared down at it, feeling hollow, broken, lost.

I wanted so badly to feel Ben's arms slide around me, for him to nuzzle my ear, making me feel safe, happy, and content.

Now I was none of those things. Scattered into a million broken pieces, and no matter how much crazy glue there was, I'd never be whole again.

I was non-fixable.

Chapter 10
Emery

"Oh girl, my feet are screaming for a massage." Marcie plopped back in a chair, putting her feet up on another one. The staff lounge was empty except for the two of us. "Just need some young, hot man giving me a foot massage." She wiggled, humming like she was picturing this fantasy. "With a glass of wine and a come-to-Jesus kind of orgasm that puts me right to sleep."

"Sounds good." I took a sip of my coffee, hoping the caffeine would kick in soon. I hadn't slept well last night, tossing and turning, my mind not letting me rest. Because *he* kept popping into my head every time I dozed off, making me hot, sticky, and agitated. The feeling seemed to follow me into my day.

Marcie shot me a look, her attention dropping to the ring on my hand. They all knew I was widowed, but not much else.

"Looks as if you might need the same."

The idea of a hot young man giving me an orgasm shifted me in my chair, causing me to down more caffeine because now he wasn't faceless.

"How long have you been wearin' that?" She nodded at my wedding ring. "After his death?"

My attention went to the diamond, flicking at the band. "Three years." I cleared my throat, feeling my own judgment and defense rising.

Marcie nodded her head. "Do you want my advice?"

"Feels as if I'm going to get it anyway."

"It's as if you already know me so well." She snorted, sitting up and turning toward me at the table. "You know I was married once." She flipped her hand. "Many moons ago. He cheated on me from the start."

"It's sounding very close to my sister's story."

"Sadly, it's too many women's stories." Marcie tucked back her naturally kinky hair, which was falling from the clip. "Each time he left, I continued to wear his ring, giving him chance after chance. Thinking I was some self-sacrificing saint for putting up with his shit."

"Now, you're just plagiarizing my sister's story."

"You know why you, your sister, me, and so many others keep wearing our ring, even though we know it's been over for a long time?" It was a rhetorical question, so I stayed quiet. "It isn't self-sacrificing. It's fear. The ring, good and bad, symbolizes security. Safety. Commitment. That you are off the market. Someone has you. Loves you. And when we lose that, we continue wearing it as a symbol, for all the wrong reasons. To protect ourselves from commitment, from love. We are still off the market. Someone still has us because we are too afraid to try again."

I stared blankly at the table, her speech causing tears to spring behind my lids.

"I'm not telling you when you should be ready, though I think there is a very cute doctor here who hopes you are. I'm just saying don't waste so much time in the past, hiding from the future. I wish I didn't let Darrell rob me of so much of my life." She stood up, straightening out her purple scrubs. "I know our situations are different. Your husband died, but at the end of the day, it's up to us how much we let our own fears dictate the rest of our lives." She picked up her cell, walking to the door. "Food for thought. Okay, back to sucking out saliva, scraping plague, and drillin' in peoples' mouths. Oh goody." She sighed, going out the door.

Marcie left the staff room in a silent loudness, the buzz from the fluorescent lights humming in my ears sounding like mosquitos, the beat of my heart strumming in cadence as the ring on my finger screamed out every insecurity and truth she uttered.

Taking it off meant I was ready to move on. I somehow accepted Ben's death, and I was okay without him. It felt wrong to be okay. To want to move on... to fall in love with another.

He was supposed to be it. The love of my life. Life was ripped from me, and the question was, did I acknowledge the terror and step forward into the future? Or stay in the shadows and memories of the past, where it was safe?

"Emery." My name jarred me to the entrance. Dr. Ramirez walked in, a warm smile taking over his face, lighting up his eyes.

"Dr. Ramirez." I went to my feet, feeling my stomach tie up.

"Daniel, please." He spoke softly.

I nodded, swiping up my coffee and snack wrapper, throwing them in the bin, pointing for the exit.

"Oh, you don't have to leave." A slight disappointment hinted in his timbre, his eyes watching me.

"Break time's over. Last patient for the day." I shrugged, my hand twisting my ring around my finger, calling his attention to it.

His mouth pressed together, staring at my ring.

"Right." His chin dipped slightly, his shoulders going down. "Of course. Well, if I don't see you, have a good night."

"You too," I replied, backing out the door.

I stopped a few yards down the hall, my hand pressing against my stomach.

Marcie was right. I was using my ring to keep me safe. To keep myself protected from life. From experiencing pain and loss again.

But the thought of Daniel asking me out?

There were no butterflies or jitters.

Only fear.

⎯⌁⎮⎯⎮⌁⎮⎯♡

"Addy, I got us pizza!" I called out, stepping in the front door and kicking off my shoes. I brought home a large margarita pizza, thinking the leftovers could be our lunch tomorrow. Pizza was becoming too much of a staple in this house. I really needed to cook occasionally.

The giggly, girly voice she never used around me unless it was about a boy resounded from the kitchen. A prickle shot down my spine, intuition turning my lungs into a butterfly cage.

Swallowing, I strode across the cozy living room, coming into the kitchen, where my eyes landed on a jean-clad ass bending far over into the dishwasher. Holy shit, his ass was round and taut. Something you'd want naked so you could fully appreciate it. Worship it. Mason's shirt hitched up, showing off the lower portion of his broad, muscular back, looking as though he worked out every day. For a guy who didn't play football anymore, he sure appeared as if he did.

Realizing I was standing there ogling him with my mouth open, I jerked myself away, clearing my throat.

"Hey, Aunt Emery." Addy sat on the counter near him, her legs swinging. "Mason stopped by to look at the dishwasher."

"I can see that." Did my voice sound rough? Clearing it, I kept my eyes off him as I moved around, setting the pizza on the counter.

Mason sat back, wiping a line of sweat off his forehead with his arm, his attention turning to me. His t-shirt was slightly soaked in places, sticking to his chiseled abs.

I found myself staring again. It was the first time I had seen him without a hat. His soft, black hair was rumpled in an alarming sexy way, like he had just climbed out of bed and had not been alone. It was long enough you wanted to rake your fingers through it.

I hissed under my breath, whirling my back to them, busying myself with the mail I had piled on the pizza box.

"Just as I thought, it needs a new motor. Think I can keep it working for a while longer."

My teeth clenched together at the sound of his voice. "Thanks," I snapped.

I needed him to leave. To not come back again.

"Mason said the washer was toast, though," Addy spoke like Mason was the guru of appliances.

"Did he?" I flipped through the bills, not looking back, but I could feel his gaze on me, ordering me to turn around. Demanding me.

"I can get the parts, but this model is so old, it will cost more than to replace it."

"Great," I said curtly, twisting around and heading for my bedroom. "I'm going to go change."

My feet took me down the short hall, their voices following me.

"Is she a nurse?" Mason's deep timbre muttered.

"No. She works as a dental assistant for Dr. Ramirez."

"Oh, the office on Main Street next to the drugstore?"

I went into my bedroom, shutting the door, sure Addy replied with an affirmative.

Why did him knowing where I work feel vulnerable? As if the more he learned about me, the more of a real person I became? Not someone's aunt or widow, but a flesh and blood person.

"Just need some young, hot man giving me a foot massage... With a glass of wine and a 'come-to-Jesus' kind of orgasm, which puts me right to sleep."

Yanking my scrubs off and tossing them into the dirty basket, I quickly got into a pair of sweats and tank, trying not to notice how hard my nipples were or how sensitive my breasts and pussy were. Maybe all this was because my body needed sex. To feel alive again. Craving it so badly after this long, it was getting jumbled and confused, looking at any male with a pulse as potential. It had nothing to do with him.

Though, when I tried to put Dr. Ramirez into that spot… I felt nothing.

A tap sounded at my door before Addy sprang in, jumping on my bed, her face bright with joy.

"Can Mason stay for dinner?"

No.

"Please?"

Hell, no.

"Um. Sure. I guess," I croaked out.

"Oh. My. God." She gripped my arm, trying to keep her squeal quiet. "I think he likes me. I mean, he's never gone to any of the other girl's houses and fixed their dishwasher."

"They probably don't have appliances from the 1970s."

She rolled her eyes, high on her hope, which I felt the need to bring down a little.

"Don't read into something that might not be there." I hated myself, but I knew in my gut she needed to not get caught in a fantasy. "As girls we tend to complicate and overanalyze things when it's not really that way to them."

"Why else is he here?" She motioned to the door, staging a whisper. "He is the most popular boy in our school, and every girl in the tri-state area is out for him. He wouldn't leave the party until I did." *Because he promised me he wouldn't.* "And he's come over the last two days to 'fix' something." She did air quotes, like it signified another meaning. *The first time he came, he knew you weren't here.*

I hated myself more for every counterthought that came into my head. Who was I to sway her from him? I could be the one overthinking everything, and he *was* here for her.

I had to find a man my age, get laid, and stop whatever was going on with me. To shut the hell up, step back, and let them be.

"Why don't you and Mason take the pizza outside and enjoy. I'm going to watch TV in here and relax." Drink wine. Forget everything.

"Really?" She leaped up, hugging me. "Thank you. Thank you. Thank you!"

She was doing so well here. Her grades and attitude had flipped completely. I wanted to show I trusted her, giving her the space to be a teenager.

She left my room in a gallop, calling Mason's name.

Huffing, I crawled under my duvet, texting my sister.

Me: Being an aunt is hard.

Harper: Tell me about it. Try being a mother to a teenager. I give it
zero stars. Don't recommend.

I laughed at Harper's text, knowing she felt the exact opposite.

Harper: She doing good?

Me: Yes.

I wanted to tell her she had a boy over now, but I couldn't. There was something about Mason. I had this strange need to keep quiet. If Addy wanted to tell her about him, she could.

Footsteps carried down the hall, too heavy to be Addison's, probably heading for the bathroom.

My breath fluttered, my heart pumping as they stopped.

Right in front of my door.

I didn't move or breathe, as though he would be able to sense it if I did. I could feel him, and I knew somehow he could feel me too. Hear his heartbeat, his body heat slinking under the door, curling around me. Feel every breath he took. Time seemed to suspend. Hold its breath.

Then the footsteps started again, the bathroom door shutting.

Letting out a huge breath, I slumped over in a mix of relief, nerves, and a feeling I wouldn't acknowledge—disappointment.

If he had opened my door and stepped in, I didn't know how I would have responded. And it was *not* okay with me.

I was the grown-up, and I needed to put whatever this was to an end. Even if it was merely in my head.

He was Addison's.

That was it.

Chapter 11
Mason

The crisp air blew into my garage, whirling together the scent of oil, gas, and Grandma's lavender laundry detergent. I stared down at the engine I was rebuilding from scratch, my mind drifting to the house down the street, like it had all fucking afternoon.

"Dammit." I slammed the hood down, knowing I was getting nothing accomplished, and feeling even worse because I skipped football practice again, unable to find the will to show up. I hated to be counted on. To have people depending on me when most likely I would let them down.

"Did your car do something to you, son?" My grandfather shuffled out the door, holding tight to his walker.

"No." I dragged my hand down my face, trying to rub the frustration away. "Guess, I'm not in the mood to deal with it today."

"Huh." My grandfather huffed in a tone where he didn't say anything, but he said everything.

"What?" I peered over at him. From the pictures on the shelf, Neal James was once a very good-looking man. He was in the Air Force, and when he retired, he found rebuilding old cars was a good hobby. The man fixed everything in the house, even if it was fifty years old.

"It's still good." He'd motion to it. "Why get new when you can fix the old?"

"Why fix the old when you can get new?" I used to tease.

"Your generation too easily throws everything away. Wasteful. Plus, the old stuff has history. A story. Just because it's broken doesn't mean it's worthless."

That was my grandpa to a T. He wasn't the hugger like my grandma, but he showed love in the everyday things. The hours he stood next to me, explaining how to fix something, letting me do it, mess up, and try again. Never getting impatient, answering all my questions. He taught me everything I knew about restoring and repairing. Except myself.

"How's school going?" Grandpa rolled his walker closer. "Keeping those grades up? Coach needs you to keep up your GPA."

"I'm doing fine."

"You're not at football practice?" He checked out my GTO, a thread of disappointment in his tone. Grandpa was also a huge football fan. It wasn't only me who was let down when I had to quit playing. He used to come to all my games. Now he watched me assist on the sidelines from the comfort of his chair. He was the one who contacted the coach when we moved here, helping me get the assistant job.

"No." Guilt ticked at my eye, hating to ever let him down.

"You can't ignore your obligations. You told them you'd be there. You need to be there." He was all about keeping to your word, a man's honor.

"I know."

"Hmmm." The sound was full of meaning too.

"Been spending a lot of time down the street." He flicked his chin. "Must be a girl distracting you, am I right?"

A sardonic laugh bubbled up, my hand scouring my face again. "I wish." No, Grandpa, it's not a girl. It's a grown-ass, sexy as hell *woman*.

How much easier it would be if it were Addison. The other night while eating pizza on her deck, I tried to make myself believe she was the reason I was there, or at least could be. I wished this blonde schoolgirl was making me hard, not the dark-haired woman hiding in her bedroom. When Addison told me it was just us two for dinner, I was really disappointed. I mean, sure, Emery was hot—sexy as fuck. But I liked talking to her. And the chemistry when we were near each other was *intense*. Normally, I could shrug that kind of shit off. I've never felt anything too deeply for a girl beyond physical attraction.

That might be where I had been going wrong. Emery wasn't a *girl*.

I couldn't stop thinking—what if I walked into her bedroom, shoved her against the wall, and kissed the fuck out of her?

I swear I felt her on the other side of the door, hearing her pulse in rhythm to mine. Sensing this push-pull of wanting me to come in and not wanting me to. I had to jerk off two times that night, and not once was it Addison I thought of.

The last few days, I stayed away, knowing Addison was reading too much into my actions, behaving more and more at school as if I was already hers. I stayed aloof, steering clear of her, making sure she understood nothing was going on, though she wasn't taking the hint.

"I think I'm gonna go for a run."

Grandpa glanced up at me with a frown.

"Yes, I'll be careful. And I have my phone on me."

His jaw strained, but his head dipped in accord. It was those tiny moments, the look in his eyes, when I knew my grandfather loved me more than anything.

"Okay, when you get back, your grandmother needs you to look under the sink again. Not draining properly, and I can't get down there as I used to."

I snorted. The sink was always clogging. The thing was so damn old. Every week, I would crawl under, knowing exactly what to do, while my grandpa stood near me, playing backseat plumber.

"Okay." I grabbed my running shoes by the door, shoving them on my feet. "I'll be back for dinner."

"It's meatloaf tonight," he belted out after me as if I didn't know. We had the same schedule of meals every week. Wednesday was meatloaf night, and I ate it every time, asking for seconds.

My legs took me down the sidewalk in the direction of the cottage. This was my normal route, no other reason. I passed the cottage every time I went on a run. I tried to keep my gaze ahead, purposely not looking as I ran by.

"Damn it! You suck!" A cry followed by a loud bang of metal had me heading to the garage. My feet stopped short, my mouth twisting up, trying not to laugh as I watched Emery flail and kick at the washer, the ground covered in soapy water again. "You piece of shit!"

"Whoa, whoa… that's no way to talk to it." I strode up, tsking her. She whipped around, her eyes slightly widening before her expression locked down. My cock reacted to how her jeans fit her ass and the desire to run my hands through her long, loose strands, which hit the middle of her back. "No wonder it doesn't want to work for you."

"It doesn't work because it's a relic."

"I told you it was pretty much dead."

Her mouth pinched together. "I was hoping it had one more in it." She leaned her hip into the machine, glaring at it. "At least until payday."

"I can get a part, get it temporarily working until then."

"No." She shook her head. "You don't need to do that. You've already helped enough."

"It's not a problem." I glanced down at her, realizing once again we were barely an inch apart. I gravitated toward her like she was the fucking sun.

Her nostrils flared, her body going still as we looked at each other. It seemed to be the most natural thing in the world to lean down and kiss her as if she were mine to do it. To toss her up on the dryer and fuck her hard, leaving the garage door open so everyone could hear her cries.

The impulse hit me like a truck. Sucking in my breath, I took a step back. Her face flushed as she looked away, as though she had felt the same thing, the air rippling with energy.

"I can get the part tomorrow, if that works." My voice went lower than normal, barely getting out of my mouth.

"Yes, fine. Thanks." She nodded. A fake smile pushed up her mouth, looking all wrong on her. "I'm sure you want to get back to your run."

"Yeah…" I didn't, though. I didn't want to leave. "I probably should head home."

"You live close?"

"Yeah, a few blocks down. The beige house with the air force flag hanging in front, and dilapidated 1967 GTO in the garage."

"1967 GTO?" Her head jerked back. "My dad had one before he died. I was really little, but I remember him loving that car. Made me love it too."

"You can come down and visit anytime you want."

She smiled. This time it was genuine and all her. "You live with your grandparents?"

"I do, but I don't have to."

Her eyebrows crinkled.

"I'm nineteen. Be 20 in December. I stay with them because they need me." I shrugged. "They're getting up in years and too stubborn to go into a home."

"You're 19?"

"I was held back a year." My throat started to close. This was hinting at the area I didn't talk about.

"You didn't get your GED? Graduate with your friends?"

"You'd have to have those first. Ones who stuck around at least." What was it about her? I was telling her far more than I would anyone else. "School is really important to my grandparents, and I guess I don't want to let them down. My grandma thinks experiencing my senior year is crucial—school dances, senior trip, graduation. I couldn't care less, but I want to do it for them."

"Like the football thing."

My shoulders shifted. Emery seemed to see right through me, which made me really uncomfortable. Most people didn't bother. "They never pressured me, but I know it's something they want. I owe them that."

"Why do you feel you owe them?" Her hazel gaze pulled me to her again, and I could feel the depth in them, the pain, like she had lived lifetimes in years, as I had. I stared at her openly, and she didn't break away. Her gaze searched mine as if she could harvest any answer out of me, even if I tried to bury them deep.

"I'd better go order the part." The gravelly words scraped from my throat. "The store can get it in by tomorrow. Don't want you running around with nothing to wear."

A soft laugh went through her nose, her eyes finally breaking, her head wagging.

I stepped back, smiling not unlike a total idiot. "You know, I don't think I know your last name. You know, for the order." Total lie. I didn't need it.

"Oh." I saw her stare absently down, her finger twirling the ring on her right hand. "Campbell." She said it as though she had finally made some decision.

"Well, Ms. Campbell. I will see you tomorrow."

"If I'm not pretty much a Mrs. Robinson," she muttered to herself.

"Who?"

"Nothing." She waved me off. "Thank you, Mr. James. I appreciate it."

Muffling my groan at the way that sounded and needing to rub it out, I jogged out of her garage. I headed back to my house, knowing I was seriously fucked, because no way was anything going to ever happen, but she was all I wanted.

Chapter 12
Emery

Staring blankly at my closet, I flipped through the tops, nothing catching my eye. I spent most of my days in scrubs or yoga pants. When Ben was alive, we worked so hard we only dressed up on special occasions, which was usually an event Alisa and John made us attend. In the last three years, any reason to get dressed beyond work or lounging around the house dropped to zero.

Marcie had made me promise I would show up for drinks tonight. We were meeting at a local pub for happy hour. Low-key, though it felt like a huge deal for me. The first real outing as a single woman.

I had been set up on a few dates previously, but this felt different. Maybe now I was ready. I was accepting my single status, where I hadn't before.

Sitting back on my bed, I pulled in deep breaths, feeling panic rising in my throat, the desire to crawl under my covers and never come out.

A thump sounded on the front door, and I rose slowly, not thinking as I moved, feeling sweaty with anxiety.

I swung open the door and sucked in sharply.

Mason was on the other side, appearing every bit the trouble he was, his cap pulled down, drawing focus to his strong jaw and perfect lips. He was a bolt to my chest.

"What's wrong?" His gaze moved over me.

"Nothing," I replied, throwing a smile on my face, moving back.

He stepped in, stopping in front of me, his attention heavy, once again tearing at my walls. "Don't give me the fake smile. What's wrong?"

"You don't know me." A flare of defensive anger jerked my

shoulders, my head popping up in insolence, tilting back to look fully up at him. I felt seen. No one had ever called me out on that. "And my smile wasn't fake. That's my smile."

"No, it's not." He spoke low, an excuse to get closer. "What's wrong?"

"I said I was fine." I folded my arms.

He tilted his head, not letting up. "And I call bullshit."

Emotion built behind my lids, bare and vulnerable, and I was pissed a nineteen-year-old guy seemed to see right through me.

I peered down at my shoes, my head shaking. "It's nothing... I'm going out to a pub with friends, and..." *Shut up, Em.* You can't tell him how you miss your husband. That you are scared as shit to be back on the singles market again. It was wrong talking to Mason like this. "Never mind. It's nothing." I turned, desperate to get away from the heat of his body, the way he watched me. The way I longed for him to wrap me up in his arms, his body engulfing mine.

"Thank you again for fixing the washer." I nodded at the tools and part he carried. "Let me know what I owe you."

He didn't respond, watching me, slicing through the barrier I was trying to keep up.

"Grab whatever you want from the kitchen. Addison should be home in an hour or so. I'm going to go get ready." I didn't give him time to respond, dashing back to my room. The walls protected me from his gaze.

From him.

Pulling on some jeans, a nice top, and heels, I left my hair down and did simple makeup before heading down the hall.

Clanks and bangs chimed from the garage, drawing me to him. Telling myself I was merely checking in on his progress, I grabbed a light jacket, purse, and keys, stepping out into the garage.

"Everything going okay?"

Mason's head snapped to me. His black eyes skimmed over every inch of my figure, like fingers caressing my skin. His expression stayed impassive, but I noticed his nostrils flared, his throat bobbing. "Yeah."

Dark, coiling heat pulsed between my thighs with an acute throb. My teeth drove into my lip. Slamming my walls up, my own expression becoming deadpan.

"Good." I nodded with an unfriendly tone. "How much do I owe you?"

His focus on me didn't relent as he stood fully up, his shirt sticking to him, cutting into his muscular torso. He looked nothing like a high schooler. The other boys Addison hung around seemed like children to me. Pompous, arrogant little boys playing grown-up. Trying to act like men.

Mason was what they were all pretending to be. He made men my own age seem young and immature.

"It's on the house."

"No." I shook my head, my hair tickling my arms. "You bought the part. Let me at least reimburse you for it."

"I don't want your money."

"Then what do you want?" The moment the question tumbled off my tongue, I wanted to swipe it up and shove it back into my mouth. I could hear the implication, the innuendo, as if I really were Mrs. Robinson propositioning a younger man.

His jaw twitched, his gaze growing even more penetrating. For one split second before sanity took control again, I let my mind imagine him striding up to me, slamming me up against the dryer, kissing me fiercely. Feeling him thrust into me, showing me true pleasure. It was not sweet or loving. It was raw, brutal, passionate, and intense.

Looking away, I flushed from desire and complete shame because Mason fit perfectly into my faceless fantasy man. I had no doubt Mason picked up on something; the air in the room was thick and carnal.

"Here's some money." I pulled the a few bills from my purse, slamming it on the dryer, trying not to picture my bare ass on it while he drove into me. Damn, it would be hot. I patted at my hairline, peppered with sweat. It was warm tonight.

Mason sauntered over, his finger curling around the money, his cap blocking half of his face from me.

"If it's not enough, let me know. If it's over, use it to buy you and Addison dinner." I purposely brought up her name, reminding myself and him she was the one he should be here to see. Should be dating.

Though the idea of Mason dating Addy didn't fit. I would want to protect her from guys similar to Mason. He was way too advanced. I loved her more than anything, but she was still immature, and too desperate for affection. Someone like him would destroy her.

"Okay. I'm heading out now. Have a good night." I cleared my throat, moving around him to my car.

"You're going to be drinking?" His timbre stopped my heels, curving me back to him.

"Yes. I'm *old enough* to drink." The lash came out harsher than I meant, but he needed to be put in his place, and I needed to be reminded how young he really was.

"And driving?" He folded his arms, leaning against the dryer, his forearms budging at the simple action.

"I'm having one." My lids narrowed, and I returned to where he was standing, getting a foot away. "Don't judge me, junior. I am an adult."

Mason's mouth twitched, as if he were finding me humorous.

"Goodnight, Mason." I twisted away, annoyed I engaged in this.

An arm reached over me, plucking the keys from my hand.

"What the fuck?" I swung to him. "Give me back my keys."

"I'll drive you."

"No." I tried to grab my keys. He stuffed them deep into his front pocket. "Mason…" Irritation huffed through my nose.

"Uber or I drive you."

"Who the hell do you think you are?" I exclaimed. "This is my house. My car."

He stayed silent; his arms still folded over his chest.

"Mason." Anger flared. "Give me my fucking keys."

No response.

I watched him for a moment, my head shaking as I tucked hair behind my ear.

"Playing this cute little game?" Challenge coated my words. "You forgot." I stepped in slightly closer, his chest flexing at my nearness.

"What?"

"I'm not a little high school girl who swoons when you walk by, too shy to go after what she wants." I knew I was crossing a line, but I couldn't stop myself. My hand slid into his front pocket, his entire body going rigid as I grabbed for my keys, my fingers brushing his cock. There was no way to avoid it.

His dick was hard and seriously huge. Humiliation and desire swept through me. I tried to swallow my gasp as I yanked my car keys out, turning quickly away, acting like I neither felt nor was affected by it.

"My father was killed by a drunk driver."

Mason's declaration stopped me in my tracks, facing him again. "What?"

He gazed off to the side, his body going on defense, as if he hadn't meant to let that out.

"I was nine."

My head bowed, realizing this whole thing wasn't about him trying to be difficult or even cocky. This was about a little boy who lost his dad.

Something I understood.

"I'm sorry."

He huffed derisively, and I knew exactly how trite the phrase was, no matter how good the intentions were from the giver. They became hollow and empty.

"I understand losing someone." Actually, many people.

"I know you do." His gaze shot back, tipping to the ring I still wore, then back to my face.

I assumed Addison told him some of my story. Enough to know I was a widow.

Silence hung between us, but it didn't feel uncomfortable. Sometimes not saying anything was the best support. Just standing by them, telling them in actions you are there for them.

Eventually my curiosity opened my mouth. "You live with your grandparents. What about your mother?"

"Who knows? She ran off after I was born." He pushed off the machine with a shrug, sauntering up to me, forcing my head to tip back. "Let me drive you."

Emotion and need shook through my limbs, my heart hurting for him. It took all I had not to go up on my toes and kiss him. It was immoral, I understood that, but the urge almost stole my breath. Forcing myself to move back, I nodded my head.

Taking the keys from me, he traveled to my car while I followed behind, slipping into the passenger seat. He commanded the space inside my CR-V, making me overly aware of every molecule he took up. He drove with a swagger. Compared to his GTO, this car was probably child's play. Anyone passing by us would think we were a couple, not imagining over ten years separated us.

Biting my lip, I kept my attention out the side window, fixated on the changing leaves falling to the ground. The only time I spoke was to tell him where to drop me. The car ride was quiet and weirdly tense, but strangely comfortable too.

"Thank you." My voice came out wobbly when he stopped in front of the pub. "I'll get an Uber home."

He nodded, his cheek twitching, his gaze going to a few guys heading into the pub.

Unbuckling, I climbed out, taking in a breath. I had the urge to get right back in again and tell him to take us home, where we could watch movies and eat popcorn.

The door swung open, and I could see Marcie and a few others already in there.

You can do this.

"Again, thank you." I gripped the door, talking to Mason. "And please get a pizza or whatever you guys want for dinner."

His jaw ticked again, his gaze swinging to me, looking anything but happy. "Have a good night."

"You too." I slammed the door, my heels clicking to the front of the pub, hearing my car peel off.

I watched the taillights disappear, my heart sinking in my chest.

"Enough, Emery." I reprimanded myself as I stepped into the busy, loud pub, hearing Marcie yell out for me, feeling like I was doing what I *should*, not what I *wanted*.

Chapter 13
Mason

My hand pumped down my shaft, my dick aching as I squeezed harder, the shower pelting down on my back. A groan slipped between my teeth as I pictured Emery's body, her back arching, her cries loud as I thrust into her, cracking the washing machine against the wall, leaving a gaping hole.

"Fuck." I stroked harder, my spine burning as I jerked, cum spurting out, my hips still moving as my orgasm continued, though it didn't ease the tension in my body. My dick understood this wasn't real. It wasn't deep inside her. With a sigh, I fell against the tile, unsatisfied.

A brush of her fingers when she grabbed for her keys, barely grazing my dick, but I still could feel her touch, as though she burned her mark into my flesh.

Then to sit there watching her walk into the pub, in those tight jeans, sexy, low-cut top, and fuck-me heels, knowing every male there would be staring at her, moving in on her, buying her drinks, flirting, trying to get in her pants.

A laugh burst out, and I rubbed my face. *Are you any different, asshole?* The only thing different was I was too young to be the one buying her drinks.

I scoured my face harder.

The thought of any guy touching her, kissing her, causing her to cry out made me want to tear everything apart. Emery Campbell was the kind of beautiful that had men lose their minds, but it was more than that for me. The chemistry between us was instant and so damn palpable it was painful. A connection I couldn't explain, but it drew me to her. I didn't just *want* to be around her; I *needed* to be, especially when she was challenging me, pushing all my buttons. It took everything I had to not kiss her tonight. To have her naked up on her dryer, fucking her until she could no longer move.

Shutting off the water, I grabbed a towel, my aggravation not ebbing at all even after jerking off twice. Torturing myself when nothing could ever come of it felt like some twisted S&M shit. Yet, it seemed exactly what I was into.

When I got back to her house, I stood in front of the washer, the job minutes from being done. And what did I do? I broke the replacement part. I was such an asshole, but it gave me a reason to come over again. Otherwise, what was my purpose? I wasn't so much of a dick to use Addison. I wouldn't deny I thought about it, but she would get even more clingy. A sweet girl I sadly had zero interest in.

My phone buzzed on the counter, and I lifted it to my ear. "Mateo."

"Hey, Mas. Just checking in to see if you want to go to a house party. I know you always say no—"

"Yes." My mouth uttered before I even thought about it.

"What? Seriously?" Mateo's shock at my response was obvious. "Shit. All right, man. Cool."

I needed to get out, take the edge off. Find a pretty girl who would get my dick wet and make me forget everything else. Like the fact I told Emery about my father. The basic truth about my mom. No one here knew that. Not even my supposed friends knew anything about me, except I played football a few years back and was really good. Because no one in high school really gives a shit. Everything is surface. As long as you're hot, popular, and play hard to get, the girls want you, and the guys want to be around you so they can pick off whatever's left.

Harsh, but true. High school was a crueler, more primitive version of the animal kingdom. I couldn't give a fuck about any of it. Tonight I needed to not feel, to escape my past, and evade my future. To be a normal 19-year-old guy who goes to a party to get drunk and laid.

It wasn't a choice, because if I didn't go, I would find myself back at the Main Street Pub, marching in and claiming her. Knowing rejection would come with a brutal slap to my face and a sting to my ego.

I needed to do anything to stop the craving I had for the woman I could never have.

Music thumped in the back of my head as knocks pounded on the bathroom door. Somebody wanted in. My head spun, my vision not able to hold on to anything.

Fuck, I was drunk. I had never been this plastered before.

I could sense my grandparents' disappointment, telling me I shouldn't be drinking. For one night, I didn't want to follow what I should be doing. Except this wasn't what I wanted to be doing either.

"Mason..." a girl breathed, her lips wrapping around my dick, sucking harder. "I've wanted to do this for so long." My hands wrapped in her hair, pushing my dick further down her throat, trying to steady my focus on her dark hair, feel what she was doing to me, pretending it was someone else. But I couldn't. She was all wrong, her voice, her body, her girlie baby talk.

"Fuck," I hissed, trying to pull back. "Stop."

"No!" She moved back for me. "I want to. Tell me what you want. I can do better."

It wasn't her words. It was the pleading in her tone. The desperation for me to remember her. To get me off. To be someone I bragged about to others. To be patted on the head and told she did good.

I felt even more disgusted.

"Nooo," I slurred, pushing away. I stumbled out the door, zipping myself up, already forgetting her face. Dick move? Yes. But I was in full dick mode tonight.

Everything was pissing me off. And as much as I couldn't have stayed home tonight, watching Jeopardy on TV, I shouldn't have come here either. I was angry. Lost. I felt like I didn't fit anywhere.

Stumbling and weaving down the hall, I tried to block out the only clarity in my drunken, fuzzy state, which didn't go away with alcohol.

She was the one thing that made me feel completely calm. Not in the normal sense—our crazy tension was anything but peaceful or gentle—but I felt comfortable. At home. There was nowhere else in the world I wanted to be.

I belonged there. With her.

It fucked with my head because it was all a lie.

Tripping over something, I tumbled down onto a sofa, flopping face first. I didn't move, just wanting to sleep and forget. I let my mind drift off.

"Mason? Hey dude..." Someone flipped me over. "Wake up. The police are coming. We got to go."

I mumbled, but even I had no idea what I was trying to say.

"We have to go, Mateo. Can you get him up?" A girl's voice spoke, one I knew because it talked nonstop when I came over.

My lids pried open, seeing blonde hair and a similar face structure as her aunt.

"Get him up." Addison egged Mateo, grabbing for my other arm.

Mateo groaned, trying to pull me up. "Come on, help us out." I think I tried, but everything felt so flimsy and spastic. "This fucker is at least three times my size." Mateo heaved me onto my feet, Addison getting her shoulder under my other arm, moving me out the door and pushing me into Mateo's Honda Civic, my body having to almost fold in half to fit in the backseat.

Mateo sped away, my head spinning until I was forced to close my eyes so I wouldn't throw up. I listened to him and Addison muttering back and forth from the front, easy and fluid like they could talk to each other for hours, lulling me into sleep... but even there, I couldn't find peace.

Because she was waiting for me there too.

Daylight broke through my lids, exploding pain behind in my head. Groaning, I tried to hide under my covers, but the blanket on me felt all wrong. My body was stiff and achy, as if I hadn't moved all night, my mouth tasting like something died in it.

"You're finally awake."

I jolted at her voice, my eyes bolting open.

Emery sat on the arm of the sofa wearing sleeper pants, a tank, and a cardigan, her hand cupping a coffee mug. Her face was bare of makeup, her hair slightly messy as if she had just woken up.

Even hungover, my cock went hard. She was gorgeous. *This is how I'd see her every morning waking up next to her.*

Wait.

I blinked, my mind finally catching up. My eyes whipped around the room, and I realized I wasn't at home. The cozy living room told me I was on Emery's sofa, smelling like booze, wearing my t-shirt and boxer briefs, with only a blanket covering my erection.

"What am I doing here?" I croaked out, every syllable making me flinch. I couldn't remember anything past arriving at the party and someone handing me several triple shots of something.

"It seems Addison and Mateo tried to take you home." She rolled her lips together as if she were keeping something back. "But you wouldn't go. They got you in here where you passed out."

Still feeling confused, I glanced at the clock. 9:43 a.m.

"Shit, my grandparents." I sat up.

"I called them." She tapped her fingers against her mug. "They know you're fine."

I sank back into the cushion with relief, my fingers pinching my nose. "Thanks."

Emery took a sip of coffee. I could feel her, her every breath, her heartbeat, the words she wanted to say sitting on her tongue.

"What?" I opened one eye.

"I find it amusing." Her brow cocked up. "The one giving me a hard time about drinking last night is the one passed out drunk on my sofa. With no pants on." Her regard rolled over the jeans, jacket, and boots strewn across her floor.

"It bothers you?" I kept steady on her.

"That a nineteen-year-old is hungover on my sofa?"

"No. That I'm not wearing any pants?"

Her attention dropped briefly to the blanket barely covering me, not hiding my hard-on, before she yanked her head away, climbing off the sofa arm.

"You should probably get to school." She sounded reserved, parent-like, trying to draw the line back, putting me on the other side.

"Wait." I scrambled up after her. My hand wrapped around her wrist, the touch like a jolt straight to my heart and dick. Emery shivered, her eyes shooting down to where I touched her. We both hung in the moment, a bubble of awareness. I knew she felt it as I did, her lungs heaving, her gaze locked on my fingers.

My cock became steel, throbbing in rhythm to the pulse against her wrist. Her gaze dipped low, pink dotting her cheeks, noticing my reaction to her.

The moment was far more than it should have been, swaying my already aching head, about to lose my balance. Dropping my hand away, I put distance between us, my fingers brushing through my rumpled hair.

"You need to get to school." She pushed out, folding her arms over her breasts. Her eyes looked everywhere but at me, while mine seemed unable to leave her. The last thing I wanted to do was go to school. To leave this house.

"Well, you know, no *kid* should go to school on an empty stomach."

Chapter 14
Emery

Kid.

I wanted to laugh. Everything about him defied that word. Shredded it into tiny bits and mocked me.

Mason James wasn't only physically beyond his years, but mentally as well. Every moment I was around him, he became even more divided from his peers or the men who came up to me last night at the bar. And his body was not anywhere close to a boy's.

Oxygen ceased in my lungs my body responding to his touch. My skin sparked with fire, my breasts swelling under my tank, my pussy squeezing as my gaze went to his cock, hard and thick in his boxer briefs. Heat filled me like a balloon, all thought and logic floating away. The only thing I could hear was the pounding of my pulse, the air going in and out of my nose.

He needed to leave. To get out of my house and far away from me. The draw to him was too much. The thread between us hummed with an energy I couldn't explain, proving my sexual drive wasn't dead, and my body hadn't closed up shop when Ben died. Right now, I wished it had. I needed an excuse for why I was not interested in any of the good-looking men who came up to me last night or when Dr. Ramirez was trying to talk to me. But it was only Mason who stirred this reaction in me.

All night it was there, the truth. Whenever I talked to someone, I kept peering at the door behind them, disappointed when someone walked through because it wasn't the person I wanted. I couldn't say how many times I looked at my phone, about to dial Uber because everything about the night felt wrong and uncomfortable.

I was drinking away the raw, desperate need to go home because what

I craved was in my garage, and because of it, I forced myself to stay. To smile and laugh. To pretend I was listening and having fun.

The entire time I tried to convince myself I was going through a glitch in my system, a natural reaction to finding myself single again and attaching myself to something that felt more comfortable to me, and it was all perfectly innocent.

Though when I walked in the door, all those thoughts went to shit.

Mason was sprawled out on his back on my sofa, his pants and shoes on the floor. The fuzzy blanket placed over him was sliding off, displaying his body. He still had on his t-shirt, but it was stretched up, showing off his cut abs and his deep V-line carving down into his black boxer briefs.

The sexual attraction I had been begging for all night from any guy at the bar, including Daniel, fired up the back of my spine, clenching my thighs.

My eyes took in what my fingers had barely brushed earlier. Like an iceberg, the extent of his size had been hidden under his jeans. Now I could see the massive outline of it.

Desire flared brutally through me. The impulse to climb over the sofa and straddle him, pulling down his boxer briefs and sinking down on him, hearing both of us moan in utter pleasure.

"Don't be mad." Addison came darting out of her room, wearing her pj's. For a moment, jealousy and rage locked through my muscles. Had they been fooling around?

"What is going on?" Angry. Demanding.

"There was a party at Noel's. It was totally low-key." Lie. I could hear the same inflection Harper used on Mom when she was caught sneaking in. "Just some friends hanging out." She held up her hands. "Mateo wasn't drinking."

"Were you?"

"I had *one*. I promise."

"What is Mason doing here?"

She tugged nervously at her messy ponytail. "He got hammered. I don't know what was up with him. He was angry from the moment he arrived. He was drinking shot after shot."

My gut pinched, a slight twinge wondering if I had been the cause of that. *Don't be stupid. You had nothing to do with it.*

"Mateo drove us home, but Mason wouldn't get out of the car, muttering something about needing to fix our washing machine. He would only get out of the car here."

The twinge turned to a spasm.

"It took us both to get him to finally calm down and inside, where he passed out."

"His clothes?"

"That was all him." She held up her hands in defense again. "I went to bed. He must have done it after."

I stared at her, seeing no lie in her features.

"I promise you, Aunt Emery. Nothing happened. Believe me, he was being a pain in the ass tonight."

I snorted, scrubbing at the headache forming.

"Okay." I nodded, believing her. "Go to bed. I'll let his grandparents know where he is. We'll talk about this party tomorrow. But you are getting up and going to school tomorrow. Not one complaint."

"We have a game tomorrow. I can't miss school anyway." She nodded eagerly, hugging me quickly. "Night." Her gaze went down to him, her cheeks reddening, and I knew exactly what she was looking at.

"*Good night,* Addison." I pointed to her bedroom.

She grinned, the schoolgirl crush still showing on her face as she skipped to her room, conjuring sweet romantic notions of Mason James.

When her door shut, a huge sigh flew from my lungs. I peered down at the passed-out guy on my sofa, pulling the blanket up to his chest.

"Emery…" Still sound asleep, my name came out as barely a whisper. My muscles froze while the rest of my body responded to the hoarse way he said my name. The power it had over me, the yearning it inflicted without my control. My notions were a lot dirtier. Nothing sweet or romantic.

Now, I watched him stroll into my kitchen, still only wearing his t-shirt and boxer briefs, his hair messy. If anyone saw us, looked at my pj's and bedhead, they would come to *one* conclusion. And I wouldn't blame them. It didn't merely look bad. It *was* bad.

Even if I explained it, the fact he was walking around half dressed, and I wasn't putting my foot down spoke even louder.

"I think you should go," I said, quieter than I meant to.

Mason opened my fridge, his eyebrows crinkling at my empty shelves, ignoring me.

"Mason?" I cleared my throat, wrapping my cardigan around my braless chest tighter. "This is... um..." I tapered off, pressing my lips together. "Improper."

"What's improper is what's in your refrigerator." He yanked out a wilting tomato, one of the last from the garden. "Do you actually eat real food?"

"I haven't been grocery shopping this week," I countered. "I've been busy."

"You have an overripe tomato, three eggs, a block of questionable cheese, mustard, and a week-old Chinese takeout carton." He picked up the Chinese takeout, sniffing it, flinching before he tossed it in the garbage. "Now minus the takeout." He gathered the rest of the items, his head shaking, taking them over to the counter.

"Addison and I order out a lot." I felt defensive, my eyes tracking how easily he moved around my kitchen, opening drawers, grabbing pans, a cutting board, and knives like he lived here. I watched in awe as he started cooking, his confidence in his actions skimming something deep inside I didn't want to acknowledge.

"You know how to cook?"

He shrugged. "There was a time I was at home a lot, not able to do much. Bored, I started to watch my grandmother cook. And slowly it turned into her teaching me." He sliced the tomato, pushing the pieces into a pile before starting on the cheese. "I actually enjoy it. It's oddly calming to me. It keeps my mind off things."

"You enjoy busy work, like fixing things and cooking," I added, leaning against the doorjamb.

His black eyes shot to me, his lip tugging up slightly before he looked back at what he was doing.

"Yeah, I guess. It takes my mind off everything, and for that time, I'm in the moment. No past, no future. Just now."

His words struck something in me, stirring me. I shifted off the wall, heading for the pot of coffee.

"Want one?"

"Yes. Black." He cracked the eggs into the pan, nodding.

I poured a coffee, setting it in front of him.

"Thanks."

"Least I can do." I flicked my chin at the breakfast he was making. "I'm not really one who finds enjoyment in cooking. My interest lay in other places. Though I make a mean salad."

"Good." He dumped the tomato and cheese into the pan, setting it on the stove. "Because salads are not my forte." His heavy gaze went to me, like we were trying to see how compatible we were. See where our lives would blend together.

My attention darted out to the garden, not acknowledging his implication.

"So, what do you enjoy doing?" He stirred the eggs, the smell of melting cheese filling up my kitchen. "Let me guess, you love cleaning people's teeth," he teased.

A laugh choked out of me. "Oh, hell no." I chuckled again. "It was just a way to survive. To pay bills while Ben was in law school."

Mason didn't react, his face staying neutral as he fussed with the eggs. I figured he knew about Ben, but it was the first time I had mentioned my husband in front of him, and it made me feel strangely uncomfortable.

"My dream was to open my own pet adoption place. Finding the perfect home for each one." I leaned back on the counter, trying not to stare at his firm, pert ass. "While my sister Harper was the cheerleader and popular one, I was the girl volunteering at animal shelters and walking dogs on weekends."

"Why did you give it up?" He glanced back at me.

"Life." I lifted a shoulder. "Responsibilities. Bills. It wasn't practical at that time. Plus, Ben was highly allergic."

"Okay, but what about now?" He shut off the stove, carrying the pan to the kitchen table, hearing the silent *but Ben is no longer here, so what is stopping you?*

"Life. Bills. Responsibilities." I grabbed plates and forks, walking them over to the table.

"Do you want to be a dental assistant?"

"It's not so easy," I snipped, feeling the judgment crawling up my spine. Not from him, but from myself. I had asked myself all of this before but continued to do nothing. Letting my life slip by, doing just enough to survive, playing it safe, but not doing anything I loved.

"Well, volunteering in a shelter would at least be a start. Be around animals again?"

"Yeah." I nodded. Mason scooped the eggs onto my plate, sitting down as if we ate breakfast together every morning.

"I'm surprised you don't even have a dog."

"Too busy, I guess." I stabbed my fork into my food. "What about you?" I shoved the eggs into my mouth. "Oh my god... this is amazing." I blinked with surprise. It wasn't as if I never ate eggs, but these tasted really good.

67

"Secret spices."

"I have those?"

Mason let out a deep laugh. The power of it hummed through me, curling my toes.

"Little milk, with salt and pepper." A grin pulled up the side of his mouth, fluttering my lungs.

Staring down at my plate, I concentrated on my breakfast. "So, what do you want to do when you grow up?"

The air in the room shifted instantly, darkness wiping the smile right off his face.

"I don't know." He sat back. "Doesn't really matter."

"What do you mean? Don't you have lofty plans of your own? At least go to college? Party too hard, hook up with the hot coeds? Isn't that what guys your age are supposed to do?"

His gaze shot to me, his lid lowering as though I had insulted him. "Ahh." He scoffed. "Party. Drink. Fuck."

A gasp knifed the back of my throat, the way he said it seeping wetness from me as if his wicked tongue had actually licked through me.

"Got me all figured out." He tossed down his fork on his plate with a frown. "Spend money on a degree I'll never use, have a job which makes me miserable. Sounds like a great, full life."

"Mason…" I tapered off, not sure where his anger was coming from.

"You know what? You're right." He scooted back his chair, ire sparking off him. "That's what I should be doing with my life. Partying and fucking everything that walks. It's not as if there can be much else for me past that." He stood up. "Thanks for letting me crash on your sofa." He strode out to the living room.

"Mason?" I sprang up, a sick dread weaving around my ribs, wringing my stomach. Everything in me screaming for him not to go. "Wait."

He yanked on his jeans, grabbed his boots and jacket, and headed for my door.

"Mason!" I darted after him, grabbing his arm as he opened the front door. "What's going on? Did I say something wrong?"

He stood over me, a sadness in his eyes. My heart was pounded with the desperate need to pull him into me.

"No." He wagged his head, his jaw straining. "It made me very aware I will never have what other people do."

"What?"

"A future." Resentment flared in his face. "By the way, your washer is broken again. Better get someone in to fix it." He turned, slamming the door, leaving me confused and shaken, gutted and hollowed out.

It felt as though he took something with him when he left.

Chapter 15
Emery

"Someone pee in your cheerios this morning?" Marcie sauntered into the breakroom, her perfectly sculpted eyebrow popping up as she took me in. "You weren't that drunk the other night to be still hungover."

"No." I shook my head. "Just tired." Because I hadn't slept in the last two nights. The heaviness in my chest, the acid in my stomach, the restlessness in my limbs wouldn't go away. It clung to me like a ghost, trailing me around everywhere I went. I was afraid it would never go away because I wasn't willing to admit why.

"O-kay." Marcie grabbed a tea from the fridge, looking at the fries I left untouched in front of me.

"All yours." I pushed them toward her, flopping back in my chair.

"You sure?"

"Yes." Nothing tasted good. It was all lifeless and bland.

"I mean, my mama taught me not to waste food. It's wrong. So, I'll do you a favor here." She yanked them to her, gobbling up two.

"Appreciate it." I pulled my knees into me, my fingers playing with the label on my drink.

"Spill it. What's going on?" Marcie dipped the fries in ketchup, her fingers wiggling at me like *start talking*.

"Nothing. I'm tired. Didn't sleep last night."

"Didn't sleep because a man from the past is keeping you up, or a new one?"

"Both."

Marcie's eyes bulged. "What?"

Oh shit.

"No! No!" I shook my head. "There's no new man."

"Because I was thinking, unless you slipped out with one of those hotties at the bar…" She pointed a red nail at me. "Because FYI, I did."

"What?" My mouth opened in awe. "Which one?"

"The tall blond one." She hummed under her breath. "You know I enjoy a little vanilla in my cup."

Laughter broke out from me. "Oh my god. I love you." I wagged my head. "Can I be you when I grow up?"

"The world couldn't handle another me." She batted her hand. "Now tell me, what's going on?"

Reclining back, I brushed my hair off my face, retying it into a ponytail. "I don't know. I'm in this weird place. It feels as if I'm having a mid-life crisis or something."

"Ready to let him go, but actually too scared to let him go, the in-between place," she said, mentioning something that had been sitting on my chest. "I can't imagine what it's like for you."

Because Ben and I didn't break up, I couldn't contact him or try to have closure. He died. There was no closure.

I nodded, pressing my lips together. "Also, just thinking about what I used to want to do with my life, you know, before responsibility came in and screwed it all up."

"You mean the dream I had of marrying some Saudi prince who lavishes me in jewels and riches, and he bestows on me a hundred young shirtless men at my beck and call?"

"Yes, exactly like that." I snorted.

"So, you are a mini-me." She popped another fry into her mouth with a grin.

"I don't know. I used to want to be more. Not that this isn't a great job. And maybe it's why it's so easy to stay and not push myself. This is safe, comfortable, and gives me good pay and benefits."

"And kids who bite your fingers, kick, and spit in your face," she added.

Billy actually threw up on me last time. His gag reflex was oversensitive.

"I wanted to open an animal adoption place."

"Sounds like hell to me, but if it's what you want, then do it."

"You make it sound so easy." And I actually didn't know if I wanted to run one anymore. The pressure of carrying a business didn't sound as appealing as it used to. I still wanted to travel. Something Ben and I never got to do.

71

"And you are making it too difficult." She leaned over, patting my hands. "As you had to brutally learn, you have one life to live. Don't waste it because of fear. When you look back one day, you always regret what you didn't do, not what you did." She stood up, wiping her hands off on a napkin. "That's why I will be dipping into the vanilla sugar tonight. Hmmm-hmmm." She wiggled. "He got me to Jesus-land. Several times."

I pressed my forehead to my knees, giggling as Marcie pumped her hands up at the ceiling in gratitude, strolling out of the breakroom.

Her words continued to loop in my head, making me feel courageous. Pulling out my phone, I typed in 'animal shelter,' bringing up the local one. It was a few blocks down Main and up a side street.

I could at least walk past it on my way home.

"Looks as if Goose found a friend." A tiny-framed, older woman in a shelter apron smiled down at me. My fingers slid through the thick, husky coat, the dog's tongue licking my hand through the bars. Joy curled my mouth seeing a hold sign pinned to his cage, telling me he was being adopted.

"He's a sweetie." I scratched him behind his ear.

"Nick told me you are looking to volunteer?" She motioned back to the guy at the front desk. "I'm Anita, by the way."

"Emery." I stood up, shaking her hand. "I used to work at a shelter a long time ago. Things came up, but now…" I tapered off. My husband was deathly allergic, so I couldn't, but now he's dead, so I really don't have a reason anymore.

"Great. It's always so much easier if you already had some experience." Anita motioned me to follow, her tiny frame moving quickly to a desk, handing me a clipboard with papers to fill out. "You can fill out these, and we can start the process. You will need to do training, and we require a weekly commitment. A two-hour shift for six consecutive months."

"I can do that." I took the clipboard, settling down in a chair.

"You'll be able to start right away?" Anita asked. "It gets crazy during the holidays, and it would be nice to have you all trained and ready to go."

"Absolutely."

Anita smiled. "I think you'll fit in great here. Glad you came in."

I took a beat, a genuine smile forming on my lips.

"Me too."

"Aunt Emery, I have nothing clean to wear." Addison stomped into the kitchen, where I was trying to actually put a meal together, my good mood earlier giving me some belief I could suddenly become a chef too. "My uniform is filthy, and I'm running out of underwear. We need to fix the washing machine."

"I put a call in. They can't fit me in until next week."

"How about buying a new one? You can order them online and have them delivered."

Yeah. I should. It was time, but for some reason I hadn't gotten around to it.

"At least let me text Mason." I stiffened at the mention of his name, my attention staying on the hamburger patties I was making. "See if he can get it working until we replace it. Seriously, I need my uniform washed before tomorrow."

"We can't call him whenever something breaks." I huffed, shaping the hamburger patties.

"Why not?" Her fingers were already flying over her cell. "Plus, I kind of want a reason to see him."

"Oh?" Neutral. Didn't care.

"He's been really standoffish since the night he stayed here. I haven't seen him at football practice all week."

"Really?" I twisted to Addy, the neutral place I was in totally crumbling.

"Mateo doesn't even know what is going on with him." She stopped typing. "Well, I texted him."

"Oh." The word came out again, sounding very different. I turned back to the meat, finishing shaping them into circles and putting them in the broiler. "We have salad and hamburger patties for dinner tonight."

"Look at you, Rachel Ray." Addy laughed. "Volunteering at the shelter and now making actual dinner. What's gotten into you?"

Before I could reply, a knock struck the door, and my stomach dropped to my feet.

She squealed, running to answer it.

What had gotten into me? I was afraid that answer had walked through the door.

Busying myself with dinner, I didn't want to think about why he made me feel so jumbled and hyper aware. He shouldn't. I mean, he was the one who stormed out of here and hadn't been back, and as much as it drove me crazy, it was for the best. We needed to reset the boundaries, end whatever odd thing we had between us, and keep each other squarely in the proper boxes.

He was Addy's friend.

I was a thirty-year-old widow who had no excuse or reason to be looking or talking to a boy his age.

"So happy you came." Addison clapped her hands, talking like a speeding train again. "Please, if you can just fix it for a few more loads. I need my cheer uniform for tomorrow."

I didn't turn around, but my skin hummed, the back of my neck feeling his gaze, my body aware of every molecule he took up when he stepped into the kitchen. Demanding every breath of air. Yanking on that thread I couldn't seem to cut.

"Aunt Emery, Mason's here to save us."

"We appreciate your help." Poker-faced, I glanced over my shoulder. I shouldn't have.

Everything I was holding on to, the distance over this last week I thought would help, all sank like a stone the moment he looked at me, almost taking my breath. His dark hair was rumpled, his broad physique dominating the room, his thick muscular thighs firm inside the pair of gray sweats he was wearing, which outlined everything.

Fuck. Fuck. Fuck.

I sucked through my nose, my body lighting up like a match. He shouldn't have been let out in public looking as he did. The way the sweats fit him bordered on indecent. The intense way he stared back at me broke every rule I was setting between us.

Snapping my head back to the salad, I tried to regain control. "Thank you for doing this. Again."

"No problem." His guttural voice slid between my thighs, making my eyes squeeze together.

Why did he affect me so much? Why couldn't I get myself together and get over it?

"Come on." Addy waved him to follow her into the garage. I kept my back to him, not glancing as he passed. Not a single item of clothing touched me, but electricity bolted into my nerves, my hand gripping the knife I was holding until the skin wanted to split.

"Stop it," I growled at myself, taking several moments to regain my control.

Sounds of him working pinged from the garage, along with Addison's yammering as she tried to engage him in conversation. Though nothing worked, she continued to fill the empty space.

I set the table and checked on the burgers.

"I told him he can stay for dinner." Addison bounded into the room.

"Oh." I gulped. "I'm sure his grandparents are expecting him."

"They're at bingo tonight," Mason replied, coming in behind Addison. "But it's fine. I have something at home."

"Come on, this is an occasion." Addy threw out her hands, showing off the table. "Aunt Emery actually cooked tonight."

His black eyes skated to me with curiosity, and I felt every layer of my walls being taken down.

"Yeah, and earlier she even signed up to volunteer at the animal shelter."

This time his gaze burned into me, demanding I look up. The power he held was a force field, and it was hard to disobey. He knew he inspired my actions, what he said to me had pushed me to follow through this time.

Afraid I could not hide what I wanted to, I forced my gaze to stay off him, knowing he would see something I couldn't face within myself.

The timer for the broiler went off, and I scrambled to it with relief.

Addison pulled out another plate, asking him what he wanted to drink, being a gracious hostess.

Not once did his eyes leave me.

I set a burger on his plate. "Were you able to fix the washer?"

"I'll have to get a part."

"What?" Addison whined. "But what about my uniform?"

"I'll soak it, and we'll hang it up near the fire to dry overnight," I suggested, which made her nose wrinkle, but she accepted it.

"I'll come back tomorrow."

My head snapped to him. It was the first time I fully met his gaze.

"You can't. We have a game tomorrow night," Addison responded, grabbing the ketchup.

"I quit coaching."

"What?" Addison's voice went high, her expression full of disappointment, knowing that was where they shared a common link. The time she could really see and talk to him. "Why?"

Mason's attention was fully on me, his finger toying with a fork. "Because it became something I should do, not what I wanted to do."

I slipped into my heels, fluffing out my hair, wishing Marcie hadn't talked me into meeting her at the pub for drinks. Her vanilla cup, Tim, was coming with his friend, Sean. A convenient, not-so-subtle setup.

Hearing the knock at the door, my stomach fluttered. There was another reason I said yes to the date.

Pushing back my shoulders, I put up my armor, strolling to the front door. My jeans were tight, my top almost backless, and my heels were red. I felt like a fraud, wanting nothing more than to get the fire going, curl up on the sofa with a glass of wine and binge-watch some show.

This outfit was trying to convey to everyone in the room I was a grown-ass woman who could go to bars and flirt with men. When the girl underneath felt the exact opposite.

Swinging open the door, I kept my gaze directly off Mason, knowing he would be showing up. Addison was at an away game, then spending the night at Elena's, which was why I said yes to Marcie so quickly.

I could not be alone with him.

"Again, thanks for doing this." I strolled over to the console, grabbed my purse, and pulled out another forty. "Here." I faced him, holding up the money. "You never told me how much the part cost."

"I'm not taking your money." His nostrils flared, jaw tight. He wore a black puffer jacket and black hat, damp from the rain. He looked as though he had stepped out of a rugged winter lodge catalog. Except he'd be the dark villain in the story. The one who would shatter your world.

I wiggled my hand. "Take it."

He ignored my offer, his gaze moving down me. "Going out?"

"Yes." I lifted my chin. "I can do that." Why did it sound almost like a question?

A slight smirk moved his lips. Walking up to me, he stopped only an inch from me.

"Never said you couldn't. But if you want my *permission*?" His voice grazed my ear, full of every dark, sinful fantasy my mind tried to block out.

My chest hitched as he strolled away. His hands were full of tools, heading out to the garage. I could feel my nipples harden with the flush he could so easily draw onto my cheeks. Damn him. He had no right. Anger weaved up my spine, and I marched after him.

"Who the hell do you think you are?" I barreled into the garage, emotion taking over, not allowing my brain to step in.

He curved slightly, dropping his tools on the machine. "Excuse me?"

"You…" I pointed, moving closer. "You are a nineteen-year-old *kid*. You have no right to talk to me like that," I shouted. "It's inappropriate."

"Inappropriate?" He whipped to me, a fire lighting his dark eyes.

"Yes," I barked. "You go to school with my niece. You are in high school! I am a thirty-year-old woman."

He growled, his feet stepping to me, making me back-pedal.

"You don't think I know that?" He leaned closer, his frame brushing against mine. His gaze dropped to my mouth, a nerve in his jaw convulsing, as if he was trying to hold himself back. Air stopped in my lungs, my eyes going to his, unable to stop the reaction, noticing how full his bottom lip was. How it might feel sinking my teeth down on it, to feel his mouth against mine.

Tension congested the air, our breaths intermingling, our bodies almost touching. We teetered on a thin blade. A precipice that warned of death if you leaped. I couldn't deny how much I wanted to let the blade cut me. Life pumping through my veins as we bled out. The pure blissful high before we hit bottom.

His gaze went back and forth between my eyes, his dark gaze hungry. Violent. Promising to completely wreck my world. And I wanted him to.

Beep! Beep!

A car horn blared from my driveway, making me jolt, shattering the moment into dust. Clarity of what I was about to do, the line I about jumped over, slammed into me with horror.

Oh. My. God.

"What are you doing?" Pushing him, I scrambled away, turning my shame into fury, directing it at him. "This is so beyond inappropriate." I gathered myself near the door, using my authoritative tone. "You are a *child*." The word was like a whip. Purposefully cruel, it curled off my tongue, wanting to mark him, to hurt him. It wasn't at all true, but it worked. He stepped back defensively, his chest rising. "And though I appreciate what you have done here." My throat condensed, struggling with the last bit. "It is better if you don't come back."

Not letting him speak, I took off, heading back into my house and out the front door, where the Uber driver waited for me. Shaking, I wanted to burst into tears because no matter what my head said, my heart was calling me back to that garage.

Chapter 16
Mason

Sliding myself out from under the GTO, my hands greasy and filthy, I stood up, grabbing a cloth to wipe them off. The garage door was open, letting the cool weather in. A hazy sun was already heading for the horizon.

The car was coming along faster than I thought because every moment I wasn't at school or helping around the house, I was here. The desperation to keep my mind occupied at all times was hitting obsessive levels.

On the outside, I acted as if everything was fine, while inside my brain, I was going insane. My mind never letting up on the moment in the garage with Emery. Seeing her lips part, knowing without a doubt she felt the same thing I did. She tried to hide it, but desire heated her body, wrapping around my dick like she owned it. I was about to kiss her before the asshole driver interrupted us. I couldn't stop thinking about what might have happened if he hadn't. Would she have kissed me back?

It was making me crazy. And the month and a half since that night hadn't lessened the need for her. If anything, I felt it grow stronger, almost as if I could hear her calling to me.

The next day after she kicked me out, I saw a delivery truck with a brand-new washer and dryer at her house, making her point very clear to either herself or me. I had no excuse to show up again.

"Mason?" My grandma opened the door to the garage, carrying something in her palm, her hair puffy and styled, a sign she had been to the hairdresser today. Grace James was all of five foot two, but she had the love and determination of a giant. She was the rock of this family, and watching her struggle to get down the steps sent fear and sadness to my heart.

"I got you." I went to her, helping her down the three steps.

"Thank you." She patted my arm. "I saw you hadn't taken these yet." She held my hand, placing vitamins and other horse-size pills in my palm.

Nodding, I flung them into my mouth, grabbing the water bottle I had on the bench and chugging them down. "Thanks, I guess I forgot."

"You can't forget, Mason." She frowned at me, her mouth dipping further at my blasé reaction. "What's going on with you? You seem lost lately."

I moved away, setting my water back down, not ready to get a lecture.

"Your grandfather told me you quit football." It should be a statement, a truth she already knew, but the layer of questions under the simple remark blared out what she really wanted to know. Why? Why would I leave something I supposedly loved? Why would I walk away from coaching football?

"I know he's disappointed—"

"Stop right there, young man." She held up her finger at me. "Your grandfather and I could never be disappointed in *you*. We're confused about why you left. Why you'd leave something you loved. We just don't want you to miss out on things. To have regrets later. Your father regretted leaving school and not graduating with his friends. We don't want you to make those same mistakes." She came around to me, forcing me to look at her. "We love you so much, Mason. What you've gone through... no one should have to experience, especially someone so young. But all you can do is make it the best you can from here on out."

My throat bobbed, biting back the conflicting emotions she was bringing to the surface. I didn't love coaching anymore. It actually hurt more than made me happy, but it also made me sad knowing I'd never be on the field again.

"And if coaching is not what you want to do, we're fine with it. But find something that gives you joy. Something that makes you end every day feeling fulfilled. Otherwise, what was it all for? All that you fought for, to merely let it all slip away? It would all be for nothing. Don't waste it. Don't give up on things you love."

My head dropped, her sentiment wrenching my chest.

"You are a gift, Mason." Her hand touched my cheek. "Don't treat my gift as though it was garbage."

My lids squeezed, and I swallowed back the tears. I had not let them come out in a very long time. I didn't think I deserved to show sorrow anymore. I had no right to.

She patted my jaw softly. "And you need to shave."

A scoff curled out of my throat. She always nagged at me to shave, wanting me to show my "handsome face," which was one thing I tended to ignore. The scruff was here to stay.

"When you're done and cleaned up, can you take a look at the sink again? It's backing up." She tottered back to the door.

"You know we can easily replace it with a new one." I grinned, already knowing what she'd say.

"Why?" She grunted, pulling herself up the steps. "This one still works fine." She paused halfway up, her hand going to her chest, taking a deep breath.

"You okay?"

"Of course." She nodded, waving me off, going back inside the house.

Falling back against the workbench with a deep breath, I rubbed at the back of my neck. She was right. I needed to find the thing that made me happy. Right now, I was numbly going through my days, as if I were waiting.

Life didn't wait; it kept moving. You had to decide to interact with it or not.

Finding what gave me direction still seemed intangible. I liked working out, restoring cars, and fixing things, but I can't say any of it made me want to get up in the morning. Football had lost its luster when I stopped playing.

So, what did make me happy?

Movement on the sidewalk across the street drew my eyes up, the fading sun behind the house making it hard to see specific features.

But I knew.

A million miles away, and I swear I would be able to sense her, feel her, experience the pull that perked up my body in awareness.

Wearing the animal shelter apron, her hair in a ponytail, she walked a handful of dogs down the street. She didn't look over, but somehow, I knew she knew I was there, and every bit of her was as aware of my presence as I was of hers.

She strolled away, and all I could do was watch her from afar.

Feeling as if my joy just walked by.

Chapter 17
Emery

"Addison, are you ready yet?" Harper called to her daughter from the living room sofa.

"Almost!" Addy's voice cried back.

"Fucksake, she's going back to a house full of her clothes, and she's still packing like she'll be in the middle of nowhere for a month." My sister brushed back her blonde hair.

"Well, it gives me time with you." I sipped at my wine, squeezing my sister's hand. "I've missed you."

"I've missed you too," Harper replied. "It's not the same without you there. I miss being able to run over and say hi. Actually, a few times I found my car headed for your house when I'd remember."

My house. The one I shared with Ben.

My gaze stared off at the Christmas tree in the corner of the room. The fireplace was going, a Christmas movie playing on the TV, and my life with Ben was starting to feel further and further away from me. The house we had lived in was no longer my home.

"Do I need my heavy jacket?" Addison yelled from her bedroom.

"Addy, we're four hours away. To a place you have grown up all your life." Harper blew out, shaking her head. "Did I forget teenagers were brain-dead?"

I laughed, snuggling into my couch.

It was Christmas break, and Harper was taking Addison back to spend the vacation with her. I never minded the quiet before, but my stomach pitched a bit at the thought of not having Addison around. Her constant chatter and noise distracted my mind from wandering too far away.

Like down the street.

She talked about Mason, but the crush seemed to have waned a bit with his absence. She still got a faraway look when he was brought up, probably getting giggly when she ran into him at school. Thankfully, he took my request to heart. He stayed away from this house and me, and he also kept a wide berth with Addison too. She talked to Mateo all the time, though she claimed they were only friends.

"Can I say again how appreciative I am? What you've done for Addy?" Harper glanced toward her daughter. "She's so happy. Thriving. She showed me she got Bs on her mid-terms."

"She's doing really well. Cheerleading helps. They have to keep a certain GPA, and Addy loves it too much not to make it a priority."

"Why do I feel like I failed?" Harper blinked, her eyes watering. "That I suck as a parent."

"No." I grabbed Harper's hand. "You are a great mom. You are so selfless that instead of keeping her with you, you did what was right for her." I tilted my head with compassion. "Harp, she needed to get away from Joe. From all the bullshit he was putting you guys through."

"Another fail on my part. I should never have stayed with him so long. I knew… but I was too scared to leave. Thinking things would be worse if I were alone when in truth, it was worse staying with him."

Really looking at my sister, I could see the change in her. The growth she was forced to do in this time.

"We're human beings. We're going to try and fail, and sometimes fall. You did the best for Addison. And look at her." I motioned back to the girl darting back and forth between her room and bathroom. "She is better. You are better, and I think this time away will help your relationship with her."

Harper laid her head back on a cushion, trying not to cry. "Thank you."

"Honestly, I think Addison being here has helped me heal. I don't think I'd be in the same place without her."

"You look happier." She nodded in agreement. "Speaking of that, is there anyone special putting that smile on your face?"

It was instant, no choice, my brain going straight to him as if it were programmed. Followed by instant shame.

"Uh… no… not really." I shifted in my seat, clasping my glass harder. "Dr. Ramirez at my office keeps expressing interest."

"Oh." Harper's eyes lit up. "And do you call him Dr. Ramirez?" Her voice went into this sexy talk. "Oh, Dr. Ramirez, what a big drill you have."

"Stop it!" I hit my sister's arm. "Ugh."

"What's his name?"

"Daniel."

"Daniel Ramirez. He sounds hot."

"He's cute. Sweet. Very nice guy."

Harper's lids narrowed. "At one time, that would be an endorsement for him. Why do I feel it's a negative this time?"

I shrugged. "He's not the kind of man who will push me up against my dryer and fuck the shit out of me." I took a huge gulp of wine, trying to dislodge the image, heat and fear coursing through me, afraid I was giving myself away.

Harper's eyes popped, her mouth dropping open, not used to hearing me talk like that.

"What about you?" I turned the conversation around on her, not wanting her to dig any deeper because I felt it was right there for all to pick up and see. "Weren't you seeing someone when we left? Is it still going?"

Harper's cheeks pinked. "Actually, yes."

"Holy shit, did you actually blush?" I exclaimed.

"Shhhh." She peered back where Addy's room was. "We're trying to keep it casual. Day by day. He recently got out of something, and so have I, but…"

"You really like him."

She nodded vigorously.

"There's something else." She bit on her nail.

"What?" I slanted my head, feeling defensive.

"I didn't really want to tell you because it might bring up bad memories, but…"

"What?"

"Kevin is a policeman. Officer Bentley."

"Why does he sound familiar?" Though my brain could not recall why it did.

"Because." She cringed. "He was one of the officers who came to the door that night… you know, for Ben."

"What?" I tipped back, that moment a blurry haze, but it still punched straight into my heart.

"Of course, I wasn't thinking about anything besides Ben and being there for you, but a few weeks later, I ran into Kevin at Starbucks and went over to thank him. We started talking and it was instant attraction. Though we both denied it for a long time. He was in a bad marriage and so was I.

83

We were just friends, but we really got each other. Could relate so much with our nightmare exes. After both our divorces became official… we couldn't ignore how we felt. Though I still feel so guilty because of how we met."

"Because of Ben? Is it why you kept it from me?"

"I felt it was inappropriate."

Inappropriate. I was starting to hate that fucking word.

"I guess, if anything, Ben showed me life is too short. You never know what might happen. We should always hold on to the things making us happy. You know?"

"I'm ready!" Addison rolled her giant suitcase out, and Harper jumped up, helping her daughter with her five bags.

Even as I rose and helped them to the car, promising I would see them on Christmas Eve, I couldn't let what she said go.

"We should always hold on to the things making us happy."

But what might make me happy would bring so much pain to others.

"You sure you don't want to come out with us tonight?" Marcie watched me grab my jacket and purse from the locker, my shift over.

"No."

"Sean has been asking about you."

Double no.

The date had been awful. He thought he was charming when he actually came across as one-dimensional. His lone incentive to talk to me was to get me in bed.

"Tonight is a fire and warm blanket kind of night." I pulled on my coat, the temperatures dipping low enough the weatherman said there was a chance of snow.

"Not only will Sean be disappointed, I know Daniel will be upset too. Think he was going specifically for you."

A knot formed in my stomach.

We had chatted a lot this week on breaks. He was smart, kind, and funny. He was similar to Ben. Dedicated to his job, stable, was easy to be around. I *wanted* to like him. I enjoyed talking with him, but once he left the room, I didn't think of him again.

"I'm sorry. I have to get up early for the shelter. It's a big adoption day tomorrow."

"You seem to really enjoy it there."

A happy smile bowed my lips, thinking about all the sweet dogs and cats I had come to love.

"I really do. And I'm happy with this right now. Watching Anita run it, I'm not sure I want to do that, but there are other things." Your dreams when you were young didn't have to go away, but I realized they could alter a bit in real life. Fit you now, not the person you were back then.

"You're coming to the Christmas party at the bar and grill next week." Marcie pointed at me with a *don't fuck with me* look. "No exceptions."

"I wouldn't miss it." I heard things got pretty wild last year. Zipping up, I stepped out into the freezing night air, exhausted from the long day. I had gone to the shelter in the morning, then came straight here and worked till closing.

Climbing in my car, I drove home. Turning down my street, red and blue light reflected off my windshield from up ahead. My stomach dropped, realizing the ambulance was in front of Mason's house.

Mr. and Mrs. James were both in their late eighties, if not early nineties.

"Oh god." I jerked my car to the side, slamming on the brakes and hopping out. Running toward the ambulance, I spotted Mason coming out of the house. Two EMTs were right in front, pushing a gurney toward the ambulance.

Grace laid unconscious on the stretcher.

"Mason?" I cried out.

His head jerked to me, and for one moment, everything stopped. His face was stone, but I could see the terror in his eyes. He was all I saw. All I felt.

Then he turned away, climbing into the ambulance next to her.

As the EMTs closed the doors, his gaze lifted to mine, our eyes locking, before the doors shut. The ambulance took off down the street, wailing and screaming.

I stood there, panic fizzling up, recalling the ride to the hospital for Ben. How helpless and scared I was. Instinct wanted me to go to Mason, to be there for him.

Moving back to my car, something caught my eye, jerking my head to the doorway. A figure stooped over his walker, his expression shattered with fear and grief. "My Gracie…"

"Mr. James!" I bounded up the house, ushering him back into the house and out of the cold. "Please, come back inside. It's too cold out here."

"But... I can't... Gracie needs me," he croaked, disoriented, seemingly to not know what to do.

"Do you want me to take you down there?"

"Mason... he-he told me to wait here. He will call when he knows something." He looked at me, his dark eyes very similar to his grandson's. His body was shaking badly. "I can't move around well anymore and am vulnerable to getting sick."

A hospital full of sick people would be too risky.

"What happened?" I asked, leading him to his chair. The house smelled of fresh bread and chicken soup.

"She-she was over at the stove. She got dizzy, stopped being able to speak on one side of her mouth. Couldn't feel her hand."

A stroke?

"Please sit." I helped him get into his chair. "Let me make you some tea."

"Thank you." His weak fingers squeezed mine tighter than I was expecting. "Are you a friend of Mason's?"

"Uh." I hesitated, rolling my lips. "Yes."

He peered at me. "Oh, are you the pretty girl who has my boy all twisted up?"

"Oh... no. That's not me." I turned away, darting for the kitchen, my skin heating like I had a fever. Grandpa didn't seem to see I was far too old for Mason. I looked young, but still dressed in scrubs, my hair in a ponytail, it was clear I wasn't a schoolgirl.

For the next two hours, I stayed by his side, getting him to eat a little before Mason called the house.

"Yes. Okay. I will try." Neal James fought to hide the tears in his eyes. "No, your pretty girlfriend has been with me. Okay, my boy. See you soon." Neal blinked. "And Mason?" There was a pause. "I love you." He then hung up.

A tear slid down my cheek seeing the man struggle knowing the love of his life was hurt and he couldn't be with her. I understood more than he knew.

"How's Grace?"

"She hasn't woken up yet." His voice broke. "But he says she is stable. It was a mini-stroke. Mason is heading home now." His entire body strained to hold back his emotion, not wanting to cry in front of me. He looked utterly exhausted and weak sitting there, breaking my heart.

"Do you need anything else? Want me to help you to bed?"

He took a shuddering breath, peering around the house like he could not understand anything without her. After a moment, he nodded his head, reaching out his hand for me to help him up.

With his walker, I slowly took him down the hall, getting him into bed.

"Thank you, my dear." His old face looked exhausted and heartbroken. "It's no wonder my boy adores you so much."

"Oh. It's not that way." I placed the blanket over him, fluffing his pillow. "He's my niece's friend."

"I might be old, but I'm not blind." He wiggled in, sighing heavily. "My boy is very special. He's had to grow up fast, been through so much." Sadness flittered in his eyes. "Grace and I won't be around forever. We only have so much time allotted in this life, and I want him to be happy, no matter what." His sentiment felt direct, as if it meant more than surface value.

Neal closed his eyes, turning into his pillow.

With a heavy breath, I turned off the light and headed out, feeling his pain, the fear of possibly losing her as if she were my own.

I drank my dinner, probably dessert too. My worry continued to wander to the James's home as I stared absently at the fire, hoping Grace would be all right. For both the men's sakes.

Holiday music and my tree felt contradictory against my current mood, though it fit with the few flakes falling from the sky. It was well past midnight, but I couldn't seem to move, and sleep seemed far from reality, even with an early morning barreling toward me.

A thump hit my front door, jolting me. My head snapped to it, my mouth suddenly going dry. I knew who it was. Setting down my glass, I got up, strolling for the door, ignoring the way my stomach fluttered.

Swinging it open, the air sucked from my lungs.

Mason stood there, his hands leaning against the frame as though it were holding him up, his head bowed, the snowflakes catching in his hair.

Slowly his head lifted, his eyes finding mine. The depth of sadness and grief etched into them, as though his soul was a hundred times heavier than others.

I didn't say anything. Words weren't needed.

He stepped inside as my arms went around him, pulling him into my embrace, wanting to take his sorrow, wanting him to feel my warmth. A pained noise came from him, his head tucking into the curve of my neck, his hands circling around my waist, holding me like I was the only thing keeping him together.

His warm breath stroked my neck, the feel of his chest moving in and out with heavy breaths, rubbing against my breasts. His heart beat against mine, his hair between my fingers, his huge physique pressing into me.

It appalled me how easily I could imagine him picking me up, my legs wrapping around him as he carried me to the bedroom, wanting him to take every fear and emotion he felt out on my body.

Sucking in with chagrin, I tried to pull back, but Mason wouldn't let go, gripping me tighter, fighting through his terror, using me as an anchor to keep him from falling.

"I can't lose her." His voice came out coarse and low.

There was nothing I could say, no comforting words that didn't feel contrived and false. Grace might get through this now, but sadly, this would take a toll on her body, which was already tiring.

After a long moment, I leaned back, my gaze searching his. Normally, he was a force. Strong and commanding. Tonight, I saw vulnerability. A guy who carried the world on his shoulders and needed for once someone to be there for him.

Taking his hand, I guided him to the sofa. Sitting down, I pulled him to me. He followed my lead, laying his head on my lap, my fingers threading through his hair.

Over and over, I stroked his temple and head, hearing his breathing shudder before he exhaled, his lids closing.

Time no longer existed to me. Nothing else mattered. Music hummed in the background, snowflakes fell outside, the warm fire crackled... and nothing felt more as if I were truly home than it did right now.

Chapter 18
Emery

Blaring, my alarm jolted me awake with a cry. My legs kicked at my sheets, tangled in my comforter. My brain did not understand where I was or what was going on.

Rubbing my eyes, I peered around my bedroom, not recalling going to bed last night. Recollections of me on the sofa, my eyes drifting closed, his head on my lap.

Mason.

Scrambling out of bed, I beelined for the living room, finding it empty and quiet. The blanket folded. The Christmas lights off. Everything in place as though last night never happened. I had dreamed it all. Except I could still feel his weight on my lap, the softness of his hair, the moment he let go and fell asleep, his expression free of worry. How his fingers wrapped around my thigh, probably thinking it was a pillow.

From an outsider, this would have been so unacceptable; the lines needing to stay in place were hazy and distorted. Yet, seeing him at my door, I didn't care. He needed me. Needed someone to hold on to. Keep him from floating away in grief and fear.

I understood that more than most.

My fingers trailed over the blanket I had put on him last night as if I could still feel him, sense his heat, his presence. Mason must have carried me to bed, which smeared the line even more. He had been in my bedroom. Put me in bed. It felt intimate. Inviting.

The clock on the wall chimed seven a.m.

"Oh shit!" I dashed for the bathroom, jumping in the shower and rushing to get ready to get to the shelter on time.

The day was a blur of pets and people stopping by our outdoor adoption event, looking for the animal that fit perfectly into their home. Getting attached to the animals as I had, it was hard to not want to adopt them all myself. Finding them a forever home, knowing the dog or cat would have the best life, was incomparable.

One family really struck me. The little girl had Down syndrome, and Max, a German Shepard at the shelter, was instantly drawn to her. The moment the family walked up, the dog picked them, as if it were his job to protect and love that little girl.

Anita and I were in tears as they filled out the paperwork, the dog already licking the little girl's face, her small chubby fingers tugging on his hair as he stood by her side guarding her. She was *his* little girl. Dogs had such keen intuition, and I had no doubt Max felt she was more vulnerable, and he instantly wanted to protect her.

"Oh goodness." Anita wiped at her face. Though the family couldn't take him home today because others had filled out an application for him too, she knew we would be calling this family later with the news they would soon be able to. "Some days this job can be hard and sad, and other days… It's the best feeling in the world to match animals with people like that."

She was right. It was such a high. It was so gratifying and made me feel not only had I given the dog a better life, but the whole family.

"Good work, team!" Anita clapped her hands at the few volunteers and workers at the event. The end of the day coming to a close. "It's been a long but good day. Almost 80 percent of the animals got at least one application."

Cheers went up, but my heart wanted to protest for the ones who didn't get picked. They all deserved loving homes.

"You guys were amazing, and we couldn't run this place without our volunteers." Anita put her hands together, giving us a little bow of appreciation. "Thank you."

The sun had long set by the time we cleaned up and got all the animals settled and fed. When I got back to my car, I felt exhausted, but I buzzed with fulfillment and a joy that felt almost foreign to me.

Pulling up to my drive, I glanced down the street, wanting to know if Grace was better, but I knew I needed to keep my distance. Last night was an anomaly. A moment of grief where he needed a friend. Support to get him through.

That was over.

Getting into my lounge clothes, I went through my cupboards and fridge, not finding much to eat. I debated if I should have another liquid dinner when a tap rattled my front door.

Heat rushed to my cheeks, my stomach knotting, already knowing, as if his knock had a signature. One I could feel in my bones.

Opening the door, I still couldn't seem to not lose my breath every time. Dressed in dark gray sweats, black hoodie, jacket, and a beanie, he was holding a bag of groceries.

"Mason." I swallowed. "What are you doing here?"

Without responding, he stepped in, brushing by me, strolling straight for my kitchen.

"Mason?" I shut the door, jogging after him, stopping in the doorway, watching him unpack food from the bag. "Did I forget I ordered a grocery delivery?" I folded my arms, leaning against the jamb.

"Yep, and I'll be expecting a tip." He grabbed a pan from my hanging rack and placed it on the stove.

I tried to ignore the dirty places my mind went after his comment.

The confidence and commanding assurance he had. He moved easily around the room, pulling out cutting boards and getting spices like this was his home.

"Fresh fish tacos with avocado, tomatoes, lettuce, and cheese sound good?" He poured oil into the pan, heated it up, and placed two pieces of tilapia in it.

"Uhhh." Completely bewildered. "Yeah."

It felt so abnormal for a nineteen-year-old to be cooking this way. Normally, they ate fast food and processed crap, not fresh fish and vegetables.

"How is your grandmother?" I tracked him back at the counter, slicing tomatoes.

His lips pressed together, his attention fully on the cutting board.

"Stable." His Adam's apple went up and down. "She was awake, but still not fully coherent. Grandpa demanded to come with me this time. They kicked us out an hour ago." He scooped the chopped tomatoes into a bowl. "He went straight to bed."

I could imagine how emotionally draining it was on Neal. On Mason too.

"I'm so glad she's doing better."

He dipped his head. "I want to thank you for last night."

I couldn't stop the warmth in my cheeks; acknowledging it aloud made it real. Something we needed to talk about.

"What you did for my grandfather?" He glanced over at me. "He told me you were with him the whole time. Helped put him to bed."

A breath of relief escaped me that he wasn't calling out the moment we shared between us the night before. "Oh, of course. It was the least I could do."

"No." His energy pinned me in place. "It was *everything*." Mason's stare transfixed me, pulling all the oxygen from the room and jogging my pulse up into my throat.

Something deep and tangible hung between us, wrapping around me, pulling me down, wanting to consume me whole.

Yanking my gaze away like I didn't feel it, I cleared my throat. "Can I do anything to help?" I motioned to the items on the counter.

Mason didn't relent for a moment, as if he knew I was trying to wiggle out of this, changing the subject. But he finally turned away, his head bouncing. "Sure." He placed down the knife. "You can cut the avocados and lettuce."

"That I can do." I went to the counter, picked up the knife, and began slicing the items. Mason didn't move, forcing my body to skim his, feeling the spark of his skin, the way his broad physique eclipsed mine, his nearness overpowering.

"What? Am I not cutting them right, chef?" I tried to tease.

"I call it butchering, but sure, you're cutting just fine." His deep gravelly voice hummed in my ear before he moved away, going back to the fish on the stove.

I needed to tell him he should go. That he shouldn't be here. I should, but the words didn't come.

"Fish is done." He traveled back, coming in behind me, his body brushing mine. I could feel him through his sweatpants as he reached over my shoulder to grab plates from the cupboard, lightning fire into my veins.

I went still, bolting down the impulse to arch into him, to feel his cock rub against my ass, to hear him groan in my ear. Unbidden thoughts sprung to my mind: Mason yanking down my pants and underwear, his fingers parting me before he thrust into me. The fantasy I always wanted Ben to fulfill, though he never did.

The pulse between my thighs was painful. Dizziness twirled all logic out of my head and had me gripping the counter, my nipples taut and aching.

For one moment, he paused as if he could feel my reaction, smell the need, hear the tiny puffs in my throat.

Mason pulled away, taking the plates to the table, acting like he didn't experience the same thing I did. This was solely a friendly thank-you dinner.

Reaching over, I grabbed my wine, drinking it like a shot. I needed to go out on a date or hook up with some guy at a bar and get this out of my system. It had been over three years now without sex, and clearly, my body was waking up out of its coma and declaring itself ready again.

Of course, Mason was here and hot as hell. Sinful fantasy level. A bored housewife's wet dream.

Finishing the avocados and lettuce, I took them over to the table.

"Want something to drink?" I asked him.

"Sure. What do you have?"

"Probably water." I joked, going to the fridge.

"I can get it." His hands grasped my waist, shifting me easily out of the way before opening the fridge and finding cranberry juice.

The imprint of his hands burned into my skin throughout dinner. I hated the way I loved how easily he could move me, how he touched me. How comfortable he was here. Mason wasn't a huge talker, so I thought it would be awkward.

It wasn't.

Even in the silent moment, it felt normal, neither of us needing to fill it. Watching how my Christmas lights twinkled in the dark, him laughing at me when I made up my own lyrics to Christmas songs, which used to drive Ben nuts.

I was on edge because it was too comfortable, too easy to want to reach out and touch him.

To *kiss* him.

We sat on the sofa and watched a movie after dinner, and I stupidly ignored the fact he shouldn't be here, that this crossed so many lines.

Losing interest in the movie, I glanced at his profile, noting he wasn't watching either.

"We can watch something else."

"Doesn't matter. Not sure my brain can concentrate on anything right now." He scrubbed at his forehead, laying his head back. "I just look at my grandpa. He's so lost without her—we both are. I don't want to think about anything happening to her. I don't think my grandpa would survive long without her."

I turned to face him more. "Did Grace and Neal raise you?"

"Pretty much," he replied, his gaze on the ceiling. "When my mom walked out, my dad tried his best, but he had to work all the time to keep up with the bills and stuff. So, they watched me all the time, and then when he died, it wasn't even a question. Not like I had anywhere else to go."

"Your mom has never been in the picture?"

"No." He lifted his head up, peering over at me. "And no, I have no interest in ever finding her either. I have no desire to know a thing about her. Who knows, she's probably dead too." He lifted a shoulder. "She was hardcore into drugs, didn't stop even when she was pregnant with me. I was a mistake to her. And her addiction came first."

"Wow," I muttered.

"She did enough damage to me. I'd rather not know anything about her," he declared. "Pretty much an orphan."

"Me too."

"Really?" He sat up, curving toward me.

"My mother died of cancer over thirteen years ago, and my dad was gunned down in a biker gang shooting when I was around six, I think."

"Shit." Mason's eyebrows went up. "Really?"

"My mom liked the dangerous, violent ones." My fingers played with the edge of my blanket. "They never married but had enough sexual attraction to produce both Harper and me over the years. Similar to your parents, my father didn't want kids either. He had days he would pretend, but he enjoyed the biker life too much and would disappear for months at a time."

"Damn, I'm sorry," Mason said, his gaze moving over me like he was seeing me in full color.

"It's fine." I adjusted against the arm of the sofa, his thigh brushing my knee. Neither of us moved, as if we needed the contact. "It's probably why I always chose safety. Security. Not venturing too far out into the unknown. Growing up, money was tight, and nothing felt stable. I went for the opposite. Everything about Ben was safe, and I think that's why it was even worse." I swallowed back. "He was supposed to be the steady thing. *My safety*. And when he died, it shattered the world I built, thinking I was safe and protected from pain."

"Fuck, I get it." He leaned over his legs; his head turned to me. "You don't know how much I get that."

I realized how much we had in common. So much loss, hurt, and agony. We recognized it in each other, felt it deeper. The strings between us seemed to multiply, linking us together, making it harder to pull back.

Our gazes met, the intimacy of sharing our grief, the undeniable chemistry that always sparked like live wires closed in around us, stinging and sparking at my skin. The air was thick, need pulsating like a drum in the room, growing louder with every second our eyes stayed on each other. The contact between us was no longer comforting. It was an electrical charge racing up between my thighs.

I tried to control my breath, but could hear his quivering in my lungs. The desire for him rattled through me. Overpowering, about to pull me under.

"You probably should go," I spoke quietly, but the implication was strong behind my tone.

His jaw clenched, his gaze finally dropping from mine, his head dipping in understanding. "Yeah."

We both knew we were riding the line of danger. We were getting too close to the sun.

He blew out and stood up, grabbing his jacket, his eyes finding mine when he reached the door.

"Good night, Emery." It felt so much deeper than the actual words. His voice licked through me, making me shudder as he closed the door behind him.

Later that night, for the first time, I let myself think of him as I pleasured myself. The featureless fantasy man had an identity now.

⎯⎯ᴧᴧᴧᴧ♡

I didn't know if I'd see Mason again, but he showed up the next few nights, coming over after visiting his grandmother at the hospital. He'd get his grandpa settled and come over with food. We cooked together, talked, laughed, and watched movies. It felt so effortless with him, so good, I lost all reasoning to stop it.

I didn't want to.

"Grandma's mad she wasn't home for my birthday." He served a heaping portion of spaghetti Bolognese onto my plate, adding a slice of fresh garlic bread, which smelled so good I wanted to face plant into it. "But at least she gets to come home in time for Christmas."

"Your birthday?" I blinked up at him, forgetting he told me it was in December. "When is it?"

His mouth twitched, as if he wished he hadn't said anything.

"Mason?" I had a warning in my tone. "When is it?"

"It's not a big deal. I mean, this one feels even more pointless than the last," he grumbled. "Still can't go to bars, and I'm an even older asshole still in high school."

95

"Every birthday is important. And this one means you are no longer a teen, right?" Why did that make it better in my head, as if I were trying to find a reason I wasn't some perverted cougar? The difference between us was still the same. "Plus, bars are overrated."

"Still be nice to be able to go to one." His gaze drifted to me. Heavy. Weighted.

"When is your birthday?" It was more an order than a question.

His shoulders rolled; he faced the pot of pasta. "Today."

"What?" I exclaimed, my mouth dropping open. "Today?"

He shrugged.

"Why didn't you tell me?" I hit his arm lightly. "At least I would have been the one to make dinner."

"Oh no, it's okay. I'd like to see my twenty-first."

"Shut up." I swatted him again. "Dammit. I feel like an ass."

"You didn't know."

"Well, Happy birthday."

"Thanks." He brushed it off. "And I said it's not a big deal."

"You should be out with your friends, celebrating."

"I guess I need to get some of those."

"You have a ton of friends. Addison tells me how many people seem to worship the ground you walk on at school."

"That makes them followers… not friends." He shoveled spaghetti onto his plate. "I don't seem to really fit with anyone at school."

"What about friends from where you used to live?"

He went to the fridge, opening it up and grabbing a bottle of juice. "They disappeared when football did. We no longer had anything in common, and then I moved here and none of us kept in touch."

I understood more than he realized. It took me a while to recognize that all those friends I thought I had were really Ben's. I was no longer part of a couple you invited to dinner, not someone you called when you had a group BBQ. Slowly, all those people who had been at the house that night drifted away, no longer in my life.

"It's your birthday. You should be—"

"Emery." My name off his lips stopped my sentence dead in his tracks, his timbre stern. "I'm exactly where I want to be." He clutched his plate of food and breezed past me to the living room.

I stood there, my mouth parted, feeling every syllable, every nuance of his response. Somehow the tables were flipping on me. He was the one in control, the one who could say something like that and walk away, while I was the schoolgirl with a crush.

Recapturing my breath, I pulled my shoulders back and went into the living room, seeing him settle into his spot as if he did this every night, not for only a few days. The last two nights, we ate dinner out here while watching holiday movies.

We stayed abnormally quiet, a weight in the space between us as we devoured his amazing pasta, though my stomach wasn't letting me enjoy it as much as I wanted. Distracted, my attention kept sliding over to him, slyly watching him through my lashes.

Mason James was probably one of the most ruggedly beautiful men I had ever seen. I could see why every girl who crossed his path was completely enamored with him. He was the kind of good-looking you saw in movies, but never real life. Though, to me, looks only got you so far if you had nothing underneath. Mason was complex. Layered. He had been through so much. He let me into just a slice of his past, and I knew it was far more than anyone else got from him. Mason was crawling under my skin, embedding himself into my life, and becoming something he shouldn't. No matter what, he was still in school and Addison's crush.

Yet, I couldn't stop myself from getting up and heading to the kitchen.

"You're missing the best part," he called after me.

"I'll be right back." I dug through my drawers, finding what I was looking for and grabbing a chocolate chip cookie out of the cupboard.

Stepping back into the dim room, glowing from the Christmas lights, I walked back to him, sitting down on the floor where he was lounging with pillows and blankets.

He watched me curiously as I stuck a candle into the cookie and lit it.

"It's all I have." I held it flat in my palm. "And I won't make your birthday worse by singing to you, but…" I swallowed. "Happy birthday."

His body jerked, sitting up, looking shocked I did this for him.

"Make a wish." My voice came out choppier and heavier than I wanted.

His regard went to the candle, then slowly drew up to me, the flame reflecting in his eyes. Dark. Hungry.

My lungs hitched at the intensity of his gaze, as if I could see exactly what he wished for.

Me.

Every night after he left, I pleasured myself to thoughts of him, and I felt he could see his stain on me. That he knew.

He leaned closer, blowing out the candle, his eyes never leaving mine.

"I know it's not a cake or anything great, but—"

"Emery." A growl vibrated from him, his tone making it clear what

97

he wanted, forcing air to stick in my throat. He got to his knees. Taking the cookie from me, he set it down, moving over me. His mouth was only inches from mine.

"Mason…" It was a plea. To stop. To not stop. I couldn't tell.

He shuffled in closer, my legs opening as he moved between them. My back arched, breasts grazing his chest.

"Mas—"

Grabbing the back of my head, he stopped the words in my throat, his mouth crashing down on mine, his fingers digging into my hair as my back hit the floor. He rolled himself into me, making me feel every inch of his massive erection.

Oh. Holy. Shit.

My entire body ignited. Every nerve scorched to ash as his mouth claimed mine brutally, his tongue slipping past my lips, wrapping and sucking so hard, my pussy pulsed. A deep, guttural moan heaved from me, his fingers yanking on my hair as he pushed himself harder against me.

"Oh god," I groaned, my skin hot, my clothes irritating my skin.

Roughly, his hand gripped my chin, letting out a growl before his lips devoured mine again.

He already had me clenching with the need to have him inside me. Being starved for so long, desire cut through me like a blade. Desperate and vicious.

I pushed down his sweats over his amazing ass. He wasn't wearing underwear, and his dick popped free, throbbing and glistening with pre-cum. My hand wrapped around it. *Holy. Fuck.* A twenty-year-old shouldn't be this massive and thick.

He groaned as I gripped him harder, my thumb rolling over his tip. "Em…"

His mouth, either kissing me or saying my name, had me close to coming. My chest heaved as his fingers pushed under my tank, ripping it over my head, leaving me in my bra.

"Fuck, Emery." His hips pumped into my hand, his eyes rolling back as his finger slipped under my bra, cupping my breasts, pinching my nipple. "I need to be in you. *Now*." His mouth came back down on mine, kissing me so deeply I felt it tug at my core.

"Mason," I begged. His hands untied my drawstring, slipping under my knickers, sliding through me.

My mouth opened in a deep moan, about to come from only his touch. *RRRIIIINNNGGG!*

My phone blared from its spot near us on the blanket, our heads jerking to it.

Everything turned in a moment.

Addison's name glowed in caps across the screen, as if she could sense what was happening, giving me a last chance to stop this. To turn back before we burned all rules and norms to the ground.

Reality came up and slapped me, dissolving the bubble I was in where this was okay, and tossed me into the icy pits of truth.

"Oh. God." I scrambled away from him, my hand covering my mouth.

"Emery?"

"No." I shook my head, getting up. I grabbed my cardigan, wrapping it around me like a shield. "Don't say anything."

"We're not doing anything wrong."

"We're not doing anything right either," I volleyed back at him.

The phone stopped ringing.

He stood up, pulling up his sweats and tucking himself back in. His jaw clenched, his forehead lining with anger and frustration.

"You need to go."

"What?" he barked.

"Nothing has changed. This was wrong."

"Wrong?" He moved up to me, taking up all my air and logic again. "It didn't feel wrong to me. And I know it didn't feel wrong to you either." His body pressed into mine. "Tell me your pussy isn't dripping for me?"

A gasp pitched from the back of my throat, my face burning with the truth of his words.

"No." I dug in. "I'm sorry, but this can't happen again."

"You act as if this were some slipup. That we weren't heading here from the day we met." He gritted through his teeth. "Don't make me feel I'm the only one here. Like I'm some stupid boy with a crush."

I felt tears building behind my lids because he wasn't alone at all. I had to be the grown-up. Do the right thing.

My phone rang again, Addison's name flashing bright, dropping the guillotine down on us, solidifying any choice I had.

His head bowed, knowing what Addison just did.

"Better answer it." He swiped up his jacket and shoes and slammed out of my house.

Wanting to burst into tears, I dug my nails into my palms, taking deep breaths as I picked up the phone, my face and voice putting on my trained smile.

"Hey, Addy!"

Chapter 19
Emery

Work the next day seemed to go on forever. I couldn't shake my dark mood, couldn't stop thinking about him, couldn't stop feeling him still on my skin like he marked me.

What if Addison hadn't called?

I knew the answer. Today I would be sitting here knowing what he felt like inside me.

"Emery?" A hand waved in front of my face.

"Oh, sorry." I shook my head, looking up at Dr. Ramirez standing across the table from me. "Spacing off. Did you need something?"

"No." A nervous smile wobbled his mouth as he sat down. "Maybe?"

A pinch of terror slithered down into my stomach.

"You're coming to the Christmas Party on Saturday?"

"Yes." Why did I sound so hesitant?

"I was just wondering if… we could go together."

Oh. Shit.

"Ummm." Panic danced in my chest, my eyes searching for an escape route. He was everything I should want. Proper age, handsome, nice, steady, and would treat me well. Daniel was a catch. He was what I needed to go for. Be someone I could have a future with. I knew he liked me.

The knot in my belly wouldn't go away, but I forced myself to nod and smile. "Sure." I had to get my mind off Mason. To date men around my age. Maybe if I gave Daniel a chance, he would be that guy.

With Ben and me, it hadn't been love at first sight either.

"Great." A huge smile took over Daniel's face. "I will pick you up around seven tomorrow night?" He got up from his chair.

"Sounds good." My voice sounded forced, making me feel worse because he seemed so excited.

He gave me a wave before heading back out, which told me he purposely came in here to ask me out.

Shit.

An agitated feeling climbed up and down my limbs, causing me to get up and move around. I shouldn't feel this much dread about going on a date, right?

I stared at the clock, wanting so badly to leave, knowing I had three hours left. This place felt like a cage I was trapped in.

I expected relief when I pulled my car into my garage, the long day finally over, but I didn't. It was just another cage I would pace, not finding what I was searching for anywhere I went.

Restless and prowling.

My body was still angry at me, and my mind was a confused, chaotic mess.

Grabbing my bag, I climbed out of my car, slowly making my way to my back door before I closed the garage. I didn't really want to go inside; the feel of him was everywhere in my house.

My gaze slid to my shiny new washer and dryer, looking all perky and unbreakable.

He was everywhere out here too.

The sound of footsteps hit the pavement of my driveway stopping me in my tracks. I didn't need to look to see who was here. I knew. The air shifted around me, my spine tingling with awareness, pulling me up straight. I felt him surround me, his presence taking over, demanding me to take notice.

I didn't move, didn't turn around. Afraid if I did, I would fail... fail at being strong.

At denying him.

"Mason..." My warning came out feeble and cracked, pleading he would walk away and do what I had no strength to do. He sensed my weakness, smelling blood in the water. Worn from my own internal struggle, I was vulnerable against his force. I heard his shoes hit the cement, moving toward me, taking no pity on me. "Please..." I uttered, beseeching any tiny mercy he might have.

He had none.

His body moved up behind me. Similar to an electrical fence I had once touched as a child, the buzzing of his skin, the heat of him, crackled against me, propelling my lungs to gasp for air.

His hands skimmed up the arms of my jacket around my neck to the zipper. His fingers curled around, slowly unzipping it, slipping it off my shoulders and dropping it to the ground.

"Don't," I uttered so weakly it held no meaning.

"You want me to stop?" He brushed my hair to the side, his mouth grazing the curve of my neck, a palm sliding under my scrub top, cupping my breast over my bra, his thumb pressing against my heart like he wanted to feel it pound under his hold, to notice the shallowness of my breathing. "Tell me what you want." His thumb glided lower, rolling over my nipple. My teeth bit into my lip, trying to control my response, wetness already seeping from me. His touch felt unbelievable, as if I had been waiting for it for so long.

"Tell me, Emery." His hands trailed down. They were rough and calloused and sparked electricity through me as he moved down, skating under my pants. His fingers glided over my underwear, rubbing my pussy.

A noise came out of me, sounding feral. "Mason." My back bowed into him.

"Tell me what you want?" He stroked harder.

"You."

Mason went still behind me, his ribs punching into my spine. A grunt snarled from him, and in a blink, he flipped me around. His eyes were so dark I couldn't even see his pupils, his jaw set like he was coming for his prey. A hand wrapped around my neck, his body slamming me back into the washer, his frame crushing me, jolting my nerves with desire.

His mouth came down on mine with ferocity. His kiss claimed and owned. Any rebuttal I had snapped, making me lose control. It crushed logic. It tore through doubt. There was no right or wrong. He was the relief I had been needing. I'd been aching for.

His breath heavy, he ripped my top over my head, unlatching my bra and tossing the items to the ground. The cold air from the open garage hardened my tender nipples, curving me into him. His teeth dragged down my neck before he took my breast into his mouth, sucking and flicking my nipple with his tongue.

A cry ripped up my lungs, an instant response to the hunger driving through me, feeling every inch of him. Hard and hot, flaring desire I had never felt before.

Pushing firmer into me, a slight moan parted my lips. His thumb pressed down a little harder on my neck, making me feel everything with greater intensity. "Tell me you don't feel this and you don't think about me. Tell me you haven't gotten yourself off to thoughts of me. That you haven't imagined how I'd feel sinking deep inside you?"

A throaty groan was the only thing that came out, his fingers tightening just enough to send electricity straight to my core. My chest heaved as desire flooded through me, soaking my underwear, my hips widening, wanting nothing more than him to do that very thing. My brain no longer cared about consequences or what was right and wrong.

"Tell me you haven't fantasized about my tongue fucking your pussy?"

Sucking in, heat spread through me again. Ben was never really a "dirty talker" in bed, but it fit Mason. And totally turned me on.

"Yes," I almost snarled. "All the fucking time. Every night after you leave."

With a grunt, he tugged off my pants and underwear, tossing me up on the washer. The cold metal sizzled against my hot skin. Just his touch had me on fire. I needed him so badly that I was past foreplay.

It was dark in my garage, but anyone walking by with their dog could see and hear us. Yet I didn't care enough to close it. The danger only heightened the passion.

"Mason." I could hear the begging in my voice.

He spread me open, naked while he was still fully clothed, going down on his knees, his tongue trailing down my stomach, nipping at my inner thigh.

A loud moan tipped my head back, my nails raking through his hair. "Fuck, Emery." He growled, his words vibrating against my folds, digging my nails deep into him.

His tongue sliced through me, and I lost all thoughts, a deep rumble coming from him. "I've wanted this pussy for so long." He pulled my legs over his shoulder, tipping me back, getting his mouth deeper into me. "Fuck, you taste amazing." His tongue licked further. A scream tore from me, my hips rocking against his mouth. I lost all sense. I only felt, as though I were tripping on a drug, all I could do was let myself go. He slipped two fingers inside me, slowly pumping them as his tongue worked my core.

This had been good before, but Mason took it to another level. To the point I almost couldn't handle it. A wild, raw noise came out of me. He seized my hips, pulling me hard to him as he sucked and licked me with brutal intensity, hitching my body higher and higher.

"Oh god. *Oh god!*"

"Come on my tongue." He rumbled, devouring me, his hands gripping my butt. "I want to taste your release." He sunk a finger inside my ass.

"Fuck!" My vision blurred, and my muscles shook, pleasure ripping through every cell in my body. Feeling my climax, he nipped on my clit, sucking it hard.

I almost jackknifed off the dryer, my body convulsing, shuddering with orgasm as I cried out, my body and mind bursting into pieces.

It took me a long time to come down, gasping for air, feeling my world was totally flipped upside down.

Never in my life had I orgasmed like that. *Ever.*

Mason licked through me again, his teeth nipping my thigh before he rose back up. "Even better than I imagined." He moved over me. "I'm never gonna get enough of your taste."

Sitting fully up, I grabbed for his t-shirt, but his hands stopped me. "No. Your turn. Down on your knees, *Emery.*" His order burned up my spine, my name sounding so forbidden on his lips.

Hopping off the dryer, I moved around him and shoved him against it, his eyes wild and feral as they went over every curve of my naked body he could see in the shadows. Lowering down, my fingers wrapped around the waist of his gray sweats, which did nothing to hide his massive erection. I yanked them down, his enormous size springing free.

"Wow." I breathed, wetness dripping from me, my mouth craving his taste. The guy was *beyond* well-endowed.

He grinned down at me, his hands tangling in my hair, cupping the back of my head. My tongue slid over him, licking off his pre-cum, and sucking on the tip of him.

"Em…" He drew in sharply as I took him down my throat. His hips rolled forward with a groan, his hands digging into my scalp. Wrapping one hand around his base, I grazed him with my lips—and a hint of my teeth.

Noises barked from him, his chest moving forcefully as I took him deeper. "Fuuucck." His hips pumped against me. The power I had over him turned me on, making me want to please him more. To hear him lose control.

My free hand curved around his ass, pulling me tighter to him, going deeper.

"Fuck. Your mouth feels incredible," he moaned. His grip turned painful against my head, but I loved it. He thrust harder against me, forcing me to take more of him, until my eyes watered, almost gagging. "I've fantasized about fucking your mouth so many times," he growled. "Look at me." His demand had my thighs squeezing together. I did what he said, seeing the heavy desire in his eyes, the flush in his cheeks, the hungry cocky smile.

He reached down, my nipples hardening as he twisted one between his fingers. My pussy clenched, my body sparking with need. My nails skated over his ball before squeezing them.

"Fuck! Fuuuuuck!" His head went back, hips snapping violently in desperation. "Shit!" He bellowed out. "I'm gonna come." I took him deeper. His throaty groans sent desire straight to my core, pulsing with another release. I hummed against him.

"Fuuuuuuccckk!" A roar came from him, his dick pulsing as he released, his taste bursting on my tongue as I swallowed his cum, my core clenching, sending another orgasm through me.

Mason slumped against the dryer. Our breaths filled the garage, my body still shaking and thrumming with blissful release and energy.

"Jesus." Mason clasped his chest, like he couldn't calm his heart. "I think I blacked out." His eyes moved down to me, a cheeky smile hinting on his lips. He reached down, his thumb wiping the remains of his seed off my lip before pushing it into my mouth. My tongue wrapped around his thumb, sucking it off. His dick twitched, already starting to rise again.

He let out a low laugh, his head shaking with disbelief. Yanking up his sweats with one hand, he swept me up to my feet with the other, pressing my naked body against his.

"That was... fucking unbelievable." He grinned, his mouth covering mine, his hands gripping the side of my face and kissing me so deeply desire pulsed with endless hunger through me.

But through the high, reality started to seep in. The cold wind blew in like the truth, nipping at my skin and my conscience.

The neighbors no doubt heard us. Anyone on this block probably heard us. What if someone saw? What if it was a kid from school or a parent? A friend of Addison's?

Oh my god, What the hell did I just do?

"Don't." He gripped the side of my face. "Don't start overthinking it. I can see you doing it."

"But—"

"No buts. Don't overanalyze it. We both wanted this." His hand dropped between my breasts, past my stomach. His fingers slipped through my folds, my mouth parting, fingers curling into his biceps.

He leaned in, kissing me again before he pushed off the dryer, sucking me off his fingers. "So good," he rumbled, stepping past me. "Good night, Emery."

Shock wrenched my head to him, watching him stroll casually out, heading toward his house without looking back.

Dazed and bewildered, I gathered my clothes, sprinting into the house and straight to my bedroom. My entire frame rocked and throbbed with the orgasm he gave me. The sensations he made me feel. The high he took me to. I couldn't control myself; I didn't care who heard or saw, and I didn't want him to ever stop. I wanted more.

He made me feel things I never had before. Face truths I never thought about, like not once had I orgasmed when I gave head to Ben. I never lost it so much I didn't care about consequences.

Mason was the first person I'd been with sexually since Ben. The reality of this gripped my lungs with panic.

Grieving came in stages. It jumped and skipped and dropped you back to zero in a moment. Coming out of nowhere, breaking through the walls without warning when you thought were getting solid.

It struck me across the chest, bending me over, gulping for air. Emotion slammed into me like a wave crashing over me.

Staring down at my wedding ring still on my hand, a sob wrenched up my throat. Guilt. Grief.

I curled up on top of my duvet, and I broke apart, crying until I couldn't breathe.

My mouth still tasted of Mason, my lips still feeling his kiss, my body imprinted with his touch. And it made me feel like I not only cheated on my husband, but I betrayed his memory, the love between us.

It felt as if I was losing him all over again. But what scared me was it didn't hurt as much as it should.

And that was what destroyed me.

Chapter 20
Mason

Craving was a powerful desire for something.

When I was young, I loved M&Ms to the point I could eat a dozen packs a day. The way the smooth shells felt on my tongue, the way they snapped when I bit down. The chocolate melting in my mouth. I had to cut them out of my diet, and I still recalled how hard it was to give them up, to not have that experience anymore.

Fuck. M&Ms had nothing on Emery.

I was distracted before, but since walking away from her last night, my mind had not shut down. My body twitched as if I had ten cups of coffee, and my dick was perpetually hard and no car engine in the world seemed to take my mind off it.

Most of my night was spent tossing and turning, ready to get up and march down the street again, climbing into bed with her. Sinking into her like I really wanted to. But walking away was the only choice I had.

I could see Emery coming up with all the reasons why it shouldn't have happened and why it couldn't happen again.

Leaving was my response. Half of it was because I felt it was the best way to lessen her freak out. Leave her a bit curious, a bit stunned, and wanting more. The other half was protecting myself because I didn't want to hear her excuses. Nothing about what we did seemed wrong. And that was exactly her problem. She needed it to be wrong, to put the barrier between us, to be the one to end it. Walk away as if she had taken the high road.

So, I walked away first. And I planned to give her space. Let her come to me.

It was the smart move, but my dick was telling me different. It wasn't something I totally was proud of, but I had been with plenty of girls. Girls had come easy to me since fifteen, which was exactly what Emery proved to me—they were *girls*. Young, insecure, and so eager to please, but not for the right reasons.

Emery was everything opposite.

So, instead of knocking on her door in the middle of the night, I had to jerk off multiple times to calm down. Just kissing her made me feel I was about to come in my pants, let alone what she did with her mouth.

"Fuck…" I hissed through my teeth, adjusting myself.

My cell buzzed on the workbench. Glancing down, I saw a text from Mateo.

Group of us are going to see the new action movie. Interested?

I wasn't, but if I didn't do something I would cave and end up back at Emery's. It took all my energy to stay away now, and with each passing hour, the sun setting behind the trees, it was developing into a monster I couldn't control. I'd end up back there, and she'd probably slam the door in my face. I wanted to give her a little time to miss me. To crave me like I did her.

I wanted her to come to me instead. All day I fantasized about her showing up in my garage. Her naked body spread over the hood of my car.

I adjusted my cock again, grinding my teeth together. I peered at the empty drive behind my GTO, the music of CCR streaming from the radio the only thing greeting me.

Yes. I texted Mateo back. I needed a distraction more than he knew.

My cell dinged. ***Cool. Meet us at 7:15 in front of the theater***.

Tossing the dirty rag onto the workbench, I went inside.

"Grandpa?" I called out. "I'm gonna head out tonight. Will you be okay?" I strolled into the living room, where he sat in his chair, Claudia on his lap, watching football.

"Of course. You think I can't take care of myself?"

No.

"Of course you can." I went over, scratching Claudia on the head before heading to the kitchen for a drink of water.

"I've already eaten, peed, and pooped. What else do I need?" My grandpa was getting crankier; his mind and body were at odds. He still thought of himself as this Air Force pilot, young and full of vigor, when he couldn't do much at all anymore. He sat in the garage with me, knowing he could no longer even get under a car and check it out. His body could no longer do what he used to, even though his mind said he could.

I understood that frustration. By my appearance and the fact I worked out, people didn't see it in me. Didn't see I was also limited.

"Speaking of taking care of yourself, have you taken your pills today? You know Grandma will get on your ass if you don't."

"Yes," he huffed. "Have *you*?"

Touché.

"Go!" He waved me on. "Go out and be young."

"You sure? I can stay here with you."

Grandpa stared at the TV for a while before he spoke again. "Mas, I've already lived a full life. Found the woman of my dreams. Don't waste your time sitting here watching TV. You should be out with your friends, being a teenager."

I didn't feel anything like a teenager. Actually, I wasn't any more. Instead of playing video games or drinking at parties, I wanted to be cooking Emery dinner, watching movies, and fucking her on the counter before we had dessert.

My grandfather's sentiment was supposed to be inspirational and all, but now that I stood here, waiting for some guys I didn't really give a fuck about—except Mateo—for some movie I didn't care about, I wanted to be anywhere else. Like at a cottage down the street from my house, between Emery's legs as I drove into her.

Was she home? Eating a crappy microwave dinner and watching TV? Had she thought about last night all day as I had?

The way her body responded to me, how loud she cried out, how I had to hold her down so she didn't fall off the washer when she orgasmed all flooded my mind. I had felt her come again when she was swallowing me down. How fast she responded to me when I kissed her after. I wanted so badly to bend her over the machine and fuck her senseless, but for once, I wanted the upper hand with her.

Did I regret it now? Hell yes.

A noise vibrated my throat, my hand nudging at my dick, trying to get it to calm the hell down. It was like it knew it had been twenty-four hours, and it was losing its shit now, craving her so badly I was starting to not see straight.

"Hey!" Mateo's voice boomed, his hand in the air, a gang of football guys behind him. "Sorry we're late."

111

I dipped my chin, nodding at all the familiar faces, not one did I talk to anymore. Again, if I wasn't involved with football, we had nothing left to say. Meeting at the movies with friends didn't fit me. I felt old, beyond this teenage crap.

If they only knew who I had been with the last night, what I was doing. I had heard many of these guys talk about Emery, muttering about how hot she was, fantasizing about fucking her.

A smug grin worked over my mouth. I knew how she tasted, how loud her cry could get. None of these assholes ever would.

"Let's go. I need to get Milk Duds and popcorn before it starts." Mateo hit my arm in greeting, heading us toward the door. Waiting for them to go in, my gaze wandered down the sidewalk, a bar and grill blaring music as people went in and out, some with holiday hats on.

Air dissipated in my lungs, my entire body flexing in shock… then pure raw possessive anger took over. Jealousy.

Emery.

She wore a red dress cut low in the front and rose several inches above her knees. Her legs looked toned and long as she strolled to the Grill in her heels, a fuzzy velvet coat wrapped around her, her hair down and curled.

She had every inch of me standing to attention, but I saw the man beside her, his hand on her lower back, ushering her in as if he had the right to touch her. The one who had the right to be by her side. Like it was his tongue inside her last night. Her mouth wrapped around his cock.

What the fuck?

Here I thought I had the upper hand, that she would be home wondering if I was going to show up or not, when in reality, she was going on a fucking date. With this douchebag.

He was all of 5'10", average build, a nice enough looking guy, and definitely older than her. Where she sparkled, he was dull and dim. He was all wrong for her.

The door shut after they entered, losing her inside. My feet moved. Not into the movie theater, but to her. I knew Mateo and the guys probably wouldn't even notice I wasn't there until later.

Striding to the Main Street Grill, I slipped into the dark, lively restaurant, my gaze scanning the space and finding a group of people in the bar area. A beautiful black woman dressed in a glittery red top yanked Emery up to the bar, ordering double shots. That man was right by her side, like a fungus, his hand still touching her. Trying to stake his claim to any man around.

I watched from the shadows, feeling like a fucking stalker, but I realized I could no longer fight the monster back… it was lying in wait for its prey.

Chapter 21
Emery

Smiling, I pretended I wanted to be here and that Daniel's hand on my back wasn't annoying me, that I wasn't thinking about Mason all day. To the point I almost found myself at his house, begging to pick up where we left off.

From the moment Daniel arrived at my house, actually from the moment I agreed to the date, I knew this was all wrong. When I said yes, I didn't know how Mason's mouth would feel on my body, how he'd taste on my tongue, how his rough hands touched me, how his moans would be engraved on my bones.

I sobbed and cried for an hour after he walked away until I had nothing left. Then I did the one thing I never thought I would. I actually took off my wedding ring. It felt as if it might be the time. That somehow the encounter with Mason had broken and healed me at once.

When I saw Daniel take notice of my bare hand, I realized it might have been a mistake. He took it as a signal to him that I was ready for this to be a real date, for him to touch me, kiss me. I didn't blame him. I dressed the part; I smiled as we chatted in the car, trying not to notice how many times he stared at me. I was trying to make myself want to be with Daniel as though I could convince myself.

He kept telling me how beautiful I looked, opening doors for me, and being the proper gentleman. Those were all very nice things. All things most girls wanted. One time I did too. What the hell happened to me?

I didn't want a sweet compliment on my outfit. I wanted to hear the dark rumble in my ear, telling me he couldn't get enough of my taste.

"Shots!" Marcie handed me another double, and I took it without question, needing my mind to stop torturing me. I needed to have fun and maybe get drunk enough I'd forget Mason and fall in love with Daniel.

Right.

"Another." I beckoned the bartender, making Marcie howl with laughter.

"See, someone is in the mood to let loose tonight." Her eyebrows wiggled at me, not so subtly darting back to Daniel. "Maybe finally in the mood for a little D?"

I snorted. Who I was thinking about was anything but little.

After downing my third shot in twenty minutes, my muscles started to warm, my head dulling out the incessant chatter. Though the one thing with tequila… I tended to get horny as hell. Ben used to tease me about how aggressive I got when I had some.

It was hard to see Ben as anything but the love of my life, but I realized I never let go with him. He wasn't someone I felt I could push my limits with, and he certainly wouldn't have pushed mine. We had good sex, and when we first were dating, we had it all the time. Then life, work, and school came between us, and later it was just something we did.

It was never rough, never so desperate we couldn't wait. It was never mind-blowing. Not like… Heat swirled in my body, memories of Mason and me, my nails digging into my palms.

Music played, getting Marcie and some of the others I worked with on the small dance floor. Everyone was having fun, drinking and laughing, enjoying the appetizers set out on a booth table we had reserved.

"Would you care for a drink?" Daniel wouldn't leave my side, and it was starting to feel claustrophobic.

"Sure." I smiled. "A margarita. Should probably stick with tequila."

"I'll be right back." His gaze went over me with a smile, then he headed to the bar, which was a few rows deep, the area filling up quickly. Many were having their Christmas party here tonight as well.

My head was light enough that I tugged my phone out of my purse, scrolling to a name. Drinking tequila was not a wise choice. I was already weak. Already wanting to find every excuse to contact him. Earlier I contemplated breaking my dishwasher.

Don't do it. Do *not* do it.

Me: My brand-new dryer has some dents in it now. I hit send.

Shit. I did it.

Dots appeared on his end, making my stomach knot up.

Mason: I think I can pound those out.

"Shit." I flushed head to toe, unable to stop the visceral reaction to the sexual insinuation.

I touched my forehead, wanting to keep going, but knowing I shouldn't. He was the one who walked away from me last night… but dammit if it didn't actually make me feel like he had flipped everything on me again.

Dots appeared again. *Mason: Unless you found another handyman?*

Another handyman? A trickle of confusion hinted at the back of my neck, wondering where that came from. Had he seen Daniel pick me up?

Me: No. I typed, biting my lip, knowing I would regret this tomorrow. Drunk texting was never a good idea, but my fingers didn't stop. *I clearly have the best handyman around. He far exceeds expectations.*

Mason: Think I need confirmation you were satisfied with my work.

More than satisfied. I couldn't stop thinking about it. Obsessively.

More dots came up.

Mason: You don't want to be here. I can tell. You had that fake smile on your face until now.

Sucking in, my head jerked around, feeling the sensation of being watched.

Me: Where are you?

My phone buzzed with a call, my gaze darting around, putting it to my ear.

"Look across from you." His husky voice had my muscles shuddering, my core squeezing as if he had the strings to it.

My gaze went over the room. My throat went dry when my eyes latched onto his figure on the other side of the bar, deep in the shadows.

Even trying to stay hidden, Mason was noticed. Besides his large muscular frame and sexy looks, at twenty he brimmed with confidence and dripped with sexuality. He was the kind of man who walked in, and every woman instinctively understood… he knew how to fuck. He would make you scream and beg for more, and just once in your life, you wanted to experience that.

Women from all around were openly staring at him, eyeing him up and down, debating their chances if they walked over to him, but his dark gaze was set solely on me.

"Having fun on your date?" His voice rasped into my ear, my body responding instantly to it. "I want to know, Emery. While he is touching you, whispering in your ear, are you thinking about how my cum slid down your throat last night, how my tongue felt in your pussy?" A bead of sweat trailed down my back, my lungs huffing in and out. "How wet are you for me *right now?*"

A puff of derisive laughter popped through my teeth, my thighs clenching, feeling myself become even more so.

"He's coming back." His eyes slipped to where Daniel was. "Make your choice. You put back on your fake smile and stand next to him all night pretending to have a good time…"

"Or?" My gaze wouldn't tear away from Mason, though I felt time ticking down, Daniel heading for me.

"Or…" A smirk tipped his mouth, and he hung up. His look heated as he sauntered for the hallway at the back of the grill.

"Emery, come dance," Marcie yelled at me, waving me over.

My head went to her, then to where I saw Daniel, drinks in hand, walking toward me, his eyes not yet on me.

It was an instant. My choice didn't even feel like one. I took off for the hallway, slipping away from Daniel before he could see me, hoping he'd think I'd gone to the bathroom.

My heartbeat pounded, my pulse thrashing against my neck. My gaze searched for Mason.

Men and women went in and out of the bathrooms, the ladies already queuing up down the hall.

A hand reached out, grabbing me and yanking me into a coat closet, shutting us in.

"Mas—"

"No." He pushed me against the door, leaning over me, his mouth brushing mine. "No more talking. You made your choice."

My chest heaved, my eyes taking him in, the dim light making this feel even more forbidden.

"I want him to hear your orgasm shudder through you. So, he will know he is not the one giving it to you." Mason's hand tugged the top part of my dress off my shoulders, exposing my breasts.

"Emery…" he groaned, his teeth biting at the bottom of my lip, tugging it, his hands squeezing and cupping my breasts, flicking my nipples.

All the pent-up energy I had kept back all day came to the surface with a vengeance. Our mouths collided. Teeth and lips, we devoured each other with desperation. It was raw and naked, drowning us in desire. We used it, exploited it, and turned it into a living, breathing thing, ready to ruin each other.

117

My hands went under his shirt, my nails dragging down his back violently. A groan vibrated in the back of his throat. Grabbing my hips, he picked me up, my legs wrapping around him, my spine hitting the thin door dividing us from the restaurant. Voices of people in the hall echoed all around as they headed for the restrooms. At any time, someone could come to get their jacket.

"Mason." I breathed his name, my fingers ripping at the buttons of his jeans, craving him so badly my head spun. The alcohol added to my aggression and need. "Fuck me." Last night was the foreplay, and tonight I needed him inside me.

"You sure?" He taunted. "Because once your pussy rides my cock," he growled in my ear, "it won't want anything else."

"Yes." *God, yes.* I yanked down his jeans. "Now."

His eyes watched me, his nose flaring, then he reached under my dress, his fingers tugging at the thin material of my panties, tearing them off. The tug cut through my folds, making me gasp before the fabric dropped to the ground.

My palms shoved down his pants and boxer briefs enough to free his cock.

He pushed my arms above my head, arching my breasts into him, wrapping my fingers around a coat hook.

"You will need to hold on." A slight grin tugged at his mouth, letting me take more of my weight as his hands explored my body, fingers pushing into my pussy.

"Fuck, you're dripping." He swallowed a moan, spreading me wider, his fingers going to his mouth, sucking me off them. "I craved the taste of you all day."

My body was clenching, so needy. I lost all control, my thighs squeezing him to me, crying for relief. He gripped my hips again, pushing my dress up to my stomach. His tip hinted at my entrance, teasing and playing with me.

"Mason!"

He wrapped his hand around my neck and squeezed hard at the same time he thrust into me.

Oh. My. God.

A moan so deep howled out of me. The feel of him, his size, had me shuddering, walking the line of pain and pleasure. Nothing ever felt like this. My brain couldn't wrap around the abundance of sensations. How unbelievable it felt.

"Oh fuuuuck," he groaned. Sucking hard through his nose, taking a moment to let me stretch to his size. "I'm not even all the way in... *Jesus...*" He pulled out and pushed in again, slow and deep, hitting every nerve I had. We both groaned loudly, knowing anyone walking by this room could hear.

I was already so deep in this craving I knew I was in serious trouble.

His hips started pumping, hitting me deeper. My eyes rolled back in my head. My tongue spouted words I didn't even recognize. I no longer cared about control or what was right or wrong. Sanity or insanity.

He drove into me with no restraint, impelling loud, uncontrollable cries from me. Our bodies moved violently together. He spread me wider, his balls slapping my flesh as he picked up the pace.

My nails raked through his hair and down his neck, inciting him more. "Oh god... harder."

His mouth nipped and sucked at my bouncing tits as he sunk in deeper. Harder. Ruthless and pitiless. I wanted him to do worse, to break me into pieces. To destroy me.

Gasping, I bucked against him, meeting his passion with my own. Our tongues were at war, our mouths hungry. It was embarrassing, but I could feel myself already starting to climax. My need for him was too primal and desperate.

"Not yet." He bit at my ear, dropping my feet to the floor and pulling out of me. He flipped me around, pressing me into the door, his hand yanking my ass to him as he thrust into me again, ramming my chest into the door, making it bang. I let out a cry as my nipples rubbed against the wood door. We were not quiet or discreet. We lost any restraint, turning feral and raw. He was fucking me so hard that I could no longer speak. The sound of his dick railing me filled the small room, our groans and cries popping in like a chorus as the door banged like a drum.

"Mason!" I pushed back into him with a throaty cry. His cock thickened and grew harder, brushing against my walls, hitting every nerve, making my knees almost buckle.

"Fuck. Emery." He hit so deep my nails dug into the wood, splintering.

"Hey, Marcie?" Daniel's voice came from right outside the door. "Have you seen Emery?"

Mason's grip tightened, a grunt coming from him as he pounded into me harder, knowing perfectly well who was there and what he was doing. He was marking me, possessing.

"Seen her? No," Marcie replied evenly. "She's probably in the bathroom."

Oh god! I bit my lip to keep my scream in. Mason reached around, rubbing my clit as he went even harder, wanting me to come now. To explode while Daniel was right outside the door.

"Okay, just let her know I was looking for her," Daniel replied.

Mason pinched my clit. It was like I had been electrocuted. I went over completely, sparks dotting my vision. I let out a loud cry when my legs buckled, and I rammed back into him, my pussy clamping down on him, strangling and pumping his cock.

"Oh fuck," he bellowed behind me, pushing all the way to the hilt, his hot cum filling me so full it dripped down my leg.

The absolute bliss shattered everything I knew or had understood. I had been utterly destroyed and remade at the same time. Our breaths heaved in unison, our bodies still pulsing and trembling.

He pulled me back into his chest, still inside me, because my body wouldn't allow him to leave, clenched around him as if it was claiming ownership. "What did I tell you?" His mouth grazed my temple. "I warned you your pussy wouldn't want anything else." He let out a groan. "It's so tight around me. Like a death grip. It feels *so fucking good.*" He twitched inside me, growing hard again, sparking desire through me. How instantly he could turn me on. He had full control over my body, making me lose all thought and logic in a second.

This level of power he had over me scared me. It felt unsafe. Dangerous. Nobody, including my husband, had this kind of command of me. To make me forget all decorum and decency.

Trying to relax, my core still tight around him, I pulled away, making him jolt and hiss out another moan. Every inch of me throbbed with bliss, with a high I had never experienced before. Though reality scraped and crawled its way to me.

"Oh god." I pulled my dress up over my shoulders, imagining if Daniel had caught us. I didn't want to hurt him. "Oh my god." I tried to flatten out the wrinkles with my hands and smooth my hair, though nothing could fix me. Sex drenched me, my orgasm flushing my cheeks.

"You're doing it again."

"I'm sorry if realizing I just fucked my niece's crush, a twenty-year-old boy, in the bar and grill coat closet, *unprotected*, with my date right outside the door was something to freak out about!" I hissed, whirling around on him. It had been so long since I had been with anyone except Ben, but it was no excuse.

"Shit." He tucked himself back in, zipping up his pants, appearing as if that fact just hit him too.

"I'm on birth control."

He let out a breath. "I've been tested. All good."

"Still, Mason." I shook my head. "What we did? There is no coming back from that."

"Do you want to?"

Even a little sweaty, the guy looked like he could go out and do a model shoot, where I looked as if I had been fucked. Thoroughly.

I rubbed at my face. He moved to me, peeling them away. "Don't overthink. Don't analyze. We can make this casual, if it's what you want."

"Casual?" I lifted my brow. "You talk like it's going to happen again."

"Believe me." He dipped into me, his mouth a hair from mine. "It will. Many, many times." He kissed me deeply, walking me back to the door. I countered in kind, sensing how easily this guy could prove himself right.

Mason pulled back, his hands sliding over my hair, brushing it down into place, his gaze intense. "You look even sexier to me." The way he said it told me he loved sending me back out there covered in him. Marked by him.

"Have a good night with your date." He reached under my dress, his hand trailing up my thigh, feeling where his release dripped down my leg and catching it. He pushed it back inside my pussy, making me gasp. "While my cum seeps from you the rest of the night."

Mason leaned down, snatching my ripped panties off the floor and tucking them into his pocket. "I'll see you later." He kissed me quickly and opened the door, strolling out, not giving a shit if anyone saw him.

Oh. Holy. Fuck.

I took a deep breath. A huge part of me wanted to follow him. To thread my fingers with his and walk out the door, going straight home.

Taking one more pat at my clothes and hair, a draft breezed up my dress, emphasizing I had no underwear. I loved that I was bare, and I could still feel him inside me. It was kind of thrilling, making me feel naughty. A secret no one else knew. I felt alive.

Stepping out of the closet, I rolled my shoulders back, putting on my smile.

The sound of someone clearing their throat turned me back to the bathrooms. My stomach dropped.

Next to the woman's room, Marcie stood there, her arms folded, her eyebrow arched, as if she had been there a while.

"Wow. Clearly you are getting some, just not with the one out there thinking he's on a date with you."

"Marcie…" Nothing else came out, guilt sweeping over me.

"Damn, girl. I'm impressed. Think they could hear you guys two blocks away. You know I'm all for you getting some, except don't lead Daniel on." She gave me a stern look. "He really likes you."

"I know." I bowed my head. I wish he was the one I liked too.

"Think we both definitely need a drink." She strolled up, linking her arm with mine. "And you can tell me where you found that hot young piece of ass I saw come out of there." She clicked her tongue. "Because you know how I enjoy those vanilla cones. And that one… my god. I could lick him all day." She fanned herself. "No wonder Daniel never had a chance."

No, sadly, he really didn't.

"So tell me? Did he take you to Jesus-land?"

"Oh yeah." I sighed. "Several times."

Chapter 22
Emery

"I had a good time tonight." Daniel pulled into my drive, shutting off the engine.

"Daniel…" I took a gulp of air, trying to find the right words.

"Emery, I know you aren't quite ready. But I'm willing to take it as slow as you want." He reached over and touched me.

"Oh… ummm…"

"I don't expect you to answer me tonight. This is all new to you. Just know I'll wait. And maybe after Christmas, we can go on a real date. Only the two of us."

"I don't think—"

"Please, just consider it." He rushed over my words like he didn't want me to end his chances yet. He leaned over, kissing my cheek. "I'll see you at work after the holiday." Christmas was in a few days, and the office was closed until the twenty-seventh.

My brain was too frazzled to respond further. I opened the door and got out, feeling my indiscretion even more as I climbed out, trying to keep my dress covering my thighs, the cold air nipping at me.

"Goodnight, Emery." He thankfully didn't get out, as if he sensed it would tip me over, and not in the direction he wanted.

"Goodnight." I felt an ache in my chest because looking at him, he was everything I should want. He was the "right" choice. Nothing could ever come of Mason and me. It was something I needed to get out of my system. The person who helped you move on, but not the one you chose for forever.

Daniel waited until I unlocked the door and stepped inside before he drove away. I clicked the door shut, kicking off my heels with a groan and falling against it. Staring at my decorated house, looking at the jacket I decided not to wear lying over my sofa, and thinking about the earlier me. If she had any idea how this night would go…

I had sex with Mason, and it was beyond anything I ever imagined. Guilt and disbelief were there, yet it didn't overrule the need coursing through my body. The intense craving for more.

The knock on my door vibrated down my spine, spearing between my thighs. My heart picked up the tempo. My breasts grew tender at the idea he was there, already primed to respond to him.

Peeling myself off the door, I circled around, opening it.

The air went electric as Mason stormed into my house, slamming the door, his hands already cupping my face, his body walking me back to the sofa. His mouth was on mine, hungry and desperate as though these few hours apart were agonizing for him too.

Desire lit my nerves, already needing him inside me so badly it physically hurt.

"Have a good time on your date with Dr. Douchebag?" He perched me on the back of the sofa, my hips widening as he settled between them.

"Daniel is a decent man."

"Decent." Mason scoffed, our breaths mingling as we spoke between our desperate kisses, his fingers already tugging at my outfit. "You don't want *decent*."

"Yes, I do." I moaned as he yanked down my dress, his hands exploring as if he knew exactly where to touch me to get me soaked. "He's the type I should date. Settle down with."

"And I'm the guy who knows how to fuck you. I'll have you screaming so loud you rattle the walls." He clasped my chin hard, tilting it to him. His dark eyes were like pools of sin. I wanted to jump in and never look back. His free hand spread me further open, his fingers trailing up my thigh, parting my folds. A small cry opened my mouth as he rubbed me. "Looks as if someone lost her panties tonight—I wonder who could have done that? The good doctor?" He tilted his head, eyes sparking. "You can pretend all you want he's the guy you'd end up with." He stroked me harder, jerking my muscles with a throaty gasp. "But we both know." His hand left my chin, trailing back into my hair, gripping it firmly, his fingers pushing into me. "This pussy is *mine*."

My control shattered, and I turned wild and boisterous. I tore at his clothes, desperate for him to fill me again. I wanted him to take the very thing he claimed was his.

He picked me up, my thighs hugging his hips, my dress bundled around my waist as he carried me back to my bedroom, his mouth never leaving mine.

"I have a condom this time." His teeth nipped at my neck before tossing me onto my bed. In the darkness, I could barely make out his outline. "I can't believe we didn't even think about it. I've never done that."

I had been on birth control since college, but we had been so lost in the moment we didn't even think about it. This guy had me rattled. But now that I had felt him, I wanted nothing between us.

"I want you fucking me." I pushed my dress off me, leaving me completely naked. I reached for him, tearing off his shirt, my palms exploring his ripped torso. I felt some kind of scar down his chest, but I was too frantic for him to focus on it. "I want you bare inside of me, covered in my cum."

"Fuck." A deep growl came from him, his jeans and boots hitting the floor before he crawled over me. "That mouth…" he rumbled before his own crashed down on mine. My legs wrapped around him, his cock sliding through me. He groaned. "You're so fucking wet…"

"For you." I slid up and down him, biting at his neck. I had never spoken this way with Ben. This kind of feral need was never us. We had comfortable, good sex.

Mason was opening me up to more. To what phenomenal, mind-blowing, dirty sex could be.

I could feel his heart pounding against mine. Then he gripped my thighs, pushing them up high as he plunged into me, making me cry out.

I knew even my seventy-year-old neighbors probably heard me. It wasn't even a choice to be quiet with him; I seemed to have lost all control. Mason cut everything else out except the pleasure, the pain, the way our bodies moved together, the way he felt inside me.

There was no question he knew what he was doing, far more than any high school, college, or even men my age knew. Mason was in a field of his own. No teenage girl knew enough about herself to handle him, challenge him.

Be his equal.

That's what it felt like. We matched each other, pushed boundaries, and explored what turned the other one on. No shyness or doubt.

Tonight, in the dark, there was no age difference. Nothing forbidden.

It was just us.

My lids blinked open to a cloudy morning, a soft milky light glowing throughout my bedroom. I stretched, feeling every muscle in my body scream in protest, achy and sore after hours and hours of being used. For a moment, I let the memories of the night before flicker through my mind.

The incredible sex didn't stop. All. Night. Long.

Even when we had to take a break, we never stopped kissing and touching, quickly to be aroused again, finding ourselves even needier than the time before.

I heard the sexual drive of a thirty-something woman and an eighteen-ish-year-old guy were on par. I could vouch that was true… for us. We matched each other in every way.

A knee bumped against my ass, and I twisted my head to peer over my shoulder.

Mason was sprawled out on his back, his leg bent into me, one hand on my thigh while the other one was tucked under the pillow, his face toward me, still sound asleep.

I wanted to feel shame. To be so appalled by my actions because that I could understand. Could defend. I just got caught up in the cover of darkness, in the moment. Something I'd had to get out of my system. But the light streamed in brightly, and I found him more tempting than before, not wanting to give him up. But I knew I had to.

Turning to face him, my gaze ran over his beautiful face, letting my fingers trace his lips, noticing where I had bitten into his bottom one, making it bleed. His shoulders and neck were covered in red marks from my teeth and nails.

The boy completely unraveled me, turning me feral.

A hum came from his throat, his lids not even opening, when a soft smile curled his mouth. I found myself smiling the same way in response.

"Hey." His lids finally blinked open.

"Hey," I whispered back.

He watched me unabashedly for a moment, like he was absorbing every molecule of me.

"Shit," he mumbled, glancing over at my clock. "I have to go soon. Picking up Grandma today."

"That's good." Sadness was creeping in, understanding this couldn't happen again, and these may be my last moments with him. "I have to get to the shelter soon too."

His eyes tracked me as if he could see beyond what he should.

"Too early to be overthinking already." He reached over, tucking a strand of hair behind my ear.

My fingers gripped the pillow tighter, my gaze drifting down.

"Let me guess." His voice was even more gravelly in the morning, striking right between my legs. "You're going to say this can't happen again, am I right?"

My tongue slid over my lips, my feelings and logic at war. "It can't. It probably never should have started." My throat strangled on the idea. "You need to be there for your grandma, and I'm busy at the shelter. I'll be heading back to my sister's house for Christmas in a couple of days. Plus, Addison will be coming back before school starts again."

"Then we have until then. You can't tell me you want this to end yet." He turned more onto his side, facing me. His palm touched my face, his dark eyes hinting with desire.

No, I couldn't. My craving for him was at DEFCON 1 after last night.

"Let's enjoy every moment we can, until we can't," he propositioned.

"So merely sex?" I countered. "No feelings involved or talk about anything more. It ends when it ends," I said, but I could feel everything in me screaming no, already knowing this was a mistake. We needed to end it now before I got in too deep. Because I would want more.

Mason's throat went up and down, a nerve in his cheek twitching, an emotion I couldn't decipher fluttering over his face before it was gone.

"Sure." He nodded. A slow smirk twisted his mouth, his gaze heating. "Just a ridiculously obscene amount of dirty sex. Who knows, maybe by then, both of us will be completely over it."

Doubtful.

By his expression, he didn't believe it either, but I couldn't say no. I didn't want to. And this gave me time to get him out of my system. To get me back in the land of the living and able to move on and heal.

"I think we better get started on the dirty sex." He rolled me over on my back, his weight feeling delicious between my thighs.

"Thought you had to get going?" I teased, my hands curving over his marvelously firm ass, dragging my nails across his skin.

"I bet I can make you come in less than three minutes." Heat sparked in his eyes, and I felt him hard against my stomach, rolling into me.

"Oh really?" I lifted a brow. "What if I make you come before that?"

"Challenge accepted." He leaned down, his mouth devouring mine. Our kiss went instantly hungry and needy, making me wet and desperate to feel him enter me again. I rolled him over on his back, straddling him, his hand brushing over my breasts and hips as my eyes took him in.

In the daylight, my attention caught on the thick pinkish-white scar tissue running down his chest. I hadn't noticed in the dark, but now it drew my focus. My finger trailed down it, making him suck in.

"What's that from?"

His jaw locked. "Nothing."

"It doesn't look like nothing."

"From an operation when I was a kid. No big deal." He sat up, adjusting my hips back, rubbing my entrance over his cock, his voice low. "My scar is not what I want to talk about right now." He lifted his hips into me, pushing the tip inside, causing me to lose my thoughts. My back arched, a groan puffing from my mouth. "I need to fuck you, to be so deep inside you I can't find my way out." He grabbed my hair, holding me down as he thrust up into me.

"Oh god…" I moaned loudly, his strokes slow and deep, his thickness hitting all my nerves. "Mason!"

"Fuck, I love when you say my name," he growled, hitting harder, our forms moving together in a violent dance.

Our rhythm picked up, our groans filling my bedroom as I rode him harder. It wasn't long before I clenched around him, already feeling my climax coming.

Dammit. He was right.

He pushed me on my back, moving over me. His thumb pressed down on my throat, dotting my vision as he hammered into me.

My spine bowed, my hands sinking into his ass, pushing him in deeper, the sounds of my wetness almost obscene.

"Fuck!" His cock twitched inside me.

My climax went around him like a fist. Mason bellowed, releasing inside with his warm cum, making me orgasm again. A scream ripped from my throat as I almost lost consciousness, my world fracturing into pieces.

Our time was limited. I understood it, but I wasn't ready to give him up yet.

Chapter 23
Emery

The days leading up to Christmas were a haze of being at the shelter, cooking dinner with Mason, and sex... unbelievable, relentless sex. In every room and surface of my house.

It became this little routine—him coming over after he helped his grandparents to bed, making sure Grace was settled. We cooked, watched movies, and fucked like fiends through it all. We actually burned last night's meal because we were too busy screwing on the kitchen table. We'd go to bed, where we'd continue to fuck all night and at least twice before he left, slipping out early enough to make sure he could help Grace with her morning routine.

How in a few days had it become so natural and comfortable, but at the same time so forbidden and reckless? Why did the thought of it ending make my chest flutter with panic?

"How long are you going to be gone?" Mason pushed me against the car, his body leaning into mine.

My gaze darted nervously out the open garage door, hoping no one was walking by. It was dangerous enough for him to be seen coming here at all, but to be caught like this? There was no excuse.

"Two nights." Making sure the coast was clear, I turned back to him. "I'll be back the twenty-sixth."

It was Christmas Eve. My car was packed with presents, ready for my four-hour journey to Harper's.

"Two nights." His mouth grazed my ear. "Of not being inside you. Not feeling your pussy spasm around my cock. Not tasting your release on my tongue. Not kissing you." His lips captured mine, his hands holding my head, controlling the kiss, flooding heat through my veins and between my thighs.

Was it selfish I didn't want to go? The idea of staying here, lying in bed with him all day, was infinitely better. Two days without him sounded miserable, and the last place I wanted to go back to was the town where Ben and I lived as man and wife.

I hadn't thought of Ben as much since Mason and I had gotten together. It scared the hell out of me. The safety of my life was crumbling around me.

"Mason." I pulled back, my eyes darting outside. "Anyone can see us."

A rumble came from his throat, and his nose flared with irritation, but he dropped his hands, stepping back.

"Text me when you get there?"

"Isn't that crossing our only sex rule?" It was half a tease, but it fell flat as his expression darkened.

"Right." He nodded. "Have a good holiday." He turned for the exit, his shoulders stiff. Angry. Irritated.

"Wait." I reached for him before my brain even weighed in, emotion taking over. I swung him back to me, going up on my toes, my hands cupping his jaw, my lips finding his mouth. A noise hummed from his chest, his hand clasping the back of my head, our lips saying more than we ever would. The need for each other constantly thrummed between us, quickly turning a simple kiss into something heated.

Regrettably, I broke away, knowing where this was heading—me on top of the washer or dryer, trying not to let my neighbors hear me getting railed by a twenty-year-old.

Shit. Why did that turn me on so much?

"I'll text when I get there." I went back on flat feet. "And tell Neal and Grace Merry Christmas for me."

"I will. I think my grandpa has a crush on you. He mentions you all the time."

"Really?" I grinned coyly. "Ex-fighter pilot? Sounds just like my type." Sadly, this world would probably accept a relationship with him more than they would me with Mason. It seemed perfectly acceptable for men to be far older than women to be.

"That's really disturbing." Mason snorted, a smile tipping his cheek. "Drive safe." He kissed me again before he reached down, grabbing the waist of my jeans. His fingers glided under my panties, sliding through me, pushing into me. A gasp hurled from my lips. His eyes flashed as he pulled his arm away, placing his fingers in his mouth, sucking me off them. "For the road." He winked before sauntering out of the garage.

A strange sound tumbled from my chest as I sucked in and out. My skin flushed with need, my core aching for him to finish. The equivalent of blue balls.

"Asshole." I huffed, walking shakily to my car. He was devious knowing I'd be horny as hell for the next four-hour drive, my thoughts focused entirely on him.

Fantasizing about him. Needing him.

"Aunt Emery!" Arms wrapped around me, Addison's frame almost knocking me down to the ground as I got out of the car. "I've missed you so much."

"I've missed you too." I hugged her back.

The guilt I seemed to be able to push away now came flaring up at seeing Addison right in front of me. The notion of making her cry or hate me pooled acid in my stomach.

"Em!" Harper ran out of the house, clobbering me in another exuberant hug. "I'm so glad you are here. We've both missed you." She pulled away, smiling at me. "Welcome home."

Home.

My eyes drifted over the familiar small blue house my sister had lived in since she married Joe. It wasn't in a great area, but it was cute and clean. I used to be here often, so it did feel like another home at one time. Yet, the moment my car crossed back into this town, I knew I'd never call this place home again. Nothing had changed; it was all the same. I passed the street where Ben and I had lived, and I could easily see myself shopping at the local market or going to the yoga studio on 11th Street. Now it seemed similar to that old sweater you used to love but stopped wearing. Then one day you put it on again, and it just didn't feel the same. This place no longer fit. It was for the version of me who was still married to Ben, who would've probably had me pregnant by now because he was in such a rush to have kids. Even though I wasn't, I would have given in. To make him happy. To make Alisa and John happy.

I carried both guilt and relief for that, one only eliciting the other... a vicious circle.

131

"Come on, it's freezing out here." Harper waved toward the house. "Addy, help your aunt with her bags."

Addy bounced up to me. I forgot how much energy she had.

"I've really missed you." She squeezed me again, reaching for my suitcase. "I'm so ready to come back."

I grabbed the Christmas presents, shutting the door.

"Mateo, Elena, and Sophie are begging me to return." She chattered on. "The spring fling dance is coming up soon. It's a dance where the girls ask the guys."

We stepped into the warm house, the place decorated, the fire going, smelling already of lasagna, our traditional Christmas Eve dinner.

"I'm gonna ask Mason."

"What?" I snapped, my head jerking to her, my body going rigid. Quickly I tried to counter my response. Smoothing out my features, I placed the gifts under the tree. "You're going to ask Mason to the dance?"

"Yeah. I know he says he doesn't dance, but it's not really about dancing anyway."

"Oh?" I cocked my head. "What's it about then?" Every word was tight.

"The dresses, the party after, being with friends and renting a limo together. Plus, they have a spring princess and prince." Her smile grew euphoric. "Mason will definitely win. He basically wins every time even though he never goes."

"And you think he'll go to this one?" *Stay neutral, stay neutral.* Perspiration heated under my jacket, my hands tearing it off, feeling my face hot.

"I know it's a long shot, but…" She dramatically flopped onto the sofa. "I thought I was getting over him, but when he texted me back the other day, I realized I hadn't. I still really like him."

"He texted you back?" My throat struggled to swallow.

Her cheeks pinked, pouring acid straight into my gut.

Needing to get away, I rolled my suitcase down the hall to the guest room, shutting the door.

I felt sick. Not only because Addison was still crushing on the guy I had been fucking for several days straight, but the idea he could be playing with me. I was the one who declared it was just sex, nothing more, but if he was chatting to Addy while he was in bed with me?

No. It was wrong.

A crazed laugh sobbed up. All of this was wrong, and I let it happen.

It shouldn't have gotten this far, and now I felt so tangled up in a mess set for disaster and heartbreak.

"Emery?" Harper called to me. "Want to come help decorate the Christmas cookies?"

"I'll be right there." I forced cheer into my voice. Taking deep breaths and pulling myself together, I went back out with a smile pinned on my face.

Holiday music played in the background, and I joined them in the kitchen. Addy was already dancing around, decorating the cookies, while Harper checked on the dinner.

"Everything smells so good. Can I help with anything?"

"No!" Harper and Addison replied, shaking their heads profusely.

"Hey now." I folded my arms. "I'm not that bad. I've actually been cooking a lot this past week." I crunched down on my teeth because of the reason why. They wouldn't link it to him, but he seemed right on my tongue whenever I opened my mouth.

"True, you've gotten a bit better." Addison agreed. "The hamburger patties were good."

"Wow, that's my extent, huh?" I ruffled her hair, trying not to recall that after we burned dinner last night, he went straight to making brownies, but he ended up licking the batter off my boobs instead.

"You okay?" Harper tilted her head.

"Yeah, why?"

"You just looked flushed."

"It's warm in here," I fibbed, fanning my face, disregarding the ache between my legs. Just the idea of him had me hot and bothered.

It was another thing I had never experienced before. I dated, had sex, and had many crushes. I had never been this riled up, smitten, or horny. Not like this. It was as though he had awakened something in me, and I couldn't get enough. And even after giving me the best orgasms of my life, the moment he left my house, I wanted him to come back.

"Actually, what you can do is help with the salad." Harper put the items next to me at the counter.

"That I can do." I set down my phone, grabbed a knife and cutting board, and got to work.

"Dinner will be ready in an hour." Harper peered at the baking lasagna. "And…" she tapered off.

"What?"

"Kevin is coming over."

"Oh." I smiled. "That's great. You guys making it more official now?"

"Yeah, I think so."

"Mom, just admit it. You looovvveee him." Addison snickered, bumping my shoulder. Clearly, Addison not only knew about him, but fully approved. I could see in the short time here, how much their relationship had mended. They were more back to how they once were.

Harper rolled her eyes. "You think you will be okay with him coming?" she asked me.

"Of course."

"It's just…"

Oh right. His connection to Ben. "It's fine, Harp. I'm happy to meet him. Or I guess re-meet."

Harper looked at me with intuition and intensity, which made me shift. "What?"

"I don't know. Something is different about you." She studied me, her eagle-like gaze going to my right hand, seeing the ring was gone. "Even from when I last saw you."

"Right?" Addy nodded in agreement. "You seem happy."

"I was happy before."

"Maybe on the surface, but there was a sadness around you." Addison shrugged. "Now, I don't know. You just…"

"Glow." Harper's tone was poignant, her arms folding. "Who is he?"

"What?" I sputtered, my face starting to burn again. "Who's who?"

"The guy putting the smile on your face."

"No-no one." I shook my head.

"Oh my god, is it Dr. Ramirez?" Addison gasped, she and her mother barreling down this road together, while I felt the same as an animal stuck in the headlights about to get run over.

"No." I swallowed. "There's no one. I swear!" Why did that sound like a lie to me too?

"Bullshit." Harper pointed at me. "I know you, little sister. And I know what a good…" She mouthed *fucking*. "Looks like."

"Harper!"

"Like I don't know what you both are talking about." Addy rolled her eyes. "I'm not a child. I'm seventeen."

"Don't remind me." Harper groaned.

Turning back to the lettuce, I tried to pretend the conversation was over, a weight sitting in my stomach.

On the counter between Addison and me, my cell lit up with a text. My brain still wound up about what just happened, it took me a moment to respond to seeing Addison look over at the screen. Her forehead lined with confusion, her eyes darting up to mine.

"Why is Mason texting you?"

Oh. Holy. Shit.

"Oh." I dropped the knife, swiping up my cell and shoving it in my pocket before she could read it, my gaze not able to meet hers. "It must be about the part... the dishwasher broke again."

LIE. LIE. LIE. It felt as if a blaring neon sign was on my forehead.

Addison's gaze didn't leave mine, her eyes studying me as if somewhere inside she sensed something.

"Hey, hey!" A man's voice came from the front entry. "I have pie and presents."

Addison squeaked, running out to the man. "Kevin!"

Relief flooded me, grateful for Kevin's timing. His entrance had me stunned for another reason. Addy was very comfortable and excited to see him, and he had simply walked in. No knocking, no being a "guest." This was huge. Harper wouldn't let a man she was dating be so casual unless it was serious. The way Harper smiled at hearing his voice, I knew my sister was in love.

"Wow, he sure has Addison's approval."

"Yeah. They hit it off. He even took her to a football game with him the other week. She said they had a blast."

"I'm so happy for you, Harp." I felt myself choke up. "You deserve it so much."

"So do you, sis." She wrapped her arm around me, heading over to where Kevin and Addy were. "And don't for one moment think the conversation earlier is over. You have this 'I'm getting a truly fucked' aura about you. I know because I had the same happy dazed look after I met Kevin." She let go, jogging for her boyfriend, leaping into the arms of a tall, toned, and handsome man.

He peered up over her shoulder, going stiff. My heart tripped over itself as I stared into the same face who told me Ben would not be coming home.

It was blurry, hazy, like a bad dream you couldn't exactly recall, but somewhere in your gut, you did.

"Kevin." I gulped back the knot in my throat, reaching out my hand.

He and Harper parted, and he stepped up to me.

"I've heard so much about you." Kevin took my hand. "It's nice to officially meet you."

"You too." With his hand in mine, I felt tears brimming in my eyes, but for once it wasn't out of heartache. It was gratitude. "I never got to thank you." I gave him a watery smile. "Your kindness that terrible night. What you did…"

"I was only doing my job." He looked down, letting go of my hand. "But something about your case stuck with me."

A full smile bloomed on my face when I glanced over at Harper. "I guess it did. I'm glad it was you who knocked on the door."

He let out a relieved breath, like he was afraid I would never be able to forgive him for the role he played that night.

"Maybe it was fate." I glanced at my sister and Addison.

"Maybe." He smiled warmly back at me. I already knew this man was a keeper.

"Come on. Dinner will be ready soon." Harper moved back to the kitchen, and I watched him follow her, his hand rubbing her back, kissing her sweetly before they stepped out of my eyeline.

Seeing him again, the officer who had to give me the horrendous news, it gave me this sensation of lightness. Maybe I was actually moving on. A sense of closure, and as much as I would always love Ben…

It was time to let myself free.

Chapter 24
Mason

I peered down at my cell again, a groan bubbling in the back of my throat, my hand rubbing over my head with frustration. She told me she'd text when she got there, which should have been hours ago. All I needed was a damn text telling me she was all right.

Shit. I sounded like a boyfriend.

Not what we agreed to be. Just sex. And fuck, was it *unbelievable.* I could not get enough of her. My dick was raw after days of relentless fucking, but I still craved her like a drug. I wanted to be inside her now. But it was more than that. From the day I saw her across the field, I couldn't explain it. I was drawn to her. It was nothing I felt before, as if I had always known her.

She was mine.

I had to walk this line, play by the rules she set, and not call her like a worried boyfriend.

"You okay, son?" Grandpa glanced over at me, his attention going to my bouncing knee.

"Yeah." I hopped up, realizing I hadn't been paying any attention to the football game. "Gonna go check on Grandma."

Christmas was usually the three of us. My father had been their only son, and since I didn't know my mother, I only had them after my dad died. We'd watch football games while Grandpa went in and out of napping, and Grandma humming Christmas songs in the kitchen as she cooked while I prepared the turkey.

Our small gathering never bothered me before, but this year, everything felt off.

Grandma couldn't leave the bed, and she slept more than she was awake. I did the cooking this year, but doing it for Grandpa and me seemed pointless. We were going through the motions, but neither of us wanted to celebrate. Grandma was the lifeblood of this family, and I feared she might not be here much longer. When she went, so would the joy in this house.

To not think about it, my brain flipped back to Emery, which had me just as agitated.

Grandma appeared so little and fragile in the bed. I never noticed how old and weak she had gotten. She was still the woman who raised me, who swung me around and taught me how to cook.

"Mason." Her voice was soft and frail, her lids barely holding up.

"Sorry if I woke you. I wanted to check on you."

"Come here." She patted the empty spot next to her on the bed.

I went over, sitting next to her, her hand wrapping around mine, her grip still surprisingly strong.

"Do you know how much your grandfather and I love you?"

"Grandma…"

"Let an old lady talk." Her shaky hand tapped at my hand, telling me to be quiet. "You know I've only wanted the best for you, Mason, and I feel your grandfather and I have let you down."

"What?" I jolted. "No way. If anything, it's the other way around."

Her hand pressed on mine, snapping my mouth closed.

"I know you didn't have the best childhood, but the moment you came to live with us, you were ours, Mason, and there wasn't or *isn't* anything we wouldn't do for you. And that's why I blame myself." Her lids fluttered. "I know you've put a lot of pressure on yourself to finish school, coach football, and experience your senior year—for your grandfather and me, *not* yourself. Like you're obligated to us, when that couldn't be further from the truth. We saw your father's regret. We saw all the experiences other kids were going through, which you missed out on, and I think we made ourselves believe it was something you wanted too, for our own selfish reasons. It took until this stroke for me to be honest with myself, to face what I've known for a while—you are merely going through the motions *for us*."

"Grandma—" My throat bobbed.

"We're not going to be around long."

"Grandma, stop. You'll probably outlive me."

"Don't say that." Her face pinched, her hand squeezing mine harder. "Don't *ever* say that," she whispered, almost in a cry.

"Sorry." I lowered my head.

"Your grandpa and I have officially put the deed to the house in your name, along with the few stocks we have. It's not a lot, but everything is now under you. We have money set aside for the funeral expenses, so nothing falls on you."

My eyes and nose burned with tears. I couldn't talk, my throat too thick to push anything out.

"Sell the house and stocks, or do whatever you want. The *most important* thing is you live the happiest life you can. *That* is our first dream for you. For you to follow your heart no matter where it leads you. And I'm so sorry for making you believe you needed to do this to please us. Whatever you do will make us happy as long as *you* are." Exhaustion fluttered her eyes. "You are my greatest gift, Mason." She patted my hand, her lids drifting lower. "Stop acting as though you owe us. If anything, we owe you for giving us such joy in our lives."

A hiccup caught in my lungs, my eyes burning.

Her mouth parted as she fell back to sleep. Leaning over, I kissed her forehead, tucking her in before sneaking out. My chest burned with unshed tears as I headed for my room. The terror of losing them had me gasping for air. They had been my rock, my world, stood by me, and gave everything up for me. Without them, I had no one.

My cell buzzed in my pocket. I yanked it out, seeing a text.

Emery: I'm here.

Nothing more, nothing personal, nothing telling me she missed me.

"Follow your heart no matter where it leads you."

Fuck it.

I hit the call back button.

Chapter 25
Emery

"Are you going to tell me who you're seeing?" Harper sipped at her wine. Addison was in her room chatting to her friends on the phone. Kevin had just left, and we were all full of pasta, cookies, and pie.

"I'm not seeing anyone," I refuted.

Harper curved her eyebrow, "Mmmm-hmm. Sure."

"I'm not!" Technically, Mason and I weren't "seeing each other." It was purely sex.

"So, you're just sleeping together?"

"Oh my god, I'm not sleeping with my boss." I shook my head, the idea of Daniel and me together making me cringe. Though if I let her believe it was him, they wouldn't suspect it was the twenty-year-old who Addison crushed on. "He asked me out on a date. That was it."

"If you say so." Harper nodded at my bare finger. "You are interested enough to want to at least try again. That's good."

Yes, but not with Dr. Ramirez. How I wished it was him. How much easier this would be.

"You really are telling me nothing happened? Because you have these radioactive waves of sex coming off you. The look that screams, *I've been so truly good and fucked.*"

"Harp." I palmed my face.

Addison's laugh drifted from her bedroom.

"Good having her home again?" I changed subjects.

"Yeah." Harper nodded. "I would love for her to move back now, but I know she's happy there and loves her friends and cheerleading. I couldn't do that to her." Harper tucked her leg under her. "And honestly, I'm about to drive her back so I don't have to hear any more about the Mason kid."

Everything in me froze, panic burning around my lungs. "Oh?" I took a heavy gulp of wine.

Kid? I wanted to burst out laughing. If she knew what dirty things he did to me on the kitchen table last night.

"What is she saying about him?" Every syllable was even and tempered.

"He's the most gorgeous boy she's ever seen." *Agreed.* "He's dark and mysterious." *Check. Check.* "When he looks at her, she feels all fluttery." *Can concur.* "I have no room to talk, but he sounds like the opposite of the guy I want Addy to like. A heartbreak waiting to happen. The ultimate playboy, someone who will toy with her."

He was using a "toy" on me last night.

"He's not an asshole at all. Actually, with his past, he's very sweet to those close to him." *Oh. My. God. Shut up, Emery.* "I mean, he's been around enough, so I've kind of gotten to know him." I sure know how he feels inside me. How he loves my nails digging into his ass as we come together. The noises he makes when he's pounding into me. It is also how smart and funny he is, how he takes care of his grandparents. Of me. How his past has shaped him to be more selective with friends, to trust very few. And how good it feels to be one of those special ones to him.

"Well, this kid Mateo sounds like a better guy for her." Harper didn't read into me defending him. "But Addy is too similar to me. I never wanted the good ones."

"Until now." I clinked my glass to hers.

"Oh, he may come across as nice, but that man is all bad in the bedroom." She fanned herself.

"I think I should be grossed out." I laughed. "But I'm happy for you."

"Thanks. I hope you let someone in again. Believe me, I wasn't looking for anyone so soon after Joe, and Kevin wasn't either. Sometimes life doesn't care about your plans. The right person comes along, and you just have to take a chance."

I stared at the ruddy color in my glass, my heart twisting because right or wrong, no matter what I said about it being only sex, I really liked being with Mason. Talking and laughing with him. It scared me, but I missed him. *Really* missed him.

As if Mason could feel me thinking about him, my phone buzzed, his name blaring on my screen.

Shit.

Jumping up, I twisted my cell away from my sister. "Um, I should get this… it's the shelter."

She nodded, waving me on, believing the lie.

Darting back to the guest room, I shut the door, my finger pushing call.

"Hey," I said quietly. Addison's room shared a wall with mine.

"Hey."

Shit. His voice should seriously be illegal. My nipples hardened instantly, my pussy pulsing like they were now conditioned to respond to his voice.

"I'm probably breaking another rule, but I needed to hear your voice," he rumbled. "Having a good Christmas?"

It would be better with you here.

Then my mind actually tried to conjure it up. It could never happen. Addison would hate me forever, and no one would accept us.

"Yeah." I licked my lip. "And you?"

"Just great." His sarcasm was thick. "Rather be between your thighs right now."

"Mason." I tried to put warning in my tone while desire poured over me at the thought of him there.

"Don't say my name that way if you don't want me imagining my tongue fucking your pussy right now."

A heavy breath surged from me, every nerve sizzling at the idea.

"Stop." I really didn't want him to, even if it was wrong. My gaze kept bouncing to Addison's bedroom wall, hearing the muttering of her voice and music playing. "Addison said you texted her the other day."

A deep hum came from him. "You sound jealous."

"I'm not jealous," I snipped a little too quickly. "I want to know if you are playing both my niece and me because if you are, I swear to—"

"Emery." He cut me off. "Hear this loud and clear. You are the only thing I want to be playing with."

My throat caught; a deep relief I didn't want to analyze simmered under my skin.

"She just texted me to ask how my vacation was going and said she couldn't wait to come back." The sound of him moving and flopping on his bed could be heard in the background. "I answered, 'it's good,' but maybe I should have said it's been fucking amazing because every night, I'm balls deep in the most stunning woman I have ever seen. Consumed with how she feels coming on my cock. Oh, and she happens to be your aunt. So how's your vacation going?"

My cheeks heated at his claim, and I strolled to the twin bed I was sleeping on, lying down, feeling the forbidden naughtiness of us.

"Yeah, probably better to go with a simple 'it's good'."

A dark laugh vibrated in my ear. Every inch of my skin tingled, every nerve sensitive and aching.

"Is it against the rules to say I miss you?"

"No." I drifted my hand up my thigh and over my core, the ache becoming acute. "I miss you too."

"Fuck," he breathed out. "I want to be inside you so bad right now."

"Me too."

He went silent.

"Mason?"

My phone buzzed again. This time he was video-calling me. Somewhere in my brain, it told me this was a bad idea, but the two glasses of wine had dulled any judgment.

I hit the button, his face coming into view, taking my breath away. He laid back on his bed, his gaze heavy on me.

"Take off your sweater and pants," he demanded. A little taken back by his gruffness, I couldn't fight how lust boiled between my legs. "Now, Emery."

My breath catching, I did as I was instructed. "You too."

He smirked, ripping off his shirt, his muscular torso and deep V-line coming into view. He pushed down his jeans and showed me how rock-hard he was under his boxer briefs. His body was miraculous, and my hands and mouth craved to worship it.

"Slip your bra off." He watched me as his hand rubbed over his erection. "Slowly."

Unclasping it, I let the fabric slowly drop away from my body.

Mason groaned. "Play with your tits for me."

My palms circled my nipples, squeezing and massaging, my spine crackling more with heat.

Addison's laughter came through the wall, stressing how wicked and wrong this was.

"Fuck." Mason gripped his cock, rubbing it harder. Knowing exactly how it felt in my own hand, how it tasted on my lips, I got increasingly turned on.

"Finger your pussy," he growled. "Let me watch."

Gripping the phone in one hand, my fingers slid down into my panties, rubbing through me, peppering sweat along my spine, getting off on the way he watched me.

I had never done anything even remotely similar to this. Not really.

One time Ben was on a business trip, and we tried to have phone sex. It felt awkward, and I faked my orgasm.

My pussy soaked my underwear as I stroked myself, loving the heat burning in Mason's eyes.

"Take them off now." He freed his cock, but his hungry gaze was on me. Slipping off my underwear, I sat naked on the bed, painfully aware of who was in this house and how easily my sister or niece could walk right in without knocking. It felt even more sinful.

"Spread your legs wide."

My back arched as I opened my thighs, continuing to rub myself, the sparks already igniting through me. "Mason…"

"Put the phone between your thighs. I want my view of your pussy, like I'm eating you out right now." His dirty command produced a moan from my throat, my teeth biting my lip to keep it back, my body burning. "Pretend it's my fingers inside you right now. Going harder. Deeper."

My lids shut, the sound of my wetness growing louder, my hips bucking as I hit deeper, making believe it was Mason.

A groan and hiss came from him, and I peered up. His expression was tight as his cock thickened, pre-cum spilling out, which only egged me on.

"Em, I want to be fucking you so hard." His eyes locked on the angle of the camera, what he was seeing. "To watch me slide in and out of you, covered in you."

"Oh god." A rough, guttural moan escaped. My hips bucked, needing a release badly. "Mason…" His name spit through my teeth.

"Push down on your clit." His voice was as coarse as mine, his hand moving faster, watching me do what he said. "Now pinch it. Don't move the camera… I want to watch you come."

I did, feeling my spine jolt, my orgasm hitting me. I chomped down on my lip as I tried to keep my moan from escaping, my vision going blurry.

A strangled sound came from Mason, and I gaped in reverence as cum gushed in waves from him, covering his stomach, a throaty sound of pleasure jerking through him.

When I caught my breath, I lifted the phone to see him. A mischievous little smile took over one side of his face, his eyes glittering, his cheeks and chest flushed.

"Fuck, that was hot." He reached over to his desk chair, grabbed a towel, and wiped himself off.

Propping up on my elbows, my pulse still beat like a hummingbird. "Yeah." I hadn't expected it to be that hot or that good. "Think it will curb you until I get home?" I teased.

"With you? It won't take the edge off for an hour. Kind of used to having you all night now."

How in the hell could I just orgasm and be turned on so quickly? It was all Mason. He seemed to bring it out in me. "I know. Same."

The naughtiest grin pulled his lips. "You have a good Christmas." He winked. "See you when you get home." He hung up before I could respond. A huge smile took over my face, still shocked I just had Facetime sex with him.

"Aunt Emery?" A knock tapped on the door, making me scramble for my sweater and underwear. "You okay?"

"Yeah?" My throat was raw and wobbly, the guilt I ignored earlier leaping back up.

"Oh, thought I heard something. Like you were hurt or something." Shame. Shame. Shame. "We are going to start Elf."

"I'll be right there." I fumbled for my suitcase, grabbing my pajamas.

A stab tore at my gut, shame over my actions and my weakness for letting it happen, no matter how good and right it felt. I was a horrible person and an even worse aunt.

Mason and I had to end. It was inevitable anyway. In two weeks, Addison would return for school.

The thought of her finding out. Hurting her…

Why was the worst thing for you, the only thing you craved?

On the morning of the twenty-sixth, I rolled my suitcase toward the front door, anxious to get an early start, trying to deny why I was in such a rush to get home.

"Wow, you're wanting to head out early." Harper came from the kitchen holding a cup of coffee. "Have a hot date tonight?" She winked, teasing me. "You know, one of these days, I'll be right."

You're not too far off now. Except we wouldn't be clothed or leaving the house.

"We'll let me see if I can get Addison up and moving." She headed for the hallway. "Addison! Better get your butt up."

"You can let her sleep. I'll call her later."

"Call her?" Harper tilted her head right as Addy came out of her bedroom, her hair rumpled from sleep.

"What?"

"Time to go."

"Oh crap, already?" She scrambled back to her room. "I'll be quick, Aunt Emery."

"Wait." My stomach sank with trepidation. "What's going on?"

Harper's lids tapered in confusion. "What do you mean? Didn't you get my phone message? I called right before you came."

Oh. God.

"No." I wasn't great at checking my voicemail, but in the Mason bubble, I forgot everything once he had me bent over the sofa or up against the fridge.

"Addison wanted to be back for Sophie's birthday on the thirtieth, and then I guess there is a cheer group thing she didn't want to miss the next week. So, she wanted to come back with you now."

"Oh." I fixed a smile on my face. "Of course." It wasn't that I was upset Addison would be back, but I wasn't quite ready. The expiration date on Mason and me just jumped ahead two weeks.

"I'm coming!" Addison called, running from her bedroom to the bathroom.

"I'll help you get your stuff to the car." Harper picked up the gifts they had given me, following me out to the car. "Thank you again for what you are doing for Addison. She idolizes you, Emery. She is so happy at her school with her friends." Harper welled up. "As much as I want her back with me, I feel so lucky to have you as my sister." She hugged me. "And for Addison to have such an amazing aunt."

"Yeah." I swallowed, feeling anything but amazing.

"And whether you're dating or not, it's so good to see you happy, moving on with your life. I know Ben will always be with you, but he'd want you to live your life. To love again."

My heart twisted, hating how that single word made me think of Mason. This wasn't love. Just lust and mind-blowing sex.

"Okay, I think I got everything." Addison came barreling out with her five bags.

"Oh." Harper leaned in conspiratorially. "If you have to slap the boy she likes around, go for it." She turned to help her daughter as a dark, crazed laugh choked my throat.

Yeah, I've done that already, and he spanked me back.

Chapter 26
Emery

Addison let out a cheer as we pulled into the driveway. "As much as I love my mom, I am so happy to be back." She peeled off her seatbelt. "It's so much better here."

Over the holiday, she realized she really didn't have friends back home anymore. The crowd she was hanging with there was no longer her thing, and she spent most of her time on the phone with all her friends here.

She scrambled out, going for the back of my SUV, getting some of her stuff out. I opened the back door into the house, letting her take her first load in, while I went around to get my suitcase.

A warm, firm body pressed into the back of mine, hands gripping my waist. "Fuck I've missed you." Mason's mouth skimmed down the curve of my neck. "I need you naked, now."

Panic jerked my body, a gasp trapping in my lungs as footsteps came pounding back into the garage.

Mason was barely able to step one foot back when Addison came to a sudden stop, her eyes widening into saucers.

"Mason?" Her forehead lined with confusion.

Color drained from my face, my pulse thundering in my ears. What did she see? How could I explain this?

"How did you know I was coming home today?" Addison wagged her head.

"Oh." He took another step back from me, his Adam's apple dipping. "I think… umm… Mateo must have mentioned it."

"Really?" Excitement widened her eyes. "I can't believe you came over." She skipped up to Mason, hugging him. He stood there, his arms at his sides, frozen. "I've missed all of you so much."

147

"Yeah." He subtly retreated. "Welcome home." He backpedaled, his eyes sliding to me, then back to her. "I better get back home. My grandma still needs me close by."

"I'll call Mateo, Sophie, and Elena. Let's all hang out soon," she added before he took off.

He didn't answer either way, but as he turned around to leave, his gaze met mine again. His questions and confusion swirled in his eyes before he walked away.

We came so close to getting caught. Disappointment wrung out in my gut as he disappeared, my chest filling with heaviness.

"Oh. My. God." Addy's eyes were enormous, her expression completely giddy. "He knew I was coming home and came to see me. Like right away. We're not even unloaded yet." She did a little prance. "I mean, who does that unless you like someone, right? I mean *really* like them. I'm so asking him to the dance."

I stared blankly at the stuff in the car.

She grabbed her last few bags. "Also, I wanted to ask—because you are the best aunt in the whole world." She talked fast. "I was thinking this would help you too because you can have your little Dr. Cutie over… but I wanted to invite a few friends here on New Year's? For dinner and stuff, and then we head out from there?"

"Why?" I turned to her. "I mean, why would you guys want to hang out here?"

"Because…" she exhaled… "Mason hates parties. He's turned down every party since the night he passed out here, and it was even strange he went to that one. He will always bail on them, but he seems to have no problem coming here. I thought, you know, once I got him with us, having fun, I could ask him to the dance." She twisted her hands nervously.

"Addy…" I tapped my front teeth together, trying to come up with the best phrasing. "I want you to be very careful. I think you're seeing something that's not there."

"Come on!" She waved back to where he left. "He came down to see me the moment we got back. He must have seen us pass and practically ran down here."

Yeah. For me.

"Addy, please. I think you might be reading too much into Mason's actions."

"But it's what mom told me to watch. Their *actions*. Words can mean crap, so watch what they do. Sorry, Aunt Emery, you are wrong about him. He likes me. I know it." She took her stuff and went into the house.

Taking a breath, I leaned against my bumper, my cell buzzing in my pocket.

Mason: Why didn't you tell me Addison was coming back?

Me: I didn't know until this morning!

Mason: You could have texted me.

Me: I should have, but I didn't know you were going to be here right away.

Mason: Haven't you been aching for me too? And if she wasn't there, you'd be screaming out my name as I fucked you in the back of your car.

A groan hummed in my throat.

Me: Addison still has a thing for you.

Mason: I never liked her that way. And I've never led her on.

Me: She thinks you came over for her.

Mason: Tell her it's because I wanted to nail her aunt.

Me: This needs to stop. A bit earlier than we thought, but we both knew it was coming.

Typing bubbles came up and disappeared, came up, and went away again.

Me: I'm sorry. But nothing else can happen between us. It's over.

My heart sank when he didn't respond. A sick part of me wanted him to fight, to tell me it was far from over. No such text came.

A silent ending to an illicit affair.

"Aunt Emery?" Addison bellowed from the kitchen. "We need groceries. There's no food here."

I grabbed my items and went inside, closing the garage door, feeling it was symbolic of Mason and me.

The idea of never being with Mason again made me nauseous, but I had to stay strong. Addison came first.

No matter how much I craved him, I had to do what was right.

"You look like shit, girl." Marcie lounged across two chairs eating chips and a sandwich when I strolled into the break room.

"Thanks." I redid my ponytail, plunking down across from her. This first day back at work was torture, every minute feeling like an hour. "Didn't sleep well." That was an understatement. My brain wouldn't relent, going over the ending with Mason while my body was going through withdrawals. I kept fantasizing about him crawling through my window, covering my mouth to keep me quiet, as he sunk into me, taking me higher and higher until I shattered.

"Not sleeping?" She wiggled her eyebrows. "Any particular reason why?"

"Not what you think." I slumped back in the chair. "That ended."

"Why?" She blinked blankly at me. "It was incredible sex, right?"

I huffed out a pained laugh, my head nodding. "Beyond incredible. To infinity and beyond."

"Wow, it must be good if you're quoting cartoon movies." She snorted. "With a hot piece of ass, if it's as good as you say, girl, you do not give it up." She waved her hand in a 'no way' gesture. "That shit is like a unicorn in today's world. You ride the horn until the end of the line."

"Think it was the end of the line." My hand absently rubbed at my chest. "It got too complicated."

Her heavy silence pulled my attention to her.

"Oh girl…" She shook her head, her gaze going to where I brushed at my heart. "You fell in love with him."

"No," I exclaimed, sitting up. "Not even close. It was only sex. Plus, he is way too young."

"What does age have to do with fallin' for him or not?" she replied. "My big vanilla beefcake is four years younger than me. We are perfectly on par together. Especially in bed."

Four years was different from ten, and Mason was still in school. It sounded appalling.

Daniel strolled into the room, ending our conversation. He did a double take, a warm smile going over his face. "Hey, Emery. Haven't seen you yet today."

"It's been crazy." The first day back after a holiday was always insane.

Marcie hopped up, brushing off her hands. "My break is over."

I glowered at her. *Don't you dare leave me.*

She shrugged, an impish smile on her lips, popping another chip in her mouth. "Can't be late when the boss walks in," she teased, taking her stuff to the trash and strolling out.

I hate you! I internally shot her, and I swear I heard her laugh. Eventually I would have to face Daniel. I just didn't want today to be the day.

"I was hoping to see you." He sat in Marcie's seat. "How are you?"

"Good." I nodded.

"Have a good holiday break?"

"Yep, went to my sister's place for a few days."

"Went to my mom's. Got the yearly why are you still single, Daniel? When are you going to meet the right girl, Daniel? Time to give me grandchildren, Daniel." He laughed, rubbing at his temple. "I couldn't wait to get back."

I smiled, though I felt every question he repeated was purposeful.

Nothing was keeping me from going out with him. Not anymore. He was such a nice guy. A total catch. Except I still wanted to run when he smiled at me because his smile was full of hope. Full of more than being my friend.

And all I wanted was to go home, to someone else.

I couldn't explain it. The moment I met Mason, I felt something between us. A pull neither one of us seemed to be able to fight. Yet, he walked away from me with no problem.

"So, this Saturday is New Year's Eve. And in no way is this any kind of pressure, but I wanted to take you out—"

"I can't," I spouted, my mind reeling, trying to find a good reason. "My niece is having a little get-together at the house with her friends." Addy didn't know this yet. I hadn't said yes. "Just appetizers and stuff. Kind of a pre-party thing."

"Oh." His head bobbed. "Yeah. Sounds nice. I can do that."

Oh hell. That wasn't meant to be an invite.

"Daniel, you are a very nice guy." I folded my hands together. "I don't think I'm ready yet. I think it's better if we stay friends. Plus, dating my boss? It might get really messy and uncomfortable." Unlike being with my niece's crush.

"Only if we broke up," he tried to joke, but it fell flat instantly, his lips pressing together. "I get it. I know you're still grieving, but I *really* like you. I enjoy being around you. If I have to wait, I'll wait. If you want a friend right now, I can be one." He got back up, heading for the door, probably wanting to run from the awkwardness I had laid out. "The party sounds fun. I'll bring my mom's seven-layer bean dip recipe. It's really good."

"Great." I smiled pleasantly as he left.

What the hell happened? Now I needed to invite everyone, get food and drinks, and threaten Marcie within an inch of her life because she left me here. She had to come now so it wouldn't be only Daniel showing up, getting the wrong idea.

Guess Addison was getting her party after all. The one which was fabricated solely to ask Mason to a dance.

Chapter 27
Emery

"Or is this one better?" Addison was in my doorway, twirling her latest outfit choice, a short champagne sequin shift dress with the same-colored heels. Her blonde hair was curled and pinned up on one side.

"Wow." I wanted to make her six again in pigtails with her stuffed bunny. It hit me I was nineteen when she was six… pretty much Mason's age. That thought felt like a bullet. "That's the one."

"You sure? Not the black?"

"Nope. The champagne colored one." I shook my head in awe. "You look beautiful."

"Thank you." She grinned. "And look at you!" She motioned to my sleek emerald green silk jumpsuit. "All the football guys already think you're hot and crush on you. I'm gonna have to put bibs on them tonight to catch all the drool."

Addy's friends were coming over to hang out, have some pizza, and then head out to a party, where I knew there would be drinking. I understood being young and wanting to celebrate with friends at her age. She told me she'd be safe, and maybe a year ago, I wouldn't have trusted her, but I did now. It was a bonus that Mateo seemed to be extra protective of her too. He had such a crush on Addy, but sadly, she didn't see past Mason yet, no matter how cute Mateo was.

Putting in my gold hoops, I tried to not think about *him*. It had been a horrible week. Long, taxing, and I just couldn't shake this sadness and restlessness. I missed him. I shouldn't miss him, but it was a constant ache in my chest. I walked the shelter dogs by his house several times, hoping to get a glimpse of him.

My time at the shelter saved me. They were the few moments I felt I could breathe, especially when a dog was brought in because he wouldn't do simple commands. It was Anita who found out the dog understood and responded to sign language.

"One of his owners must have been deaf." Anita curled her fingers, signing him to sit. The sweet pitbull mix sat down instantly, looking so happy when Anita gave him a thumbs up. "He doesn't understand verbal cues."

"We should put it in his profile. See if we can match him with someone who at least knows ASL." I patted Blue's head. "Someone out there is looking for you, Blue. I know it, and I will find them for you." I promised the dog. After seeing the shepherd with the little girl, I felt this need to find the perfect dog for people with special needs. Giving both the best life.

"So?" Addison's salacious tone brought me back to the present. "Dr. Ramirez is coming tonight, right?" She wiggled her shoulders. "Is that why you look so hot?"

"It's not that way." I tugged at my ironed, straight hair, giving myself a last look before turning to my niece. "We're only friends."

"*Sure*. Friends." She kept teasing, determined for me to like him.

I rolled my eyes as I strolled out, heading for the kitchen. I'd never acknowledge I took a little extra care in case Mason came by, though he probably wouldn't. Addison couldn't get a definite answer out of him, which I didn't want to tell her probably meant no.

He wouldn't be coming because of me.

"Hey, hey!" Marcie opened my front door, peeking in.

"Come in!" I grinned seeing her. She wore velvet pants and a glittery top. Tim, her 'vanilla cup,' walked in after her, followed by his friend Sean, who still seemed determined to take me out again, though I thought the first group date was enough.

"Happy New Year!" she sang out, her hands full of champagne, Tim and Sean carrying more beer and alcohol.

"I'll definitely need this." I grabbed the bottles from her hands, motioning them in. My house wasn't huge, but we put heaters in the backyard, the hot tub was bubbling, and music played throughout to give us all more space inside and out. Addison got Mateo and some of the other players to help set up earlier today.

More people from my work came, followed by a flood of Addison's guests, escalating the sound level to high decibels. I didn't realize how loud teenagers were and was relieved when Addison's group separated from us, hanging outside.

"Someone's at the door." Marcie nudged my arm, directing my head over. For a moment, hope filled my lungs but quickly deflated.

Daniel.

He looked nice in slacks, a white button-down shirt, and a jacket, his hair short and styled. A smile curved his mouth as he spotted me coming over to him.

"Kelly let me in. I hope it was okay." He nodded at one of the dental assistants I worked with standing near the Christmas tree.

"Of course. Come in." I waved him in farther. "Let me take that." I grabbed the plate from his hands, bringing it over to the food table.

"It's the seven-layer dip. Hope it tastes good. Didn't quite look as good as my mother's." His hand touched my lower back, his gaze intently on me.

"I'm sure it's delicious." I shifted to face him, forcing his arm to drop away from me.

Daniel's gaze wandered down me. "Wow." He blinked a few times. "You look absolutely breathtaking."

"Thank you," I responded politely. "You look nice too."

His eyes warmed, his demeanor coming across as if friendship was the last thing on his mind.

"Your hair is caught in your earring. May I?" He reached up without waiting for my reply. He was inches from me, his finger grazing my cheek as he tugged a strand. "There." He didn't move, his regard dropping to my mouth.

Suddenly, my skin prickled with awareness, my body thrumming as if it had come back to life. But it wasn't from the man in front of me.

My head turned slowly to the door, the pulse in my neck pounding in my ears, spotting the source of my reaction. Oxygen balled up in my throat, the blood in my veins flooding me with heat.

He had come.

Mason stood in the doorway, dressed in his normal dark jeans, t-shirt, and jacket, looking ten times sexier than any man I had ever seen.

Time stopped when our gazes met. His brown eyes bore into me, so dark they looked black, as if he was some demon coming here to punish me for my sins. Stripping me bare, ready to corrupt me. Imprisoning me for my wrongs.

His attention trailed from me to Daniel. Not one emotion escaped Mason, but I could feel his anger, the wrath bubbling underneath his stoic expression. The truth behind the guise he wore as armor. It was as familiar as my own. While mine was a fake smile concealing my pain, his was indifference.

From the corner of my eye, I saw Marcie's head whip from me to Mason, her mouth parting with recognition. Even from a distance and in a dark restaurant, Mason was not someone you could ever forget. His height alone had him standing above everyone. She knew who he was, what we had done in the closet and many times since, which made the next moment feel like a slow-moving car accident.

"Oh my god, Mason!" Addison's cry cut across the room, her feet running to him. "You made it!" She bounded up to him, wrapping her arms around him with a small squeal. "Come on, we're in back." She linked her hand to his. "I told Mateo you'd show up." She tugged him toward the backyard. Her face showed her feelings for him like a neon sign.

I saw the moment understanding clicked on Marcie's face, widening her eyes more, her attention snapping to me in shock and disbelief.

I kept my eyes down, not able to look at anyone, struggling to keep my own feelings hidden. It didn't matter if I didn't acknowledge him. His presence was felt in every molecule of my body anyway. Mason was a force I couldn't fight. One I couldn't deny.

His body moved around me, energy crackling at my skin and knocking on my barriers. So subtly and quick, he skimmed his knuckles over mine as he passed, triggering thousands of electric charges through my entire body. A whimper trapped in my throat, my teeth diving into my bottom lip, my lids shutting briefly, trying to keep my body in place, to not react to him as my soul screamed to do. Our chemistry was palpable. The air around us held so much power, I felt like where he was, my entire being wanted to follow. My heart and soul cried out for him, craving to reach out and touch him. My body shook with need while I bore the shame of what I had done, feeling even more real under the weight of Marcie's eyes.

"Mason!" His name cheered out from the backyard, pulling my focus for a moment, watching the back of him. Aching. Longing.

"Sorry, Daniel. Can you excuse us?" An arm hooked around mine, snapping my head back to Marcie coming in beside me. "I need her for a moment in the kitchen."

"Oh yes, of course. Anything I can help with?" Daniel responded.

"No!" she exclaimed, then laughed. "No, we got it." She practically dragged me into the room, moving us the farthest away from the door, glancing over her shoulder to make sure it was clear.

"Please tell me the guy who just joined your niece is not the guy I saw coming out of the coat closet with you?"

Nothing came out of my mouth.

"Are you kidding me, Emery?" she hissed. "There's young, and there's you can be arrested young."

"He's legal." Wow, that didn't sound any better. "He's twenty."

"Twenty?" She was taken aback. "I'm confused."

"He was held back or missed a year."

"But he is in high school now?"

"Only because his grandparents wanted him to experience what he missed out on."

"You know you're not making this better."

"I know. God, I know. I'm an awful person." My face went into my hands. "I don't know how to explain it. It just happened. He's barely twenty. It was totally a mistake—"

"Excuse me." Mason's voice froze my lungs and body.

Marcie's eyes bulged, whipping back to him stepping into the room.

"You're out of cups." His deep voice moved through my bones like an earthquake, his eyes zeroing on me with accusation, his jaw rolling.

He heard me.

I couldn't move, feeling as if I were drowning under him. Both Marcie and I seemed inconsequential compared to his physical body and presence. Mason took over a room. He didn't even try, but he commanded every molecule around him just the same. I wanted to run to him, to feel his arms around me, to kiss him.

It took me a few moments to realize I was openly staring at him. "Oh." I swallowed, tearing my eyes from him. "Of course." I pointed to the cupboard. "They're in there."

"I know." A low scoff derisively came from him. "I know where everything is." He reached up, grabbing some before his intense gaze met mine. We stayed locked for a few moments. A nerve in his cheek twitched. He strode out of the room, leaving the air gutted and empty.

"Okay. Wow." Marcie's mouth was open. "Forget what I was saying. I get it." She shook her head, fanning herself. "And the chemistry between you two? Holy fuck, my panties dissolved. Damn, no guy should look that way at twenty." She shook herself, her expression becoming serious. "You need to be careful. There's no one in the world blind enough not to see it. To feel it. And it was clear Addison has a huge crush on him. Though he seems to only have eyes for you."

I blinked, tears blurring my vision. "I know. And I know I need to stay away from him."

"But you can't." A sadness tipped her head.

"I have to."

"You trying to convince me or yourself?"

"What do I do?"

Marcie's shoulders fell, sympathy etching her features. "I wish I could tell you. You know I'm all for you getting freaky with a young hottie, but this…" She flinched. "This is more than that."

"The thought of hurting Addison…" A tear escaped, and I wiped it away quickly.

"There's that too, but I wasn't talking about her."

Confusion wrinkled the space between my eyes.

"Oh, Emery." She drew out my name, her tongue clicking. "You've got it bad. Really bad. And from what I've seen, he feels the same."

"No." I shook my head vehemently. "It's not that way."

She let out a laugh. "Sure, you keep lying to yourself. This isn't only sex for you. It never was." She patted my arm and sauntered out.

Tears burned at the back of my throat from the burden of her claim.

Ben's death had almost destroyed me, yet I pulled my way out of the darkness. Survived. Persisted. Began to live again.

The truth was Mason should have never happened, but at most, he should have been nothing more than a steppingstone. Helping me heal and move on. A moment in my life.

He shouldn't have this much power. This much pull. To knock me so far out of my safety bubble. From the moment I saw him, we were set on this collision course.

"You okay?" Daniel popped into the doorway.

"Y-yes." I cleared my throat, forcing a smile. When I headed past him, he followed me back into the living room, where the TV reflected festivities all over the world, the music weaving along with the chatter. More people than I thought showed up, filling my house with cheer and exuberance, their laughter and carefree smiles emphasizing the falseness I had on my face. Keeping myself busy, I was able to get Daniel into conversation with Kelly and Mike from work.

"I don't think you've stopped all night." A form moved in next to me at the food table, where I was adding more plates. I peered over at the blue eyes looking back into mine, a cocky smirk on his face.

Sean.

On the one "date" I was hoodwinked into with him, he came across nice enough but boring in his cockiness. It was a night full of sexual puns and shallow talk. I don't think he asked anything past what show I last binged, yet he made it very clear he wanted to come home with me.

"Life of a hostess." It was a lie. I could have easily left everything, but keeping busy stopped me from constantly searching for someone I shouldn't. To ignore the incessant awareness I had of Mason no matter where he was.

"I think the hostess can have a little fun too." Sean stepped closer to me, his eyes moving over me blatantly. "I don't think I told you how hot you look."

"Thanks."

"We never got to go out on our date." He inched in further.

I was hoping he had forgotten about that. About me.

"Everything okay here?" Daniel was suddenly beside me, his hand going to my back again, as though he had the right to claim me. As if I were his.

Sean's eyes narrowed on Daniel. "It was until a moment ago."

"Didn't look that way," Daniel replied coolly.

"Good thing you're not an eye doctor." Their testosterone knocked into each other, a display of chauvinism, acting as though I had no say in what I wanted.

What I wanted, I couldn't have.

"Looks as if I'm not especially needed for this pissing contest." I pushed away from both men, heading down the hallway toward the restroom, needing to get away. Emotion built up behind my eyes, feeling like I was about to break.

From behind, fingers wrapped around my bicep. A tiny yelp chirped from me as I was hauled inside my bedroom. The moment the door shut, my frame was shoved up against it, a body pressing into mine, igniting fire through me instantly.

Dark eyes looked down on me. Hungry. Angry. Possessive.

"Mason." I breathed, shivers running through me, tightening my core. "What are you doing? We can't—"

Growling, his mouth crashed down on mine, taking control, dominating and ruling. His tongue wrapped around mine, sucking, producing a moan from my soul, breaking all my resolve. My mouth claimed his back in a frenzy, my fingers sliding up his neck and digging into his hair.

He sucked in, pinning me harder against the door, pressing his cock into me, saturating me with need. His physique enveloped me, and all I wanted was to be consumed entirely by him, for him to devour me completely.

"Oh god…" I rubbed against him, needing to feel him. My hands moved under his shirt, feeling the curves of his abs, the scar running up his chest. "I need you."

A strangled noise produced from his lips as he pulled away. "Fuck." He ran his hand through his hair, moving back, fury riding his shoulders.

"What?" I couldn't catch my breath.

"Wouldn't fucking the barely twenty-year-old be a mistake?"

Flinching, I curled up my fingers. I knew he had heard me. "I-I didn't mean that…"

"Then which one of us are you lying to, Emery?" He scoffed. "You seemed quite clear last week this was over. You tell your friend it was a mistake… now you want to ride my dick?" Embarrassment burned my cheeks. "Guess I should have taken you more seriously when you said this was only sex."

He reached around me, grabbing for the door.

"Wait." I slid over, blocking his exit.

"No. Move," he growled. "I think I know my place."

"You think this is easy for me?" I hissed. "I'm sleeping with someone not only younger than me, but the guy my niece is obsessed with. I have to look at myself every day in the mirror, no matter what, knowing what I did. I can't do that to her."

"What about me?" he spat. "Do I get a say? Or do I just have to stand there watching two guys all over you, knowing how it feels to kiss you, to be inside you?" He moved in closer. "I have never been interested in Addison. I'm here tonight because of *you*. Because I'm an idiot and can't seem to stay away."

"Really?" I spat. The hurt I tried to bury came slithering out of its grave. "Didn't seem so hard for you to walk away." I glared up at him. "One text, and you didn't even respond. I didn't see you fighting for this."

"Oh." His chin lifted. "Is that what I was supposed to do? Crawl on my hands and knees and beg for you to keep fucking me?" His frame seemed to expand above mine, making me feel tiny. "And here I thought girls grew out of playing games."

"I'm not playing games," I hissed. "But we both know this can't go anywhere."

"Why?"

"Why?" I sputtered. "Because…" I motioned to him. "You're too young—"

"What a bullshit excuse. How many men date women ten years younger, and no one gives a shit?"

"It's not that. It's how those ten years separate us. I've been married, widowed… you are still in high school."

"Actually, I dropped out. I'm getting my GED."

"What?" My mouth opened. "Did you do that because of me?"

"Seriously?" He tilted his head, his lids narrowing. "Stop making me out like some lovesick puppy following you around. I make my own fucking decisions. I never wanted to be there, but I was for my grandparents. They thought it was what I wanted. We both realized that in making them happy, none of us were happy." He stepped back up to me. "I'm not your plaything, Emery. To come running when you suddenly want me or scamper off when you're done with me again. You are so worried about what *others* think, you'll turn away from something you want." He placed his hands on the door over my head, locking me in. "This week has been hell. And staying away from you was the hardest thing I had to do. It took everything I had not to sneak through your window at night."

My breath hitched as he hit on the very fantasy I had envisioned.

"I saw your expression when Dr. Douche touched you or when fuckboy was hitting on you." He clutched my chin. "I know the difference between your fake smiles and real ones. I've seen your face when you're coming around my cock. I know when you're pretending, hiding your pain so no one else will notice. I *see* you, Emery. I fucking *feel you*. Even when I'm not near you."

My chest fluttered as though he cracked me open, seeing everything inside.

"I'll ask you this once." He leaned in closer, his mouth hovering over mine. "Tell me you don't want this. That this week wasn't torment for you too. Tell me you want me to walk away." His throat bobbed. "And I will."

I knew what I was supposed to say, what was right, but I couldn't get my mouth to open. The terror I felt he would leave for good was like drowning, and I couldn't catch my breath. This week had been excruciating. And I felt even worse for it. Not only my guilt over Addison, but the realization I had never really felt this way with Ben. He'd leave on business for weeks at a time. I was sad and missed him, but it was never physical pain. Never an ache so deep I couldn't seem to settle, or the need to go to him didn't overpower my every move.

"Tell me to go, and I will." He leaned down, his nose grazing my neck, his warm breath sliding between my breasts. His mouth drifted across my jawline, suspending over my lips, waiting for my answer. "Emery?"

Hearing him call me, the command in his whisper, broke me. My mouth struck his with a needy force, biting his lower lip. A deep thunder came from him. Our desire was instant and desperate, clawing and biting. His hands seized me, pulling me closer, knotting through my hair roughly. Just the way Mason kissed created hysteria in me, whirling out all logic. I needed him more than I wanted air.

"Fuck, I missed you." He easily picked me up, his hips pushing hard into me, making me feel every inch of him. Rock hard and pulsing. I groaned, my spine arching, my hips pushing back into him.

"Mason." Begging, pleading, I no longer could muster any shame, my hands flicking the buttons of his jeans, sliding my hand behind his boxer briefs, gripping him. My thumb skimmed over the tip of him, rolling and rubbing.

He hissed, rocking into my palm, his fingers pushing down my top and bra. He dug into my thigh as his mouth covered my breast, sucking hard on my nipple.

I tried to keep my cry back, my vocals burning with hoarseness. "Please. Now."

"Fuck, I'm thankful this is two-piece." He pushed my pants and underwear down just enough, and his fingers slipped into me, his moan going deeper when he felt how wet I was.

"Aunt Emery?" The door against my back tried to open, Addison's voice coming through. "Are you in here?" The knob jiggled.

My bedroom door had no lock on it.

I froze. My breath, my muscles. The heat that had been peppering my skin turned cold. Mason's eyes met mine, his fingers still inside me, panic filling both of us.

Oh. Holy. Fuck.

"Yes. Just a moment." Dropping away from him, I shoved him toward my closet. "Go!" I mouthed to him, my heartbeat thwacking against my ribs. Mason crawled inside as I straightened my hair and clothes, my stomach twisting into a braid as I reached for the door. Would she know? Did she see him walk back here?

Plastering my face in a smile, I pretended the door was jammed before swinging it open.

"Sorry, this door is sticking lately."

Her brows were furrowed together, taking in my slightly disheveled appearance and dark room. It seemed as if Mason marked every inch of my skin, burning his name across me like a scarlet letter A.

161

"You okay?" She slanted her head. The girl was far from stupid, sensing something was off.

"Um. Yes." I tucked strands of hair behind my ear. "I just needed a moment."

"Oh." Her face softened. "I know the holidays are still hard without Uncle Ben. I miss him too."

I was going to hell. If I believed in such a place. Maybe I was already there.

"I wanted to let you know we're heading out for the party." She motioned to where her friends were. "I promise to call if I'm not home by two. And we will be careful." Her forehead crinkled again. "You haven't seen Mason, have you?"

Yep, I was already in hell. I could feel the fire burning into my bones. "Uh. No. Why?"

"He disappeared." She shrugged with disappointment.

"I'm sorry. You know he hates parties."

"I know. I was still hoping he'd stay. For me…" She sighed. "I was about to ask him to the dance."

I had no response. Her hurt solidified what I had to do.

"Addison, let's go," Elena called out for her.

"Have a good night. Happy New Year!" She grinned, hugging me. "And maybe we can get Mason to look at your door," she said innocently. I watched her dart toward her friends, Mateo staying back and waiting for her before they all headed out.

I slammed my door, my forehead falling against it. I took in deep, uneven breaths.

"Hey." Mason came up behind me, his hand touching my arm.

"Don't." I jerked away from him. "Don't touch me."

"Emery…"

"No." I flipped around, staring up at him. I wanted to cry, this huge divide splitting me in two. Mason on one side and Addison on the other. It should be simple. My niece came first, and I knew I would pick her over him, but I couldn't stop the utter devastation crumbling the ground I felt had barely begun to build under me again.

I shouldn't have these feelings for him. I shouldn't be so aware of him, even when he wasn't in the room. I shouldn't crave him and need him like he is the one solid thing in this world.

But I did.

"Mason."

"No." Ire gripped his jaw. "We are not back to this shit, again."

"Did you hear her?" I exclaimed, my voice going louder than it should, hoping the music and chatter in the other room would drown us out. "She's still in love with you, Mason. She wants to ask you to the spring dance."

"Yes, I heard her." He tapped his fists against his head in frustration. "You seem to keep forgetting I have a say in this too," he yelled hoarsely. "First, Addison is not in love with me. She loves the *idea* of me. Of being the one who "gets" the unattainable Mason James. And though you look at me as if I'm some kid, you have no idea what I've been through in my life. How much older I feel than all of them. They feel like kids to me. Not one has a clue what real loss is. And maybe it's why you and I connect so much. We have known darkness so bleak that you don't even want to come out of it. You hope it swallows you whole so you don't have to wake up to another day of bottomless pain."

His words hit me—the raw truth no one wants to hear or talk about, but it's there, a ghost, a whisper in the back of your mind. The hope you'd close your eyes and they wouldn't open again. The shame and guilt for even thinking it breaking you down more. I could see it in his face; he knew that feeling too, experiencing something most twice his age had not.

"I was never going to go to the dance with her, and I think she knows it. Even if I was still going to school or you weren't in the equation." He strode up to me. "I don't want to be with her. I never did, nor am I going to. Stop treating me like *her* crush is somehow *my* fault. I have no control over her. But I know how I feel. *What. I. Want.*" Raspy, his voice pulsed my core, gripping my chest. "I think you need to figure out what you do." He moved around me, opening the door and storming out. His boots hit the wood floor in sync with my heartbeat, and the hollow bang of the front door slamming echoed in my soul. The emptiness I felt as he drifted farther and farther away, as if the threads between us were stretching in agony. Unnatural. Wrong.

The sound of the party, music, and laughter on the other side of my bedroom wall felt conflicting to me, draining the energy I didn't have. I inhaled, rolled my shoulders back, and acted like I was happy they were all here as I stepped back into the living room.

Marcie's gaze was the first I found. Her head was already wagging, looking at the door and back to me with a scoff.

"Don't say anything," I muttered as I walked up, stealing the glass of champagne out of her hand and gulping it all down.

"Not sure I have to." Her gaze went over my wrinkled outfit with understanding. "Think someone's actions speak louder than her words."

"It won't happen again," I replied, more to myself than her.

"Girl, stop." She poured more champagne into the glass in my hand. "I know what Tim is. We're having fun. And once it's over, we'll part with no hurt feelings. But you…?" She tsked. "You are already in too deep. Your bit of fun? You've already fallen for him."

Chapter 28
Emery

Avoid.

That was what I did all week. I avoided Daniel, I avoided Sean's texts, I avoided my thoughts, and I even avoided Addison as much as I could.

She found out Mason had dropped out of school and was so crushed she couldn't stop talking about him. My limit on hearing his name reached its peak within an hour, and I felt even worse because there was a part of me who unfairly resented her for making me choose between them.

I threw all my attention into my shifts at the shelter, focusing on finding a perfect match for Blue, which was my one joy in my bleak week. A deaf older man who had lost his wife a year before came in. His son saw my ad for Blue and brought his dad to see the dog. It was instant love. When the man signed to Blue with his fingers, I swear the dog lit up, prancing with excitement, doing everything the man indicated him to do. Sharing a language no one could hear but was felt between them both. It was as if he knew he found his new forever home. His person.

Again, Anita and I sobbed as they filled out the paperwork, and we prepared Blue to head home with them. Seeing the older man tear up with happiness, petting his new best friend, who stared lovingly up at him, had tears running down our faces. Even his son was choked up, telling us it had been a lonely time for his father after his mother passed.

"You are really good at this." Anita turned to me the moment they left, still wiping at her eyes. "I think you found your calling."

"I want to find the perfect home for all the animals here, but it does feel extra special to put a pair like them together." It filled something in me I never knew was empty, a peace I had been looking for. Animals were the one thing keeping me happy this week.

Taking my dog pack on their daily walk to the park, I ignored the idea I was purposely going the long way to walk by Mason's house. I mean, how old was I? Women at thirty didn't do this kind of shit, but I couldn't seem to stop myself. The pull to him was unbearable.

This time I did it, I saw his garage was open. I suddenly regretted my plainly obvious walk by. Stopping the dogs, about to turn around, the rumble of an old car engine came up behind me, a GTO pulling into Mason's driveway, dropping my stomach. He stopped the car inside the garage, the squeaking of the car door opening and slamming shut found me outside.

There was no way he didn't see me, notice the four dogs around me. To my surprise, he didn't come out, like he was waiting for me to make a move instead.

I was going to be an adult about this. He was still my neighbor, right? I could at least pass and say hi if he saw me.

Holding my chin up, I continued the dogs forward, my eyes sliding inside the garage as we started to pass. The hood was up, his back to me as he stood at the workbench, busying himself. He was purposely not looking. I could feel his awareness of me as I could him. It wasn't something we could help. It just was. Tangible and invasive. It took over every cell of my body until it felt like I was burning alive.

I should have kept walking. It was the right thing to do in our case. He was giving me an out. A chance to go on with my day. With my life. And maybe it's what fastened my feet to the ground, panic gurgling up my chest.

My impulse took over any logic.

I stepped off the sideway, entering the garage. The noise from dozens of dog nails hitting the cement ground stiffened Mason's shoulders. I could see him inhale and exhale, feeling me there.

"I was passing by. I don't want to bother you. Just wanted to say hi."

"Why?" He continued to work.

"Because we're still neighbors. We're still going to run into each other now and again."

"Is that what we are?" He turned around, leaning against the bench, his expression completely unreadable. "Neighbors?"

"Yes," I replied stiffly. "It's all we can be."

His gaze dug into me. It seemed as if he could uncover every falsehood I hid behind. He finally broke his gaze from me, going down to the dogs. Ozzy, a Bernese-Labrador mix, lurched for Mason, his excitement yanking me forward as he wiggled and danced up to Mason.

"Hey there." Mason held his hand out for Ozzy to sniff before he started scrubbing his head. Ozzy licked him, continuing to smell him, the Labrador nose working overtime. He sat, lifting his paw to Mason's leg.

"Huh." I blinked. "He's never done that before."

Ozzy was one of my favorites. Everyone wanted to adopt him because he was so beautiful, but twice he had been returned because he was "higher maintenance" than they expected. Some people liked the idea of pets, not realizing they were a living, breathing life who took care, patience, and time, similar to a child. So now I was on a mission to find the perfect home for him, not only someone who wanted him, but who Ozzy would be happiest with.

"Aren't you a sweet boy?" Mason rubbed his head, petting all the other dogs begging for his attention. Stella, our Rottweiler, shamelessly flirted with Mason, rubbing all over his legs and licking him.

Yeah, Stella, I totally get it.

"Come on, guys." I tugged on their leashes, feeling I was crossing the line of being polite and trying to find reasons to stay. "The park is waiting." None of the dogs, especially Stella and Ozzy, seemed keen to leave.

"Think they want to stay." He gave them all more love and pets.

"Yeah, you scratch their butts and ears. Of course they're not going to want to leave."

He stood fully, strolling up to me, forcing my head to tip back a little.

"Is that all it takes?" he said with no innuendo, but I could feel the implication skating over my skin and dipping between my legs. His timbre scraped the floor. "Why are you here, Emery?"

"I-I told you."

"Just being neighborly?" he derided. The heat of his body penetrated my layers, my fingers itching to reach out and touch him. "Right." His gaze dropped to my mouth. I wanted him to kiss me so badly it hurt, my willpower evaporating as it always seemed to around him. Without even moving, our lips were only inches apart.

"Mason?" Grace's weak voice came out into the garage from the house, the hood of his car blocking us. We both jerked back, moving away from each other. "You have a call—" She looked up, spotting me over the top of the GTO. "Oh, Emery, I didn't know you were here. So good to see you, dear."

"Out walking the dogs," I offered as an excuse. "And it is so nice seeing you too. You look good. How are you doing?"

"I'm doing better."

I noticed she now had a walker next to her.

"You shouldn't be up, Grandma," Mason gritted through his teeth.

"Mason, I am eighty-nine years old. If I don't move every once in a while, I'm afraid the vultures will start thinking I'm dinner."

I burst out laughing as Mason shook his head.

"Grandma…" He rubbed his temple. "Tell whoever it is, I'll call them back.

"It's the parents—" She stopped herself, her gaze drifting from me to him. "It's important. They want to set a date."

Mason's demeanor shifted, everything in him closing down. "Yeah, okay. I'll be right there."

Grace nodded, her attention going to me. "It was lovely seeing you. Please come by more often."

"Thank you. I'll be sure to come visit you when you're feeling better."

She smiled, her gaze darting between us again before shutting the door, seeming far more perceptive than she should be.

"Well, I better go." I turned away, dragging the dogs away, pretending I didn't feel his gaze clawing up my back, nipping at the base of my spine.

"Emery?" His call swung my head back around to him. The wickedness in his gaze pumped my heart faster. "You came to me."

"So?" My pulse tapped harder, feeling I had fallen into a trap of my own making.

His cocky grin curved the side of his mouth. "All bets are off now."

"Are you all right?" Marcie watched me from across the breakroom table, both of us finishing the soup and bread we got at the place around the corner. It was a cold, rainy, crappy day, and I felt less and less like being here as every hour went by.

Daniel was pretty much ignoring me. He had been standoffish since New Year's. From the daggers he was throwing at Sean that night, I think he assumed my disheveled appearance later was because of him. I'm pretty sure Sean thought it was Daniel.

The truth was worse… but also so much better.

After walking away from Mason a day ago, I was tense, like at any moment he was going to jump out, and then I became unbearably disappointed when he didn't. I almost texted him when Addy spent the night at Sophie's last night. Instead, I drank half a bottle of wine, got off on my vibrator, pretending it was him, and still felt unsatisfied, making me crankier.

The boy was driving me mad. What did he even mean by 'all bets were off'? Then to do nothing?

"Emery? Hello?" Marcie clicked her long nails in front of my face. "Damn, girl. Don't you know? First rule of using a hot piece of ass for sex is not to *fall* for that hot piece of ass."

"I didn't!"

She raised a brow.

"I swear." I tossed my spoon on the table. "I'm fine."

She barked out a laugh.

"You know, I thought you'd be another boring, run-of-the-mill white girl." She spooned another scoop into her mouth. "You have surprised me, which is a high honor in my book."

"Thanks?" I brushed back a loose strand. "I think I've shocked myself."

"So, what are you going to do about it?"

"Nothing." I stood up, dumping my items into the trash. "I can't do anything."

"Why? He no longer goes to school with Addison. He's completely legal."

"Not in a bar."

"Bars are to get drunk and meet someone to take home. You already got him in bed."

"I still can't. Just because he's not at school with Addison. He *was*... and she still really likes him."

"Yes, and someday she will learn not everyone she likes will like her back. Something I doubt she had to deal with before."

No, Addison was never hurting for male attention. She had never been broken up with or not liked back. Maybe that's why Mason was such a mission for her.

"Addison is not in love with me. She loves the idea of me. Of being the one who "gets" the unattainable Mason James."

I wagged my head, trying to push away his words. "It doesn't matter. She comes first and foremost. She will get her heart broken someday, but I will not be the cause of it."

"Okay. I get it. I do." She stood up, tossing her stuff away. "But I also see it as you are missing out on something great for something that was never going to be hers anyway. Think you're letting your fear keep you in a safe bubble."

I shrugged her off, heading for the restroom to brush my teeth.

169

The day became even more strained when I had to assist Daniel with a root canal. He was direct and professional to the point of being awkward. He was purposefully treating me coldly.

"I need a break." I pulled off my gloves, walking out of the room, relieved to get away from Dr. Ramirez after two hours of stress.

"One more." Marcie pointed to the far room on the end, the one we nicknamed the cave because of how this old building was designed. It was tucked in the back with no windows.

"I will pay you to take it for me."

"Nope. This one is all yours."

"This is a trick, huh? Is it Billy?" I had seen him on the schedule. "You trying to get out of doing him yourself?"

She snickered, pointing me toward the room. "Just a little polishing."

Annoyance wound through me, my mood plunging lower as I stomped back to the room. My irritation was high, my patience low. Stepping in, I reached for the glove box, wanting to get this done so I could go home.

"How are you doing tod—" The rest of my standard greeting halted on my tongue. My feet stuck to the floor.

He stood on the other side of the dental chair, wearing his gray sweats, jacket, and a black hat pulled down low, still dotted with raindrops. Everything about him enticed me to want him, invited me to touch, encouraged desire.

"Mason, what are you doing here?"

His mouth tipped up. "I'm here for my appointment." He went around the chair, moving in on me, his body lining up with mine. "I think your friend, Marcie, said I get a free polish or something." He grinned down, the insinuation warming my skin like a heating blanket.

"Mason, you can't be here."

"I told you." He leaned into me, his hand skimming up my neck to my jaw. "All bets are off."

He attacked my mouth. Fierce and demanding. Sucking and nibbling on my lower lip before his tongue claimed my mouth. He yanked on my ponytail, forcing the kiss to deepen.

Everything in me was set on fire. All my anger, guilt, and rage centered on him. Had an outlet. A focus. And I battled back, needing him to ruin me. To take everything I had left.

He broke away from me with a snarl, twisting me around and pushing me up against the wall. My cheek pressed against it as his hands came around, shoving up my bra and top, cupping my breasts. Every nerve was coiled tight, feeling everything with extra intensity.

"You're gonna need to be *very* quiet, unless you want your doctor to hear us." Mason bit into my ear as he yanked my pants and panties over my ass, his fingers sliding through me. "Fuck," he hissed as I tried to hold back my moan. My body had never craved something so bad.

Sex at work would never have been something I considered. *Ever.* I always stayed in the lines. But with Mason? I couldn't seem to do the appropriate thing. He made me want to break every rule, to burn down everything that kept me safe.

"Emery." He breathed against my neck. He withdrew his fingers, replacing them with the head of his cock. He rubbed it against my entrance. Teasing. Taunting.

My nails curled into the wall, my teeth biting into my lip. "Mason…"

He thrust into me, and I slapped my hand over my mouth, choking over a moan as he filled me, stretching me around him.

"Fuck, fuck, fuck," he hissed against my ear, taking a moment before he pulled back and drove in again.

Paint chips dug under my fingernails, and I blinked back tears of agony and bliss.

How did I ever think I could give this up? Nothing compared to how good he felt inside me, how unbelievable it was. It overwhelmed me, pulling me under, making me crave him.

One of his hands stayed on my hip, holding me so he could plunge even deeper, while his other hand fingered my clit, our pace picking up like were both on fire.

A drill from the room next to us tapped at my eardrum, heightening every nerve he hit, turning us into a frenzy of lust. The days we weren't together contributed to our desperation, the vicious way we both demanded more, as if we needed to make up for every hour we'd been apart.

"Jesus, you're so wet," he growled in my ear. "They're gonna hear me fucking you." His fingers rubbed me harder. The sound of him thrusting into me was loud, but I couldn't stop, hoping the office noise would still drown us out. "Do you like that? Knowing your boss is next door while you are getting fucked by me?" I clenched around him, his dirty words turning me on more than I expected.

And he felt my response.

I would never want to hurt Daniel. But nothing prepared me for someone like Mason. I had no choice to be the good person, to be considerate and appropriate. Mason wiped all that off the board and then bent me over it.

He pushed me harder into the partition, my sensitive nipples rubbing over the textured wall. Small cries jumped from my throat; I couldn't keep them inside.

Mason pulled out of me and I hissed in displeasure. He dragged me with him, sitting back on the dental chair. I climbed over him, straddling him, his cock glistening with my wetness. Gripping him, I sunk down on him. Mason jolted, my hand slamming over his mouth to keep his moan quiet as I rode him. Hard.

Both of us watched how his cock thrust in and out of me.

"Fuck," I hissed. His hand covered my scream this time. I could no longer stay silent, my pleasure taking over, making me lose all control as I moved faster. He pushed up into me over and over, his free hand rubbing over my clit.

My orgasm hit me with a vengeance. My teeth sank into his finger, biting until I could taste blood, my body gripping his brutally. He jerked under me, slamming into me twice more with bruising force before he released inside me, spearing a current of bliss through me, shattering me into a million pieces, floating me away into oblivion.

It took me several moments to come down. My breath was ragged, my body still pulsing around him. He reached up, grabbed my face, and kissed me, licking his blood off my lips. "Jesus, woman." He groaned against my mouth. "That was…" He shook his head.

I felt the same. There were no words. Mind-blowing, amazing, earth-shattering all felt so trite and overused. There were no words for what this was. Until Mason, I had never felt anything even close to this before.

"Shit." The reality of work and the activity around me cut through my haze, realizing how easy it was to get caught. Climbing off him, I pulled my bra and top back down, getting myself together in case anyone stepped in, although I was doubtful they would be fooled. My skin was flushed, and both of us oozed sex, the air reeked of it.

"I'll have to give this place a great review." Mason got up, tucking himself inside his sweats, the outline of him dragging my gaze down. "The dental assistant did amazing things in my mouth… though I had to bring my own drill and I didn't get my free polish."

I groaned at his terrible pun, scratching at my brow.

"Em." He was in front of me, his hands cupping my face. "We didn't do anything wrong."

"Except violating health code, a work violation, sexual misconduct, patient misconduct, and probably a dozen other rules, plus just general decency." I shrugged, not feeling anywhere near as bad as I should have.

"Don't tell me you wouldn't do it again, and you didn't want it as bad as I did." He spoke against my cheek, his mouth dragging to mine. "You didn't fuckin' love it?"

I did, which was the problem. I felt out of control, and it frightened me how much I didn't care. He was changing something in me.

He kissed me lightly and stepped away, his focus going to his finger, looking at the teeth marks cutting his skin. "And here I thought it was the patients who bite." He smirked, replacing the hat that fell off during our encounter. "I'll see you later." He stepped out of the room.

Peeking out, I watched his firm ass saunter away. Marcie waited at the end of the hall, and they nodded at each other before he dipped out the back door.

Her gaze danced to me, her head wagging with the biggest grin on her face. "Mmm-mmm. Told you that one was all yours. Won't deny I'm extremely jealous." She turned, heading for the front, pointing past me. "Better make sure you fully disinfect that room."

"Marcie." Her name was chock full of all my questions and worries, not able to say them out loud.

She stopped, her head shaking. "Stop punishing yourself. Seriously, enough with the guilt. At one time, you never thought you'd be happy again, but here you are. I don't know what you were like with your husband, but I've seen you around Mason. How you look at him… and I'm telling you, don't give him up."

"But Addison…"

"I'm not saying you need to flaunt it right now. There is something fun about keeping it quiet for a while. See if it even has legs before you cut them off."

"You mean lie to her."

"Not lie. Just not tell her the complete truth until you figure out what it is you even want. Who knows, it might fizzle out, and you won't even need to worry about it." She tilted her head. "Though, from what I have felt being in the same building as you two, there's no chance of that."

Could I do it? Take a moment to figure out if there was even something there? Give Addy time to get over this crush and move on with someone else?

It was a risky game to play, but I knew I couldn't walk away from Mason.

He was a force I couldn't fight from the moment I saw him.

Chapter 29
Emery

"Elena, Sophie, and some of the other girls are going dress shopping after school today." Addison stabbed her spoon at her oatmeal. "Elena wants everyone to stay over at hers after. Is it okay?"

"Sure." I poured another cup of coffee, not that I needed the extra jitters. Since Mason walked out of the dentist's office last evening, I felt like I was strung out on drugs, going between a blissful high to paranoia, thinking Addy would see right through me. "You going to ask anyone or go as a group?"

Addison shrugged, peering down at her breakfast. "I don't know. They all have dates."

"What about Mateo?"

"Mateo?" Her head bounced up. "We're just friends."

"Why can't you go with a friend? You guys get along great. You have fun with him, right?"

"Totally." A grin hinted on her mouth, which I don't think she was even aware of. "He did this impression yesterday of this guy on TV, and oh my god… it was spot on. None of us could stop laughing."

I wanted to shake her, to wake her up and see what was right in front of her. He was everything she didn't realize she wanted. It wasn't until you were older that guys making you laugh, making you feel good when you were around him, were the best catches.

"So ask him."

"I don't know. I think Janel on my squad said she might ask him." She got up from the table, putting her dish in the sink. "Is it okay if I stay over at Elena's? There's a basketball game on Saturday. We were gonna go straight from her house."

"Sure." I nodded.

"So, what about you?" She glanced over at me. "What happened to Dr. Ramirez?" She grinned at me. "He wouldn't let you out of his sight on New Year's."

"We're just friends." I gave her the same line back, generating an eyeroll from her. She started to walk out, then stopped.

"You know, I think Uncle Ben would be okay if you dated someone. I will always miss him. But I think he'd want you happy. I want you to be happy." She turned and left.

I stared out the window, my eyes misting, knowing the one man who seemed to make me happy was the one who would hurt her.

Yet, the power to stay away from him seemed to be my biggest weakness.

"Bye!" Addy called out, the front door slamming before I could respond. I had off from work today but a shift at the shelter for a few hours.

Heading out, I tried to pretend I didn't know exactly where I'd end up later, no matter what my conscience screamed at me.

The dogs pulled me like they knew exactly where I was headed, my feet stumbling to keep up with their exuberance. Ozzy beelined directly for the open garage, galloping to Mason next to his car.

"Hey there, boy." Mason bent over, rubbing his back and head before Stella, Millie, and Poppy who were fighting for his attention. Mason's eyes drifted to mine as he gave them all love and attention, his gaze heating. "Hey."

"Hey." I tried to keep the giddy smile off my face but failed.

"You know I'm blaming you."

"For?"

"The fact I kept waking up last night, hard as a rock, and then getting angry because I was alone in bed." He strolled up to me, his boots hitting my tennis shoes. "All your fault."

"Funny, I was gonna blame you for the same thing."

"For getting hard?" He smirked, leaning in closer.

"My nipples were."

A groan bubbled from his throat as his mouth took mine. Just his kiss had me melting from the inside out. He pushed me into the side of his car, pressing me hard against it, our mouths becoming brutal. His tongue wrapped around mine, sucking until my core pulsed with need.

"Okay." I leaned back, my hands on his chest. "We seem to escalate quickly."

He grabbed one of my hands, placing it on the erection trying to break through his pants. "This is how I've been since about three minutes after I left the parking lot last night." I gently rubbed him, loving the feel of him. "I can't seem to get enough."

"I know." My forehead tapped his, our breathing labored.

"I don't want this to stop."

"Me either," I replied. "But…" With a pained noise, I slipped away from him, sucking in the cold air from outside. "If we're going to do this, we need ground rules."

"Ground rules?" He folded his arms, smirking at me.

"No PDA in public." I held up a finger. "No coming over whenever you want. We must keep up appearances. Addison cannot find out. Not now. We keep this secret for a while." I licked my lips, the last one making me curl my hands at the idea. "And no sleeping with anyone else if you're sleeping with me, especially unprotected."

He fell against the car, coughing out a laugh. "You think I'm going to sleep with someone else?"

"If you find you want to."

He wagged his head with a huff, his tone gravelly. "Believe me, you are the only one I want to be inside of."

His words had my lungs expanding for air.

"Is that it?" He popped off the car, petting the dogs again before stopping in front of me.

"For now."

"Good." He grabbed Ozzy and Stella's leash. "Let's head to the dog park, or you're gonna find yourself bent over the hood of my car."

A shiver ran down my spine, my body responding instantly with a *yes, please.*

He herded me to the exit.

"Mason, what did I just say?"

"You said no PDAs in public, not that we can't go out in public." He grinned with his cocky smile. "Afraid you won't keep your hands off me?"

Yes.

"You know what I meant."

"Sorry, you already established the rules. Not my fault I already found a loophole." He leaned in, running his gaze over me with a wink. "And I'm going to bend every rule and find every hole I can."

"I hate you."

His laugh burst out into the cold sunny day, swelling my chest like a balloon. I loved that sound.

We walked for a while before I asked, "How's the GED coming along?"

"Good." He nodded. "I'm testing out next month. I'm studying and taking practice tests. Want to tutor me?"

"Sorry." I snorted. "Did okay in school, but don't ask me to recall anything now."

"What about in sex ed? Might need a little more tutelage."

"I think you'd score off the charts." I grinned coyly at him. "Can I ask where a twenty-year-old learned some of those things? I know guys far older who don't perform at your level."

"Oh, do you?" He twisted his head to me, an eyebrow lifting. "Can *I* ask where you learned some of those techniques?"

"You mean how many I've been with before you?" I stopped, letting Millie pee.

His silence suggested that was exactly what he wanted to know.

"Actually, not many. There were two guys in college, and then Ben." I shrugged. "Ben and I knew each other for so long, dated, and then got married. It was never my thing to sleep with a bunch of people."

"For a while, it was mine." There was not an ounce of pride in his claim, more like regret. "I thought it would help."

"Help what?"

"Help me forget, help me feel normal, help me be someone else."

A sadness swirled in my chest at his words.

"And why was that?"

"Guess at the time, I felt life had no purpose. I was going through some shit. Could no longer play the game I loved. Lost my supposed friends. I felt adrift. We moved here, and I guess it was my way of starting fresh. Being someone else. Distracting myself from reality.

"I know the feeling."

"I know you do." His eyes held mine with intensity. "You know, you don't talk much about him."

"Ben?" We reached the gate of the dog park, and I let the dogs off their leashes to play. Mason unleashed Ozzy and Stella, walking with me to the bench. "I guess when I came here, I also wanted to forget, to feel normal, be someone else." I repeated his phrase, sitting on the bench. "He was all I talked about back in our town. Even before his death." I leaned back. "He was all anyone talked to me about when they saw me. I stopped being Emery and became Ben's wife, then Ben's widow. I started to forget I was a whole person. That Ben's death wasn't my entire identity. That every breath was just trying to live to the next moment, and I wasn't drowning in grief."

Mason's throat bobbed, his head bowing like he understood.

"It may be selfish, but it was nice coming here and not talking about him, you know?"

"Yeah," he agreed, his attention on the dogs. "And it's not selfish. You have the right to live your life, to not be stuck because it makes them feel more comfortable. To be seen for more than this one thing."

"Can I ask what happened to you?"

"You *can*." He leaned over as Ozzy ran up between his legs, licking his hand and getting scratches before Millie raced by, and he ran off after her.

"I can." I huffed, hearing what he really meant. "But it doesn't mean you'll answer me?"

His arms rested on his legs as he peered over his shoulder at me. "You already try to find excuses to push me away. I don't need to give you any more reasons."

I stared at Mason, realizing his depth, owning up to my own shame. I was trying to keep him at arm's length. Trying to keep him as this young, inconsequential fling. Use his age as an excuse without seeing how well we got along so I wouldn't have to admit how much I liked him.

We were silent for a little while before he stood up.

"I better go. Grandma might need me. And I need to study." He stuffed his hands in his pockets. "See you."

I nodded, feeling oddly choked up and sad at him leaving. I wanted to kiss him, make plans, to tease and joke with each other.

He got several feet away when Ozzy about knocked him over. He petted the big floof, tossing a stick before continuing on. My heart cried out with urgency to stop him, to do something.

"Mason?" I called across the park, turning his head back to me. "Addison will be at Elena's tonight. Was going to order pizza."

"I make a much better one." He winked and strolled out of the dog park, my eyes watching him until the last possible moment.

I already knew Marcie was right.

I was falling for him.

"Stop. Stop." He grabbed my hips with a laugh, coming up behind me, peering over my shoulder. "What are you doing to that poor dough?"

"What?" I feigned innocence. "You told me to knead it."

"Knead it, not punch the living crap out of it."

"It deserved it." I was pretty sure I had more flour in my hair than on the pizza. "It was being a naughty dough. I had to punish it."

"Emery," he gritted. "Do you want to eat dinner?"

"Yes." I was starving.

"Then stop talking like that," he rumbled in my ear, his hands running up to my breasts. "Or you're going to be the one laid on this counter getting punished."

I gulped down my response, wanting him to do exactly that. "Okay, then show me."

He reached over, covering my hands with his. Our fingers massaged the dough, feeling far more sexual than it should. "You got it?"

"Y-yes."

He kissed my temple before moving back to the sauce on the stove he made from scratch.

"You know it would be so much easier to order delivery." I flattened out my crust, trying to copy his already on the pan.

"Not nearly as good in your mouth." He winked over his shoulder.

I laughed, loving how easy it seemed between us. Tonight, I wanted to forget the guilt. Forget what was right or wrong. Without the influence of Addison, his age, or even Ben.

Just him and me. Nothing else.

See what was there.

"You really enjoy cooking." I placed my dough on the pan, walking it over to him.

"I do." He popped the sheet into the oven to cook for a bit before we put the toppings on. "I find it calming. Also, I want to know what I'm putting into my body. I had to be on a strict diet for a while. Cut out processed foods and sugars, and I didn't go back. Need to keep as healthy as I can be." He motioned down his body. "You've seen this masterpiece."

Grinning, I wrapped my arms around his waist. "Yes, I have. I mean, if you like ripped abs, corded arms, deep V-line, a firm ass, and muscular back... it's okay, I guess."

"Okay, huh?" He smirked, shutting off the burner and turning to me. "Think you need to be shown how to appreciate a work of art." He bent, his arms sweeping me up, flinging me over his shoulder as he carried me back into the living room.

"What about the pizza? I'm starving." I draped over him, laughing.

"We've got ten minutes." He slapped my ass before tossing me back onto the sofa, making me squeak. "I can do a lot of damage in ten minutes." He pulled off my tank top, crawling between my legs, his mouth covering mine. I liquefied at his touch, forgetting all about the pizza.

When I let down my barriers, being with him was so comfortable. Fun. I didn't stop smiling, laughing, or wanting to rip his clothes off.

He teased and taunted my body with feral expertise. He had me coming so hard I bit into his neck, drawing blood, forgetting all about dinner or anything outside of us.

The pizza ended up a little burnt, but sitting with him, naked, eating, talking, watching movies, and having unbelievable sex, I couldn't remember being so happy.

Before, I thought I was breathing. That I was happy. Living. Tonight destroyed that standard, making me feel truly alive. The light at the end of the tunnel wasn't the distance I had made it out to be, and I found even more on the other side than I expected.

Deep in the early hours when I sank down on Mason again, gripping the headboard as I rode him, not trying to be quiet or careful, it alarmed me to consider the idea—what if Ben hadn't died? I wouldn't be here with Mason. I would be with Ben, thinking I was happy and content, never knowing this. How unbelievable Mason felt inside and out. He had me smiling so much my cheeks hurt. He filled something in me I never knew was missing.

We were drawn together instantly, fate bringing me here. To him.

It wasn't fair to play the what-if game because there wasn't a moment I didn't wish for Ben to be alive. But to never know this? Mason? It felt worse. If someone showed me both doors and told me to pick, I no longer could say for sure what I'd choose. Actually, I did, and that petrified me.

The connection to Mason felt like even if I didn't know about him, still happily Mrs. Roberts, somewhere in my soul, I would be missing him.

He had been the one in my fantasies the whole time. The one I dreamed about.

Chapter 30
Mason

I couldn't catch my breath, my release almost blinding as she swallowed me down, a guttural moan echoing through the room, my back hitching off the bed. Everything going black for a moment.

"Damn," I breathed out, feeling the pulse of my dick and heart throbbing wildly together, making me lightheaded. My muscles went limp with sedation.

"Good morning to you too." She sat up, grinning mischievously at me, wiping her mouth. I had woken her up to my tongue between her thighs, making her cry out in a piercing orgasm. She wanted to return my morning wakeup call.

My palm went to my heart, beating so hard against my ribs I had to close my eyes and try to relax, the world still spinning on me.

"Guess I got that free polish after all." I muttered.

She snorted, falling next to me. My eyes opened, staring at her with awe. This woman was unbelievable. A fantasy come to life, and not merely because the sex was insane, but because of her. I had never smiled and laughed so much in my life as I had in the last twelve hours. I never thought this kind of happiness was meant for me.

It was easier when I thought it wasn't. It was better for all if we didn't see each other, but Emery was like a drug I couldn't wean myself off, no matter the costs.

"Wow." Her eyes went to my neck where she bit me the night before, her fingers grazing over it with a flinch. "That's bruising badly. I'm so sorry."

"Don't be." My hand cupped her cheek, my thumb dragging over her bottom lip. "I liked it." My mouth took hers, pulling her into me, showing her the words I couldn't say.

Last night I could feel the difference. She didn't keep me at arm's length. Her barriers were down, letting me glimpse what we would be like together if there were no obstacles. And I wanted it. I wanted even more.

And that actually had reality set in.

I wasn't a fool. It was more than Addison or my age that would end this. And deep down I knew it was better to hurt now than later when we were both in far too deep.

"I better go. I need to check in on my grandma." I kissed her again before rolling off, my legs tangled in the sheets, recalling everything that happened in this bed. I think we slept maybe three hours total. My body ached and the lack of sleep was making me feel a bit off, but it was so fucking worth it.

"And here I was hoping you'd cook me breakfast naked."

"I've tried it. Not recommended. Hot oil and butter hurts like a bitch."

"Okay then, only an apron."

I stood up, searching for my boxer briefs. "How about I run down, check on them, and come back and make you my banana pancakes, in only an oven mitt. Need to keep one thing protected at least." I yanked them on, crawling back on her bed.

"Those sound… healthy."

"You'll love them, I promise." I crawled over her, kissing and tickling her.

"Stop!" She giggled, trying to get away from me. "Mason!"

In any tone, I loved her saying my name. It confirmed it was me she wanted here, me she chose to be in her bed. And fuck if I couldn't get used to this.

You can't. This is only short-term. My mind shot back. *This is not a future you can have.*

"I'll be back." Kissing her as I climbed off, I grabbed my jeans, knowing if I didn't go now, it would be at least another hour before we left this bed. My grandparents were early risers, and at eight, they had already been up for a while.

Guilty about my obvious absence, I rushed to get on my shirt and shoes, which were scattered in the living room, and headed out the door, forgetting where the hell my jacket was. The cold morning had me grappling for air, not seeming to get enough as I jogged down the street to keep warm. My mind went through moments of the night, how we ate our burnt pizza in our underwear, still glowing from sex. How we sat up late talking and laughing, our hands always touching each other. Then how we stayed up all night fucking. Hard, soft, fast, slow, we covered it all, every time feeling the bond between us tightened, though we both knew it shouldn't.

I knew I was grinning like an idiot by the time I pushed through my front door.

"Hey, I'm home." I stepped in, my skin sizzling after coming in from the cold. They kept the temperature far above seventy degrees, causing me to become even more flushed and sweaty. "Grandma?"

Silence.

Fear coiled in my stomach. I ran down to their bedroom, peeking in.

Empty.

"Grandma?" I bellowed, tearing back down the hall to the living room, my feet coming to a halt.

Grandma sat on the sofa, the cat on her lap, but Grandpa's chair was empty.

"Hey?" Nerves fired off alarms up my neck. "Didn't you hear me? Where's Grandpa?"

"Oh." She looked up, startled, as if she just realized I was there. They were both really hard of hearing, but she usually wore her hearing aids. "Mason." She touched her chest, looking so weak and fragile still. "You scared me."

"Where's Grandpa?"

"Now, don't worry, he's okay, but..." A buzzing in my ears started, panic rising. "He fell trying to get out of bed this morning."

"Fell?" I exclaimed. "Is he okay? Why didn't you call me?"

"I did."

I yanked the phone from my front pocket, the one I completely forgot about, not caring about the outside world when I was with Emery. Ten missed calls glowed on my screen.

"Fuck." I gritted my teeth, the weight of guilt crashing down on me, the pounding in my head thumping louder. "I'm so sorry. I didn't even look... I should have."

"It's okay, Mason."

"No, it's not." I shook my head. For all they had done for me, been by my side, sat at my bedside for months, this was how I repaid them? "Where is he? Was he hurt?"

"I think more his pride," she responded. "Caroline's husband, Peter, from next door, took him to the hospital to make sure. But they've already called, saying he's fine, only some bruising. They're on their way home now."

I dug my fingers into the back of my neck, rubbing so hard, I could feel my skin burning, as if I were trying to punish myself.

"I should have been here."

"No, Mason. You are not shackled to this house. Your grandfather and I aren't expecting you to stay here. You will get your GED soon, and you should head off to college."

"I don't want to go to college." I paced in front of her, my internal rage coming out cross.

"Mason, you can't live your life tied to us."

"Why not?" I practically spat back.

"Come here." She patted the seat on the sofa next to her. My body was restless, not wanting to sit, but her steady look had me plopping down on the cushion next to her. "My baby boy." She touched my cheek, pain watering her eyes. "So many people have left you, whether in death or their own selfishness. This is why you hold on so tightly or keep people at a distance. I hate that someday your grandfather and I will cause you more pain and loss."

Emotion strangled my throat. I felt sick at the notion.

"I know you're scared." Tears filled her eyes. "But don't waste your time being our caregiver. You have to live, Mason. Staying here is not a life. Don't you want to find someone, get married, have children, do something you love to do?"

My chest echoed Emery's name, feeling like I had, but it was all water through my fingers.

"What's the point of any of it?" I swallowed, wiping the beads of sweat gather at my temple. "Then I'm the one causing others pain."

"Don't say that."

"Why not? It's true. No one in their right mind will jump into my mess."

"You sure about that?" Her head tilted, her gaze dropping to my neck, something in her gaze suggesting she knew more than I thought she did..

"Yes." I nodded, feeling the decision I knew I had to make like an impact of a truck. I had to cut it off with Emery now. I was an idiot thinking I could have this time with no consequences, and it wouldn't affect others. Selfish and cruel. Emery already had too much pain in her life, and she deserved happiness and love. Security.

"Mason?"

I bolted up from the sofa. "Do you need anything?"

"No, but—"

"Being here is not holding me back, and I'm done talking about this."

She exhaled, the disappointment on her face shredding through my gut even more.

"She called again." She changed the subject. "Wanting to set up a date to meet. I think it would be really good for you too."

I scoffed, my lids closing, but I nodded. "Yeah." Another layer of pressure landed on my shoulders, strain stretching across my ribs. The ache in my head moved down my spine, forcing my lids to close for a moment, feeling a little shaky.

The front door opened, and I rushed to help Peter and my grandpa into the house.

"I'm fine," Grandpa said, but I took on a lot of his weight, walking him to his chair. His eye was black and blue, and he hissed as I eased him down like his whole right side was bruised.

"Thank you, Peter." Grace appeared as if she wanted to get up.

"Oh please, don't get up." He went to her, taking her hand. "And you know it's no problem. Caroline and I are here whenever you need us."

Peter was a good guy and he meant it, but it only made me feel shittier, as though I weren't the one here for them.

"Thanks." I shook his hand.

"No problem." He nodded. "Glad I was home."

He didn't mean it as an attack on me, but it was another dagger to my chest. Another thing telling me the bubble I had been living in, when it came to Emery, had just popped.

Peter and Grandpa said their goodbyes before the house was back to the three of us.

"Can I get you anything?" I went to my grandpa, fear swimming in my stomach, seeing him look so frail and old.

"Just some water. Gonna take some painkillers and nap."

I got water for both, standing over them like a helicopter parent.

"Mason, we're fine. Please stop hovering. Go on with your day." Grandma waved me off. "He's going to be asleep in ten minutes with the game on, and I'll probably be napping in five." Grandma curled up with the cat, her lids already drifting closed. "Please."

"Okay, but I will keep my phone on me, and I'll only be gone a little while." I still hesitated, not wanting to leave them and not wanting to do what I knew I needed to. Going back to Emery's was no longer something good. It wouldn't be pancakes and sex.

It would be gutting raw agony.

My hand went to my head, everything spinning on me, my muscles wobbly. My stomach growled, but acid burned through it, making me nauseous.

Soft snores came from my grandpa, my gaze jumping between them, seeing my grandma's lids flutter closed. Blocks of emotion stacked on top of the other. I wasn't ready for them to go. To be without them. They had been my rock, and I was terrified of how adrift I would be once they were gone. Would everything feel even more meaningless?

The only thing I knew was this could never happen again. They were my priority. The ones who had loved me through all the dark times. No matter what my grandmother said, I needed to be here. Emery and I both understood our little fling couldn't go anywhere...

Jogging back to Emery's, my skin sticky, my head pounding, knowing I wasn't coming back to make breakfast, but to end it.

It was the only right thing to do. For her as well.

My head a blur, my heart hammering, I walked straight into her house, struggling to catch my breath. "Emery?"

"Mason?" The girly voice shot my head over toward the hallway in shock.

Oh. Fuck. Addison. She wasn't supposed to be home.

She stood there, holding a pair of her white cheer shoes like she had forgotten them, her forehead wrinkling in confusion. "What are you doing here?" Addison's attention went to the door I causally walked through, drifting to the bruising bite marks I had on my neck.

Emery came out of the kitchen, stopping dead. Panic widened her eyes for a moment, then she jerked her head to Addison.

"Oh... I asked him to look at the dishwasher again."

It was so slow, or maybe it was fast; time seemed to have stopped. Addison's head twisted back and forth between us, then her gaze slowly went to the jacket hanging over the end of the couch closes to her. The one I left here.

Her attention stayed on it, then slid back to me, stopping on my bruised neck, her chest starting to rise and fall as if she was putting pieces together, understanding what had been right in front of her this whole time.

It was like more bricks crashed down on my chest. My pulse drummed in my ears, my hand grabbing for the wall, trying to keep steady. Sound hazed out, making everything far away, my lungs gasping for air. Blackness seeped into my vision, and I felt myself tip to the side. Somewhere in the distance I heard my name being screamed, but then everything went silent. Dark.

Time hadn't stopped.

I had.

Chapter 31
Emery

"Mason!" A scream bellowed from me as his body dropped to the ground. Fear carved through my gut, my legs already darting for him, knocking Addison out of the way. "Mason!" I screamed again, falling down next to him, flipping him over on his back. A deep-rooted guttural terror rose into my chest, pounding my heart with panic. *Don't leave me. Don't leave me too.* "Mason?" I leaned my ear against his chest, trying to hear his heartbeat. My body was shaking so badly I didn't know if it was him or me.

"Oh god! Mason! Is he okay? Oh my god!" Addison squawked around me, flipping and flapping.

"Call 911. Now!" I screamed at her. She nodded, grabbing for her phone and dialing. I tuned her out, concentrating on him.

"Mason, please…" I batted back my tears, starting CPR. My training was rusty, but it made me focus on my steps instead of my terror.

Addison stayed talking to the operator, telling her everything, until we both heard ambulance sirens wailing in the air, pulling up in front of my house.

They rushed through my front door, taking over for me.

"Is he okay?" Addison continued to wail.

"He's breathing." A woman nodded, she and the other two EMTs getting him on a gurney. I didn't hesitate, running alongside them. I would not leave his side.

"Addison, take my car. Phone Grace and Neal. Tell them I will call them as soon as we arrive."

Addison nodded at my directions as I climbed into the ambulance, sitting down next to his unconscious form, my hand wrapping around his, biting back the tears strangling my throat.

I can't lose him. I can't…

The state of being so hyper aware that nothing felt real had swooped in like a bad dream. The same bitter taste on my tongue, the feeling my brain couldn't quite register anything around me. The panic, the terror, the grief already choking me.

My fingers laced with his, squeezing. "Please, Mason." I reached up, brushing back his hair, watching his chest rise up and down until we got to the hospital. It was a blur of nurses, doctors, and words I didn't understand.

"Miss, you can't go back there." A male nurse stopped me as they rolled Mason past me.

"But…"

"You have to stay out here. Someone will be out as soon as we know anything." The man turned and disappeared behind the door.

Minutes or years could have gone by. I stood there, my life replaying itself. It was a horror that left me a shell once again, though it felt worse this time, because I knew what was on the other side.

Numbness kept me in that spot until I felt someone touch my arm.

"Aunt Emery?" My head turned, and I blinked at the girl, taking a beat to register it was Addison. "Come sit."

I didn't want to, but being no more than a zombie, I let her lead me to the seating area, where a tiny, fragile-looking woman sat.

"Grace?" I jolted at her appearance.

"She wanted to come with me," Addison explained.

"You shouldn't be here, though. You are still recovering." I went to her, suddenly having another focus to put my energy on.

"My grandson's life is far more important than that." She gripped my hand, a tear sliding out. "I feel this is my fault."

"Why?"

"Mason works so hard to please us and takes on so much. Neal fell this morning getting out of bed and had to be taken to the doctor by our neighbor. He feels he let us down by not coming home last night. Not being there."

On the other side of Grace, I saw Addison's head snap my way, but my gaze wouldn't meet hers.

"Neither of you are to blame."

"Mason takes everything on himself. He acts like he doesn't care—"

"But he cares too much." The sentiment slipped out of me, knowing where she was going.

Grace peered at me, a smile ghosting her mouth, her gaze seeing more than I wanted her to.

189

"Ms. Campbell?" A nurse stepped out. I rose, feeling a sick sense of déjà vu. I barely recalled giving my name at the counter.

"Is Mason okay?" I continued to hold Grace's hand, Addy taking her other.

"He's fine." The nurse nodded. "Looks as though lack of sleep, stress, low blood pressure, and skipping his meds today caused his heart to beat irregularly, leading to him not receiving enough blood and air to his brain, which is why he passed out."

"But he's okay?" I heard the hitch in my voice, wanting to crumble to the ground in relieved sobs.

"He's resting, but you can come back and see him. We're finishing up his tests, but he'll probably be clear to go soon after."

"Thank you," Grace replied when my voice couldn't, trying so hard to fight back the emotion swallowing me up.

Helping Grace up, we slowly followed the nurse, but Addison hadn't moved.

"Aren't you coming?" I asked.

Her mouth pinched, her head shaking. "No. I'm gonna go home."

"Okay." Concerned, I watched her grab for her purse, shocked she wasn't the first to be checking on Mason. "Call me if you need anything, okay?"

Her head bobbed again, and she took off, almost running out.

Trepidation strummed at my nerves as if someone were playing them like a guitar, but the moment we stepped into his room, everything else vanished.

"Mason." Grace went straight to him, kissing his cheek. "You scared us so much."

"Sorry." His voice was rough and raw, his eyes going over her to me. They captured mine like I was prey. The impulse to consecutively run to him and run away yanked at my body. Because I understood—I was completely his.

And he could ruin me.

"Emery…" He said my name with so much depth that he didn't need to add anything. His hand laid on top of the covers, his palm inviting me to him.

I didn't resist. My fingers slid in with his, not worried about what Grace would think.

"Guess I owe you."

"You owe me pancakes." My smile fell flat quickly, emotion blinking my eyes. "Don't scare me that way again."

A pained expression flicked over his brow, his thumb rubbing the top of my hand, but his gaze not meeting mine. Something in the pit of my stomach twisted at his response.

"Well, Mason, it seems you had a lively morning." A tall man in a white coat walked in, holding a clipboard. "Maybe next time, try not doing that."

"Sure," Mason scoffed.

"Your tests look good. Your blood sugar was *far* too low when you came in, but we are getting you back up to normal levels."

"Everything is fine?" Grace asked, worry still on her face.

"Yes, though I think you should take it easy for the next couple of days." He spoke to Mason. "Nothing stressful… and maybe keep intense physical activity to a minimum." The doctor looked between Mason and me with a knowing look, seeing clearly the bruising bite mark I gave him on his neck. My face flushed red, only deepening when I heard Mason scoff.

"We'll try."

"Just until we make sure it was a one-time irregularity and nothing to do with the actual heart. You just got it. Let's try not to break it already."

"What?" My hand slid from Mason's, intuition squeezing me, my head snapping to him.

He wouldn't look at me, his jaw ticking. "Anything else?" Mason spoke directly to the doctor.

"Nope. You'll be free to go in an hour. Please do not forget to eat and take your medication. I don't want to see you here again anytime soon."

"I won't."

"All right. Take it easy and call if experience anymore dizziness or shortness of breath." The doctor nodded at both Grace and me and headed out.

"I'm going to call your grandfather and tell him you are okay." Grace struggled to get up, shuffling slowly out of the room, leaving us purposefully.

"I didn't want you to find out this way," he muttered.

I couldn't move, already sensing what was coming but needing him to say it. The scar I traced so many times but never wanted to think about because, perhaps deep down, I already knew.

He swallowed, lifting his chin to me. "I was born with a bad heart. Blame it on my mother continuing to do drugs while pregnant with me, who knows, but we really didn't notice it until later, when I was a teen. I wanted to play football so badly, even had scouts looking at me. I ignored all the signs, kept it hidden as much as I could. The plan worked, until the day it didn't. I spent the next year and a half in and out of the hospital waiting for a heart. And knowing even if they found one, I still couldn't play ever again. My grandparents never left my side. They put all their savings into treatments and medication. And when I was sick of being looked at as the kid with the broken heart at my last school, they picked up their entire life and moved here for me. Everything they've done has been for me."

A tear slid down my cheek, understanding so much more of his relationship with Grace and Neal and why he felt he owed them so much. I was heartbroken for the child who had to go through all of that.

"Why didn't you tell me?"

"Like I said. You already were looking for any reason to keep me at arm's length. This would have shut the door forever. Not only too young, but damaged as well. Though, I should have let you. You deserve far more than this."

"What are you talking about?" I stepped closer to him. "You're not broken, Mason."

"You don't get it," he bit out, his lids blinking, emotion bobbing in his throat. "You know how I never answer any questions about my future?"

I frowned in confusion.

"It's because I don't have one."

"That's not true," I sputtered.

"Do you know how long someone lives after a heart transplant?" Anger flashed in his eyes, but it wasn't at me. "No? The *max*, not the standard, is thirty years. Most are far less. I'll be lucky to get twenty-five more years."

That would put him in his forties.

Acid rolled in my stomach, terror bleeding into my veins. "Wh-what about another heart transplant?"

"Yeah." He laughed mockingly. "Those are even rarer. Hearts aren't offered like going through a fucking drive-thru."

"I know." I trembled, still not accepting the reality of this new revelation. "But you can't give up."

He looked away from me, his shoulders lowering. "And take someone else's chance at a full life?"

"Yes!" I shouted, tears spilling over. "For you… yes! If I have to give you my own, I fucking will."

His head snapped back to me, his eyes full of emotion. "Come here." Reaching for me, he pulled me into him, his hands cupping my face, wiping away my heartbreak. "I won't make you go through it. You deserve better than this. It was supposed to be just sex, remember? A fling. You weren't supposed to get this deep." His forehead pressed into mine. "I was being selfish. I couldn't seem to stay away from you. But you have lost way too much. I will not put you through this again."

I yanked back, my head shaking. "You're not—"

"Emery." It was a command. "It's better to end it now than later. We both knew deep down this couldn't go anywhere."

"No—"

"Yes. It's better for *both* you and Addison."

My lids squeezed together, recalling the flicker of pain in her eyes earlier. "I think she knows."

"She *thinks* she knows. But now you can be truthful with her. There is nothing going on."

"You think I'm going to walk away so easily?" Anger weaved through my devastation. "Like everyone else has?" Resentment flared up my spine. "Fuck you."

His brows curved in shock at my response.

"I went through hell and made it out. I've always tried to stay safe, to be protected, thinking it was the best thing so I would never get hurt again. It didn't matter how secure I was. Life is never safe. You made me see that. I realized I'm not some delicate little girl who doesn't know what true darkness is. I've danced with my demons and flirted with death. So don't treat me like I'm some fragile thing who needs to be protected."

"You are the strongest woman I know, which is why you deserve happiness. A life with someone who will love you… have a love like my grandparents."

"You sound as if you're dying tomorrow!" My voice rang through the room, though it was the echo of his words embedding in my gut. *Who will love you.* As in, he didn't. This was him trying to break up with me, telling me it was over nicely.

"I might," he shot back at me. "That's why it's best we end this now."

My head shook, not accepting his claim.

"Do you see us having this happily ever after, Emery? Growing old together?" The beeps of his heart monitor picked up, his arms going out. "Do you?" His dark eyes pierced mine, digging into my soul for the answer. One I didn't have. I didn't know what our future was, if we could even have one with all the obstacles in our path. All I knew was I didn't want to be without him.

But he picked up on my hesitation. My own fear of the future.

"What I thought." His voice was detached. "It's one thing for someone you love to die suddenly, but it's different going into it knowing *they will*. We had an amazing time. Now it's over." He stared forward at the wall. "Goodbye."

"What?" Dumbfounded, I watched him in denial. "Mason…?"

"It's over, Emery." His throat bobbed, and he still wouldn't look at me. His voice was hard. Final.

"Fuck you, Mason James. You're doing this because you're afraid, *not me*."

"Afraid?" He scoffed. "I've been looking death straight in the eyes since I was a kid. I'm not afraid of dying."

"No." I seethed, my heart cracking into a million pieces. "You're afraid of *living*."

Anger and pride marched me straight out of the room toward the exit, my vision blurring when I hit the corridor.

"Emery?" Grace's soft voice came behind me, whirling me around.

"Oh." I stuffed back the emotion wanting to explode from me. Hurt, anger, agony, my heart being the one ripped out of my chest. "Do you need a lift home? Addy took the car. I was going to call an Uber."

Grace walked up to me, taking my hand.

"Don't give up on him."

"Wha-what?"

"Too many in his life have hurt him. He has built a shield around to keep people at a distance. Or he walks away first before they can leave him," she patted my hands. "But he is worth the fight, and I think you know it." She shuffled down the hall, going back into Mason's room, leaving me eviscerated.

Addison sat at the kitchen table when I came in, a Coke and chips sitting in front of her, both untouched.

"Hey." I poured myself a glass of water from the fridge. "You okay?"

She didn't look up, her head nodding in response.

"I know it must have been scary." I sat across from her, my stomach tightening when she still wouldn't look at me. "He's doing fine. Probably already heading home."

She twirled her can of Coke.

"Addison?"

"Your reaction... it was intense."

"Yeah." The bubbling of nerves filled my belly. "I think it reminded me of what I went through with Ben. Triggered a lot of memories."

"No." She wagged her head, finally lifting her gaze to me. "It wasn't about Uncle Ben... it was one hundred percent Mason."

My throat dried out. "What?"

Her jaw rolled, her gaze piercing me.

"Did he stay here last night?"

My mouth opened, words sticking in my throat.

"Don't *lie* to me." Emotion flushed over her face. "I'm not stupid. I saw the hickey on his neck... the way you touched him in the ambulance. The way you looked at him." Hurt flooded her eyes, making my heart twist. "The way he *always* looks at you." She rolled her hands into fists, her gaze glancing back at Mason's coat still on the sofa. "His jacket is here because he came over last night, didn't he?"

"Addison, you don't—"

"No!" She stood up. "Tell me the truth! Don't you dare bullshit me!"

"Please let me explain," I pleaded, my voice breaking.

"He was here with you last night, wasn't he? You are the one who gave him the hickey, didn't you?" she shouted, her face turning red. "That's why he wasn't home when Neal fell... because he was here!"

My teeth bit into my lip, my vision blurring.

"Tell. Me!"

"Yes," I choked.

Pain struck her features, her head wagging. She knew, but hearing me confirm it stepped her back in agony. "I can't believe you," she whispered hoarsely, bolting from the room.

"Addison!" I leaped up, grabbing her arm. "Let me explain."

"Explain?" She ripped away from my touch. "Sure, explain to me why Mason was here *all night*. How he got bite marks down his neck." I stared at her, my mouth not responding. "Or maybe you can tell me how long you two have been going behind my back?"

"It wasn't like that."

"Not like what?" she screamed, her face turning almost purple with rage. "You're *fucking* him!"

I flinched at her harsh words, but the fact I didn't refute them made her lose all control.

"How could you?" she bellowed. "You knew I liked him. How could you do that to me?"

"Addy—"

"You fucking *slut*." I coiled back at the cruelty in her words. "What kind of person are you? He was in *high school*. You're thirty! That is so repulsive. You're like some sad, old, cliché cougar! Can't you go to jail for something like that?"

No. At twenty, he could actually get in trouble for going out with her since she was still underage, but I knew none of that would help.

"I can't believe you." Tears broke free, falling down her cheek, crushing my heart into dust. "Was it only last night?"

Tears fell down my face too, pain squeezing them shut because I wouldn't lie to her anymore.

"Oh. My. God," she whispered through a sob. "How long?"

"Addison, that's not—"

"*HOW LONG?*" she shrieked, her feet and hands moving like she was losing control.

"Before Christmas." I prepared, knowing my answer would light a fuse since we were now well into February. This wasn't a onetime accident. We had been keeping this from everyone for a while.

A noise strangled from her, disbelief and betrayal rocking her backward. I could see her mind flipping back to all the things she might have missed, the times he had been here since.

"So, when he texted you on Christmas that wasn't because of the dishwasher… or when he showed up here when we got home. I-I thought he came for me, but he didn't, did he? Oh god, on New Year's, he disappeared. You were in your room…" She blinked, realizing why I had looked so disheveled. "He was in there with you, wasn't he?"

"I am so sorry. I never meant—"

"Shut up," she demanded. "Don't dare tell me you didn't mean to hurt me. Because you knew I liked him, and you still slept with him. The whole time letting me believe I had a chance. You lied to me, made me look like a fool."

"No. I wasn't lying to you; I was lying to myself. I tried to deny it. We both tried to stay away, but we couldn't. I am so sorry. It should have never happened. Just know the last thing I wanted was to hurt you. You were my main concern."

"Until you got a taste of his dick, spread your legs, and decided you wanted that instead?"

"Addison!" I stepped up to her. "I know you are mad at me, but *do not* disrespect me." I shot back. "I have made mistakes—"

"Made mistakes?" she spat. "You slept with a kid from my high school!"

"He's twenty and—"

"I don't want to hear it. I don't want to hear any excuse coming out of your mouth." She stomped to her room, grabbing clothes by the handful and stuffing them in her bag.

"What are you doing?" I came into her doorway.

"Going anywhere but here." She slammed past me, heading for the door.

"Addison?"

"I wonder what Uncle Ben would think if he could see you now." She shook her head, disgust spewing out at me. "I fucking hate you."

The door slammed, ricocheting through my bones and soul.

I stood there for a minute before a sob shattered through me, my legs giving out and dropping me down the wall, crying until I couldn't breathe.

Letting my demons pull me back into hell.

Chapter 32
Mason

"Mason?" Grandma knocked softly on my door. "You awake?"

Awake? Yes. Functioning? No.

I hadn't been for two weeks, doing the bare minimum. I got up, ate enough to take my medication, did chores around the house, studied for my GED, ate dinner, and went to bed. Rinse and repeat. I hadn't worked on my car or barely left this house since I was discharged from the hospital. I moved around as if everything was fine, but nothing was.

The pull down the street only grew stronger. The need to see if she walked by with the dogs was almost unbearable, but I never looked. I avoided people, ignoring every one of Mateo's calls and texts.

Grandma kept trying to get me out of my rut, but I couldn't get past the notion of my expiry date and find the stuff in between worth getting up for. I had no direction, no dream, and the lone thing that gave me any joy lately, I had pushed away.

She sent me one text: *I miss you.* I deleted it instantly, knowing if I gave myself a moment, I would be running back to her. She would be grateful later. She'd find a man she could love completely for the rest of her life.

This didn't ease the constant emptiness in my chest, and I found myself staring off or sighing repeatedly. Agitated and exhausted, but neither sleep nor exercise helped.

"Mason?" A knock tapped at my door again.

"Yeah, I'm up." I tossed off my blanket, put my feet on the ground, and rubbed my head. The scruff along my jaw had grown thicker, my hair untidy and annoying the hell out of me. "Can you run to the store and pick up our prescriptions? Yours are ready too."

We should get a group discount for the number of drugs this house took together. We all had our own pill cases, telling us which one to take on which day. I'd be taking immune-suppressants for the rest of my life so my body wouldn't suddenly decide my heart was foreign and attack it.

"Sure," I grunted, standing up and stretching my knotted muscles. "Let me jump in the shower."

"Okay. I made some eggs. You need to eat soon."

She'd been on my ass since the scare at the hospital. I understood. I know I terrified them both. They didn't wait in fear for ten months for me to find a heart and then sit by my bed as I recovered, for me to fuck it up now.

Jumping in the shower, the water sprayed over my skin. My dick was hard, but lately jacking off didn't even bring me relief. It *only* wanted her. The few times I had ventured out of the house, I'd found myself at the dog park, like a sick stalker hoping to "accidentally" run into her. Other women, beautiful women, had tried to make small talk when I was there, blatantly hitting on me. And all I felt was exhausted and bored.

They weren't Emery.

She seemed to be the only one who jolted life into my veins. It was that way from the moment I saw her. And it seemed especially cruel to have a taste and know I would probably never have it again.

Dressed, I pulled on a cap and headed out to the kitchen, the eggs waiting for me with my box of pills next to my plate.

"Thanks." I sat at the counter, shoveling them in, downing my medication. Grandpa sat in his chair watching war stuff on the History Channel while Grandma was doing a crossword, with Claudia asleep beside her. Domestic. Boring. Expected.

Anxiousness wiggled through me, knowing I'd never get to their stage where life with my wife became monotonous. Though at their age, it was acceptable. They had lived very full lives.

At the ripe age of twenty, I was already living that life. Colorless and tedious. It screamed to the part in me which wanted to escape. Travel. Explore the vast reaches of the world. Live life to the fullest. Take a cooking class in Italy, taste beer in Belgium, go zip-lining in New Zealand.

Instead, I got up, tucked my wallet into my back pocket, nodded at my grandparents, and left. My GTO rumbled down the street, rolling into the parking lot of the drugstore. My knuckles clenched around the steering wheel. Spotting a familiar SUV a few spots away, my eyes drifted down to the building at the end of the shopping strip.

The dentist's office.

My cock hardened instantly with the memories of my last visit there. How I sunk into her, fucking her against the wall, before she rode me on the chair, how our orgasms tore through us both. It had been risky, wild, and so damn hot.

"Shit." I blew out, my head falling back on my headrest, scrubbing my face. *Block it out, asshole.* I climbed out of the car, trying to flee from my memories. Head down, I barreled into the store, set on the far wall where the pharmacy was, wanting to get in and out. Curving around an aisle, a petite frame ran into mine.

Light brown eyes widened when she stepped back in shock. "Mason."

My lungs clipped, dread pouring through me.

Addison.

"Hey." I swallowed, keeping my face blank. She had barely passed through my thoughts lately, except seeing her reminded me of Emery, taking me back to the day it all came to an end. She was there when I passed out and had called 911.

Her shock flipped like a switch, becoming aloof. "Glad to see you're all right."

"Yeah, thanks." I shifted on my feet. "Was going to come down and thank you guys, but…" But I would lose my shit seeing your aunt again. "Things got busy."

"Well." Her jaw rolled. "I'm not staying there anymore."

"What?"

"I'm staying at Elena's. Not like you'd be coming down for me anyway."

Oh fuck.

She swallowed roughly, peering down. It was then I noticed her basket full of makeup and some bathroom essentials, as if she hadn't been home for a while.

"I know, by the way." Her voice was strained, no longer disguising her hurt and anger. "So, you don't have to stay away on my account."

"I don't know what you think—"

"Don't," she hissed, her eyes filling up with anger and grief. "Don't you fucking bullshit me. I know you've been screwing since Christmas."

My jaw clanked, crunching my back teeth.

"I can't believe you guys." Her blonde hair whipped around, her head wagging. "She's my aunt," she exclaimed, looking around to see if she caused any attention. "It's *disgusting*." Her eyes watered, bearing even more weight on my chest.

"Addison…"

"I liked you." She choked out. "Really liked you. You had to know that."

I did, but it didn't stop me. Emery was by far more powerful than Addison's crush on me. I know it made me a real asshole, but I doubt I'd do anything different.

"I feel so stupid. The whole time…" A sob sucked in her chest. "How could you?" Her voice cut out, a tear sliding down her face. "Was it worth it? Was fucking my aunt worth it?"

Hell yes. But that wasn't what she wanted to hear, so I stayed silent.

Her eyes went back and forth over me, seeing my answer there. Her face crumbled, my non-answer speaking volumes.

"Oh god." She blinked rapidly, her hand going to her stomach.

"I'm sorry," I muttered. "You probably won't believe me, but know Emery fought it a long time because of you. It was me. I wouldn't let her be."

Addy shook her head, trying not to let my words sink in.

"She still knew better. She's *thirty*, Mason."

I felt far closer to Emery's age than I did to her.

"You guys no longer have to pretend or hide it from me anymore."

"We haven't spoken since the day at the hospital." And it hurt like hell.

"What?" Addison's lids narrowed skeptically.

"We thought it would be better."

In truth, it was me. I wanted better for Emery. I still did.

"Don't hate her. She loves you. Believe me, she never wanted to hurt you. Neither did I." I tucked my hands into my pocket. "And I'm sorry I didn't feel what you wanted me to, but I never led you on, Addison. I never promised or said anything that was otherwise. You made it into something you wanted, but I apologize if my actions in coming to the house made you believe I did. It wasn't my intention." I shifted on my feet again, feeling the hollow ache I had since I forced Emery to walk away. "I couldn't stay away."

Addison's chin trembled, hearing my declaration, the honesty I couldn't hide even to myself.

"What the hell is taking you so long?" A girl strutted up to us. "Oh, Mason." Her tone completely changed, a coy smile curling her lips.

"Elena." I greeted her, watching her gaze move up and down me. Elena wanted to be the girl every guy wanted. She put out all the subtle

201

signals she would backstab her friend in a moment if I gave her any hint I was interested.

"We've missed you at school. Was *so* heartbroken to hear you aren't coming back," she purred. "Especially Addison here."

My eyes slid to Addison, her face pointed down, trying to hide how upset she was, though her gaze met mine briefly before looking away. I knew in that moment Addison hadn't told Elena anything about Emery and me.

"Any chance you own a tux? Addy is in need of a date for the dance tonight."

"Addison has plenty of guys hoping she'll ask them." I knew one in particular.

"What about the party back at mine after? Gonna be insane. Addison is staying in my guest room. Sooo…" She peered up at me with a coy smile. Although she was pimping her friend, it was clear if I made a move for Elena, she would be on me in a heartbeat.

"Sorry." I cleared my throat, stepping back. "You guys have fun." I signaled my head toward the pharmacy. "See ya." I stepped around them, walking a few feet when I glanced back. Elena was already sauntering away while Addison stood in the same spot. "Addison?"

Her head bopped up to me.

I licked my lips. "Go back home. She doesn't deserve this. She's been through a lot… and you know this is killing her. She loves you more than anything."

"And I haven't been through a lot?"

"Didn't say that. I think this is hurting you too." She really did look miserable. "You can't hate her for taking something that was never yours to begin with." I tried to keep it soft, but she still flinched at my bluntness. "Plus, Elena is a catty bitch. That's got to be exhausting to be around all the time."

A snorted laugh came from Addy, a glimmer of a smile telling me she knew it too.

I tipped my head again before I turned away, assuming I closed the chapter on both aunt and niece, able to step out of their lives.

Life seemed to want to torture me. Walking out of the store and heading for my car, my attention went to figures stepping out on the sidewalk. Oxygen seized my lungs. As if a needle was scratching across a record, everything came to a jolting halt.

Emery and Marcie came out of the dentist's office, bundled up against the chilly breeze, engaged in their conversation. I couldn't move. Any solid reason for staying away from her dissolved into the slush around my feet, feeling like I had woken up from a coma.

Her long dark hair was in a ponytail, her cheeks pink with cold, appearing exhausted, but she was insanely beautiful.

As if Emery could sense me, her gaze flew up to mine, her shoes squeaking to a stop on the frozen pavement. Marcie took a few more seconds to register what was happening, but she was nothing but a blur to me. All I saw was Emery.

We stared at each other, neither of us making a move, lost in emotions and unsaid things hanging between us. I wanted nothing more than to go over and kiss her. Tell her to forget whatever bullshit I said at the hospital.

Emery's gaze caught on something past me, her face paling.

My stomach dropped, my head twisting to follow her gaze, already sensing who was behind me.

Addison had paused right outside the store doors, her eyes darting between us. The three of us were frozen in a silent stand-off, with so much to say and nobody saying it.

"Addy, come on." Elena griped from her car, jerking Addison's attention away for a moment. When she glanced back, her expression flashed with hurt and anger before she turned fully away and ran for Elena's car, climbing in and driving away.

I already knew when I looked back at Emery any tiny piece I had of her was gone, replaced with guilt and grief.

Regret.

My throat thick, I witnessed exactly what I feared. Misery covered Emery's features, tears filling her eyes. She twisted back for the office, darting inside, needing to get away from me.

Marcie's mouth pressed together in pity, her gaze soft with empathy before she retreated into the office after her friend, leaving me the only asshole still standing here.

Standing alone, feeling my chest had been cracked open, and my heart removed. *Again.*

Chapter 33
Emery

Dr. Ramirez sent me home after seeing me sobbing in the breakroom. His eyes were full of concern when he told me to rest and call if I needed anything, which merely added to my misery. He had asked me out a few days earlier, and again I had to tell him I only wanted to be friends. But he still seemed to be waiting. Waiting for me to suddenly wake up and see him as more. To find myself falling in love with him.

Even without Mason, Daniel and I were never going to happen. Daniel deserved far better than me. He needed someone who got butterflies every time he walked into the room. Who couldn't wait to see him, who wanted to be with no one else but him.

Being home alone, stalking Addison's social media, and seeing her getting ready with her friends for the dance only sunk me further in despair.

What a mess I had made. Addison hated me, Harper was mad at me, and I could barely look at myself. What really cut me was the one person I wanted to talk to about all this had walked away from me.

Seeing him today pulverized my façade and fake smile like a tornado. Every emotion I had pushed back, focusing on getting through the last two weeks, cracked. My heart leaped up my throat. The need to go to him, to burrow in his arms, was painful. It should be easier now. I shouldn't feel like the whole world stopped and started because I saw him.

On my third glass of wine, my will was weak, and my heart was heavy, scrolling through Addison's newly posted pictures. She appeared to be having fun at the dance. I kept going further back into her posts, knowing secretly what I was looking for. My heart still stopped when I landed on the few shots she had of Mason. Almost all were taken here in our backyard.

Stopping on the first one she had of him, I sucked in, remembering the night clearly. The first night he came over after the game. It was odd to think shortly after this picture, he had come into the kitchen purposely to see me, bringing dirty dishes to the sink. How that night started it all.

He affected me from the moment I met him, but if I knew then what was ahead, would I have changed it? Stopped it?

A sound worked up from my throat, curling me deeper into the sofa, bringing more desolation because I knew I wouldn't. The thought of never being with him caused panic to simmer under my skin, an anxiety in me that had me flinching in agony.

I wanted to call him. To walk down the street or open my door and have him on my stoop.

It was well after midnight, but my fingers punched a number into my phone. The darkness I lived in for so long was nipping at my heels, wanting to pull me back down in it.

"Hello?"

"Harper…" My voice cracked, holding back my tears.

My sister stayed silent for a moment. I could feel her anger at me. I had called her when Addison left, knowing she needed to know. I broke down and told my sister everything, which ended in another pummeling of my character. I deserved it, but it didn't seem to change my feelings on the matter.

"I'm sorry," I whispered hoarsely. "I know you hate me too. I just—" Feel lost. Have nothing keeping me afloat. Miss my family.

"I don't hate you, Emery." Harper sighed. "Disappointed? Yes. Protective of my baby girl because she's hurting? One hundred percent. Mad at you? A little. Did I want to drive up there and bring her home? Absolutely." Addison begged her not to. Harper realized she was too close to graduating and really happy and settled here with her friends to make her leave now. "But I don't hate you. I could never *hate* you."

Pressing the phone to my ear, I dropped my head to my knees, choking back a sob.

"I hate myself."

"Em." Harper let out another long exhale. "I don't condone what you did. My head still can't wrap around it, but you are both *technically* adults." The jab hit its target. It took everything I had to not defend him, telling her how much older he was compared to his actual age. "I hate you lied to both of us, but then Kevin reminded me I had kept our relationship secret for a long time because I didn't want to hurt you. He made me see it more from your point of view.

"You've been through a lot. And I was scared you might never move on from grieving Ben. I really wish it wasn't the same boy my daughter was crushing on who helped you get past your grief. Though, seeing you at Christmas, I noticed a huge change. You glowed… I thought it might be Daniel. Or maybe I hoped."

"I wish it wasn't Mason either—" The sentiment stuck in my throat because deep down, I didn't actually wish that. I hated the thought of it not being him, not kissing him, seeing his smile, hearing his laugh, feeling him inside me. It was why the guilt kept circling around in an endless loop.

"I'm not blind or dead. Addison showed me pictures of him. He's *exceptionally* good-looking. I could totally see the attraction. I could tell he was way too old for her just by looking at him," Harper declared. "I mean, if you had met him randomly, no connection to Addison, I could see using him for a bit of an ego boost."

"It's not that way," I gritted. "I didn't ruin my relationship with my niece for an ego boost. And I'd never use him. Jesus, what he has gone through in his life. What he's lost and fought for. He's older than any of the men I've met who are double his age."

Harper was silent, causing my stomach to clench.

"Oh my god…" she breathed.

"What?"

"I can't believe this." She laughed dryly. "You're in love with him."

"No, I'm not!"

"Holy shit." She ignored me. "Of course, it's so obvious now."

"I'm not!" My defenses rose like porcupine quills, hating both her and Marcie for accusing me of this. "I *like* him. He's an amazing guy. We have fun together." Fuck, did we. "But I don't love him." I could hear the pitch in my voice peak.

"Em, you're right. You wouldn't hurt Addison for something that didn't mean anything. No matter how hot the guy was, you wouldn't have done anything if it was purely physical attraction. I know you."

Nothing came out of my mouth. No response, no counter to her argument.

"Addison is everything to you," she stated. "You would never hurt her just to get laid."

"Maybe the sex was that good," I disputed, feeling how flimsy and awful the claim sounded. The sex was phenomenal, but it wasn't what kept me going back, willing to risk everything.

It was him.

"Keep telling yourself that," she scoffed.

The sound of the door opening made me jump to it, my mouth dropping in shock.

Addison, still in her dress, bags in hand, wrestled through the front door.

Harper heard my sharp intake of air.

"What?"

"Addison is here," I muttered, my lashes blinking faster.

Harper let out a relieved noise, her voice thick with emotion. "Oh, thank god." She sniffed. "Call me later, okay?"

"Okay." I hung up, standing up from the sofa, facing my niece. "Addison—"

"I haven't forgiven you yet," she blurted.

My head bobbed. "Okay."

"And I'm home because if I spent one more day at Elena's, I would be in jail for murder."

"Probably only juvie. You're not an adult yet."

I could see Addy trying to hold back a thread of amusement, instead shaking her head with annoyance.

"I still can't believe what you did." Her eyes watered. "It still hurts to look at you."

"I know."

She gathered her bags, walking into her bedroom, and I followed quietly behind her.

She tossed her stuff on her bed, kicking off her heels, her back still to me. "I kissed Mateo tonight."

"Oh," I responded, not ready for the turn in conversation. "That's good, right?"

"No." She swung around, her eyes blazing. "Because he was at the dance with Janel. She likes him... *a lot*. But seeing them together... kissing. I wanted to throw up." Addison's hands rolled up. "He and I were talking at Elena's party, and I kissed him." She threw up her arms. "He's Mateo! He's my *buddy*, but suddenly I looked at him and thought, damn, he's hot. How did I never notice that? And realizing I didn't want her to have him." Addison sat back on her bed, a tear sliding down her face. "I took off... because Janel is my friend, and if she found out. She'd hate me. And suddenly I realized I was no better than you."

Ouch.

"Addison, I lied to you because I didn't want to hurt you, but I was also lying to myself because I didn't want to admit what I felt."

"She asked me point-blank if it was okay if she asked him, and I said yes, that we were only friends."

"Oh."

"It was strange. I saw them laughing and having fun, and when I saw them kiss? Something shifted, and I realized I wanted to be the one he was laughing with. It was always *us* together. Not her."

"I'm sorry Janel will be hurt, but she has to know Mateo is completely head over heels for you."

"You think?"

"I know." I leaned against the doorjamb. "And so do you. Sometimes it takes the idea of losing someone to wake us up."

Her gaze lifted to mine.

"Is it how you felt with Mason?" Hearing her say his name immediately made me want to put up walls. Deny. But the only way forward with Addison was if I was completely honest with her.

"Yes." I swallowed. "Though I think I knew way before."

"Me too."

"Talking about Mateo or me?"

"Both." She dropped her shoulders. "Looking back, I see how obvious it was now. You two were drawn to each other from the beginning. How many times I would see him looking at you. Near you. Coming here all the time, even more when I wasn't here. The looks or smiles you'd share when you thought I wasn't looking. You guys couldn't seem to stay away. I mean, even the first time I introduced you to him, he stared at only *you*." She shook her head, pain flickering her featured. "The *way* he looked at you. It was so clear. It was how I wanted him to look at me. I should have seen it then. Though, I think I did, but I just didn't want to acknowledge it. I feel so stupid now."

"You are not stupid. Do not blame yourself. This is completely on me. I made bad choices. I kept the truth from you."

"It's on him too."

I tucked my arms against my ribs, nodding with acknowledgment.

"I want to know." She pressed her mouth together. "Would you do it again?"

"Hurt you? No," I replied adamantly.

"That's not what I meant." She shifted on the bed. "Take me out of it. Would you still be with Mason if not for me?"

Once again, my mouth didn't move. I wouldn't lie, though the truth still felt too harsh to say out loud.

Addison didn't need my confirmation. My expression must have given her enough.

"I thought so." She wiped at her eyes.

"I never ever wanted to hurt you." I fought back my own tears.

"I know." She used the back of her hand to mop up her eyes again. "And I feel so hypocritical sitting here after kissing Mateo though he was with Janel and still being so hurt about Mason."

"You have every right to be." I could barely get out my sentence. "I betrayed you. And I am so sorry."

We stayed silent for a long time, Addison staring at the wall, taking in everything.

"Grace told me about his heart transplant. That they almost lost him."

"Oh." I tucked my arms against myself. I never got around to telling her, though I figured she knew something. "I'll let you get some sleep." I stepped out of her doorway. "I'm glad you're home." I reached for the knob, about to shut her door.

"If it matters, when I saw him earlier, he looked miserable." It took her a lot of strength to get that claim out. "I think Mason really likes you. Actually, I think he's in love with you."

All I could do was nod at her before shutting the door.

I went straight to my room and cried.

The week went by, slipping into routine. Addison and I weren't even close to where we used to be. Her anger would flare up in moments, her hurt in another, but every day I worked at making it better between us. She started to talk to me more about Mateo. They hadn't really talked since the night she ran out after they kissed, and I knew she was missing him. I think she didn't realize how much he was in her life. It wasn't Sophie or Elena who was her best friend, it was Mateo.

One topic we avoided was Mason though he was constantly the elephant in the room. Always there, either unsaid or in my thoughts.

No matter how much I forced a smile and tried to pretend everything was all right, it seemed to get harder. I couldn't get over this empty feeling in my heart. Even when I was playing with the cats or out walking the dogs, it was always there—sodden and heavy with sadness.

Today was cold but sunny, and I was taking the pack to the dog park.

209

Millie had been adopted, so I had Ozzy, Poppy, and Stella, all full of energy and ready to play.

Honestly, I couldn't say if I was aware or it was just my subconscious, but I found myself near his house, my feet leading me back to the source of my pain like he could fix it.

The garage was open when I walked by. Holding my head high, pretending my heart wasn't bleeding and my soul wasn't screaming for him.

Ozzy let out a happy yelp, lurching out of my hold, his fluffy form barreling forward.

"Ozzy!" I shouted as he tore away from me, galloping straight into Mason's garage.

Shit.

Stella and Poppy went tearing after him, yanking me behind them. Entering the garage, my gaze landed right on him. He was crouched down, scrubbing Ozzy's head, greeting the rest of the dogs as they leaped up, licking him.

"Hey, guys." Scratching each one in hello, a smile spread over his face, his gaze turning to me.

My breath tripped over itself, my lungs struggling to take a full breath.

"Hey." He gave them all more pats before rising.

"I'm sorry," I burst out, gesturing to Ozzy, who was sitting in front of Mason, staring up at him as if he were a god. "He broke away from me... I wasn't meaning—"

"To see me?" he finished.

"No, I mean yes." I took in a shaky breath. "I mean, I think you have a fan." I nodded to the dog. "He really seems to like you."

"He's the only one." Mason was a foot away from me, but he had the power to make me feel him without even touching me. His physique took over every molecule.

Peering at my shoes, I clenched my teeth, my body quaking with the intensity surrounding us.

Mason took a step back, his hands going to his hips. "Mateo told me Addison was back home."

"Yes." I nodded, still not able to look at him. "Things aren't great, but I hope in time it will get better."

"I'm glad," he responded, both of us being polite and uncomfortable. "I hope it all works out for you." He rubbed Ozzy's head, taking another step back. "Have a good time at the park."

Dismissal. A goodbye.

He gave me the opportunity, a clear exit out of this awkwardness. But I didn't move. He turned back around, going to the workbench, cutting me off.

"Mason?" My expression and voice filled with torment.

He twisted back, waiting for me to say anything, but I couldn't get anything out. What I really wanted to say got bottled in my throat, pushed back with sensibility.

"What?" he said softly.

Nothing came out.

"What?" he exclaimed louder, the politeness snapping in half. "God damn it." He strained, his hand running through his hair. "What do you want from me? I am trying to be respectful. I'm trying to stay away from you. Trying to do the right thing."

"Staying away from me?" I exclaimed. "You're the one who ended things."

He let out a harsh laugh. "Like you wouldn't have eventually. Don't tell me you wouldn't have sent me another fucking text, telling me it was over, *again*, after Addison found out."

In the moment, I didn't realize how shitty it was for me to have done that to him after Christmas. How it much hurt him. Because now I could see how I'd respond if he sent me a text telling me it was over.

"I'm sorry."

"For which part, Emery?" He flung out his arms. Ozzy seemed to sense his agitation, pawing at his leg.

"Everything. Nothing… I don't know."

"That's the problem." He placed his hands on his hips, frustration pulsing off him. "You are trying so hard to do what you think is right, thinking you're protecting Addison, that you ended up fucking us all."

The sting of his comment hit home, causing me to lash back. "I wasn't the only one. I sat at your bedside at the hospital. I knew how it appeared to everyone. I realized Addison was suspicious, but I didn't walk away! *You* forced me to leave."

"You were looking for an out."

"I thought so too."

"What does that mean?" He squeezed the back of his neck, looking as if he wanted to punch a wall.

"I don't know." I fiddled with the leashes, not able to stop what wanted to follow. "I just know I miss you." My voice shrunk, going very small. "I can't eat, I can't sleep… I can't *breathe*." *Without you.*

Mason froze, his muscles locking up. It took him a while before he heaved out a sigh. "Same."

It was not some great love confession. It only tangled us more in the unknown, the area between lovers, friends, and strangers.

Ozzy whimpered, circling around Mason, pulling my focus to the dog's distress, reminding me of a golden retriever I had worked with when I was in high school. She could smell when someone's blood sugar was low, coming from a home of a diabetic. She did the same thing Ozzy was doing.

"Have you eaten?"

"What?" Mason peered around like one of us had lost our minds.

"Dog senses are powerful. They can pick up on things such as your blood sugar being low."

He rubbed his forehead, looking down at Ozzy, stroking his fur to calm him down. "Haven't been much in the mood to eat lately either."

In a moment, I made a decision, not wanting to think past it.

"There is a sandwich truck next to the dog park." I licked at my lips nervously. "If you'd like to join us."

He half scoffed and snorted, his head wagging, bemused by the flip in this conversation.

"He loves the meatball one." I nodded at Ozzy, who sat close to him, whimpering softly.

"Well." Mason smiled down at the dog, picking up his leash. "Guess we need to get Ozzy his sandwich."

I had no idea what I was doing, if this was smart or not, but being near him… it felt like my lungs could finally inhale air.

My heart could beat again.

Chapter 34
Emery

With a few days off work, most of the week I found myself back in Mason's garage, with or without the dogs, sitting on a stool, watching him work.

We hadn't spoken about our fight, both of us knowing we were still at an impasse, acting like friendship was the only thing being offered, while my hormones said differently. Observing closely how his body would lean over the engine, showing off his round ass, his muscles flexing as he fixed a part, his t-shirt clinging to his chest. It was hard to remember anything past wanting to jump him.

"Oh, I forgot to tell you." He finished tightening something in the engine, twisting around to me, a smile hinting on his lips, leaning back on the car.

"What?"

"I passed my GED. I'm officially graduated and out of high school."

"Mason, that's incredible. Congratulations!"

He folded his arms over his chest, his grin turning more sheepish. "Got a seven hundred."

"What?" I gaped. That was exceptional. The highest score you could get was an eight hundred. "Holy shit! That's amazing!" Not thinking, I jumped off my chair, leaping for him, my arms circling around him in a congratulatory hug. The moment he wrapped me up in his arms, I felt it deep in my bones. It was like coming home.

He tucked his face into my neck, inhaling deeply, the feel of his breath heating my skin, igniting my veins on fire. We held on for a long time before I tipped back. Only an inch apart, his eyes dropped to my mouth, our breaths mixing, our chests moving in sync.

213

"Really, I'm so proud of you," I said softly.

"Thanks." His finger lifted, brushing hair behind my ear, his eyes tracking mine. How could a simple touch make me tremble? Mason had a power over me I couldn't explain. I had lived so long wanting security, choosing safety over what might actually make me happy.

And he made me happy.

No longer wanting to fight what was between us, I leaned forward, my mouth grazing his. He let me move first before his lips responded, claiming mine wholly. Our kiss was slow and deep, filled with so much passion and emotion. It felt different from any of our others. There wasn't any rush, no timeline.

As if we had a future.

His tongue parted my lips, deepening the kiss, letting me feel it penetrate my bones. Declaring me as his, etching his name into every fiber.

"Mason?" Grace's voice sang out to us, her head peeking into the garage. "Oh, I'm so sorry."

I tried to jerk back, but Mason didn't let me go, holding me so close there was no mistaking the intimacy between us. His attention remained hungrily on my mouth for another beat before he exhaled and slowly dropped his arms away from me.

"What do you need, Grandma?"

"Just wanted to tell you they are driving up now," she reported, then smiled at me. "Hello, dear."

"Hi, Grace." I gulped, still shocked by her nonplussed attitude at seeing Mason and me together. Did she not realize who I was? Or think I was some other girl?

"Shit." Mason frowned. "I forgot."

"You forgot?" Grace replied.

"I had my mind elsewhere." He smirked, his gaze moving over me as if I were the cause.

"Well, I have some refreshments inside." Grace shuffled back for the door. "Good to see you, Emery." She smiled warmly at me again, her focus sharp and clear, not mistaking who I was, before she closed the door.

Taking in that Grace seemed perfectly okay catching us kissing, I barely gave notice to the silver-colored Lexus parking in front of the house.

"Sorry, I totally forgot about this."

"About what?"

"You don't have to stay," he continued, his attention going to the car. "Honestly, I'd run while you can. Going to be pretty intense." His mouth brushed the crown of my head, kissing it softly, his mood shifting to somber. He turned for the exit, his shoulders stiffening, his head tipping back as if he was preparing for battle. An emotional one. I instantly wanted to protect him. To shelter him from what was coming.

He stepped out of the garage, heading for the visitors climbing out of the car. I came out right behind him, my hand threading with his, giving him support. I instinctively knew he needed me by his side. I watched an older couple come around together, their attention on Mason.

"Hi, you must be Mason?" The woman was the first to speak.

My world slid from under me.

My brain stuttered, not comprehending what I was seeing. The woman turned to look at me politely, but her head snapped back, her eyes going to where my hand linked with Mason's, widening with shock and confusion. "Em-Emery?"

Her husband approached her side, his gray eyebrows furrowed in a bushy row. "Emery? I don't understand." He shook his head in confusion. "What are you doing here?"

I stepped back. *No. This can't be happening.* The ground dissolved, pulling me down like quicksand, ripping the oxygen out of my lungs. How was this possible? Why were they here?

Alisa and John Roberts stood right in front of me. Not belonging in this world, not fitting here at Mason's. My past and present collided and crashed into each other, shattering me into pieces.

My lungs collapsed, making it hard for me to breathe, slowing time.

Mason looked back and forth. "How do you know each other?"

Alisa's mouth pinned, her frame rigid. "Emery is our daughter-in-law." Her eyes went between us, her voice taut. "She was married to our son Ben."

"Ben?" The name clicked in and Mason went so utterly still, I couldn't even see him breathing. His head snapped to me like he wanted Alisa to be wrong, begging me to refute it. "Your married name was Roberts? I-I thought it was Campbell?"

"I changed it back to my maiden name," I whispered. Even focusing solely on Mason, I could feel Alisa's penetrating gaze on us, picking up every nuance.

"You dropped my son's last name?" Alisa gripped her purse tightly. "Our last name?"

Accusing. Condemning. Bitter.

"Emery?" John cluelessly peered around. "I still don't understand how you are here." Because fate was twisted and sick. "We thought when you moved away, gave all his stuff up, you no longer wanted to be part of his life."

I couldn't breathe, dots sprinkling my vision, sensing I was about to be swallowed into the void. Mason's eyes were the one thing keeping me afloat and the very thing drowning me.

"How did you know about Mason? Only Alisa and I had the paperwork." John still utterly befuddled.

"Please," I said so low it only hummed in my throat, my attention still on Mason, acid lining my throat. "Please, no." I mentally pleaded for this not to be true.

I took another step away, wanting to flee before they could say it, escape the truth, live in the innocence of a few moments ago. To not face this unbearable certainty.

"How did you know Mason received Ben's heart?" John stared right at me.

His words snapped my last hold on hope, plunging me under. Everything blurred, time no longer making any sense. My body and mind separated, taking me back to the day Ben died. To the despair I thought I had finally escaped.

It came flooding back to me in the most cruel, horrendous way. Punishing me for moving on. For daring to be happy.

A sob hurtled up my throat. My mind and body went on the defense, pulling me away from what was happening. The pain. I turned and ran, hearing my name being called behind me. I couldn't stop, feeling fate crawling up from the grave and pulling me back down under, smothering me with the thump of my husband's heart, turning me crazy, like I could hear it beating under the floorboards.

Haunting me. Tormenting me.

Ben was dead, but his heart continued to live on… finding me once again.

"Emery!" My name rang out louder behind me, my legs not moving fast enough, tears burning my vision. I reached my front door, pushing through with force, causing Addison to leap up from the sofa, her eyes widening seeing my state, then to the person charging in behind me.

"Emery, wait!" Mason caught the door before it could close on him, reaching for me.

"No!" I screamed, whirling around to face him, though I couldn't directly look at him. "Go back! Alisa and John are waiting for you."

"Alisa and John?" Addy's voice tapped at my ear, her confusion at hearing Ben's parents' names, but I wasn't able to put my focus on her, my legs barely able to hold me up.

"Fuck them!" Mason growled. "What the hell is going on?"

"What is going on?" A wild laugh burst out of me. "Fate really wants to screw with me because for one moment, I found happiness again. I'm being punished for moving on. For being with you!" Anxiety pumped my lungs roughly. "Did you know about Ben? Was this some sick joke?"

"You think I planned this?" His arms went out wide, his emotion matching mine. "I somehow got you to move down the street so I could seduce the widow? What the fuck, Emery?" he bellowed. "If anything, I should ask you that. Maybe it was you tracking me down. Screwing me to get close to him again?"

"Fuck you!" I shoved at his chest, and for one second, I felt his heartbeat against my palm. The heart which was out to break me again. I tore my hands away with a cry.

"All I knew was his last name was Roberts. Nothing else. I didn't want to know anything more. I left it up to them if they wanted to meet me or not. I thought it was done until they contacted me a few months ago." He moved up to me, anger locking up his muscles. "I knew nothing about you. You introduced yourself as Campbell. How the fuck would I have known?"

"Get out, Mason." I felt vomit pooling at the back of my throat. "I can't do this."

"Tough!" His feet stumbled me back into the wall. "You don't always have the final say. You don't think this is freaking me out too? That I don't feel terrified and gutted?" he roared.

"Hey!" Addison yelled, trying to get in between us, but neither of us paid her any attention.

"That everything I thought I felt, what you felt, was real? The only thing you might even care about me is this organ in my chest? As if you two found each other again, like some sick romance story, and I'm actually inconsequential and don't fucking matter." He slammed his hand against his heart. "All you were drawn to was *him*."

"What are you talking about?" Addison stepped back, her eyes popping wide between us. "What is he talking about?" She looked at me, piecing together the agony on my face with what he had just said. "No, no way." She gaped at Mason's chest. "That's not true, right?" She pleaded with me, but I could not save her from the pain I was already sinking in. "You're the one who got my Uncle Ben's *heart*?"

217

Hearing her say it out loud, my legs bowed, his nearness ripping me into shreds. "Go..." I begged, sobs hiccupping in my throat.

"No," he snapped.

"Mason, go!" Addison yanked on his arm, moving him away from me.

"No!" He tried to move back for me, my body folding over itself, the misery no longer staying in.

"Can't you see you're making it worse?" She wiggled in between us, pushing him back. "Please, Mason."

Agony carved over his face, a noise of grief coming up his throat. "Emery..."

"Leave!" Addy demanded. "You are hurting her more."

His lids shut briefly, his shoulders sagging, grief breaking him. A noise came up his throat, sounding like utter agony. He turned and left the house, slamming the door with a crash.

I buckled to the floor, wails curling me over.

Addison's arms came around me, holding me tight as my life came apart again, reminding me...

This was how a heart breaks.

Chapter 35
Emery

Once again, I lived in suspended time, where nothing made sense, and time held no meaning to me. Even when the sunbeams reached my room, all I felt was darkness. This almost felt worse than Ben's death because I was not only reliving that, but I was in a fresh hell. Another level of grief and loss.

Day or night, it was the same to me. I barely noticed when my sister showed up, trying to get me to eat or talk. I knew Addison must have called her, probably scared and confused herself, which made it all so much worse because I couldn't comfort her. Even during my dark times after Ben's death, I was there for my niece, knowing how much she hurt too.

This time, something felt broken. Whatever core belief I had once in myself was gone.

I questioned every moment I was with Mason. Did I subconsciously know? Was it why I was drawn to him? Was anything I felt real? Or was it this cruel cosmic joke?

Every time Mason was deep inside me, his heart pounding wildly against mine... it was *my husband's* heart. It seemed like I was sharing the bed with my husband and my lover at the same time. My mind couldn't accept it. Couldn't face this new level of guilt, finding myself apologizing to Ben as if I should be punished for moving on.

For moving on with Mason.

"Brought you some dinner." Harper came into my room again, a tray in her hands.

I didn't move.

A heavy sigh came from her, and she sat the tray on my nightstand.

"You need to eat something." I felt the weight of her body press down on my mattress. "Emery, I know this is a lot to deal with, but you're going to get through it."

It felt just the opposite, grief blinding me to anything beyond pain, where simple things like breathing was a burden.

"Both work and the shelter called. I told them you were really sick."

Silence was her only response.

She blew out again. "I can't imagine what you must be going through. What you must be feeling." She rubbed my shoulder. "I know this must bring back so much pain and guilt. As though you didn't have enough of it already. But maybe you are looking at this all wrong." Harper paused. "Maybe this isn't some sort of punishment. What if this was Ben's way of leading you to happiness? To your future?"

I squeezed my eyes together tightly.

"You can pretend all you want," Harper stated gently. "But you *love* him."

My lids squeezed firmer, fighting back the emotion that stirred up.

"And it terrifies you. It would be to anyone who's lost someone before. Deep down, you're petrified of going through all the pain again."

Because I would. Mason might have years ahead, but it was still limited. I would go in knowing I'd lose him down the road. Lose Ben *and* Mason at once.

"Mason might have Ben's heart, but he's *not* Ben. So don't let the memory of one take away your future with the other. Maybe coming here was for a reason. Maybe against all odds, Mason *is* the reason. He's not meant to break you, but to heal you." Her hand squeezed my arm. "I had never seen you so happy. You *glowed*, Emery. So, fuck what everyone thinks, including me, and especially Alisa and John. They don't get a say in your life anymore. And I want to believe Ben would want you to be happy, not hating yourself for living your life."

She dropped her hand away, and a long silence grew between us. "Just think about it. If it wasn't Alisa and John who got out of the car, just another couple, would you be with him right now, even knowing you had a limited time with him? Because that's your answer. That is where your heart lies." The bed creaked as she rose up. "Next time, I come in with a bucket of water and soap. Time for some tough love." She closed the door behind her, leaving me with my thoughts.

I knew where I'd be right now if it wasn't for John and Alisa showing up. I knew what my heart wanted, which didn't change the facts.

Now, I feared any time I saw Mason, all I would see was Ben.

Chapter 36
Mason

Could you detest your own heartbeat?

The very thing keeping me alive, I wanted to rip out of my chest just so I could breathe again. To stop feeling every thump like it was mocking me. It was his life I was living, not my own, as if I were a backseat driver. I both hated and was indebted to a man who gave me life, but then took it away anyway.

Because he would always have Emery.

The day we got the call telling me they found me a match, I remember Grandma crying while my grandpa tried to hide it, but I heard him in the bedroom later, sobbing his heart out with relief.

I was happier for them than myself because my grandparents had lost their only son. Losing their only grandchild would have destroyed them.

There was a mix of fear and surreal anticipation when I woke up having someone else's organ pumping in my chest, keeping me alive when the man no longer was.

A man who had a life, a family, a *wife…*

Acid drove up my throat, and I leaned over the engine of my car, trying to stay balanced. For three weeks, I stood out here, pretending to be occupied with restoring the GTO. Fixing things had always kept my mind busy, but my mind barely stayed on the tasks. I moved mindlessly around, not caring at all about the object I spent so much time on. Everything felt pointless, and I couldn't seem to get my feet under me.

My emotions were a whole other beast. I would swing from numb to so fucking angry I was shaking, punching the shit out of my weight bag until I broke it off the chain. Furious at fate, at Emery, at Ben, myself, and at Alisa and John for wanting to meet me. For showing up right when I got her back.

For just a few minutes before they got out of the car, I had her. In my arms, choosing me. Now, I'd never know if it was me or not, and the only thing she saw when she looked at me was Ben. The life they could have had together if he lived instead of me.

The thought had me rolling my shoulders, moving around the garage, heading for the weight bag I had strung back up, needing an outlet. My knuckles cracked against the surface, spearing pain through my hands. It gave me a rush, an indication I was still in there, that I was alive.

Out of the corner of my eye, I saw a car pass down the road toward Main Street. I didn't even fully look, and I knew who it was, my gut twisting with awareness. A thousand spider webs linked me to her, making me feel her every move like a vibration. It had been this way from day one. Before, I might have found satisfaction in it, but now I felt only doubt and resentment.

What if the part which felt her, connected to her, was never me… but her husband?

Grunts huffed from me as I hit harder, sweat dripping down my back, soaking my t-shirt.

"Don't want to know who you're imagining that bag to be." A voice came from behind me, stopping me in my tracks. My head snapped around to see a girl standing at the entrance of my garage.

I wheezed in, taking a moment to make sure I wasn't hallucinating.

"Addison," I muttered her name in almost a question.

Addison folded her arms across her ribs, her lips pursing, gazing at the ground. I didn't move or speak, just watched with reserved curiosity. It hurt to see her. She was Emery to me, the connection which brought me into their lives. There was enough family resemblance to stab the knife in deeper.

Her shoe nudged at the crack in the foundation, taking a deep breath. "I never thought I'd come here." A slice of grief shook her voice. She licked her lips, clearing her throat, walking in deeper into my garage.

Okay.

I slowly followed her to where she stopped at my workbench, her fingers tracing over some of my tools, picking one up. "What the hell does this even do?"

"Hose clamp pliers." What the hell was happening right now?

"I won't go into all the jokes you could make about that." She snorted, putting it down.

222

"Addison?" This time the question/warning was clear. "You're not here to talk about tools."

Her entire torso moved as she blew out. "No, I'm not." She turned away from the bench, nervously moving to the chair, though she didn't sit. "I'm here for my aunt."

My shoulders jerked back, putting up a barrier around me, ready to get leveled by her.

She perched herself on the edge of the stool, her arms crossing again.

"I don't know if I'll ever be okay with what you guys did." Her lashes batted faster. "It still hurts."

"I know," I uttered. "I'm sorry."

"God, that makes me feel even more pathetic." She tucked her blonde hair behind her ear, not looking at me.

The phrase I'm sorry wanted to replay again, but I swallowed it back.

"But yeah, I liked you a lot…" She bit her lip. "Or maybe I thought I did," she muttered. "Because as much as it hurt, I realized watching my aunt over the last few weeks, I didn't even come close to actually hurting."

I stayed utterly silent, letting her talk.

"It took me a while to get over my own shock. It's hard seeing you now. Though I think it cured my crush on you." She laughed, then made a face, trying badly at humor. "Like trying to kiss my uncle or something now."

"Funny."

Her expression went somber. "You don't understand… my Uncle Ben…" Her voice broke off, emotion clogging her throat. "He was everything to me. My dad is a real piece of shit most of the time. Uncle Ben was the dad I never had. And when he died? It was awful." She shook her head, blinking back the tears. "I honestly didn't know if my aunt would be happy again."

My gaze dropped to the ground, hating I was so fucking jealous of this man I didn't know but could never escape.

"That was…" She waited for me to peer back up at her. "Until you."

Her declaration sunk me against the workbench.

"She laughed, she smiled, she was the person I remembered. She came back to life. Because of you." She wiggled as if this were hard for her to say out loud. "And maybe even from the start, I knew deep down, there was something between you two. I mean, I look back now and think… hello? How did I not see it? It was so obvious. The sexual tension… I was such an idiot." She rubbed her temple with a dry chuckle. Her gaze returned to me after a few beats, her expression somber. "What I'm saying is, I might not be totally okay with you two being together, but I think I will be eventually."

"Eventually?" My forehead crinkled. "What are you talking about? There is no eventually for your aunt and me. It's over."

"Why?" She pushed off the chair, going on defense, confusing the hell out of me.

"Why?" I repeated. "What do you mean, why? Did you miss the whole I have her dead husband's heart?" The anger at the situation boiled up again.

Addison flinched but grew more forceful. "So?"

"So?" I sounded like a fucking parrot. "That's not something either of us can easily get over. It's not as if she likes pineapple on her pizza, and I don't."

"She likes margarita pizza. She hates pineapple on pizza."

"Missing the point, Addison," I growled.

"Am I?" She tilted her head. "Maybe you are. I'm not saying it's not bizarre and kinda creepy."

"See!"

"But…" She held up her hand. "What if this was all meant to be?"

"I don't believe in that crap."

"Normally I don't either, but my god, Mason. Of all the people in all the world, *you* got my uncle's heart? And we just happened to move to not only the same town as you, but the *exact* street you just happen to live on? And I happen to get a crush on you and introduce you to my aunt?" She wagged her head in disbelief. "What are the chances? The one guy, out of all the ones she could have chosen. It was *you* she has fallen in love with."

"What?" I jerked back, feeling like I had been punched in the gut, all the air leaving my body. "No, she hasn't."

"You think I'd be here otherwise? Jesus, Mason, it took everything I had to come here," she retorted. "I have seen her go through loss, be crippled by grief and agony. But this is worse."

"Worse?"

"At least with Uncle Ben, you could see the emotion. Even if she faked her smiles and pretended to laugh, she had something still in her trying to survive." Addison choked up. "There is nothing now. She goes to work, to the shelter, and home. The animals don't even bring her much joy. There is nothing behind her eyes. She's there, but she isn't alive."

Shit if that didn't sound like me. Two lives destroyed by a single heart.

"I'm sorry, but I'm not the person to help."

"Why not?" she wailed. "I know you're in love with her too."

I could think of no defense, no rebuttal, because it was true, but it didn't change anything.

"Tell me I'm wrong."

"You don't get it!" I practically roared. "We were fighting a losing battle anyway. Everything is against us. Even time. But now?" I shook my head. "I can't ever trust when she looks at me she won't see him." I slapped my hand on my heart. "It was never me she wanted, that somehow it was always about him. She found her way back to him because *HE* is the love of her life, not *ME*."

Tears fell down Addison's face, her head dropping.

I tucked back my ire, bringing my voice back down. "I can't live my life in the shadow of someone else."

Addison sniffed, her hand wiping at her eyes, making me feel even more like an asshole.

"I'm sorry," I muttered.

She sucked in a shaky breath, taking a step back.

"You're wrong, you know." Her voice barely came out a whisper.

"About?"

"You wouldn't be living in *his* shadow." She swallowed. "He'd be living in *yours*. I think it was always you she was supposed to be with. You were her future. The love of her life. It was my uncle who gave you guys the chance to have it." Addison retreated to the exit. "So, don't you dare waste it." She darted out of my garage, disappearing back down the street.

Days or minutes passed; I didn't know. My guts were strewn over the floor, my soul gutted, my mind whirling with Addison's declarations.

My ears drummed with my pulse, like my heart was trying to communicate with me. My palm slid over my left pec, feeling the pounding of the organ. From tests, the surgeon had been nervous my immune system wouldn't accept the foreign object, rejecting the heart and putting me back at square one. Which we all knew would have been the end for me.

I didn't. My body adapted to it faster than they thought, taking it on as though it was always supposed to be there.

Maybe it was.

Maybe instead of my enemy, Ben Roberts was my ally. The man who gave me a chance at a future he could no longer have, pushing me to finish the story.

A life loving the same woman.

Chapter 37
Emery

"I'm starting an intervention."

I peered up from blankly staring at the table. Marcie dropped down on the other side of me, a cup of macaroni and cheese steaming in her hand.

"Think you need more than one person to have an intervention," I replied, poking at my untouched lunch in front of me.

"Girl, the whole office would join me. And I'm sure if I called your sister, she'd be right over."

Probably true.

"It would take Harper at least four hours to get here. I'd already be on the run by then."

Marcie shot me a look, digging into her pasta. "She went home?"

"A week ago. She has a job and life to get back to." I actually had to push her into her car, forcing her to leave. I outright lied and said I was fine. I went to work, paid my bills, and dressed myself. A fully functional adult.

Barely.

Culture praised people for "being strong," for smiling through a devastating event, for keeping their chin up and being remarkable through horror. It was only so society didn't feel uncomfortable. To have to acknowledge someone else's pain, to take it on and feel it. We lived in a world where someone would ask you how you were, but they really didn't want to know, especially the truth. The pressure to be "fine" tripled the weight on your shoulders to keep everyone else comfortable when you didn't feel strong or brave. You wanted to be home under the covers, hoping sleep could numb you for a while longer. Except I was numb all the time. I had cried my tears and screamed in anger. I had nothing left to give.

My blasé state ticked Alisa off again when she called last night.

"I know you were seeing that *boy*," she hissed in my ear. "What kind of person are you? How could you do this? He's a child, Emery! I can't even imagine what Ben would think. He'd be disgusted."

Good thing Ben won't ever know.

"Alisa…" I heard John in the background, a warning in his voice.

"No, John. This is unacceptable," she screamed into the phone. "You were married to our son. And moments after his death, you're jumping in bed with not only a child but the kid who has Ben's heart? How do you live with yourself?"

Moments after? I mourned and grieved Ben for over three years, and honestly, without Mason, I probably still would be. I was chastised if I didn't move on and punished if I did.

"I told Ben you were not the right girl for him, that you were low bred, but he didn't listen to me. He was set on marrying you."

"Alisa!" John yelled louder, but she didn't pay him any attention.

"I guess it's good he's gone, so he doesn't have to see what a manipulative little whore you are." she shrieked before hanging up on me.

John called me ten minutes later to apologize, telling me she was just hurting and lashing out. They still wanted me in their life, which was a lie.

Not even John wanted the constant reminder of his son's widow, especially now they knew I had been with someone else. I was no longer the person who could sit and reminisce for hours about Ben, my life with him staying frozen in time.

"Emery?" Marcie waved her hand in my face, waking me out of my stupor and fighting with myself. "Should I schedule Mason for a *cleaning* so you two can work it out?" She tried to tease, but at my flinch, her face softened. "Sorry."

"Don't be." I absently rubbed at the pain in my chest. "I need to move on, right? Maybe I should go out with Daniel." He had been slyly hinting again, he probably sensed my vulnerability.

"I will kill you." Marcie stabbed her fork in her pasta. "First, you don't even like him more than a friend, and he likes you too much, so don't do that to him. He doesn't deserve it." She tapped her finger on the table. "And second, I've seen you with Mason. Girl, I'm telling you, he is what the rest of us search our whole lives for. Don't give up on it so easily."

"Easily?" I sputtered, a streak of fury striking so fast I had to grip the table. "You think any of this has been easy?"

"No, you've fought like hell for it, mainly against yourself. That's why I don't understand. After all that, you're giving up now?"

"He has my husband's heart!" I cried out. "How can I possibly get over that?"

"Yes, it is some crappy made-for-TV-movie shit right there. Or possibly a horror flick." She picked up her fork, licking it. "Dead husband takes over the body of her new lover, pretending to be her new beau as he stalks and kills her... called, The Haunted Heart, or," she chirped, "The Killer Heart. Nah, that's to on the nose."

"Marcie." I palmed my face, my mouth twitching with a laugh. "You are seriously sick."

"That's why you love me." She bit down on her macaroni.

"This is not funny."

"Maybe not, but if anyone needs to laugh, it's you." Marcie jabbed her fork in my direction. "Come out for drinks tonight."

It was the office cocktail night.

"No." I shook my head.

"Actually, you don't have a choice." She stood up, taking her garbage to the bin. "Just for one hour at least. Then you can run home and hide under your blankie."

"Marcie."

"I will come get your ass if I have to, Emery." She gave me the look that said not to test her. "Two hours, that's all."

"You said one!"

"It will keep going up the longer you fight me," she threatened like I was a kid about to get a whooping. "See you at six thirty."

"Yeah." I huffed, feeling like a brooding teen.

When you felt dead inside, the last thing you wanted to be around was cheerful people. It reflected what you didn't have.

Happiness.

$$\sim\!\!\!\wedge\!\!\!\upharpoonright\!\!\!\wedge\!\!\!\upharpoonright\!\!\!\wedge\!\!\!\heartsuit$$

Happy hour was in full swing by the time I stepped in. It took a lot of encouragement and blatant threats from Marcie to finally get me dressed and out.

"Fifty-nine minutes left," I muttered to her the moment she came to pull me further into the pub.

"You have 119 minutes left," she stated. "Remember, it went up to two hours."

"I hate you."

"I'm okay with that." She looped her arm in mine, heading us straight for the bar. "Two margaritas," she said to the bartender.

The music was loud, and the bar was packed, everyone feeling spring was officially in the air. My gaze ran over the room, spotting most of the people I worked with. Daniel was chatting with the newest hire, a sweet girl named Molly, who worked the front desk. I watched her laugh at something he said, her hand touching his arm. He chuckled, leaning in closer, their body language pointed toward each other as if no one else existed. I had no idea if they were just being friendly or something might be kindling, but there was no doubt she was who Daniel deserved. Someone who didn't see anyone else but him.

"Here you go." Marcie handed me a drink, peering out at the full bar. "Guess you can be my wing woman. Ohhh, he's hot. He and his friend are both staring over here."

"What about vanilla cup Tim?"

"Oh, we ended it. It was fun, but it ran its course." She shrugged, already wiggling her fingers in hello at the new prospects. "No big deal."

No. Big. Deal.

No heartache or misery. No pining or an ache so deep, she could no longer breathe. No being curled up in the fetal position staring blankly at her walls for days. Feeling gutted and empty.

Just over. Simple. Clean. No hard feelings.

What Mason and I were supposed to be. What we agreed on, but we never were.

I missed him so much. I felt adrift. Dull and heavy. Nothing had meaning. Nothing felt right. My chest constantly hurt, making it hard to breathe.

Like missing a piece of my soul.

The loss of Ben was horrific, but the loss of Mason…

"Oh my god," I whispered, realization hitting me.

"Oh, their coming over!" Marcie muttered over to me, flattening down her hair.

The two nice-looking guys nodded at us, heading our way. A strange panic ruffled up my spine, urging me to run. They held no interest to me. Not one bit.

All I wanted was *him*. All I *ever* wanted was him.

Mason James.

"I can't be here." I sucked in, understanding crashing over me in waves, waking me out of my numbness, like I was woken from a coma.

"What?" Marcie swiveled to me. "What's wrong?"

"I don't want to meet anyone else."

"It's okay. You don't have to tonight."

"No." I shook my head, my eyes burning. "You don't get it. I don't *see* Ben." I knew it came out wrong, my head jumbled. "I see *him*. I want *him*." His laugh, his smile, his voice, his soul. I heaved in and out. "I'm in love with Mason." The need to be with him roared through me like he was calling me to him.

"Yeah." She grinned. "You're now figuring that out?"

I shoved my drink at her. "I've got to go."

"Oh, girl, finally." Her hands full she flicked her head at me. "Go get your man!"

I shoved past the guys heading for us, running out of the bar and to my car. Every light seemed against me, a panic fluttering between my ribs as I grew more and more desperate to get to him. It seemed like hours before I skidded my car in front of his house, climbing out. My stomach wobbled when I noticed the garage door was open.

He was here.

I strode into the garage, gulping back at seeing him again. His tall, broad frame bent over the car. His dark hair was messy. He looked so hot. Everything about him made me come back to life; I could finally exhale. "Mason?"

He jerked up, his eyes taking me in. "Emery?" He stood up, his throat bobbing. "What are you doing here?"

"I was out tonight." I stepped further in, nerves taking over my voice as butterflies banged against my rib cage. "Some guys approached us. And I realized I didn't want to be there. I didn't want to meet anyone."

He slammed down the hood, turning away from me. "Thanks for letting me know."

"What I mean is…" I was messing this all up. "All I could think about was you."

His shoulders strained, his head bowing.

"All I want is you."

He inhaled, his voice low and thick. "I can't keep doing this with you." He slowly circled to face me. "Tell me, what changed from a month ago? When I was the one begging for you to talk to me? You kicked me out. Wanted nothing to do with me."

"Jesus, Mason, I needed to process everything." I took another step closer. "Finding you have Ben's heart is not easy to accept. I'm still struggling with it."

230

"And you don't think it's hard for me?" he gritted. "It didn't absolutely destroy me? That the worst thing about that day was finding out my donor's wife was the same woman I was sleeping with? And the fact when you looked at me, you didn't see me anymore."

Biting my lip, I dipped my head. "I didn't know how to handle it. I'm sorry."

"I won't live in his shadow," he growled, the power behind his voice mounting. "Knowing every time you look at me, you see him. Want him. It will kill me far more, knowing the woman I'm *so fucking in love with* secretly wishes I was someone else." He lashed out at me. "I will not settle for second best."

"Second best?" I exclaimed, my head shaking in disbelief. "Oh my god, you don't get it!" I marched up to him. "I loved Ben so damn much. I never thought I could love someone else again." My body shook with life, with the truth I was about to utter. "Then I met you, and you ripped everything I was sure of to shreds. You forced me out of my safety and comfort and made me see and feel things I never had before. Everything was against us, yet I still couldn't fight you. I never feel more alive than when I'm with you. If anything, you have this all backward. I dreamed of you before we even met. You somehow have always been there, casting a shadow on *him*. The moment you looked at me across the field, deep down, I knew. It's *always* been you." My voice wobbled with emotion. "When I look at you, I only see the man I'm falling for."

He took a staggering breath, his chest moving up and down violently, staying silent for a long time.

"Mason?"

"That's even more reason I can't consciously do this to you."

"Do what to me?"

"Leave."

"You going somewhere?" I snapped back, my anger rising.

"You know what I mean."

"No, I don't. Explain it to me." I grabbed at his arm. "Because all tonight showed me is I don't want to be with anyone else."

"You want to be with someone you know will die?" Fury coated each word, and he stretched his arms, daring me to really look at him. "All I will cause you is grief and agony all over again."

"Yes!" I yelled. "Because I'd rather live a short life with you, living it the fullest we can, than live a long life feeling as if part of me is missing. I'm just filling time until I go," I bellowed. "Plus, you don't know what will happen in the future. I could die first."

231

"Don't say that."

"Why not? You don't know. I could get into an accident tomorrow. Look at Ben. He was healthy, was supposed to live a long life, but he didn't. You are jumping us ahead to something we don't know yet. You could find another heart. There might be technologies we don't know yet." Tears formed under my lids. "And I want to believe he saved you on purpose, and all this wasn't for nothing. And this life, with you, is where I'm supposed to be." I motioned to us. "I want to be by your side during all the ups and downs. I want my life with you. My future with you." I took a huge gulp of air. "I love you," I croaked out. "I am so completely in love with you. I have been since the moment we met."

For a moment, he watched me, his nose flaring, his dark gaze wild. A growl vibrated in his throat.

It was my only warning.

He moved in a blink, cupping the back of my head, his mouth covering mine, seizing me like he would raze me to the ground. Searing hot desire rushed between my thighs. His mouth was desperate and hard, overflowing with pain, love, grief, and desire.

"I'm so fucking in love with you too," he muttered against my mouth before he claimed it again. Taking our emotions out on each other, vicious for blood, ruthless to feel life pumping in our veins. His tongue pushed deeper into my mouth, forcing a moan from my throat. He picked me and tossed me up onto the workbench, pushing between my legs, his mouth devouring mine.

"Fuck. I've missed you," he rumbled, biting down on my lip, tugging and sucking on it, making my pussy throb with need.

"I've missed you too." I pulled him closer to me as he kissed my tears away.

Ripping my shirt over my head, he unhooked my bra, baring my breasts to him. With the garage light on, anyone could see us clearly, giving us that extra dose of raw need.

"Fuck," he rumbled, taking one in his mouth. My back arched as his tongue flicked, his teeth scraping over my nipple.

"Oh god." My whole body pulsed with need, the time apart only adding to my desperation. I tore at his shirt, wrenching it off him. He paused as I followed the scar down with my fingers. "This scar is mine." I leaned over, kissing the raised skin. "You were marked for *me*."

His chest heaved as he recaptured my lips, consuming me. He breathed me in and took everything left of my soul, possessing the rest of me. "I need you now." He grabbed my hand, yanking me off the table and pulling me toward the house.

"Mason." I stumbled after him, one arm covering my bare chest. "What are you doing? Your grandparents?"

"They are asleep and deaf as doornails." He marched me down the hall, kicking his bedroom door closed the moment we were inside. He took me in with hungry eyes. "Strip," he demanded.

Heat flooded my skin as his hungry gaze watched me take off my jeans, slinking down my underwear, leaving me in nothing.

He grabbed me, pulling me into him, his lips taking mine. "I want to take my time with you. Lick every inch of your body."

"You can do that after." I went on my toes, my mouth grazing his. "Right now, I need you to fuck me, Mason. Show me you're mine."

A guttural noise clawed up his throat. He tossed me back on his bed, yanking off his jeans and briefs. As he climbed over me, his hands wrenched my legs wide apart, and his mouth dipped between my legs, licking through me as he traveled up. "I've craved nothing but this pussy." He dragged his cock between my folds.

A loud moan curled me up into him, my veins on fire. "Mason."

"I'm not going to be gentle."

"I never want you to be." I wanted it rough and dirty, deep and passionate.

I wanted us.

His heavy erection rubbed against my entrance, making me cry out. "Please." I bucked into him, my muscles shaking with need.

"Jesus, I can feel how wet you are. How bad you want me." He grunted as he drove into me. Both of us cried out, his dick stretching me, my fingers digging into the sheets as he pushed in deeper.

I would never get over how he felt, how our bodies moved together, how much pleasure he could draw from me. I became obsessed. Addicted.

"Shit!" He drew back, slamming into me again, my head hitting the headboard. "Emery?" His teeth clenched together, and I could feel him trying to hold back.

"I want it all. Ruin me. Make me only yours."

He growled, pulling out of me and flipping me over. Gripping my hips, he thrust back into me.

My cry got stuck in my throat as he took control, taking all his anger and pain out on me. Pummeling me so hard, tears leaked down my eyes as both pain and pleasure consumed me, taking control of my vocals and my mind.

He pulled my hair, making my pussy clench down on him. He hissed, pulling me up. "Ride it." He shoved a pillow between my legs. "I want you on my pillowcase. Dripping on it. Soaking it."

Damn, his dirty mouth turned me on. A cry pelted from my lungs, utter bliss taking over my body as my clit rubbed against the fabric, his cock spearing me so deeply my nails embedded into the wood.

One palm wrapped around my neck as he thrust in deeper, squeezing his fingers just enough for my entire body to ignite.

I lost all control, no longer trying to stay quiet, my eyes rolling back. "Mason…" I rasped out. "Oh god!"

He yanked out again, flipping me on my back. "I need to watch you come. Know you are mine." He wrapped my wrists with one hand, yanking them above my head as he torturously sank into me, inch by inch.

"Mason." I snarled, my muscles quaking, my hip pitching up, trying to get him deeper inside me.

"Watch me, Emery. Watch my cock sink into your pussy. Watch me fuck you."

Fire crackled through me as he rolled his hips, the sound of him entering me echoing off his walls. A deep moan hummed in my throat as he worked my body. Harder and harder, he hit deeper and deeper.

"Fuck!" Something snapped in both of us, unleashing. He hammered into me, stretching my body, making me feel every strike. "This is mine. Always." He sat back on his heels, grabbing my hips, pulling me closer, making me cry out. I started to spasm around him. "Fucking come for me."

My body exploded, my sight going dark as sparks danced behind my lids. I know I screamed, my body almost convulsing as my orgasm engulfed me.

"Fuuuck!" He drove in with craze, splintering more quakes through me, before a loud bellow tore from him, his hot cum releasing inside me.

His body fell over mine, his weight solid and amazing against me, his cock still twitching. Our lungs duked it out against each other, trying to claim the air in the room.

It took us several moments for us to regain reality.

"That was… unbelievable." His lips trailed over my neck, kissing the spot behind my ear. "This is what I want. Now and forever."

"We might have to get out of bed sometimes. Especially for those pancakes you still need to make for me."

He scoffed, his teeth grazing my skin. "I meant I want you. *Us*. We live life the way we want, and we don't give a shit what anyone else thinks.

Because they will. They will try to tear us apart."

Mainly me. I would be the villain. The harlot. The cougar. They'd call me names, saying our relationship was wrong. Judging us on their values and not the truth of our story. Not understanding what we had been through, that the fates led us to each other.

He was worth every insult, every obstacle, every fight I would battle.

I cupped his face, leaning him back to look into his eyes. "I don't care. You are worth the fight."

Kissing me, he rolled off me, pulling me against him. "You sure you can handle everyone knowing you're fucking a twenty-year-old? Because my grandparents might be deaf, but I'm pretty sure our whole neighborhood heard us, and I plan on making you scream as much as I can. Very loudly."

Hell yeah, I could. After all we had been through, I could take anything, knowing I was crawling into bed with him every night.

"Fuck them all." I snuggled my head on his chest.

"Going to be a full bedroom then."

I laughed, my fingers running up and down his scar, feeling I finally found peace.

Home.

We had a lot of hurdles ahead of us, but nothing felt insurmountable as long as his heart continued to beat, and he was by my side.

We'd fight like hell for the rest.

I lived so long staying in my box. Picking safety because I feared being hurt. And in the end, I got hurt anyway. There was no security in life. With Mason, I didn't want to fear anything. I wanted to live life the way we wanted, not how we should.

With my ear pressed against his chest, I listened to his heartbeat.

The heart that caused me to break into pieces.

The heart that helped put me back together.

Two men.

One heart.

And a love, that found each other, against all odds.

Epilogue
Emery

Six years later

The warm spring breeze flittered through my hair, brushing lightly at my face as I lowered to my knees in the grass. My eyes misted as I placed the flowers in my hand on the grave. My fingers brushed over the engraving on the stone, tracing the name James.

I won't cry. I won't cry.

Death had taken so many people I loved. Every day, I tried to live in remembrance of them, for what they had given and taught me while they were here. Life ends, but love doesn't. It continues on in the living.

"Ma-ma!" My fourteen-month-old son waddled up, still struggling to keep steady steps, his hands flailing the flowers he demanded to hold. Dark mop of hair, almost black eyes, and a slight dimple, Benjamin Neal James was the spitting image of his father, reminding me each day of the gift I was given.

My son's birth coincided with death, as though life had to balance itself, taking and giving with joy and heartache.

"Put them here." I pointed to the headstone.

Ben toddled up to the grave, kissing the name on the stone with a loud smack, completely melting my heart.

"Very sweet." My throat choked with tears.

Still gripping the flowers, he plopped down on my leg, whacking them around, dusting pollen all over me. I pulled him tighter, kissing the back of his head, trying to keep the sorrow at bay.

So much loss, but at the same time, I had gained so much.

Ben squirmed out of my grip, never wanting to sit still for long, leaping back up, waving his flowers.

"Dada!" he belted, drawing eyes from all around the cemetery, pulling my gaze to the figure strolling up the path. Instant joy and desire mingled through me, sparking my heart to life as only he could.

"Hey, little man." Mason swung Ben up into his arm, kissing his chubby cheek. With a devious smile, he strolled over to me, bending over. "Hey, sexy." He kissed me, happiness bubbling into my veins.

My husband was a total FILF. At twenty-six, Mason was sexy as hell, and he would keep getting hotter. He got the attention from everyone he passed by, but with Ben bundled across him, I could hear ovaries exploding from all around me, including mine.

I never really wanted kids, or maybe I didn't want them with Ben. Because with Mason, I never had any doubt, even when he was terrified of having a child. Petrified he would leave his kid as his father had left him, but the moment I got pregnant, Mason couldn't have been more ecstatic. Every day he made sure our little boy knew how much he was loved. He stayed with him during the days, his job more flexible, while I worked, to spend every moment he could with Ben.

"You going to give those to Grandma and Grandpa?" Mason pointed at the bedraggled flowers, the stems limp in my son's grip. Mason set him down, and Ben ran to the graves, giving Grace and Neal the flowers—what was left of them anyway.

Neal passed away over three years ago, not long after Mason and I got married. And Grace passed a few days after Ben was born. Like she waited to meet him before she let go.

Mason's fingers laced with mine, pulling me up to my feet, his mouth claiming mine again. Six years together, and we only seemed to get hornier for each other. The way his mouth moved over mine, I knew the moment Ben went down for his nap later, Mason would be between my thighs, making me come so hard I'd pass out.

We lived every day as though it could be our last.

For many years, we traveled whenever we could. Zip lining in New Zealand, going on a safari in Africa. He took a cooking class in Italy, and we tried twenty-two beers in Belgium on his twenty-second birthday. He proposed to me in Cappadocia, Turkey, on my thirty-third birthday.

We planned to keep traveling. Ben already had his passport, and we were looking forward to beach time in Mexico in a month.

"Happy birthday, Grandma." Mason crouched next to Grace's

headstone, Ben snuggling between his legs, both their hands touching Grace's name. "Miss you both so much."

"Ganma!" Ben tried to mimic his dad. "Ginpa!"

Mason blinked away his sadness, kissing Ben's head and standing back up. "Ready to go to the park, little man?"

"Pak! Pak!" Ben jumped up and down.

Mason wrapped an arm around my shoulders, pulling me into him, his cheek brushing over the top of my head as we walked back to the car, Ben trotting not far in front of us.

Mason exhaled deeply.

"What?" I twined my fingers with his at my shoulder, feeling his emotions like they were my own.

"Some days it really hits me." He squeezed my hand. "Our life. How fucking lucky I am. And how easily I could have had none of this."

It was why we named Ben after my first husband. He was the very reason our son even existed. That Mason lived to be a father.

"Did you ever think when we saw each other at the game, when I came over that night—it would lead us here?"

"Strangely, yes." I leaned my head into him. "Like I said, it was always you."

"Wasn't there some fantasy of yours you thought I was in?"

"Yeah." I laughed. "One where you couldn't wait and fucked me up against the sink."

"We've done that many times now." He smirked. "Also against the washer, dryer, on my car, in my car, in the garden, on the table, in the hammock, over the hammock."

"Don't forget in a bar coat closet."

"I'll never forget that one." He leaned in, kissing my nose. "Think we need to revisit our special closet."

"Addison is coming over Friday to babysit." I wiggled my brows.

"We can pop over to the pub, see if we still got it. Wear a slinky dress like you did that night?" His mouth moved down to my lips. "Shit, I'm hard now. Don't really want a hard-on when you're going to a kid's park."

I snorted, my head shaking.

"When is nap time again? Can it be now?"

"I wish." My body was tight, ready to feel him sink into me, to have him arching my body in pleasure.

Barking caught the air, making Ben squeal and run faster for our SUV.

"Ozzy! Ozzy!" Ben chanted, the Bernese-lab wiggling around the backseat, waiting for his favorite people, which sadly was not me. Mason was Ozzy's person, next Ben, then me.

I adopted Ozzy when I realized the home he was meant for was mine. Even more so when Mason moved in and I noticed he seemed to pick up on Mason's moods. When his blood sugar got too low or something was off, he was in front of him, his paw padding his thigh before Mason had a clue anything was wrong. They became inseparable. He went with Mason on every run or even to the store. Where Mason was, Ozzy wanted to be, and when Ben came along, it was love at first sight for both of them.

Ozzy was what made me finally decide to go into service animals. From the moment the German Shepherd guarded the little girl with Down syndrome—Anita and I heard they still have never left each other's sides—I felt this drive to find matches like that. I stayed at the shelter for a long time, moving to a paid position after leaving my dental assistant job. I quickly moved to another company, which handled service animals specifically. It was crazy, and I was flying around the country a lot, a matchmaker for people with special needs and their future best friends. Some days were tough, and it wasn't all roses and happiness, but it was so fulfilling. It was even better than my dream as a teenager.

"Let's go to the park." Mason rubbed Ozzy's head through the open window, picking up Ben. Ozzy licked Ben's face until he was squealing with laughter. Mason egged it on with his own laugh.

I loved the sound of my men laughing. Their joy. I wanted to bottle it up and hold on to it when days got dark, because I knew someday they would. A day when his laughter was ripped from me, taking away my air. My heart.

The now was what I focused on.

"Hey, Mateo wants to know what to bring this Saturday?" Mason palmed his phone, stuffing it into his pocket and getting Ben into his car seat.

It was my thirty-seventh birthday this weekend. Mason was taking me out on a special date on Friday, while Addison and likely Mateo were coming to babysit Ben for the night. Then there was going to be a party on Saturday.

"Have him call Harper or Marcie. They both told me to stay out of it." I held up my hands. "Threatened they'd have Kevin arrest me if I tried." My sister and Kevin had a son, William, who was four now. Kevin, year after year, tried to get my sister to marry him, but she nixed the idea. After Joe, I think she no longer felt she needed to have that piece of paper and was perfectly fine with their life. They lived together, had a son together, and they were pretty much married, but Harper was happy forgoing the last part, and I totally supported her.

Addison was kind of following Harper, not in any hurry to get married. During a college break, Addison came back to stay with Mason and me, where she met up with some of her old friends. One of those was Mateo. They spent the whole night talking and were inseparable the rest of the vacation. All of us could see they were totally in love. They had been together almost five years now, and Mateo wanted to get married, but Addison wanted to wait until she was done with school. Following my path into dentistry, she was working on finishing her DMD. She was studying to be more specialized, which took longer. She was now working at Dr. Ramirez's office with Marcie. She and Mateo shared a small apartment across town, near Marcie. Marcie and her vanilla cup, Tim. It was six months after they ended things, they ran into each other again. They both found they hadn't moved on like they thought. They had been married five years now. Drove each other crazy, fighting passionately, but loved each other even more enthusiastically. Think their neighbors complained more than ours did.

"Kevin wouldn't mind if I borrowed those handcuffs, would he?" Mason winked at me, getting both Ben and Ozzy settled before closing the door and strolling up to me. "I could keep you very occupied while they set up."

"You're going to have to." I slipped my arms around his shoulders, tipping my forehead to his chin, feeling his mouth against my skin. This party gave me a sick sense of déjà vu, and I had already told Mason he wouldn't be going anywhere. No running, no going to get ice or beer. It was silly, but the last time I had put on a party in my backyard, my husband never came home.

A moment without Mason sent me to a dark place, bringing back all the trauma.

Loss wasn't linear. It flowed and ebbed. It snuck in on you, pulling you out like an undertow. Sometimes it was grief you hadn't even experienced yet but could feel the dark cloud hovering, moving closer.

"Hey." He brushed my hair back, his brows furrowing. "I'm right here. Be in the now with me." He muttered our mantra. I said the same to him when I saw the shadows darken his face, his eyes off in the distance.

I could never ask him not to leave me. To always be by my side. That was a promise he couldn't make; no one could really make.

"I can promise you right now." He cupped my face, knowing what I was thinking.

I blinked up at him. "I love you."

"I love you too." He kissed me softly. "Now, let's go to the park, wear out our child and dog, and then go home and fuck each other until our neighbors call the police again."

My cheeks heated. A true story. It was really embarrassing, though it never stopped us.

"Fuck them all, right?" He winked at me, his hand tugging me toward the car.

"Going to be a crowded bedroom." I winked back.

His laugh filled the air, his eyes sparking with love.

My heart encapsulated the single moment in time, holding onto it forever.

Whatever was in our future, I would always know I had loved the two men who carried this heart, but only one had my soul.

Mason
Age 44

Death no longer scared me. It was the missing out. Missing my wife's smile, her laugh, my son graduating from high school, my daughter getting her driver's license. Though that did scare the shit out of me. Olivia Grace was a better driver than her brother. I sat many hours in the passenger seat teaching her, but it still frightened me she was old enough to even be behind the wheel.

I understood what it was like to let someone you love so much out in the world and have no control over what might happen to them. They might get hurt, and you couldn't do a thing to prevent it. My kids had made me come to understand my grandparents much more, and to see everything they did for me wasn't a sacrifice to them. It was love. I spent so many years believing I owed them, and I needed to make them happy so they didn't regret giving up all their money and retirement to get me a new heart.

I understood it now. It was what you did when you loved something more than life.

When Grandma asked me to find something that gave me joy and do that, I never knew it would be marrying Emery and raising our kids, four rescue dogs, three cats, chickens, and a rabbit. I worked part-time doing handyman stuff and reselling cars I fixed up, making a decent enough living, but it was being the stay-at-home dad while Emery worked that ended up being our joy.

Looking back on my life, I didn't regret one thing. Except maybe not fucking my wife more. And we fucked *a lot*.

"Mason." Emery's voice pulled me from my thoughts. Her hand gripped onto mine, and I could see her fighting back the tears. Damn, she

242

was even more beautiful than the day we met. And I was even more in love with her. Still couldn't keep my hands off her. "I'm right here. Be in the now with me."

I nodded my head, blinking back the tears. The beeps of my weak heart echoed in the hospital room like a Ping-Pong match.

And both sides were losing.

Twenty-eight years Benjamin Roberts had given me life. I had a family because of him, had a wife... *his wife*, but hey, we kept it in the family.

Emery always cracked up when I told strangers that joke. The shock on their faces, wondering what sick shit we were into. She'd play it up, her sense of humor as dry and twisted as mine.

"Well, Mr. Roberts, we had a good run." I patted my chest, covering up the grief I felt. I didn't feel this sad when my own heart was taken.

"You're not funny." Emery's throat bobbed.

"Yes, I am. It's why you love me."

"I love you for your cock."

I snorted, my head shaking with amusement. Exhaustion already leaning me back into the pillow. "Good, because that still works."

"Mason." Her grip on my hand tightened, her throat thick with emotion, her gaze noticing the nurses and doctors moving around outside the room.

Ben's heart was worn out. I pushed it to the extent it could go, gave it a fucking full life, but now it was done.

I noticed over the last two years I was getting tired more often. I was out of breath and couldn't go on runs or even do stairs. I tried to pretend it wasn't happening, but we all knew it was.

Our new dog, Pepper, a lab doodle mix, was trained to sense heart problems. The damn thing never let me alone anymore. I loved her, don't get me wrong, but shit, did I miss Ozzy. The day we had to put him down at the age of seventeen, my heart shattered. He was seriously my best friend. He was family, and I missed him every day since.

Emery's grip crunched my bones when the doctor stepped into the room, her body stiffening.

"Mrs. James." He nodded at her, coming around to talk to me. "How are you feeling, Mason?"

"Like I'm dying."

"Mason." Emery clipped, her body trembling.

"Don't lose your sense of humor on me." I pleaded, needing to laugh or I would lose it. "Not now."

She dipped her head in agreement. I was asking a lot of her, but I needed her smile. I needed the woman who had been my rock for the last twenty-five years.

"Mason, everything is ready to go on our end. The anesthesiologist will be in soon to prep you." The doctor patted my shoulder. "You are young and healthy, and I don't foresee any complications."

"Unless my body rejects it." I gritted my teeth.

The fact I was given this opportunity to get a second heart transplant was a miracle. My age and health contributed a lot to it, and pure luck of finding another match. Not many got a heart transplant at sixteen, and I was still considered young to be getting one at forty-four, let alone a second one.

I was scared.

Ben Roberts had become not just my ally, but my constant companion. My relationship with a man I had never met threaded through my soul. He was part of our lives, the reason for everything I had in mine. Why I could have all that I did.

A part of me wanted to believe I was always supposed to have his heart. Why we matched, why my body accepted it so easily, but now they were taking him away. And I felt lost. Terrified. Sad. Like I was losing a friend.

I was afraid this time my body wouldn't want this unknown heart. A stranger who had no connection to us or my life. An even deeper irrational part of me was terrified that without Ben's heart, I would lose my bond with Emery. That he was the thing which brought us together.

From the day we met, something neither of us could explain had always been there between us. A force we couldn't fight. A tie that drew us together. I always thought it might be Ben who had played a part in it. He had loved my wife too. We had that in common. A bond.

So what if it was taken away?

"Okay, I will see you when you wake up, Mason." The doctor sounded positive, noticing the nurse wheeling in a tray of syringes filled with anesthesia. He spoke to my wife as he left, but I couldn't hear anything but my heartbeat.

The final time I would hear it.

"Emery?" Terror strained my voice as the nurse came around, wiping down my arm, inserting the needle into my vein, and wheeling the drip closer.

"The kids are in the waiting room. We will be by your side the moment you wake up." She croaked over her words.

"You'll still love me, right?" I couldn't hide the deep insecurity. "It will no longer be *his* heart."

"Listen to me." She leaned over, her hand running over my scruff. "I don't care whose organ you have in your chest. As long as it's beating, keeping *you* by my side. It's not the heart I love. It's your soul. It's all of you. And you own mine, Mason James. You have since the day I saw you. Ben had nothing to do with it. It was always you." A tear fell down her face. "So please come back to me, okay?" she whispered hoarsely. "Come back to us."

My lids started to close, the drugs kicking into my system. I fought it so I could look one more time at her. We had never made each other a promise, knowing what my future held, but I heard myself mumble, "I promise," before everything went dark.

I would keep my promise because it didn't matter whose heart was in my chest.

It beat solely for her.

Thank you to all my readers. Your opinion really matters to me and helps others decide if they want to purchase my book. If you enjoyed this book, please consider leaving a review on the site where you purchased it. It would mean a lot. Thank you.

About the Author

USA Today Best-Selling Author Stacey is a lover of hot fictional bad boys and sarcastic heroines who kick butt. She also enjoys books, travel, TV shows, hiking, writing, design, and archery. Stacey is lucky enough to live and travel all over the world.

She grew up in Northern California, where she ran around on her family's farm, raising animals, riding horses, playing flashlight tag, and turning hay bales into cool forts.

When she's not writing, she's out hiking, spending time with friends, and traveling more. She also volunteers helping animals and is eco-friendly. She feels all animals, people, and the environment should be treated kindly.

To learn more about Stacey or her books, visit her at:

Author website & Newsletter: **Author website & Newsletter**: www.s-marie.com

Facebook group: www.facebook.com/groups/1648368945376239/

TikTok: @authorstaceymariebrown

Instagram: www.instagram.com/author.s.marie/

Facebook Author page:
www.facebook.com/profile.php?id=61554199619604

Sex, Lies, & Blank Pages Podcast: https:/linktr.ee/sexliesandblankpages

Pinterest: www.pinterest.com/s.mariebrown

Bookbub: www.bookbub.com/authors/stacey-marie

Acknowledgements

The love for this series has seriously been beyond anything I expected. Thank you all so much for living the Savage Lands Series as much as I loved writing it.

Kiki & Colleen at Next Step P.R. - Thank you for all your hard work! I love you ladies so much.

Mo - Thank you for making it readable and your hilarious comments!

Jay Aheer - So much beauty. I am in love with your work!

Judi Fennell at www.formatting4U.com - Always fast and always spot on!

To all the readers who have supported me: My gratitude is for all you do and how much you help indie authors out of the pure love of reading.

To all the indie/hybrid authors out there who inspire, challenge, support, and push me to be better: I love you!

And to anyone who has picked up an indie book and given an unknown author a chance.

THANK YOU!

ALSO BY S. MARIE

Contemporary Romance

Down For the Count

How the Heart Breaks

Buried Alive

Smug Bastard

The Unlucky Ones

Blinded Love Series
Shattered Love (#1)
Broken Love (#2)
Twisted Love (#3)

Royal Watch Series
Royal Watch (#1)
Royal Command (#2)

FANTASY BY STACEY MARIE BROWN

Paranormal Romance

Darkness Series
Darkness of Light (#1)
Fire in the Darkness (#2)
Beast in the Darkness (An Elighan Dragen Novelette)
Dwellers of Darkness (#3)
Blood Beyond Darkness (#4)
West (#5)

Collector Series
City in Embers (#1)
The Barrier Between (#2)

Across the Divide (#3)
From Burning Ashes (#4)

Lightness Saga
The Crown of Light (#1)
Lightness Falling (#2)
The Fall of the King (#3)
Rise from the Embers (#4)

Savage Lands Series
Savage Lands (#1)
Wild Lands (#2)
Dead Lands (#3)
Bad Lands (#4)
Blood Lands (#5)
Shadow Lands (#6)

Devil in the Deep Blue Sea
Silver Tongue Devil (Book #1)
Devil in Boots (Book #2)

Fairytale Retellings

A Winterland Tales
Descending into Madness (#1)
Ascending from Madness (#2)
Beauty in Her Madness (#3)
Beast in His Madness (#4)

The Monster Ball Anthology
The Red Huntress

Foreign Translations

Italian Editions

L'oscurita Della Luce Serie (Darkness Vol. 1) (Darkness of Light)
Il fuoco nell'oscurità: serie (Darkness Vol. 2)
Gli abitanti dell'oscurità (Darkness Vol. 3)
Il sangue oltre le tenebre (Darkness Vol. 4)
Blood Beyond Darkness (Darkness Vol 5)
West (Darkness Vol 6
City in Embers (Collectors Vol 1)
The Barrier Between (Collectors Vol 2)
Across the Divide (Collectors Vol 3)
From Burning Ashes (Collectors Vol 4)
The Crown of Light (Lightness Saga #1)
Lightness Falls (Lightness Saga #2)
The Fall of the King (Lightness Saga #3)
Rise from the Embers (Lightness Saga #4)
Savage Lands (Savage Lands Series #1)
Pezzi di me (Shattered Love) (Blinded Love Series #1)
Broken Love (Blinded Love Series #2)
Twisted Love (Blinded Love Series #3)
Descending into Madness (Winterland Series #1)
Ascending from Madness (Winterland Series #2)
Royal Watch (Royal Watch Series #1)
Royal Command (Royal Watch Series #2)
The Unlucky Ones
Buried Alive
Down For The Count

Portuguese Editions

Savage Lands (Savage Lands Series #1)
Wild Lands (Savage Lands Series #2)
Dead Lands (Savage Lands Series #3)
Bad Lands (Savage Lands Series #4)
Blood Lands (Savage Lands Series #5)
Shadow Lands (Savage Lands Series #6)

Silver Tongue Devil (Croygen Duet #1)
Devil in Boots (Croygen Duet #2)
Caindo na Loucura (Ascending into Madness) (Winterland Tales Livro 1)
Saindo da Loucura (Ascending into Madness)(Winterland Tales Livro 2)
Beauty in Her Madness (Winterland Tales #3)
Beast in His Madness (Winterland Tales #4)
Má Sorte (The Unlucky Ones)
Sob a Guarda da Realeza (Royal Watch #1)
Royal Command (Royal Watch #2)
Down For The Count

Polish Editions

The Boy She Hates
Shattered Love #1
Broken Love #2
Twisted Love #3

Czech Republic Editions

Divoká říše
Savage Lands #1
Wild Lands #2
Dead Lands #3
Bad Lands #4
Shattered Love #1

French Editions

Savage Lands #1
Wild Lands #2
Dead Lands #3
Bad Lands #4

Israel (Modern Hebrew) Editions

Savage Lands #1
Wild Lands #2
Dead Lands #3

Bad Lands #4
Blood Lands #5
Shadow Lands #6
How the Heart Breaks

Turkish Editions

Savage Lands #1
Wild Lands #2
Dead Lands #3

Russian Editions

Savage Lands #1
Wild Lands #2
Dead Lands #3
Bad Lands #4
Blood Lands #5
Shadow Lands #6

Printed in Poland
by Amazon Fulfillment
Poland Sp. z o.o., Wrocław
25 May 2024

7440f0c2-205f-41a7-9bd3-da325806c6c0R01